DAUGHTER OF THE DARK SUN

Songs of the Night, Volume One

D. Kathleen McAteer

Copyright © 2025 by D. Kathleen McAteer

Cover designed by Matisse Luisa Designs
Chapter headers & scene breaks designed by MG Designs
Part pages designed by D. Kathleen McAteer

All rights reserved. No portion of this book may be reproduced in any form without written permission from the publisher or author, except as permitted by U.S. copyright law. The scanning, uploading, and distribution of this book without permission is theft of the author's intellectual property. This includes any and all uses for training AI programs.

This book is a work of fiction. The names, characters, and events in this book are the products of the author's imagination or are used fictitiously. Any similarities to real people, places, or events are entirely coincidental.

DAUGHTER OF THE DARK SUN

First edition. August 2025
ISBN PB: 978-1-950879-87-8
Wednesday Ink, LLC

If you would like permission to use material from the book (other than review purposes) please contact the author directly at mcateerdk@gmail.com. Thank you for your support of authors rights!

Website: dkathleenmcateer.com

THE FIRST SONG

Author's Note   VIII

Playlists   IX

Map   X

Pronunciation Guide   XIII

City of Av Madhira, Second Era 3783   XV

Darkness Gathers

1. The Silent Dove   3

2. Crossing Boundaries   11

3. The Silver Tree   23

4. A City with People   31

5. Little Cub   48

6. Echoes   55

7. Stolen Glances   69

8. Ready To Fall 78

9. Discord 91

The Maiden's Doom

10. A Black Land in a Black Sea 109

11. Dead Voices 119

12. White Gems 122

13. The Visitor in White 130

14. Fate Twisted 139

15. Spider Silk 153

16. The Coming Storm 161

17. The Black Jewel 175

18. Push and Pull 186

19. An Unkind Touch 202

20. Deadly Urges 207

21. Another Life 215

22. The Nameless One 230

A Shadow Dance

23. Stagnation 247

24. Stumbling Blind 260

25. Hunter 266

26.	A Path to Tread	273
27.	Impossible Choices	279
28.	The Maiden of Shadow	285
29.	Shattered	302
30.	Upended and in Disarray	323
31.	Metamorphosis	338
32.	Evocation	344
33.	The Watching Sword	356
34.	Goddess Divine	369
35.	From the Oracle's Mouth	375
36.	The Shadow-Queen	384
37.	A Life Given	398
38.	A Life Gained	404
Glossary		413
Thank you!		425

To all those who have lost themselves along the way and thought themselves the villain.
Let the world burn, if it must. But never you.

AUTHOR'S NOTE

This is a **DARK romance** as well as a **dark fantasy** and details part of the MC's traumas on page. These characters are guaranteed a HEA, but the road is dark and difficult to navigate. Please ensure you are comfortable with all topics below.

Depictions of adult themes such as: child abuse (one scene), psychological abuse and manipulation, suicidal ideation & attempt (flashback), murder, death, gore, alcohol abuse, slavery (prisoners of war), and open door scenes with a virgin FMC and MMC including dubiously given consent, knife play, and blood play.

PLAYLISTS

MUSIC PLAYS AN IMPORTANT part in this story; it's only fitting that I have a playlist to help introduce the mood and journey of Mireithren and Therat. Scan below & enjoy!

APATTAR MIREITHREN

THERAT

Nithrin Sea
Madhir
Narnarán
Eithros Nar'iri
Zironde
Ombad Na
Ruins of
Bethwen
Narárenir Cez
Andesiri
The Afaras Sea
Godless Wastes
Ruins of Andeshar

Eás
N
Legend
City
Town
Mountain
Tir is Vielen
Dead Sea
Vathir River
Siusir Forest
eriath
Henith Cet-i
Eithravali
Dawning Valley
Hénar
Tir is Eabhiri
Tir is Isneha
Irие River
Apathren
The God Fists
Vamase Ri
Sea of Grass
Navathel Cet-i
Madhira Desert
Âr Madhira
Aemyn Cet
Cidhen's Rest
Sere Aesli
Bay of Sere Aesli
Rislirii
Nava
Green Bow
Twins' Port
Gisamir
Hylaea
Aeslirin

PRONUNCIATION GUIDE

OF IMPORTANT PEOPLE & PLACES

Adairen (Ah-dare-en)
Adon (Ah-dawn)
Aesirhelí (Ey-sear-hel-ee)
Amaren (Ah-mah-ren)
Apattar (App-uh-tar)
Aslyren (As-leer-ren)
Av Madhira (Ave Mah-year-a)
Eás (Ey-awhs)
Eásirí (Ey-awhs-ear-ee)
Émerin (Ey-mare-in)
Eithros Nav'iri (Ee-throws Nahv-ear-ee)
Evranenith (Ehv-rah-neh-nith)
Hénav'an (Hey-nahv-awn)
Hylaea (Hi-lay-uh)
Ishfasnith (Ish-faas-nith)
Isht'iri (Isht-ear-ee)
Kathiél (Kath-eye-ey-el)

Laisha (Lye-shuh)
Liraes (Leer-ays)
Madhiri (Mah-year-ee)
Mahkaeren (Mah-kay-ren)
Mireithren (Mere-eth-wren)
Myrniar (Mur-nee-ar)
Ninann (Ni-nawn)
Oneriath (Oh-near-ee-ath)
Pherisa (Fair-ee-suh)
Saiya (Sigh-yuh)
Sera Aesiri (Sare-uh Ay-sear-ee)
Therat (Thair-aat)

CITY OF AV MADHIRA, SECOND ERA 3783

T HE SCHOLARS CALLED IT an eclipse. A simple movement of the stars and moon above, part of the natural order of the universe set by the gods themselves. The Shadow-weave would reign for but a moment, and then the sun would return. A mere evanescence.

Many things evoked fear in Émerin—the Dark Goddess most of all—but the sun was never one of them. More accurately, *had* never been one of them. Yet, fear gripped his heart for the last three days at the sight of the flaming orb, wondering when it would die and cast the world into shadow. Some claimed the eclipse a blessing, a new sun to greet his daughter flowing with divine blood. But in his dreams, the man saw only chaos and destruction, the girl cursed by the Shadow-weave. Raven-haired and black-hearted she would be if the darkness claimed her.

Émerin's predictions of the future never lied before. Dreamweaving gifted him everything in life. The Named Houses raised him from the caste of Weavers with his marriage to Nessaeren on the condition that he warn them of any who would harm the Madhira Desert. What would they say if he brought an *evranenith* into their midst?

Dropping to his knees, Émerin stared at the sun, a flaming crescent swallowed by the endless black of the cursed moon. The world underneath grew dim, shadows creeping into place, ready to strike. The air clung to the world, thick with dread. The eclipse would soon peak.

"Émerin!" Nessaeren screamed, breaking the deathly silence. Her voice dripped with panic.

Tearing his eyes away from the sun—now only a thread of light in the dark sky—Émerin bolted across the breezeway. The far side opened into an atrium lined with a rainbow of colored silks and cushions. Deep in the throes of childbirth, his wife Nessaeren lay in a small built-in pool. Five women tended to her with such haste that Émerin could hardly keep track of them.

Nessaeren waved them away with her hand when she saw him enter. He rushed to her side, sliding into the pool behind her without bothering to disrobe.

"I ca-can't. I can't, my sweet, she is coming! She will kill me to come screaming into this world amidst the dark. I'm scared, I do—*AUGH! MAKE HER STOP!*"

Émerin pulled Nessaeren against his chest, her ragged breath calming with his touch. He stroked her bright scarlet hair—damp with sweat—with one hand and wiped the tears from her face with the other. Her skin sparkled like a rich brown diamond as he swept the salty tears away.

"Shh, shh, Nessaeren, I am here. I will not let anything happen. Fate has not been decided yet, the gods leave it up to us. You can do this, my *apat*. Our daughter will not be cursed." Émerin seemed to say the last sentence for himself, repeating the words under his breath.

"*Mahkiri* Lady Nessaeren," an older woman interjected. "I must insist you drink this wine the *Makhaeren* blessed, it may delay the baby." She extended a golden-bronze hand to Nessaeren, who only slapped it away.

"Just. Let. Me. Wait." Nessaeren said through gritted teeth.

Émerin placed his hand on her belly and focused on the soft, near imperceptible music of the Sun. He called forth a strand of the Sunweave, letting the bright, joyful music fill his mind. He shaped it into a ball of warmth, heat radiating from his hand. It helped for a moment, a weak smile tugging at the corner of Nessaeren's mouth. Then, a new wave of contractions hit, tearing a roar of pain from the soon-to-be mother.

The last golden light of the sun slipped away; an empty void took its place. An eerie hush swallowed the land. The temperature plummeted as the shadows of the Dark Goddess tightened their grip on the living.

Émerin blinked hard; when he opened them again, tall figures cloaked in black danced in and out of his vision. An ear-splitting scream broke the silence. The wail of pain cut through the pitch-black like a hot knife. Shadows surged forward, enclosing the two in a cold, silent embrace.

Nessaeren slumped back against Émerin's chest. A woman shouted something unintelligible. Hands splashed into the water. The pale amber glow of a lantern tried to break through the thick darkness. Émerin could only form a hazy image of two handmaids searching in the water. After what seemed like only a second, a pair of hands emerged holding a scrunched-up body.

The baby lay still for a moment before wailing ferociously. The tiny face grew redder and redder as a pair of light brown hands curled into fists and began pummeling the air. The handmaid holding the babe cut the umbilical cord with one swift motion and swaddled it in a thick purple blanket. The others rushed around in the shadows, the confusion of voices impossible to untangle.

Nessaeren shuddered against Émerin as she took a raspy breath, her eyes fluttering, struggling to open and bring the world into focus. Through the dim chaos, he saw thin threads of shadows weaving their way across his wife's bare breasts, crawling up toward her face. He tried to wipe them away, but they only faded for a moment before forming again.

"Nessa, Nessa!" The words died in the storm of frantic voices.

He shook Nessaeren, but she did not respond. Threads of Shadow-weave crawled over her face. Her eyes trembled before opening. Black pools of nothingness stared up at the dark sky.

She spluttered and gagged on the darkness spreading through her body.

"Ness, oh gods, what is happening? Wake up, wake up. Please! Fight it; come back to me!"

Émerin pulled Nessaeren's face up to his, her shallow breath cold against his lips. The black, unseeing eyes did not change. A thin, weak voice trickled into Émerin's ears. It did not sound like the woman he loved—hers a soft symphony—but rather that of a puppet, as if Nessaeren fought to regain control.

"She... save her. You cannot... cannot know. Not cursed, blessed. A gift..." The voice faded away. Convulsions wracked Nessaeren, body twitching as the black faded from her eyes.

"Nessaeren!" he screamed. "Ness, follow my voice. You must return," Émerin sobbed, voice breaking as hot tears rushed down his face.

Nessaeren's body stilled at the sound of Émerin's voice. Seconds felt like hours, eternity stretching on as his beloved *liraes*, the only reason he needed to live, lay still in his arms.

Émerin's heart turned toward the newborn still squalling in the dark. He would kill the child, swift justice for killing her mother. A curse sent by the vengeful Dark Goddess—it was true, he knew it all along. But never in his dreams did he see this future. Never did he think this would be the death of his *liraes*, the lover fated to him by the gods themselves.

As the rage and hatred for the daughter whose face he hadn't even seen built, life crawled back into Nessaeren. With great effort, she reached a hand up to his face creased with worry, touching trembling lips with cold fingers. Émerin thought his heart would stop, his spiral of grief halted in an instant.

"I'm sorry, I'm sorry... I tried..." She opened her eyes, looking up at Émerin. "Hold me, my love." She pressed her head against his chest as he pulled a tangle of bright scarlet curls out of her face.

"Shh," he whispered into her ear. "No, my *apat*, it is not your fault. You are here, you are here. Stay with me, Ness."

Time seemed to stretch on, each passing moment in the chaotic darkness moving in slow motion. The attendants moved with wild energy from babe to mother, to poultices, then back to the babe again. Nessaeren shuddered against Émerin, her face once a dark amber brown now pale and wan.

In the blink of an eye, light crept back into the world. The babe screamed as the first rays of sunlight hit her skin, eyes scrunching shut in pain. Her mother in the pool began laboring again, sucking in breaths between the contractions as the pressure crescendoed again into dizzying waves of pain. Nessaeren smiled at the sight of the sun, looking back at Émerin with those sandy brown eyes he first fell in love with.

"She—ah! She has a *soerl*, sh—" A scream swallowed Nessaeren's words.

Nessaeren squeezed Émerin's hands until her knuckles turned white. She reached a hand down between her legs and pulled a second baby girl out of the water. A cascade of laughter erupted from Nessaeren as she clutched the babe to her chest. The tiny girl lay quiet at her mother's breast, her twin screaming a few steps away.

"You are perfect," Émerin breathed. "I knew you could do it. You always were my brave girl, Nessa." Émerin stroked a cheek soft as calm water, neck bent forward to deliver a shower of gentle kisses. "Ninann... she is perfect, just like her mother." He reached another hand over to his young daughter, sliding an arm under Nessaeren's.

As soon as Émerin laid eyes on the second girl, her cursed twin became a distant memory. An inconvenience, but dealt with the same way all *evranenith* were. A dagger to the heart was a mercy. Children of the Dark Goddess must be purged, her tainted shadows kept at bay, eager to devour the world if given a chance. Nessaeren would surely not argue. She had the daughter she always wanted at long last.

Cradled in Nessaeren's arms, Ninann—his Ray of Sunlight—would make this moment worth it.

"Where is my other daughter? Why is she screaming so?" Nessaeren moved as if to get up, but Émerin held her back.

"Nessa... She is an *evranenith*."

"Bring me my daughter! I must see her face, please!"

A nursemaid shuffled over with the other babe. Her body convulsed as each scream tore through the newborn, face nearly purple from the effort. The moment her fingers touched her sister, the child stilled. A slow, steady thrum of music broke the silence, a heart-wrenching sound that almost seemed like a dirge.

"*Soerl...* But Ness, you know what must be done..." The words slowly drifted from Émerin's mouth.

"Life cannot grow with Death; ones who are soulbound can never stray too far. Look at her, she is a reflection of Ninann. Myrniar blesses both my daughters, Émerin. Her Light is stronger than even the cursed moon."

Nessaeren cooed at the twins nestled at her breast while deep furrows formed on Émerin's brow. This was not the Nessaeren he knew, the woman who dedicated her life to the Sunmaiden, never alone in the dark without a light to part the shadows.

He wanted to argue and fight back, to tear the cursed babe from her breast. But never had Émerin been able to deny Nessaeren, forever succumbing to her beauty: more goddess than woman, in his mind. He could not bear the thought of causing her pain, even if it meant swallowing all his fears and hatred.

É MERIN COULD NEVER FORGIVE himself for letting Apattar live the day she came screaming into the world. He promised not to kill the girl but would try everything to purge the tainted Shadow-weave, even if it broke her. Apattar stood as a reminder of the past he never asked for. No one could know or look too deep into the man's lineage and his family. For a moment, Émerin almost came to believe he outran fate.

As a girl, Apattar could never quite understand the hatred behind her father's eyes or the furtive tender moments with her mother. The only semblance of love in the little girl's life came from her twin sister. Ninann's glittering smile became a bright light in Apattar's dim world. Yet, their hours spent together—always under strict supervision—dwindled over the years. Given no explanation, Apattar's days of relative freedom became a relic from an all-too-brief childhood.

As the girl approached womanhood, one thing became abundantly clear: Apattar was her father's ultimate failure. A descendant of Myrniar, cursed by the Dark Goddess, born from the seed of a lowly Weaver. Émerin worked tirelessly to hide his eldest child from the world, the circumstances of her birth known to only a few. Yet, the shadows of the cursed Goddess run deep.

Fate is impossible to outrun, even in the desert.

PART ONE
DARKNESS GATHERS

Under the silver moon my Mother wept,
A maiden fair under Death's cold shadow.
Sorrow-bound and bereft of joy,
she walked in silence under the moon's glow.
There in the land where sun does not show
The Shadow Siren fell to woe,
Heart turned cold under the willows.
When last she stood at the edge,
the world turned away,
Away, away.

Ever-fair!
I will seek you there where the light ends and void begins.
Your first and last, from a time lost to the past.
For you, I would give birth to the idea of sins.

THE SILENT DOVE

APATTAR

L OW ON THE HORIZON, the pale silver half-moon looked innocuous as it faded in the western skies. A simple thing, treading the same path each year. When the fullness of the moon illuminated the vast night sky, people gazed in wonder. For a moment, they would forgive its creator and call it beautiful, the sum of all starlight gathered by the gods.

Apattar wondered how that felt. What it would be like to look at the moon and bask in its pale glow, a reminder of simpler times—if such a thing ever existed. Did the Eldest fear the night when the moon disappeared and even the stars seemed to dim? The woman blinked and turned back to the simple leather-bound journal in her lap.

It's funny, the way I used to crave a meaning to all of this. Trying to delude myself that the pain was worth it in the end. If a god cursed me, then surely my divine foremother would save me if I proved myself worthy. Now I think the gods are truly dead, or gone, or just don't care about us anymore. I want to believe that, desperately. But I sometimes find myself doubting my convictions. It terrifies me.

The scratching sound of the quill stopped. The sudden silence felt tense; Apattar held her breath, waiting for some disaster to unfold. But nothing came, only the soft *whoosh* of wind through the crumbling tower walls.

The hot summer days blurred together, the changing weather the only indication life continued beyond her four walls. Her nineteenth nameday had come and gone, as all others had. Miserable and forced to wear a smile, paraded around as if nothing was amiss behind closed doors.

How could there be? Apattar hailed from one of the many exalted families of the Named House of Isht'iri. The Sunmaiden's divine blood coursed in her veins: a living memory of when the Seven Goddesses walked amongst their people. Admitting the Dark Goddess's curse could touch even the descendants of Myrniar was an impossibility. Even as the hatred in her father's eyes pierced the young woman's heart, he spoke of how much he adored the twins—but especially his youngest, Ninann. It never stopped sounding strange, the way the man always found a way to insult Apattar in public.

Apattar's one day of freedom from her chambers already felt like ages ago, her father's mood particularly black the last two weeks. At least the nights were still hers to claim. It had gotten easier to sneak out, the lord of the House not bothering to post guards outside her chambers anymore. Apattar wanted to believe it was a sign of his trust, but she knew he didn't care if she died. Maybe *hoped* she would. It would be a gift, an answer to a wish he never vocalized but harbored all the same.

These days, even Apattar found herself apathetic about the thought of dying. Life did not offer anything anyway, each day blurring into the next. Confined to her room with shelves full of books for company, not a living soul to be seen except the passing mouser cat. Most often, only Apattar's thoughts accompanied her, hollowing out happiness and the hope of youth over the slow turn of time.

Once, Apattar thought life held meaning—if only she could find it. But then pain became her constant companion as daggered words turned to cuts and bruises, and suddenly the idea of meaning became terrifying.

Her father claimed he would purge the girl, abuse masquerading as an attempt to chase out the evil festering inside the then fourteen-year-old. Somehow, she was to believe every black scar on her cheek a sign of his love, marking Émerin's desire to lift the Shadow-weave cursing his eldest child.

It was a pretty lie.

Once, Apattar might have believed it. But the Goddesses did not dole out curses. How could they, when they'd been dead and silent for over 3,000 years? Émerin cursed his daughter the day she came screaming into the world; the moon passed in front of the sun, and irrational fear ruled over reason. Spared from death, and given a tortured life instead. Some days, it was almost easy to envy the slain babes.

With a deep sigh, Apattar sat forward, pushing away all thoughts of her vile father. The silvery moon would soon dip below the western horizon, chased away by Narán's blistering golden fingers of sunlight. A frown curled at the edges of Apattar's mouth as the first rays broke through the eastern rise of great dunes.

As a child, the cursed daughter screamed at the sun until her voice gave out and tears streamed down her face. But now she only felt hollow, too tired to keep fighting. Was there even a point to trying to survive?

Leaving a life of torture shouldn't be so hard. Even if Death awaited her, every day Apattar thought longer about taking her chances walking west to the great sea of golden grass. Not today, but maybe one day. At least Saiya would be waiting for her in the gilded cage of her family's estate today.

Springing up from the hammock, Apattar slid the small leather-bound journal onto a shelf of others before running her finger along their spines. Twelve years of her life fit on the shelf. She wondered what anyone would think if they stumbled across the collection. Would they think any of it was real? A woman coursing with Myrniar's divine blood, born an *evranenith*. One fate dictated she should be a priestess to her long-lost foremother, while another claimed she would end the world. Who could even come up with such a ludicrous idea? Apattar laughed bitterly at the thought.

Fate.

An idea the religious clung to, desperate to find comfort from the gods even after they abandoned Eás and their Children.

Apattar scoffed, turning away from the journals. Her eyes settled on the rising sun through the broken tower wall. With a sigh, she ran a hand covered in bright blue tattoos through her long, raven-black curls.

"Well, time for another miserable day," she said to the sun. The young woman took one last wistful look at the empty sky where the stars had danced for her the night before.

She leapt from the top floor of the crumbling tower, curling forward as the air rushed past. She rolled out of the landing with a graceful ease only learned from years of practice. The moments falling felt like flying; as a girl, Apattar would imagine she kept flying and never landed. The soft ground greeted her, a reminder that even this escape proved only temporary. Apattar stood, shaking away the sand and stretching her limbs to prepare for the long walk back to Av Madhira.

A gust of wind kicked up, sand scratching at Apattar's face—a deep, ruddy brown like clay soil after a hard rain. Looking south, she saw puffy orange clouds racing north and a golden sheen in the air. The height of the Sunbless months brought near-daily sandstorms. Sometimes sandraiders, too.

"Of all times..." Apattar muttered.

She shook her head and pulled the shawl from her shoulders over her mouth, wrapping the loose ends around each other and her neck. Soft, round fingers fell away; a slight tremor of nerves coursed through her arms in anticipation of what the day would bring.

It took nearly an hour to walk back to the oasis city of Av Madhira, yet it may as well have been five minutes. The last precious moments of solitude were always bittersweet. The desire to run away grew each day. But Apattar could only imagine how her twin would begin screaming, the sweet dove's heart broken forever. Ninann loved her sister. The two always found ways to defy the limits placed on their interactions. Apattar tried to wear a brave face, but it became harder as the years wore on, her father's torture worsening as her coming of age drew near.

Two more years. Then, she would be free.

At least, that's the lie Apattar told herself. It was a foolish dream to think her father's hatred would suddenly disappear, that the *Makhaeren* would let her walk free. Death was the more likely gift, a dagger to the heart or a pyre burnt by the radiant Sunweave. She almost wanted it.

Despite walking back on the edges of a sandstorm, Apattar thought the journey peaceful. Wind whistled past her ears, a harsh scream distracting her mind. The oasis grew taller on the horizon with each step, a swath of verdant green in the otherwise brown and yellow world. In the distance, Apattar could just make out the tall golden spires of the Sunmaiden's Temple. The familiar sight of gold rising from a sea of green stood as a beacon for nomads and the lost, though few of them would ever set foot on the white marble floors. Yet, to Apattar, they reminded her of everything she lost, mocking her no matter where she went in the city.

A strange feeling, like a hand strangling her neck, overcame Apattar. It had become disturbingly common over the years, much like the woman's voice that came to her in the dark of night. Some unseen guide, providing comfort when none among the living would.

Apattar hummed a quiet melody to herself. The pressure faded, yet the anxiety only grew inside. Each passing minute took her closer to the verdant prison she desperately wished to escape. Humming louder, Apattar tried to drown out the voice of fear that always reminded her of what cruelties lay within the walls of House Isht'iri.

Lost in the melody, Apattar nearly tumbled over a small cliff edge to the red rocky ground below. Stepping back, she turned to a well-worn staircase carved into the side of the cliff, running down two steps at a time. The Eyes of Vanyaseá watched her every move. The twin jackal statues had stood guarding the oasis since the Discordance. They towered even above the cliff ledge, their white stone cracked and eroded with age. For almost four thousand years, the glowing amber eyes saw all. No one knew exactly what powers they had, if any, for none had ever dared to attack the heart of the Madhira Desert.

Whatever their commands, to Apattar, they always felt ravenous, as if they would spring to life, gulping her down into a black oblivion.

Once down the short staircase, Apattar sprinted underneath the Eyes and up the great Black Stair. An involuntary shiver ran the length of her spine as she passed under their sweeping gaze. The steps of the staircase were steep, but soon enough, she reached the top and looked at the sprawling oasis below.

The desert city of Av Madhira stretched out nearly as far as the eye could see. A sea of greens interspersed with wide patches of golden sand and brown rock, crammed with brightly colored tents and clay buildings. Smoke rose from the Reapers Quarter nearest her, while to the right, the sound of chanting and song floated by.

Blanketed in a warm orange glow, the red and orange towers of the Named Houses and the golden spires of the Temple towered over all. Apattar took the sight in for only a moment before hurrying down the steps on the other side of the ridge, almost tumbling over her feet in the rush.

Two

CROSSING BOUNDARIES

O F THE FEW PLEASANT experiences Apattar had in her locked chambers, she enjoyed most the feeling of her hair being twisted, pulling at her scalp as her handmaiden braided the long curls.

"Do you think my father knows?" she murmured, breaking the peaceful silence. "Or does he even think about me outside of our... sessions?"

The handmaiden standing to the side braiding her hair paused for a moment to think, then resumed weaving the strands of black. She worked with deft hands despite the scarring and burns covering her arms and fingers.

She stood near Apattar's height, though significantly thinner, with a flat chest and hollow cheeks. The physique of the laboring caste. A pale blue veil covered a head of brownish-black coils, pinned at her ears and cascading down over a simple white dress held up with a gold hoop around her neck. Though disfigured and wearing plain garba regal air surrounded the handmaiden.

"I think you bear his wrath quietly enough, he thinks you broken. Perhaps too quietly." The woman finished tying off the braid and, reaching a hand forward, gently touched the crisscrossed line of black scars on Apattar's right cheek. "Why do you not fight back, *neha*? What do you tell Lady Nessaeren? Surely she wou—"

"My mother cannot do anything. *Makhaeren* Ánnarsera has given him special permission to..." Apattar paused, the Shadow-weave within squirming, sinking into her flesh. A cool blanket settled across her mind. "... permission to cleanse me. I am officially under the command of the High Priestess until I come of age. He said I should count myself lucky, the only *evranenith* in all Madhira not slain when I took my first breath. I suppose he never clarified if good or bad luck came my way." Apattar laughed, but no mirth filled her eyes, only emptiness.

"He is a hateful man," the handmaiden said under her breath. "Two years, then. Does the night heal your wounds so well that you can hold on that long? This is..."

She paused as if searching for the words to say what she wanted without betraying her lord.

"This is madness, my lady! I cannot stand by and watch him ruin you as he ruined me!" A wail ripped from her throat as she cast her arms around Apattar.

"Saiya," Apattar breathed. She froze, unsure how to reciprocate. It had been years since anyone besides Ninann embraced Apattar. Then, as quickly as it came, Saiya jerked away from her mistress, eyes wet with tears.

"Saiya, you are not ruined. I mean, look!" Apattar grabbed one of her many small braids and showed it to her handmaiden, grabbing one scar-covered hand in hers. "You bring me the only beauty I have in life."

Saiya only sniffled in reply.

"Fa—he had no right to hurt you so. And I will make him answer for it, this I promise you. I will endure; I must. For us. Then we will run away to freedom." Apattar let go of Saiya's hand, aware they had both crossed an unspoken boundary between the castes, though she did not care.

About five years her senior, Saiya served as Apattar's handmaiden since birth, given up by her mother to enter the service of the newest High Lady. An honor, she thought, though time quickly proved her wrong. Over the slow years, mistress and handmaiden became friends in those rare moments when they were alone together.

"I am sorry, Lady Apattar. I should not have spoken so freely." Saiya wiped the tears away and stiffened her back, lapsing into the formal training ingrained over years of service. "I would never imply any harm should come to your father."

Apattar stood and looked into Saiya's hazel eyes, clouded with doubt and something else.

"You should speak however you feel, for you are my friend. And you are right, he *is* a hateful man. Being a High Lord does not exempt him from judgment."

"You speak nonsense, to say I could be a friend of someone from a Named House." Saiya chuckled as a timid smile took over her golden brown face. "Yet, I suppose this life we live is nonsense."

The two women sat back down. Saiya resumed braiding Apattar's hair, idly talking about the latest news of the city. Apattar let the words float by, picking up snippets here and there. This had become a ritual of theirs: Saiya talked about nothing of consequence as Apattar relaxed, stretching out the time she spent with another friendly soul.

Saiya offered true companionship, the one luxury Apattar had since the death of her previous *danren* five years prior. Two hours with Saiya every morning, with Myris joining her once every Sandei. During these hours, Apattar would find her strength, a reminder of the good the world did possess, should it ever decide to let the woman partake.

A knock at the door to Apattar's chambers startled her out of the shared moment of fleeting happiness. Apattar groaned, grinding her molars together as her seemingly ever-present anxiety returned.

"Come in," she said in an automatic reply.

The door slid open without a sound, slow and smooth over the uneven stone floor. Apattar looked up, but no one stood at the entrance. She blinked, opening her eyes to the same empty threshold. As if by some trick of the light, a tall, thin shadow took form, growing into the silhouette of a woman with her hair tucked into a high bun.

Apattar's heart took off, racing in her chest, trying to escape and run. She wanted to look away but couldn't, watching as dull brown eyes formed in the shadowy face. They stared back, piercing deep through her mind and into memories she tried desperately to lose to the void.

A woman's shrill voice shrieked in Apattar's ear, incomprehensible, but enough to send a shiver of cold fear down her spine. Sharp nails seemed to claw at her scalp, rending flesh from bone, hot blood sliding down her forehead. Apattar tried to scream. Bloodshot, lifeless eyes loomed large in front of her, the shadows melting to reveal a thin and angular face with light brown skin stretched over high cheekbones. The mouth opened, a gaping maw of eternal nothingness. A voice slithered out of it, the whisper worming into Apattar's ears.

"You... killer, murderer. Forsaken... the void calls, yearning. You did this to me... you..."

"No! No, I didn't me—"

"Who are you talking to, my lady?" Saiya touched Apattar on the arm, wrenching her focus away from the black shade of her past.

"Th-the knock. I... I thought I heard a knock." Apattar turned around to a blank space. She glanced back to the door, but it stood closed, the room empty except for the two of them. "Something else, it seems. I... sorry."

Apattar kept staring at the door, waiting for it to fly open at any moment.

ALL WARMTH LEFT THE room with Saiya's departure not long after the strange apparition appeared. The next three hours crawled by, only broken up by the arrival of one of the estate cats. Her father brought them in as mousers, but they found equal use as companions.

Apattar curled up on the balcony overlooking her mother's gardens, idly petting the furry visitor. She stared at the white Wall and its crimson-red twin towers, forever watching to keep the Named Houses separate from the impure masses. Apattar could only imagine life past the Wall and off the Blessed Path. She observed the remnants of the day when all slept and the prisoner broke free, bounding across the lake bridge to the world beyond. But she missed the people, the din of conversation and laughter. Though millions lived in Av Madhira, they only existed as blurry figures in the distance.

Sometime in the early afternoon, Apattar heard another knock at her door. The cat curled on her lap sprang up in alarm, darting through the balcony railings to safety. She wished to go with it, petrified of who waited on the other side. Either her father or some delusion of her mind, conjured from guilt she refused to acknowledge.

Apattar's lungs tightened, her throat seizing as thoughts spiraled. Eyes, bloodshot and milky with death. The garbled pleas for mercy—how pathetic they sounded. How much she relished the feeling, watching life drain away into the black embrace of shadows.

Monster! She was a monster, a killer, a sc—

"My lady? Are you awake?" The raspy voice of Saiya halted the downward spiral of guilt and self-hatred, a ray of light banishing the encroaching void. She knocked again, this time quieter.

Apattar cleared her throat before yelling out, "On the balcony!"

Their allotted time together ended, and dusk was still hours off—though her father always oversaw her march to the dungeons personally. What on earth did Saiya want?

The door slid open, catching on the broken stone tiles. Saiya walked in, clutching a small bag in her hands, now wearing faded blue pants and a loose cream-colored tunic covered in stains. She hurried over, dipping her head before speaking.

"Come with me, my lady. I have a surprise for you, but I must bring you there." Saiya's eyes twinkled as she spoke.

"Wh— a surprise? Does my father know about this?"

"Of course not!" Saiya snorted in reply. "But as you said, I am your friend. And as a friend, I would be bereft to not share my talents."

Apattar never knew this side of Saiya existed—confident and bold. She tried to discern some hidden meaning from those colorful hazel eyes.

"Your talents? I'm not the only one with secrets, it seems. So tell me, what does the handmaiden Saiya have to offer?" Apattar chuckled as she spoke, enjoying the playfulness, even if it bewildered her.

"Do you have any idea how a surprise works, *neha*? I know you live in isolation, but surely they have those in your books."

Ignoring the jibe, Apattar stood, indicating for Saiya to lead the way. She unlocked the door at the far end of the balcony with a key drawn from under the folds of her veil, a sly smile forming as she worked. Apattar already had a dozen questions, but curiosity kept her mouth closed.

The two women walked through the back gardens, away from any exit out of the estate. The sun began its long descent into the west, the heat rising to a swelter as the day dragged on. A stale silence blanketed the overgrown gardens, as wild and free as the heart of their mistress, the Lady Nessaeren. Creeping vines and fountains of bright blooms fought for space amidst the tall grasses towering above the women.

"Where are you taking me?" Apattar piped up after walking for a few minutes through the winding paths.

"Shh, you'll see," Saiya replied.

Knotted roots and fallen debris cluttered the path ahead. A chill ran up Apattar's spine as she recognized the familiar surroundings. There were no exits from the back wall. None... except the crack in the red clay that offered a nightly flight for the black dove. Her secret. What did Saiya know? Before panic rose from the knot of dread forming in her stomach, Saiya stopped abruptly and bent down near a collapsed stone bench, almost tripping Apattar.

"Saiya, what are you doing now?" Apattar asked, watching as she fumbled in a bramble of low-lying bushes before pulling out a large knapsack. A thin layer of sand covered the otherwise clean pack, as if recently placed behind the bench.

Saiya's eyes darted around before she spoke in a hushed voice.

"Shhh, I'm breaking you out! There's a new waveweaver who came from Isneha. Well, rather, came back here from Isneha. I remember watching her shows with my mother as a little girl, before I entered your family's service. It hurts my heart to stand by and watch this continue. Your father is a cruel man, and I cannot change him, but maybe I can distract you for a while. Here, change."

As Saiya spoke, she stuffed a pair of plain dusty brown pants and a faded red tunic into Apattar's hands. The course cloth scratched at her skin, nothing like her own clothes. Though cursed, Apattar belonged to a Named House and dressed as such. Fine silks and buttery-smooth cottons provided the only soft touch she knew in life. Though a reminder of the life just beyond reach, Apattar was drawn to the finery, determined to at least look like a beautiful caged bird. She scrunched her nose at the new clothes with disdain.

"Saiya," she hissed. "Are you mad? What if someone recognizes me!"

Apattar stopped, laughing at the ridiculousness of it all. Who would ever recognize her, save a few? The thought of anyone paying enough attention to even notice the color of her eyes—the same muddy brown as her father's—was laughable indeed. Once beyond the Wall, the woman would be a stranger, the world strange to her in return.

"Right. Ignore me."

Apattar's cheeks flushed with hot anger. Not at those who imprisoned and tortured the girl, but at her foolishness. Not wanting to talk about it anymore, she reached up to untie the silks looped through golden rings at her neck. Fingers trembling, she let out a frustrated sigh before clawing at the contraption. Always pressing in, wrapping around like a boa constrictor ready to squeeze the last remaining life from its victim.

"Here, let me. Curse these stupid dresses," Saiya murmured, reaching toward her mistress's neck.

With a practiced hand, the two strips of silk intertwined with the rings came free. The pale green dress dropped to the sandy path. Apattar drank in the dry desert air, filling her lungs while stretching her neck out. Gods, did it feel good to be free from torture. The scratchy fabric of the tunic sliding over her head paled in comparison to the wretched dresses tied at her neck. The shackles loosened as the new clothes came on.

Could this be her chance, the opportune time to slip away into the masses? She looked the part, at least, like one of the thousands of petty laborers who lived in the Slums far to the north side of the lake.

"There—no. Wait." Saiya reached down and curled her fingers into a small hole of wet sand and dirt under one of the shrubs. "Your beauty betrays you, my lady. We must commit to the disguise if we are going this far!" She dipped a clean scar-covered finger into the mud and smeared it across Apattar's unmarred cheek.

Apattar leaned into Saiya's touch, the warmth sending a wave of relaxation through her body. Muscles taut with anxiety and fear loosened ever so slightly. Saiya's eyes flicked up to her mistress. Time crawled to a stop.

The void of Shadow-weave inside Apattar seized in recognition of something in the older woman. Something... kindred?

No, no, it cannot be. Saiya is nothing like me.

Apattar remained the exception to the rule, much to her father's everlasting regret. *Evranenith* never lived long enough to get a name, much less live in secret for twenty-five years. Yet, even as she dismissed the strange sensation within, thin rivulets of black seemed to float across Saiya's eyes. Saiya blinked, and they disappeared, those colorful hazel eyes looking anywhere but at Apattar.

"Mm, ah—" Saiya cleared her throat and pretended to re-tie her pants. "We should go."

Apattar stared at her handmaiden while she placed the discarded clothes in the knapsack and slung it over one shoulder. A million questions burned in her mind, but before she could speak, a soft woman's voice sang in her disquieted head.

Another child lives. Keep her close, my sweetling. I... I will come... I will try.

The voice faded with such quickness Apattar almost missed it. But she knew the voice, had heard it before over the years. It first came on her seventh nameday, an unseen guardian in the night. Alone and afraid of near everyone in her life, she never thought to question who—or what—spoke to her. Why it took an interest in someone so insignificant never crossed her mind. Over the years, the musical voice comforted Apattar when the night swallowed her whole, doing what it could to heal her mind torn apart by unimaginable fires under the hands of her father. But it had been quiet for many long years now, a relic from her shattered childhood.

It could not be the voice of a god or a divine being, but rather the delusions of a child who could not accept reality. But, even if her insanity crept ever closer, why not listen to a voice that gave hope?

From somewhere in her childhood memories, a story Saiya told came back of how one day the Shadow-Cursed Children would find their way back to the sun, led by the long-lost daughter of Shadows and Night. Though a foolish thought to believe Saiya meant to reveal some secret kinship, beacons of hope were too few to turn away from—even if it seemed an impossible reality.

Taking a breath, Apattar hurried after Saiya, shimmying through the cracked outer wall and onto an unknown adventure.

What a thrill, escaping during the day! If these rules could be broken, what else might await the caged dove outside Av Madhira?

Three

THE SILVER TREE

THERAT

EACH MORNING UPON WAKING, Therat kept his eyes closed as long as he could. In those fleeting moments before reality pressed in, he imagined waking up in a different body—one free from the weight of sorrow and guilt, instead brimming with hope and laughter. Though but an ephemeral fantasy, it gave him enough strength to push through the fog. As sleep fell away from his eyes, reality set in. He only lived for a few seconds of delusional happiness each day and his brother's smile—though it came less frequently these days.

Tonight, Therat wandered the Sun District, meandering between the mineshaft entrances dotting the base of the cliffs enclosing Av Madhira. One of the few places he felt at ease, the darkness of the mines called out, crooning voices in the shadows his haunting companions.

For the past year, Therat worked in the fields by day, weaving together rainclouds and storms with the other Sky-weavers. At night, he crept into the mines or other dark places in the city, trying to avoid the living. He couldn't trust himself around them, not anymore.

Taking one last look at the moon overhead—a constant reminder of his curse—Therat plunged into the inky blackness of the goldmine. As he entered, the dim sun-orbs overhead sprang to life and cast a pale amber glow over the empty carts and stacked pickaxes. Focusing on the gentle hum of the light, Therat let a small piece of the Shadow-weave out of its cage. The black mist engulfed the lights; oppressive darkness once again shrouded the mine.

With one tattoo-covered hand pressed against the wall to guide him through the labyrinthine tunnels, Therat strode deeper into the mine. Specks of gold glinted here and there along the walls, aglow as if lit by the Sun itself. Humming to himself, a deep blanket of Shadow-weave cloaked Therat. Cool tendrils of the Dark Goddess's tainted gift wrapped around his muscular dark brown arms. The Song of the Night settled into the back of his mind, pulling him into melancholy.

As he journeyed further, the passage broadened into a maze of smaller shafts branching out in all directions. Therat knew his destination well; he could picture each turn in his mind and how many entrances to skip along the way. The winding path led him to the underground lake he first heard whispers of in a tavern a year ago. Shrouded in darkness, his fingers brushed against the uneven walls as he counted the side entrances, ticking them off in his head until he reached the seventh tunnel from the right.

With each step, the air grew colder. A biting chill crept into Therat's bones as he came to the hidden lake. It had quickly become his favorite place to spend each restless night, a refuge amidst the turmoil of his cursed heart. The water was colder than anything he knew, a thousand needles pricking his skin each time he submerged himself.

A pale blue glow filled the end of the tunnel, urging him forward. Therat quickened his pace, body eager to feel the cold embrace that reminded him he was—unfortunately or fortunately—still alive. The tunnel opened into a large cavern streaked with seams of gold. Stretching out to the back wall, the clear pool of water sat as a hidden gem in the heart of the Madhira Desert.

In the center of the lake, perched on a small island, a silver leafless tree stood like some relic of the Seven Sisters themselves. It cast an ethereal glow over the cavern, the lake a mirror reflecting the pale giant up to dark recesses above. Its silvery bark gleamed in the dark and cast shadows that danced along the walls.

None could explain the presence of the lake and tree in the middle of the gold mine. It baffled even the scholars from the City of Books; no one had seen such a tree before. In the northern forest, trees with silver bark dominated the land, but none possessed such an otherworldly radiance. It was as if it came from another land altogether.

Whatever the tree was, Therat thought the small underground lake enchanting. In this cold sanctuary, the constant, gnawing whispers in his mind dulled to a gentle murmur.

Therat stripped naked on the shoreline and threw his clothes against a small rock nearby. The cold air pricked his ruddy brown skin. Goosebumps rose in reply. He rubbed the scar across his chest, feeling the jagged edges where his flesh did not properly heal. His heart bucked at the touch; Therat dropped his hand, fingers quivering as the memory of his failure came rushing in.

"Why am I here?" he asked no one in particular.

He knew the Goddesses would not answer. They did not care about him. His cries for help as a boy went unheeded, just as those from the rest of the world.

"I can't die when I want to, I kill even as I beg the voices to stop. Is this some game? Did I die, and this my eternal torment instead? Why won't you answer me?" Therat's screams echoed around the cavern, pressing in on him, mocking the man as he stood naked under the pale glow of the silver tree.

He shook his head, then took a step forward in the lake; ice gripped his very soul, sucking all warmth from the man. He took another step, a hiss escaping as the frigid water rose above his calves. Therat stood there for a minute as the numbness spread up his legs. He took three more steps and was hip-deep in the water. Every muscle contracted under the gelid touch of the strange lake.

With a weary sigh, Therat let the last of his constraint fall. The Shadow-weave surged forth from his heart, racing through every sinew of the man's body. This cold—unlike the lake—somehow comforted, a cool hug rather than a thousand needles. A song settled into the back of his mind, the Shadow-weave filling every thought, pulling apart his consciousness until he felt one with the Night.

Taking a deep breath, Therat dove into the water and swam to the small island. He reached it with little effort, gliding through the water with a layer of shadows between his skin and the near-freezing lake. He crawled up the sandy banks and rested his back against the gnarled trunk of the ancient tree.

Embraced by the night and the silver tree, Therat stared at the seams of gold overhead. He slept little these days, his nightmares now more frequent than dreams—or, even better, a dreamless sleep.

As Therat settled against the tree, his thoughts wandered to the love his parents once shared. It was a bittersweet memory. His heart fluttered at the thought of the family ripped from him as a child. Though he wanted to deny such feelings, Therat once dreamed about finding his *liraes*, if he had one. If not that, a lover to accompany him through life.

He gave up that dream long ago. No one could want him now—who would ever love him once they learned the truth of his lineage? They would simply run away in fear or betray him to the *Makhaeren*, who would give him the death he so craved.

And why not do it myself? If you weren't such a coward, you'd turn yourself in. But you cling to Adon, use him to justify why you cannot.

Even if someone did see his tainted heart and wish to embrace it, he could not trust himself to be so vulnerable with another person. Therat's thoughts drifted to Ethed, the one friend he had aside from his twin brother, Adon. Ethed's trusting brown eyes and warm smile had always greeted Therat as they reported for work in the fields.

What did the helpless man think when he saw the Shadow-weave take over, when he saw how cursed Therat was? Did he know it all along, harbor some vain hope he could save Therat with friendship? Or was it a surprise, some horrible, macabre nightmare that ended with his wheezing breath, coughing up blood, unable to beg for mercy?

Therat wanted to scream, but he felt catatonic. As he drowned in the memories of killing his friend, urged on by dark whispers he could not ignore, Therat wished—not for the first time—to die. When would the torture end?

"Good morning, dearest brother. Out for an early stroll before the heat rises?"

Therat looked up to see his twin, Adon, standing outside the blue front door of their clay house, a small raincloud at his fingertips watering the roses their mother once planted long ago. The cloud disappeared with a hiss as Adon's light gray eyes studied his brother. They softened with his smile.

"Something like that. Is Papa up yet?" Therat eyed the front door.

"No, he is still sleeping. Didn't you hear him sleepwalking last night?"

Before Adon could think any longer and recall Therat's empty bed, he blurted out, "Yes, yes, of course. Did you already eat, then? I don't want to disturb him, I'll go to the Market and get something there."

Adon shook his head. "Lead on, Therat. But I can't stay long, I am meeting with Lord Émerin from House Isht'iri today. I know Ninann is not of age yet, and maybe she has a *liraes*, but I think he wishes to ask if I would consider a marriage. At least, I hope he will. She is a lovely little dove."

Adon's eyes gleamed silver in the sunlight as he spoke of Ninann, his friend since childhood, and a woman from behind the Wall. Therat knew he should be happy for his brother and the chance to join the Named Houses, but his jealousy of Ninann made it impossible for him to feel anything other than despair. The woman with a glittering smile, silken black hair, and perfect ocher skin would take his twin away. She would give Adon children and a happy life, while Therat faded into the Night.

It wasn't fair.

But then, life never had been. Why should that change now?

Forcing a smile onto his face, Therat held his hand out. Adon's tattooed fingers interlaced with his as they took off walking to the Market.

"I am happy for you. I'm sorry if I don't show it," Therat said after they could no longer see their house. "I see so much of Da and Mama in you and Ninann. I see the way she looks at you, and her smile reminds me of the way Mama looked at us when we all came home, dripping in mud, Da grinning from ear to ear. I know how you love her, and I hope nothing ever comes between that. I just... I just don't know if I can be a part of that life. It hurts too much."

Adon stopped walking. He pulled Therat into a hug. Though twins, Therat's muscular frame enveloped Adon. He was unused to being the one comforted and protected. That was his role, his sacrifice in life. He took the tainted Shadow-weave into his heart, and now he would do everything he could to protect Adon from the same fate.

After a minute, Adon pulled away. A sad smile stretched across his warm brown skin.

"I wish you did not feel so broken, *maí soerl*. I love you fiercely, and I will do anything I can to help you find the light again." Adon reached out and touched Therat over the heart; he flinched on reflex, reminded of the scar he tried so hard to forget. "This night... this torment, and grief, and guilt. I will never let you feel this way again, Therat. You hide your pain so well, like a wounded cat. Please let me help you."

Therat tried to find his words, but they did not come. He leaned his forehead against his brother's, letting the warmth of Adon's skin radiate through his face.

With a heavy sigh, Therat placed a gentle kiss on Adon's cheek, then took his hand again and kept walking to the Market.

A CITY WITH PEOPLE

APATTAR HAD TAKEN ONLY a few steps outside the clay wall of her family estate when she looked down. A string of curses flew from her mouth. Saiya whipped around, concern painting her face.

"What is it, my lady? Are you hurt?" The genuine concern in her voice surprised Apattar. No one besides her beloved sister Ninann showed they cared about Apattar's well-being.

"No, look, my *hands!* I'm an idiot, I'll never pass for anyone else!"

Apattar waved them in front of Saiya's face, the bright blue doves surrounded by stylized suns on the back of her hands impossible to miss. Telltale markings of her caste and House, rarely seen beyond the Wall. Every ounce of excitement vanished, replaced with the encroaching blanket of dread and nothingness emptying the woman a little more each day. How childish to think escape would be so easy.

"Oh!" Saiya's raspy voice kept Apattar's thoughts from running wild. "Wait! I forgot I brought these for you. Here." Saiya stuffed a hand in the pack slung off one shoulder, digging around before emerging with something black in her grasp.

Apattar unfolded the long, black half-gloves; a small loop in the center hooked over one finger. Hot, most likely, in the sweltering summer heat, but inconspicuous enough given their popularity among the Weavers.

"You are marvelous!" Apattar exclaimed, pulling the gloves on as quickly as she could. She looked down at herself, now no more remarkable than one of millions.

The fabric ran up the length of her arm past her elbow, fitting snugly across the doughy flesh of her upper arms. She found the pants comfortable despite the fabric; the air trapped between skin and cloth was cool in the heat. Reaching up to her braids piled high on her head and kept in place with a simple wooden hair stick, Apattar wondered how strange she looked. No makeup, no elaborate hair, and certainly no fine silk clothes. All the things she used as armor to survive the day.

Maybe she could find happiness in simplicity. The thought thrilled Apattar. No one came for her during the days, so who would look for someone they did not think missing? They hadn't even left the Towers District, yet already Apattar wanted to plan another escape.

Saiya said something in reply. The wind carried it away. When Apattar looked up again, her handmaiden already bounded across a sandy path cutting between a stand of thin palm trees. Apattar took a step forward to follow, then stopped.

For the first time in her life, Apattar felt hot sand beneath her feet. The realization overwhelmed her.

How many thousands of things had passed her by in life while she decayed between four marble walls?

Knowing something and experiencing it are two different things. Her books may have taught her a hundred ways to manipulate the harmonic music that wove all life, or how to navigate by the stars, but they never told her how blissful the feeling of sun-hot sand under bare feet felt.

Apattar stood for a moment, digging her toes into the earth before slowly walking toward Saiya, who stood waiting in the shade. A giggle rose in her throat with each bounding step off the sand so hot it almost burned, a prickling heat spreading up her legs. It neared unbearable, but the line between pain and pleasure had blurred long ago.

I've never felt so alive!

Once by Saiya's side, the two women left the warm sands for the familiar wide path of white cobblestone snaking through the Towers District. The Blessed Path. The only place the Named Houses would step foot outside their homes, clinging to a relic from long-lost ages. As the sand on the bottoms of their feet wore off on the stones, Apattar smiled. The thought of defiling her father's sacred path brought her immense joy. An uncontrollable boom of laughter thundered forth as her smile widened, sides rolling and jiggling with the effort.

Laughter!

Not a bitter, sarcastic sound, but her genuine laugh. Apattar almost forgot what it sounded like. Loud and braying, erupting like a geyser from her heart.

"What is so amusing, my lady?"

Saiya couldn't help but laugh a little as she spoke, Apattar's sudden joy an infectious thing. It took a moment for her to reply, sucking in deep breaths between the lessening waves of giddiness.

"I," Apattar started, pausing for another breath. "I've already broken at least four rules, and we haven't even left sight of the estate! I never knew it possible to feel so... so..." Apattar searched for the right word, but nothing came.

"Free?" Saiya offered, a warm, gap-toothed smile spreading across her kind and wide face. Apattar loved that face as much as she did her sister's. Maybe even more so over the last few years as duty and life spiraled the twins away from each other.

"Free, yes," Apattar breathed, trying out the word, seeing if it could fit.

Yes, true freedom! Even if temporary, it proved better than stalking the empty city during the dark hours. Then, loneliness still found Apattar, only with a different backdrop. "You offer me more than you know, Saiya. Thank you."

"You need not thank me," Saiya murmured, dipping her head before resuming their walk.

After a short time, they arrived at a tall tower with a large red orb floating above the top parapet. A large walkway cut between the center of the smooth red stone wall, a shimmering barrier at the nearest end blocking the path forward.

Next to the opening stood two guards, and another four sat at a table under a large palm tree not far from the others. Several dressed in layered crimson robes cascading down to the ground, carefully pleated over the chest and held in place with a shiny gold pauldron over each shoulder. The belts of gold and orange ropes at their waists seemed to glow. The others dressed in similar colored tunics down to their mid-thigh, stark white pants and golden sandals underneath. All wore a veil of white wrapped over their faces. Only their eyes and the occasional loose strand of hair betrayed their appearance.

The sight of the white-veiled guards made Apattar hesitate, stuck in between steps as her brain told her to flee but her heart urged her forward. Apattar took a deep breath.

This is just like any other night. The city is asleep, and I can do as I please.

Apattar walked up to the guards, though she had no plan beyond that. Before the closest guard—a man, she thought, judging by the thick hands—could speak, Saiya rushed over and pulled Apattar to the side.

"No, this way," Saiya whispered. "That is only for the Named Houses."

Apattar looked over and saw a small booth leaning up against the bridge entrance. They walked over hand-in-hand, Saiya's touch calming Apattar's addled mind.

"House and reason?" said the nearest guard with a high but commanding voice, looking up from the drink she cradled with both hands.

"House Isht'iri," Saiya replied without hesitation. "We have a day off." It sounded rehearsed. Had she done this before? Did she sneak out often?

The guard let out a grunt and motioned for Saiya to stand in front of the booth. She walked to a small black square, another above her on the tunnel roof. As she stood, a thin glimmer of red passed over her body. The guard stood deathly still, eyes locked on Saiya. A moment later, life surged back into the woman. She waved at Saiya, who passed through the shimmering barrier between the bridge and gatehouse.

Without a word, the guard pointed at Apattar, who scurried over to the stone, trying to mimic everything Saiya did. She had no idea what to expect, but she knew something would spoil their fun.

Blessings never found the young woman before—why should they now?

The buzz of a mosquito filled her ears. Apattar squeezed her eyes shut, bracing for pain. Nothing came. A gentle, rhythmic pulse vibrated throughout her whole body. Her heart—which had been on the verge of panic—settled down to a slow and steady beat. A wave of serenity washed over Apattar. Opening her eyes, she saw the red lights fading around her.

Apattar expected more. Was this not some test meant to weed out the escapees from the lowly laborers? The guard shoved a piece of paper in Apattar's hands and waved her away. Confused, but not wanting to make a scene, Apattar walked through the barrier, relieved when it, too, did not object to her presence.

"What just ha—"

"Not here, too many ears."

Saiya grabbed Apattar by the wrist and led her down the wide bridge until they were a safe distance from the gatehouse. Once they came upon a set of benches, the two sat for a moment while Saiya talked.

"I'm sorry, I'm so used to the Gate I forgot to tell you. They make it seem so scary, but it's not. The guard is a Heartweaver, and the red lights are Suncraft. She acts like she's scanning you or doing something to mark you, but they're filling out paperwork while she listens to your heartbeat. Sometimes, she'll mess with you, make your heart race until you collapse. I've seen it before. The guards are all pricks if you don't have blue tattoos. But she was nice today, she relaxed us. Come on, I'll keep track of our ticket back in."

Already confused—yet still deliriously happy—Apattar relinquished the piece of paper without a fuss. Saiya tucked it in an inner pocket of the knapsack with a smile. Before they stood, Apattar looked at the lake she studied for hours each day from her balcony, marveling at its massive size.

Beyond the ring of trees around the glittering blue lake, she could make out the tiny, crammed huts and half-decaying buildings of the Slums, where the lowest castes lived. The red clay huts of the Weavers District clustered together against the right side of the lake, while smoke rose from the mines far behind them. Apattar wished they could explore the Weavers District more. Every morning, as she snuck back to her prison, music and song rose from the clay homes.

The Weavers District seemed like a wholesome place—perhaps the only good place in Eás. The people leaving there always smiled and laughed. Though shackled to their masters like all in Av Madhira, Apattar heard stories about how many still used their powers in secret to help the millions who lived in the city instead of sitting behind walls and gatehouses. She sometimes wished she had been born to one of them—if they spared an *evranenith*, no doubt the child would be loved.

"M Y LADY? MY LADY, did you hear me?" Saiya touched Apattar's shoulder, bringing her out of the trance.

"Sorry, the lake is so mesmerizing! I had no idea how beautiful it could be when the sun illuminates the ring of trees." Apattar tore her gaze from the shore edges teeming with life and looked back at Saiya, a smile painted on her face.

"I forget how much of this is new to you. We can stay a while if you'd like." Saiya spoke with a kind understanding. Apattar shook her head, not wanting to miss anything the city had to offer.

"Then listen to me carefully. This is important," Saiya continued. "Here, you are Sera and I am Aesiri. You must not wander off alone, tempting as it might be. This is a wild place; the same rules and order of your high towers do not apply beyond the Wall. It is safest in the Market, and the Weavers District." Saiya's voice held a sternness Apattar had not heard before, but regardless of delivery, she had no intention of breaking the rules.

"Sera and Aesiri?"

The names caught Apattar's attention, an epithet once said to have been given to the Green Goddess Kathiél by her youngest sister. The one all tried to forget, to erase from existence. The one said to have cursed the *evranenith*, sending them forth to ruin the world as her vengeance. Despite the curse supposedly laid down on her, Apattar grew fond of the tale she once overheard at a campfire when wandering the Weavers District at night as a girl. Maybe good did exist in the world. Hard to imagine, especially in this city.

"A fan of the old stories of Kathiél?" Apattar asked.

Saiya blushed, something she had never done before in front of Apattar. Reassuring, in an odd way, like a confirmation of their friendship.

"My mother's family passes it down from mother to child, she recited it every night before I left her side. Maman said the Night Goddess was the first to walk Eás. Empty and alone, happiness only found her when the True Star sacrificed her perfect bliss and left the realm of the gods." Saiya paused, chewing the bottom corner of her lip before continuing. "I felt like her for so many years. Then I entered your service, and in time, this"—she gestured to the two of them—"happened. It felt fitting, two rebels in a world they don't belong in."

Apattar didn't know how to respond. She read about these displays of intimacy between friends, memorized the adventures of characters living in her books and all the things they said to each other. But somehow, nothing felt appropriate here. It felt as if Saiya meant to say something deeper without saying it, reveal some taboo secret about herself to her mistress. But whatever she meant, it refused to register with Apattar.

She was the only *evranenith* alive. She had to be. Any who did escape the blade when born became mad, deranged, twisted people. Murderers, kinslayers! No such words applied to Saiya, while Apattar, well... she did not want to acknowledge the ghosts in her head.

"You are too sweet," Apattar mumbled while the thoughts tumbled in her mind.

She wanted to know everything about her handmaiden. Perplexed, but not wanting to waste her afternoon of freedom, Apattar kept walking toward the guardhouse at the other end of the bridge, identical to the first.

"So, what does Aesiri have planned for Sera today?" Apattar asked after collecting her thoughts. Her eyes sparked as reality set in. Already she could hear the once faint whisper of music growing louder, voices overlapping each other, and strange noises that she couldn't even describe. Was this what it felt like to be truly alive?

"The waveweaver, Tylei, if it's the same as yesterday, will start her show again in a couple of hours. I know you have your talents, and it's probably not as exciting when you can manipulate the harmonic waves too, but you'll love her, I promise. And lots of food, of course!"

Apattar smiled at the suggestions. "Anything you suggest will be amazing, Aesiri. This is all new to my eyes, and I am glad to have you here to guide me."

The second watchtower—the last thing between Apattar and the rest of the city—loomed large in front of her. A dozen guards stood near the gate, several armed with sharp glaives, polished silver metal glinting in the sun. They stood taller than the rest and had an interlacing pattern of blue running the length of their bare arms. Sons of the Named House of Kelenath.

Apattar's blood ran cold when she saw them. They would recognize her as one of their own—of course they would. Those who touched the harmonic weave of the universe could feel each other, sense the latent energy held within their bodies even as powers slept. One of the many ways the Named Houses kept themselves powerful: allowing marriages between their lesser daughters and the most potent from the Weavers District.

As if sensing Apattar's sudden fright, Saiya reached a hand out, interlacing her fingers with the younger woman's. Apattar felt the warmth from Saiya's hand spread through her own. Taking a deep breath, the raven-haired woman tried to chase away the fears. Perhaps the Kelenath guards would be mistaken, confused by the aura of energies radiating from the mill of people not far beyond the gatehouse. She could sense them, but did it work with one who touched the Shadow-weave?

Apattar looked down as they walked across, shielding her face from the guards. As the colorful bridge turned to the familiar white stones of the Blessed Path, she began laughing, a nervous sound whisking away all her anxieties and fears.

I made it!

For the first time in her life, Apattar stood past the Wall during the day. The Sunmaiden's Temple and its impossibly smooth golden towers topped with spires loomed straight ahead.

"You did it... I mean, we actually did it!" The words verged on a hysterical scream.

"The first of many escapes, I hope. Come now, let's not revel here when there is so much more to be seen!" With a tug, Saiya pulled Apattar forward, bounding toward the source of songs and the tangle of voices.

THE REST OF THE afternoon passed by in a blur of colors and sounds, exquisite new tastes, and unimaginable smells. Though wide-eyed and seeing the world like a child for the first time, a deep ache lay underneath Apattar's awe. At nineteen years old—almost a woman by rites—each discovery made it painfully obvious that Apattar never felt like a curious child in love with the world. Instead, she knew isolation and pain, with brief interludes of love when her father allowed her sister and mother to visit. The freedom the woman longed for now left a bittersweet taste in her mouth.

Even so, Apattar found moments of happiness and times when she forgot the strangeness of being this amazed by everyday life.

A flurry of activity filled the Market, thousands of people pushing and shoving each other between stalls. Musicians tucked themselves away in corners or sat on top of flat rooftops, sometimes with groups of artists between them painting the scenes below. Silence became an impossible concept to conceive of with the thrumming pulse of the city at her ears.

Sweet-smelling poultices, acrid smoke from the smithy's forge, and the mouth-watering smell of roasted mint goat would linger in Apattar's nose long after returning to her lavish prison. The sights and sounds of everyday life proved to be beyond anything she had imagined. She spent many long hours gazing at the colorful Market and the large fountain in the black stone square from her balcony. To finally participate in life was a breath of fresh air.

Apattar thought each place they visited more enchanting than the last. Glittering jewels and bracelets of glass beads, as dazzling as the sun, were strung along the outside of one building, with more gems sparkling from within. The sound of chanting emanated from a tent, while nearby, a short woman haggled with a boy selling coconuts from a large basket. A bakery tempted them the longest, the taste of sweet berries and layered honeycakes hard to resist.

The two women passed unnoticed among the throng of people, Saiya weaving a path for them with practiced expertise. Apattar figured Saiya must have come here often. How many other secrets did the handmaiden have behind her bright hazel eyes?

After passing a large meadhouse, a runesmith, and a tattoo parlor, they came to the center of the Market. The Fountain of Maidens loomed large over the people below. Apattar saw it dozens of times at night under the silver moonlight, enchanted by the delicate carvings of seven naked women holding up a budding lotus.

Under the warm glow of the sun, it looked to be a preserved relic from the Blessed Era. The smooth white stones glowed from within, water shimmering with a golden hue as it cascaded over the Goddesses. Water poured over round faces and soft curves, a music of its own dominating the world around it. Apattar stepped closer, letting the sound drown out the chaos around her.

Apattar heard Saiya speaking, but she only wanted to listen to the music of the fountain. The sunlight awoke a song so radiant and pure it made the woman forget her name. In her reverie, the world melted away, eyes only seeing the golden water flowing over the maiden closest to her.

The figure turned away from the others, face downcast. The maiden's stony eyes held a deep sorrow. Bright, silvery tears fell from dark eyes down her cheeks before flowing away with the falling water. Grief overcame Apattar, a feeling of complete and utter loss, irreplaceable with anything but pain. Lifetimes of hurt, a thousand cracks racing over her heart, threatening to shatter it beyond repair. Apattar wanted to look away, but couldn't. Instead, she embraced the grief, yearned to understand it. The face drew her in, stone eyes now so life-like.

"Sera, Sera!"

Saiya jerked on Apattar's arm, breaking the spell placed over the woman. She blinked; the desert rushed back, people pushing up against her, cramming into the square clear only moments before. "It's about to start, the show! Come on, let's get a better view."

Apattar followed Saiya without complaint, trying to understand why the face made her feel such sorrow, but her thoughts soon scattered. After finding a ladder up to one of the flat roofs overlooking the fountain, the two women settled down to watch the show. Apattar looked around, taking in the smiling faces of those around her.

A tall, black-haired man with a mess of curls and a beard framing mournful, gray eyes seemed to watch Apattar's every move. Their gaze connected, and the sounds of the Market faded. The faintest twinge of a smile lifted the corner of the stranger's mouth. Apattar fell into his eyes, searching for something that seemed so oddly familiar. But even as the man drew her in, a deep ache settled in her heart, grief mixing with a fiery rage to rival that of the sun itself.

You will end me. What is this, why are you pulling at me? Let me go!

A booming voice broke their connection. Apattar's gaze shifted to the southern end of the fountain square, and the rage subsided.

"Welcome, my friends! Let me offer respite for a moment. A chance to see the beauty of the First Harmonic, a fragment of the powers used to shape the earth we stand upon and the air we breathe. Many of you know me, but for those who don't: I am Tylei the Greenweaver, at your service!"

A lithe woman with light brown skin—silvery blue hair piled in knotted coils on top of her head—stood on a stage opposite the fountain. She wore a pale blue dress, plain and unremarkable, but something about her drew everyone in. The tell-tale mark of waveweavers, ones who had the natural talent—or education—to manipulate the world's harmonics.

All, except Apattar. Why had the guards not sensed her? Pushing the question aside, Apattar tucked a stray black braid behind her ear and settled in to watch the show, ready to see what powers might amaze her.

Butterflies made of sunlight floated in the air, ethereal doves of cloud and mist cooed overhead from canopies and rooftops, and strange creatures like tiny cats with wings flew from person to person. A talented Greenweaver, Tylei wove threads of her harmonic together with the world to create life.

As the show wore on, Apattar looked for the man with soft gray eyes, but he disappeared into the crowds. Though she couldn't say why, she almost missed his presence.

The sun hung low in the sky when the show ended. The masses filtered out to the rest of the city, back to their segregated districts to wait out the shadowy night. It brought a strange thrill to pretend to be one of the commoners, rubbing shoulders with those considered unclean and only fit to serve. Oh, what would her father think! Apattar wanted to stay here forever.

All too soon, the sky began to darken as the sun started its long goodbye. The hours spent with Saiya brought a sense of happiness that had long eluded Apattar.

Tired and leaden feet trudged back across the colorful bridge, through the gatehouse, and down the secret path to the back of the Isht'iri Estate. With the promise of another escape, Saiya left Apattar in the gathering dusk.

Apattar knew just how long the night ahead would be after tasting life in the sun. Resolved to find one last moment of happiness before the heavy tap of her father's cane came at her door, Apattar gazed at the Fountain of Maidens in the Market. She could remember with perfect clarity its sweet and sorrowful sound.

LITTLE CUB

THERAT TUCKED A LOOSE black curl behind his ear, then thumbed the smooth, rounded stone in his palm, letting the weight settle into his calloused hand. With a flick of his wrist, it flew across Lake Anataerl, kissing the water three, four, now five times before sinking into the depths below. He pulled another rock from a pouch tied around his waist, yelling as he hurled it through the air. It felt good to let out the rage bubbling over inside.

Nights like this gave Therat the only release he could find from grief and the whispers yearning for retribution. Sixteen years and one day ago, he lived a life much like any other child in Av Madhira, with a heart full of love and a head filled with wild fantasies. Those days felt like the stolen memory of someone else.

Another rock whistled through the crisp evening air. The Withergreen months faded into the Moondark, bringing with them cool nights. Yet, they did not reinvigorate Therat—much to his demise. The gnawing thoughts of the bodies left in his past grew louder with each passing day. A tainted heart beat within his chest, the man a walking bundle of ravenous shadows and haunting memories of unending sorrow.

"You cannot throw away the pain, *neha*." A wrinkled, warm brown hand stroked the back of Therat's neck. He turned to see his grandfather looking up with sorrow in his pale violet eyes. "It hurts more today than most days, I know."

Therat recoiled from his grandfather's touch, face twisting into a snarl. "Does it? How could you know what I feel? At least you knew my parents! I barely have enough to even remember their faces!" With a howl, the stone in Therat's hand hurtled through the air before crashing into the calm lake. A chorus of dogs replied in the distance, then all fell quiet again.

For too many years everyone told Therat they understood his pain to one degree or another. They lost a child, a sibling, or a parent to old age. But no one could even begin to relate. Who else became an orphan and lost themselves in the same night? How many others felt tainted, knew the taste of murderous rage and bitter hatred lurking in the darkest parts of night? Despite their torment, Therat still found solace in the shadows when only the faint silver moon lit up the world below.

Therat's grandfather stepped back, voice still full of warmth as he spoke. "You are angry, as is your right, but you need not push me away."

It is for your own good. For everyone. Even hers. Even if she did smile at me, even if her eyes captivated my heart and made the world fade.

"Then just leave me alone so I don't have to. You have given enough of your life to me, Papa." Therat took a step back, letting the cool lake water lap at his heels. He tried to focus on the sensation and ignore the anger of his grieving heart.

"I would give it all to help you heal, Therat. I love you, you know this, yes, Little Cub? Come here, come." The older man spread his arms wide, waiting for his grandson to come to him.

Therat's heart softened hearing the name his mother once called him those many years ago. Of course his grandfather meant no harm. A thin smile crept into the corners of his lips. He stepped forward, embracing the old man.

Nazith had an indescribable and comforting aroma: a mix of ripe mangoes, dirt, and something impossible to place, like a rainstorm during the darkest hours of night. Therat sank deep into wiry russet brown arms that never seemed to falter. Even on the day when the twins returned to Av Madhira, and Nazith learned he lost his daughter and son by marriage, Therat saw no tears fall from his eyes. A fountain of strength, the man bent with age set aside his grief for his twin grandsons.

Therat knew this. He tried to make the anger he had toward the world disappear. No one could fully understand his pain, but he did not need to suffer alone. His grandfather understood the best anyone could. Hailing from a line with a unique blood gift, Nazith first taught Therat's mother, Renata, how to shadewalk as a girl. After her tragic death, when nothing made sense in the world, shadewalking with his grandfather gave Therat a small sense of comfort. They spent hours on the shores of the great Lake Anataerl each night, honing his skills and unknowingly helping Therat contain the hunger lurking in his mind.

"I'm sorry, Papa." Therat stuffed his face into Nazith's chest as he spoke. He pulled away, eyes cast toward the ground. Feet shuffled in awkward silence before he spoke again. "It's not just them. I... I am lost. And scared. But there is nothing that can help me now."

"There is always hope, *mai nithat.*"

Therat winced at the words. Once, he would have agreed. But he couldn't save Ethed, and all hope fled as his friend's blood stained the golden sands of the desert.

"Then why does my heart feel empty?"

Nazith did not reply but sat on a bench behind the two of them, motioning for Therat to join him. The gold band on his forefinger glinted in the moonlight. Therat sat with a reluctant sigh, shoulders drooping in resignation.

Therat tried never to think about the night his parents were murdered, much less the way he despoiled his soul with a wild part of the Shadow-weave beyond control. The shadows stirred from their slumber at the thought of that night. He swallowed hard, trying to force the darkness whispering for death back into the cage he struggled to keep shut.

"Before Mama died, she taught me to shadewalk. I heard a woman's voice calling to me, so gentle and welcoming. So when Mama and Da..." Therat's voice faded out as the moisture left his mouth. Stones replaced his limbs, pulling him into the earth. He curled one hand into a fist, clenching with all his strength before continuing. "I thought she would protect us. And the shadows did, Adon and I are here. But I made a mistake. I... I can't always run away from these thoughts. I'm too weak." Therat's voice dropped to a whisper, tears building behind his grief-stricken eyes.

"Oh, my dear boy." Nazith settled a hand covered in knot-work tattoos on Therat's head, fingers raking through the soft black curls.

"I'm losing my mind, aren't I?"

"Only the Seven know, but I think not. I cannot see the future any better than I can read your heart. Yet no matter what, you are still our Little Cub."

Nazith spoke with a quiet calmness, but it did little to reassure Therat. Shadewalkers were driven from the desert—or so the Madhiri thought—after two of them obliterated a city early in the Second Era. Now all but a feared myth in the Madhira Desert, Shadow-weaving passed into history as a remnant of the First Era. Those born near a new moon found themselves ill-favored, at best, while *evranenith* received a dagger in their heart.

Even if the bodies from his unwilling descent into madness never surfaced, the *Makhaeren* Ánnarsera would inevitably find out what foulness tainted his blood. Therat's luck ran out long ago. A fate worse than death awaited him now. His heart felt ready to explode, chest squeezing out what little air he could suck down.

"What are you saying? I wanted to hide us from the people who... who killed them! They had daggers and powerful magic and chanting and, and, an—" The words tumbled out like an overflowing waterfall.

A gentle squeeze from his grandfather cut off Therat from spiraling into the mess of memories he tried never to acknowledge. Why was it so hard? Adon could talk about his memories, never acting as if he wanted to shrivel up and disappear. Somedays, Therat's love for his twin twisted with hatred, bitter jealousy rising. What was it like to be unburdened by such unwanted malice and guilt? To have grieved properly, let the heart heal instead of decay and rot?

"I know, hush, child. It is fine. You are *fine*." Nazith drew Therat into a tight hug, tracing his fingernails up and down his back.

Though he came of age last year and was deemed a free man, Therat still felt like a lost child in the world. It felt good to let someone comfort him. Hold him, like his mother should have for so many years.

"We walk with the Night because it calls to us, yearns for us as much as we yearn for it, but the dead who guide us are angry. You are strong, Therat. I know you can win whatever fight you have with yourself. The alternative is not something I would even utter. You must find the strength to heal. I cannot fight this fate for you."

Though his tone harsh, the soft look on Nazith's face reassured Therat he was, in fact, fine. Or would be, one day. Therat nodded, unable to find any words on his tongue. He could not shake the feeling that the Shadow-weave in his heart would serve as well as torture.

He didn't know what to think. Hope sounded sweet, but it left a bitter taste in his mouth.

"I'm scared, Papa," Therat whispered before burying his face back into his grandfather's chest. The air grew colder as evening passed into the long dark hours of night.

Six

ECHOES

A PATTAR THOUGHT IT STRANGE, having something to look forward to. The last three months sneaking out past the Wall brought a new sense of life to the near-lifeless woman. A tangible goal and purpose: explore all the city had to offer.

Saiya took her to the Market most often, a colorful patchwork of canvased tents and painted stone buildings. There, the two women wandered through the merchant stalls, hours spent gazing at the beauty of the artisan workshops filled with intricate metalwork and such life-like paintings they looked as if reflections in a mirror. But most of all, Apattar loved to sit under the crying maiden of the fountain. She had grown fond of *kunishfa* over time, the sweetness of the dates in particular. In the afternoon sun, Apattar would share one with Saiya, observing everyone passing by as the fountain's musical water gurgled in the background.

For the first time in her life, Apattar felt happy. Her father had stopped coming in the dusky hours before night took hold. Sent away for political reasons to the capital of the Federation past the edges of the desert, in far-away valleys Apattar knew little of. In their father's absence, Ninann spent every evening with the sister she held so dear, her warm embrace satisfying the craving for affection always gnawing at the older twin's heart. Isolation became a tolerable thing with the guarantee of Ninann's glittering smile at the end of each day.

If not for the overwhelming sense of impending doom, Apattar might have even thought herself in perfect happiness, content with what life had to offer for the moment.

But the clouds only grew darker. Apattar felt it deep in her bones. The calm before the storm, a false sense of safety to make the wounds that followed rip deeper through her tender flesh. She tried with desperation to accept the blessings sent her way, but a lifetime of fear made it impossible.

Apattar's breath stuck in her throat, heartbeat quickening to match the beat of a crazed drummer.

You are fine, you are fine, you are fine.

Chanting in her mind, Apattar forced the breath out and slumped back against the warm wood paneling at her back. In her lap, a sleeping cat rolled onto its back, exposing a soft, faded ginger belly. Taking another measured breath, Apattar curled her long fingers through the fluff, heart calming with each stroke.

"What would I do without you, my sweet friend?" whispered the woman, tracing the outline of the cat's pointed ears, tufts of white fur sticking out like antennae.

Apattar loved the small white ginger tabby, her favorite of the mousers on the estate. A tiny thing, she was the runt of her litter ten years ago. Apattar remembered how Ninann begged to save the poor thing when its mother rejected the kitten, how even through closed doors her cries echoed through Apattar's chambers. Her father—the vile man who carved into her soft flesh with a dagger and claimed to hurt the girl out of love—he said yes without pause, without trying to dissuade Ninann or declare it a mercy to kill the tiny thing. Apattar grew to love the kitten with a fierceness to rival her love of Ninann: living proof her father's mercy did exist.

"What is it like, Lirande?" Apattar murmured as she stroked the cat's head, tracing the dark orange pattern on her forehead. "To know his mercy? Does he ever think of you with a fond heart? Remember how his choice delighted Ninann? I wonder if he knows how much I mean to her. Maybe that..." Her voice trailed off as the feeling of choking surfaced again, invisible hands strangling her until life became blurred.

The cat opened two bright green eyes, sharp fangs flashing in the light as she yawned. The feeling of choking lessened as a giggle escaped Apattar's mouth. No matter how many times she had seen it, the way Lirande yawned always made her smile. One incisor was longer than the other and stuck out past the cat's closed mouth. When she yawned, the cat would always hold her head at an angle, shaking her head until her mouth closed and the long fang poked out. A ridiculous thing to find amusing, but Apattar did not care. Everything about the cat enchanted her.

"Hmm, you are right. It has been a long several hours sitting on the balcony with you. Off you go, little one. Go find a nice mouse for dinner, okay?" Apattar spoke with a tenderness reserved only for the small cat. The pale ginger tabby left after a minute, her tiny squeaking meows goodbye breaking the woman's heart.

Alone again, the uneasiness returned with a vengeance, waves of nausea washing over Apattar. She tried to stand, but her head felt light—as if it might float away and leave her body behind.

Why was it so hard to be alone with her thoughts? They always turned to dark and dismal things, voices reminding her of the inescapable fate laid out before her. These last months proved to be a temporary distraction. Simple, meaningless things that would disappear like everything else in her life. Everything, except the memories of pain and hurt, the terror of what she would become. What she already was. Water cleansed the blood from her hands, but not her heart.

Closing her eyes, Apattar tried to focus on the sensations of the hardwood at her back. The feeling as grooved paneling pressed in at awkward angles against her spine. How the smooth black stone felt beneath her legs, somehow always cool no matter the temperature outside. Apattar learned long ago to force herself to think of the physical sensations she knew to be real.

Her mind imagined too much, conjured darkness when it didn't need to. She didn't need to panic, not now, she told herself.

A cold wind blew past, sending Apattar's loose curls flying into disarray. A knock came at the door as it passed, heavy and slow.

Deliberate.

It knocked again.

Impatient.

Without waiting for a reply, a third knock came, so heavy it seemed as if it would break the door down.

Demanding.

Apattar pulled the hair out of her face and stood, gulping down a lungful of cool air. A knot formed in her stomach. Had her father returned unannounced? Apattar intended to face him, not cower away. It was the least she could do—pretend these last few months meant something, somehow changed her. She strode to the door and whisked it open, the wood gliding over the broken tiles near the threshold.

No one stood outside, only a single guard a few paces away, sitting with their back to her. A symbolic gesture meant to keep the woman in her quarters. Apattar stuck her head out and looked around, wondering what trickery this could be.

"Sentry," she hissed toward the guard, who did not stir. "Sentry!"

No reply.

The guard sat straight, looking up at a slight angle, as if observing something on the ceiling. Apattar looked up but saw nothing. With a huff, she walked forward and tapped them on the shoulder, rage growing. She might be cursed and a prisoner behind the Wall, but she was still a Named Lady and above their caste.

The guard did not respond, body cold and stiff. With mounting panic, Apattar tugged at the shadows within, trying to awaken the Shadow-weave. They did not stir.

Terror gripped Apattar's chest. Why did the Shadow-weave not come forth? Had someone grown bold enough to kill the *evranenith* harbored behind the Wall? Did they bring a Blight-weaver, drain her connection to the First Harmonic? With tentative steps, Apattar circled to the front of the guard.

A scream built in her throat at the sight of the face before her.

The hauntingly familiar face of a middle-aged woman with light chestnut brown skin and flat brown hair loomed large. Around her neck bloomed deep purple bruises and black welts. A trickle of blood ran from a small cut near one ear. Apattar tried to turn and run away, but her muscles refused, feet melting into place.

A thin, piercing scream like a whistle assaulted Apattar, ripping through her mind like a hot knife. Blood rushed past her ears, a warm liquid pooling in them before dripping down her neck.

Apattar heard herself screaming, but it sounded miles away, a faint sound carried by the wind across the wide open plains of the desert. Darkness gathered at the edges of her vision, forcing her to stare at the dead woman sitting in front of her. Forcing her to witness the crime she wanted to erase. Remembering the months after the woman's death, ruminating over it hour after hour until madness descended.

A grin slowly stretched across the dead woman's face the longer Apattar looked. Without warning, the corpse's eyes opened. Though pale and cloudy, the dull brown eyes could only belong to one person.

Tela.

The name thundered across Apattar's mind, worming into every crevice, unlocking every memory the woman had forced away. Flashes of the past came back.

Her hands around Tela's throat, tendrils of Shadow-weave wrapping around the slender neck. Pulsating, squeezing, hungering. The shadows gathered around the two women, a thousand whispers of anger and pain coursing through her mind. Apattar's sobs as she tried to stop, the voice of reason drowned out by the seething hatred taking over every thought.

As Apattar stared at the corpse's dead, baleful eyes, the Shadow-weave inside awakened from slumber, the void spreading like a wildfire of icy nothingness.

Wake up! You must wake up! My daughter, oh my daughter. Do not descend into madness! Do not listen, hear my voice. Wake up! Please, Mireithren!

A PATTAR'S EYES FLEW OPEN, vision swimming as the smooth black stones came into focus. She had fallen on her side, curled up on the balcony floor like a newborn child.

A cold wind blew past her wet cheeks, the last rogue tears still falling from her aching eyes. Reaching a hand up, Apattar wiped them dry, lingering over the crossed scars. Tiny little valleys across her once beautiful face. Apattar jerked her hand away, pulling a mess of curls over the marks of her father's twisted love.

The gloaming hour claimed Av Madhira. Deep purples painted the sky as night began its reign, growing each day with the approaching winter Solstice, marking the start of another year. Ninann should have arrived long ago, curled up on the balcony hammock with her twin as the sisters watched the sun set over the golden land. Why had she not come?

Apattar's head pounded as she sat up, trying to come up with a rational reason for her twin's absence that didn't include their father. They would have had warning, no doubt. If not Apattar, at least her sister. Perhaps she lost track of time, still wandering in some far corner of the Temple or the Weavers District. The woman had grown close with a powerful Skyweaver from beyond the Wall, fast friends bound for Tír is Isneha with the next waveweaver recruits.

The grumble of her stomach reminded Apattar she had also missed dinner. Another alarm rang in her mind. If Ninann had not come, then surely Saiya would have arrived with food, found her mistress and helped the woman wake from her black nightmare. Apattar stood and stumbled into the main room of her chambers, wincing as each step sent blood rushing through her aching head.

She could see little beyond shadows and dim outlines. With a flick of her wrist and a thrum of bright music, a string of orbs overhead lit up. Polished cut glass dispersed the warm amber glow from within. Apattar's eyes quickly settled on a silver tray in the center of her bed. A small wooden bowl and a note sat on it. Panic crept over the woman. She rubbed her eyes, desperately hoping she never left the dream world. The bowl remained.

Chipped and rough around the edges as if made with a hasty hand, the dark wood sat in stark contrast to the fine linens around it. Edging closer, ignoring the quickening of her heart, Apattar saw a handful of cheese curds, some dates, and a small chunk of bread in the bowl.

The panic creeping through her body rushed past the broken dam of her resolve. A high-pitched ringing in the background came to life, growing into a deafening roar. One trembling hand reached for the cream-colored parchment, her name written in harsh, bold letters across the top. Sucking in her breath, Apattar turned it over.

We begin again, evranenith. I will reclaim what the dark stole. Eat.

With a yelp, Apattar dropped the note like a burning coal, terror stilling her heart. The hands around her neck returned, suffocating, squeezing, throbbing with anger and malice. Reality came roaring back, the pretty veneer of the last three months torn away with three little sentences.

Why didn't the black dove flee from her cage when given the chance? Apattar knew her father would not be away forever. What naivety let her think the torture would not return?

The words circled Apattar, closing in, sending every neuron into a dizzying frenzy. Pressure built from within, expanding into every crevice until it became too much to bear. Apattar wanted to scream, to lash out and run away, far away until either death or freedom found her. But she could only force out a silent cry, her throat closing in and swallowing the pain back inside. Dread slithered through each cell before pooling in the heels of her feet. Why use chains and locks when fear worked as well? Perhaps better—chains could be broken, locks picked. Nothing could break the hold her father had over Apattar's heart and mind.

Numb and guided by habit, Apattar stumbled to the balcony with the meager bowl of food and sat on the cool black stone. She let the ceaselessly hungry void wash over her, felt it pulling the pain from her body, easing her mind of the dread choking like a vine. The void hungered for more than she could sate, taking with it her happiness and joy, consuming everything the woman could give.

Apattar learned long ago to embrace the emptiness, how to hold onto scraps of memories to find enough strength each day. Her journals held the woman's life, reminders of the things too painful to keep inside as well as the joy taken without remorse. It made it easier to endure her father's attention when the cool Shadow-weave waited to give its relieving embrace.

Pushing the note from her mind, Apattar choked down part of the bread and two cheese curds. The bread scratched at her throat going down. Swallowing hard, Apattar finished the rest of her meal and looked for the rising moon on the eastern horizon. It would be full soon, the last one of the year before the dark days of winter and the Moondark months began. Apattar shivered, wrapping her arms around her chest.

The pale silver orb crested the eastern horizon, a sheen of white illuminating the world below. The stars followed, one by one. First came the bright northern star Eleuran, then hundreds more. The sight brought with it a wisp of joy, but it did little to rouse Apattar, now curled up on the floor.

Evranenith.

The word terrified her when it came from her father's mouth. Cold fear dripped into her veins at the thought of what might come. But she had time, a chance to run and hide. She knew where Saiya hid the knapsack with their disguises, after all.

Before Apattar could decide what to do, a faint shuffle in the room drew her thoughts away.

No, no! Gods, please, no! Anyone, anyone?

"Get up. Come, now."

The words sliced through Apattar, a million tiny daggers eviscerating and shredding the girl to ribbons. Through some reserve of hidden strength, Apattar stood, body taking timid steps forward to the tall man in golden-yellow robes. "I see you ate. Good. Your body will need the strength." Apattar could not find the will to look up at her father's face, though she knew the exact expression it bore—lips set in a hard line, eyes narrowed and burning with malice.

A heavy hand clamped down on her shoulder, guiding the young woman out of the chambers and down long, twisting staircases and black corridors. Apattar floated, unable to feel anything except cold fear coursing through her veins. She tried to keep track of where they went, but the depths of the estate swallowed her until she could see only black.

After some time, they arrived at a small room with a single bed, a chair with armrests, and a basin of water. Old blood still caked the walls next to the bed, almost black around one of the cracked dirty yellow tiles. Her head ached at the sight, a bitter taste on her tongue.

Hello again, old friends.

"Sit," barked her father, pointing at the chair. Ducking from his gaze, Apattar obliged without protest and slid onto the wooden seat, placing her hands palm up on the armrests like an obedient dog.

Apattar's heart took off, racing faster than the beat of horse hooves across the golden racetracks of the desert. But what else could she do? Any attempt at disobedience in the past left a permanent mark on her face, a reminder of who controlled the woman's life. To think she had free will only led to pain.

As her final arm slid into place, a thrum filled the room, growing higher and louder like the buzz of a million bees. Squeezing her eyes shut, Apattar took a breath and prepared for the inevitable pain.

A gasp tore from her throat as threads of blinding sunlight wrapped themselves around chair and wrist, squeezing and pressing into her bone, sending liquid fire racing through each arm. Apattar wanted to scream but she could only suck in enough air to keep from passing out. Her father circled the chair, voice slithering into the woman's ears like poison.

"I believe my daughter is alive in there, somewhere. The Sunmaiden forgives all. Even you, *evranenith*, tainted by her dark sister who grasps and claws at your soul. The Sunmaiden's child Narán will vanquish all shadows the vixen may wield in the end." His mouth drew near, hot breath assaulting Apattar's face. "Long have my dreams foretold the destruction you will cause. I will end this future, one way or another."

Apattar scrunched her eyes closed, trying to imagine anything else.

"Fa-Father," she whimpered. "Father, please, wh-why do you keep doing this?"

Why did her comforting whisper not come, or the black Shadow-weave that lashed out and saved her life when a man attacked her in the Market? Silent, empty... *hopeless*. Apattar crawled to the void, wanting to submerse every last spark of her life into the empty black spaces where pain and hopes died.

Her father did not respond. A pained look crossed his face before disappearing off the other side. With a click of his fingers, a bright amber glow filled the room, warm like the touch of the sun.

He began chanting, a low, guttural vibration deep in his throat. As it grew louder, the prick of a million burning needles spread across Apattar's body. Pleasurable, at first, in the sick way her tolerance of pain became a game of wills with her father. But it extended past what anyone could tolerate, leaving her mind an ashen wasteland.

Threads of heat worked their way to her core, searing everything in their path with radiant fire. The sun itself exploded inside Apattar. Shadows lashed out from the void, cooling the pain for a moment before another torrent of liquid fire came, erasing all remembrance of comfort.

Through the blurred waves of pain, Apattar saw something silver moving toward her face, her father's thick hand covered in blue doves and half-moons coming with it. Lost in the din of agonizing pain, a voice told her to turn away, to kick and scream, do whatever it took to keep him away from her. A whisper among shouts and screams. Paralyzed with fear, every neuron struggled to survive the purging fires of the sun.

The silver came closer, angling toward her cheek, the outline of a blade coming into hazy focus. Everything vanished, leaving only a mind-numbing emptiness. The world slipped into a deep and impossible black around Apattar.

Through the blackness, Apattar felt herself deposited into her bed, the scent of lavender passing by the woman. Tendrils of Shadow-weave curled around her, excising the horrors of the night from a mind near-broken by incomprehensible pain.

For the first time in years, Apattar cried herself to sleep, wet tears and blood the only companions in the empty darkness. Sleep soon took her from the tortures of the day, but death haunted her dreams, and in time, she awoke and heard the vast emptiness of the desert calling her name.

Seven

STOLEN GLANCES

T HERAT WOKE UP AND immediately tried to will himself back to sleep. Too late. His mother's face faded, her dark gray eyes the last to disappear. Always the same gentle words, the same smiling face looking down. For a single heartbeat upon waking, Therat could almost pretend his life was the nightmare and his dreams reality.

What a foolish child, to think such things.

With a heavy sigh, Therat crawled out of bed, taking care not to disturb his brother on the other side of the room. The cool air pelted his skin. Muscles seized out of protest, longing for the warmth of his bed before surrendering to their master.

He wondered the hour. If, sixteen years ago right now, his parents were still alive. He often thought about the exact moment they were taken away from him. They had all stayed up late, the night sky streaked with shooting stars and shimmers of deep purple lights. What if Therat did not notice the first shooting star? Would they have left to fly back home? Would his family still be here today?

"N-no, stop!" Therat cried out before clasping his hands over his mouth. He looked back to Adon, who stirred in his bed but did not wake.

Therat tried to protect his twin from the nightmares and disturbing thoughts plaguing his troubled mind. Though Adon was the eldest by almost an hour, Therat grew fiercely protective as a young boy even before the death of their parents. The two quickly became known as "The Boy and his Cub" throughout the Weavers District where they lived. The sight of a cougar cub plodding alongside a skinny, ruddy brown-skinned boy certainly made a lasting impression. Through the years, the Boy grew into Man, Cub into Cougar. Rare were the times Therat walked alongside his brother with his own skin during the day.

Though uncommon among the Madhiri, the people grew to accept the presence of a Formweaver so blatantly in their midst. So too did Adon grow to accept his guardian-brother. It would not do to have two broken orphans. Therat thought it the least he could do with his life—ensure his brother had a happy one.

But tonight, he needed to escape.

Though his grandfather spoke true and the words of hope echoed in his mind, the screams of the dead pulled him into an abyss of dark memories. Nothing good ever came from looking too closely at the past, lest he awaken the hunger again.

Creeping to the foot of his bed, Therat pulled on a loose pair of black pants. He paused, hesitating to put on a shirt or shawl. No need for adhering to customs when none roamed the city with him. As bold as he wanted to be, the thought of walking bare-chested, the mark of ultimate failure splayed across his torso, made his skin crawl. The jagged white scar over his heart burned for a moment before fading. A relic from his weakest moment. Therat's fingers quivered as he touched the scar.

Forcing a breath through gritted teeth, Therat threw the shirt down.

Stop being such a fucking coward about everything.

Grinding his molars, Therat stalked out of the room and down the short hall, the gentle snores of his grandfather floating from the back corner. Forgoing sandals, Therat slipped through the front door and closed it with care. Cool, gritty sand brushed over hard rock greeted his feet as he stepped off the modest porch. He took a deep breath of the crisp air.

The silver moon sat high in the sky, on the cusp of its full glory. A shiver crawled up Therat's spine. Sharp claws sank into soft flesh, icy pangs of pain stabbing at his brain. He hated the full moon, but especially the one in the cold and dark month of Mireile, when the year came to an end and Death stalked the world. Three days after his parents had been murdered, the full moon rose blood red, oozing from the sky onto the boy as a reminder of all he had lost. Therat wanted to claw it from the sky and tear down the monument to his failures.

Beyond reason, tonight, Therat found himself compelled to stare at the glowing orb in the sky. The shadows curled around his heart stirred as if responding to something. For the first time since his parents' death, the Shadow-weave did not lash out and fill his head with dark thoughts. Instead, the hushed whisper of that woman's voice he heard those many years ago tugged at the back of his mind. It begged to be heard, but grew fainter the more he tried to focus on it.

Something glinted in his peripheral. Therat did not break eye contact with the moon. The woman's voice faded altogether; the shadows slumbered once more. It all happened so fast Therat almost thought it all a hallucination.

Life had gotten too confusing too quickly, hope now a commodity he could never afford. It would not do to cling to fragments of the past, even something like a voice he heard once before. What good did it bring him now? Why did it not help when the boy feared for his life? He rejected whatever comfort it used to give. Help did not disappear when needed most. The voice did not exist, only his mind playing tricks on him again, leading him down a path which always ended with someone dead at his feet.

How many had it been now? Four, five times? Alarming that he had already forgotten—though perhaps for the best.

He had to get through two more years, then the summons from Tír is Isneha would inevitably come for his brother. Therat could make his escape after Adon left. Scour the desert for some clues about the ones who murdered his parents, or go insane trying. And if the plan failed and he got lost, it would be a blessing to let the harsh wastes do what his hand could not.

Therat shook his head, touching the scar over his chest without thought. He began to walk toward no destination when another glint, this time something gold in the moonlight, caught his attention. Without hesitation, Therat shrank into the black edges of the trees lining the watery blue heart of the oasis.

The tangle of shadows wrapped around his broken heart surged forth, pulsing and writhing underneath his skin. The melody stricken with grief that always echoed through his mind hummed to life. Tendrils of black danced at the edges of his vision, ready to take over at a moment's notice. Crouching in the dark, Therat scanned the buildings ahead of him. He stooped low near the northern edge of the Market square as acrid smoke from the smithy filled his nose. If anyone lurked in the dark, they did not betray their position. Or perhaps he imagined it. Who else would be out when the blackness of night ruled the land? It was a feared thing, like him.

Therat called himself mad when a young woman with raven-black hair stepped out of a building. Her hair shone under the silver moonlight, black as the deepest shadows of night with tiny strands of gold, like gossamer threads of sunlight. The soft curls billowed out behind her with a passing breeze; it looked as if the star-lit sky itself wrapped around the maiden. Intrigued by someone else wandering in the dark of night, Therat followed the strange creature.

She did not seem to care about hiding her presence, walking without even glancing around to check for danger. The black silks flowing around her almost looked like shadows themselves, caressing the young woman with her every movement, moving as if they had a life of their own. She walked with the carefree ease of someone intimately familiar with the Market at night, taking her time to stop in front of gilded windows and locked displays, knowing exactly where to step to avoid the traps some shopkeepers set up at closing time.

A gasp slithered through the silent night as the strange maiden passed under a lantern still flickering with flame. The inky black silks around her disappeared for a moment before forming again. In their absence, Therat saw a woman, tall and slightly round, her hands and forearms covered in the shocking cobalt blue tattoos signifying she belonged to one of the Named Houses. She wore only a simple black dress with thin straps; clearly, the woman had no intention of being seen.

"It... it cannot be," Therat breathed to himself, almost forgetting to quiet his voice as shock ricocheted through his mind.

It was the woman he locked eyes with at the Fountain. The one with scars on her face but a smile brighter than the sun. The one that almost, for a moment, made him think love still existed for him.

Now she was here, wrapped in the Shadow-weave, commanding the Song of the Night as if she were its creator.

He stood, unsure what to do. Excited whispers wormed into his brain, overlapping voices almost impossible to discern.

Kindred... kin returned. Go, hurry! Again and again... Help! No, claw and tear and shred! Hope.... love, forgotten... darkness, endless...

The woman paused and turned around. Her gaze settled on Therat less than a dozen feet away, but she seemed to be looking right through him. Therat could find no sign of life behind those deep brown eyes, only flat emptiness and pain. A look Therat knew all too well. He studied her face, this time holding back his shock.

Illuminated by the bright silver moonlight, two thin, curved cuts raced across the young woman's cheek, like deep canyons carved into the warm brown earth. A thin line of bright crimson blood trickled down from the highest cut, below her swollen right eye. Deep purples and blacks painted her round face.

Therat's rage bubbled over. Who would do this to anyone, much less a woman from a Named House? Despite the blood on his own hands, Therat despised violence against women, always seeing his mother's dying eyes and hearing her screams. The first man he ever killed attacked a woman and beat her to death. She was an Unseen, a beggar the man thought no one would care about dying in the back alleys of the Slums. This woman looked young, maybe young enough to not have officially come of age.

As Therat studied the woman's face, he took in more clearly the pattern of black scars carved like crosses from her upper cheek down to the jawline. All thin and curved, as if carved by the same hand.

She is an evranenith. Alive. Is she the reason why?

The thought nauseated Therat. Why keep her alive, only to torture and maim her? Any who associated with the black corruption of Night—whether by blood or by moon—were seen as monsters, killed if any knew their secret.

Revelations about the cruelty of the world never surprised Therat. Nothing could, he thought.

Until tonight.

Until he saw *her*.

Everything stopped, and for a moment, Therat wanted nothing more than to embrace the maimed woman. He would find the person who hurt her and make them pay. He did not stop to wonder why he felt this way—kinship with a fellow Shadow-weaver, surely. It did not matter that Therat proved an unpredictable threat himself or that she belonged to the god-like caste of the Named Houses.

Deep within, something recognized the woman as more than a stranger in the night. They had always known each other and were bound to meet before either drew breath.

She would twist me, end me. I can feel it in my soul. She could never love me.

Even if he wanted her love, Therat's heart held no room for such a thing. His love for Adon twisted over time, fueled by obsessive protection and duty out of guilt. What else could he offer but terror and pain?

Why are you doing this to me?

Whatever drove Therat forward, it came too late. By the time his legs moved again, the woman with raven-black hair streaked with sunlight turned and ran into an alley. She melted into the inky darkness. Therat stumbled after her. Was she safe, running from someone? He must know, the whispers now screams in his mind. He rounded the corner to see the alley empty and devoid of any sign of life, as if she disappeared into the night itself.

A single drop of blood on the sands remained the only sign the maiden existed, a crimson reminder of the cruelty carved into her achingly beautiful face. For the first time since the shadows sank their claws into him, the sight did not send them into a frenzy, choking as they clawed their way out, demanding more. Therat shuddered at the thought.

He didn't want her to be special, didn't want to have a fate set out before him. The acceptance of fate would mean accepting he couldn't change anything... about his parents, about the shadows, about the blood on his hands. These were evil things, things done by men.

Hot anger flooded the man's body. Therat sat, drowning under the crashing waves of painful memories. Tears fell from his light gray eyes, head sinking into hands covered in interlacing spirals from fingertip to wrist. The cool night winds of late fall picked up. Therat sank himself into oblivion, letting the pain wash over him until numbness made it impossible to move.

Sixteen years and one day ago, he said goodnight to his parents for the last time. He had long since forgotten what his mother's hair smelled like when she would lean over and shower him with kisses. As he drifted off to sleep, Therat wished he had written down every tiny detail about his mother and father.

READY TO FALL

F OR THE PAST SEVEN days, Therat could do little but think of the mysterious shadow-cloaked woman in the Market. Seven days marveling over the strands of gold that seemed to catch on fire in the depths of her black hair. Recalling the bright blue tattoos on the back of her hands and forearms, the shapes too small for him to make out. The beauty of her face despite the scars. But most of all, the far-away look of emptiness in her muddy brown eyes that once blazed like the sun. Seven days of reliving the anger when he saw the harm done, fighting to understand feelings that did not belong in his black and decaying heart.

Therat sat on his heels in the shadows again, perched atop a flat rooftop taller than most buildings in the Market square. This marked his fourth night waiting to glimpse the woman again, swathing himself in darkness as the hours passed by and night gave rise to day. He gave up trying to understand his actions partway through the night before. Each time he did, an uncomfortable sensation like someone squeezing his heart overcame Therat, gripping harder until he felt he would shatter. Wrenching his thoughts away from the woman proved impossible. His body would rather die than give up seeking the strange creature.

Mireithren he named her, the Maiden of Shadows.

Death from a broken heart. A fitting way to go, Therat figured—a beautiful irony after all the pain he caused. Maybe the woman came as a scion of Death Herself, sent to hurry him along to the end. The jagged white scar across his heart ached at the thought.

Therat stood, a hushed groan escaping his parched throat as he stretched heavy limbs. Muted pinks painted the eastern horizon, stars retreating from the once deep blue night sky. He doubted the woman would show again; perhaps she had seen him the night before and ran from him instead of someone else.

Could the shadows around her have been a hallucination, a willful conjuration of his mind to assuage his grief? They had looked so real, *felt* so real. Tendrils of her Shadow-weave pulled at him, drawing Therat in like spider silk.

"Who are you, Mireithren? Not my *liraes*, this I know," Therat muttered as the first rays of sun peeked over the far dunes.

Even as he spoke the words, disappointment colored his thoughts. Try all he might, Therat could not ignore the part of him yearning to mean something to someone other than his brother. He climbed down the tall ladder leading to the rooftop and tried to push thoughts of Mireithren away.

The chill of night clung to the man dressed in thin cottons, hurrying his feet along the cool sand back to the red clay homes of the Weavers District. There were few on the streets this early, but he kept to the tree line, ready to disappear from notice if need be.

Soon enough, Therat arrived at the front steps of House Anatnará's ancestral home. A bright blue-painted wooden door trimmed with white raindrops and crescent moons stood ready to welcome him in. He paused and traced tattooed fingers over the trim, remembering when he helped his parents refresh their family's door that had stood for generations. Once, he thought he would do the same with his child.

Choking back his grief, Therat pushed the door open. The smoky aroma of burning wood and sandalwood incense welcomed him home. His sorrow melted in an instant.

His twin, Adon, stood in front of the hearth on the far long wall, warming his tattooed hands close to the flames. Black curls longer than Therat's, half knotted into a simple bun at the back of his head while the rest brushed the tops of his shoulders. The older twin stood as tall as Therat but lacked all of the toned muscle. Despite their differences in physical size, the twins were unmistakable, sharing their mother's gray eyes.

"It smells nice in here this morning," Therat said as he closed the door with a soft *thud*. "Up early today?" He crossed to a set of chairs near the fire, sitting as the warmth breathed new life into his cold limbs. The frigid nights of the winter Solstice came fast.

"Ha, not as early as you, it seems," Adon said with a playful grin, turning to face his twin. He had a broad and kind face, one you could trust as soon as it broke into a smile—which happened often. Therat lost track of how many countless hours he had spent basking in its glow, seeing the reflection of his father in the young man.

"Here, eat," demanded Adon as he shoved a plate of steaming pastries toward Therat. "You know, those muscles might eat you instead if you don't feed them."

Therat smiled, an easy thing to do around his brother. Though the pastry was simple—a creamy goat cheese with herbs—Therat devoured two, hungrier than he realized.

"Did you make these?" he managed to ask between mouthfuls.

Adon shook his head before replying.

"Papa, he could not sleep." Therat looked up from his plate, aware of Adon studying him intently. "Did you sleep, *darhir?*"

"Mmm, you know," Therat grunted in reply. He forced the remaining bite of pastry down his throat. It tasted sour going down.

"Therat..." Adon said, placing a gentle hand on his brother's arm, muscles quivering under his touch. "Is it happening again?"

Therat nodded before replying in a whisper. "I keep remembering the way she smelled, how her hands felt tracing down my back. Her face, the one she used to make when she'd scrunch her nose and call us her rascally boys. And then I wake, and it is over. I lose her all over again." Therat didn't want to talk about the other dream he kept having, the one where the woman with blue tattoos led him to the silver moon.

Adon's smile dropped at the mention of their mother, a pained look crossing before settling into heavy sorrow.

"It's not only that," Therat continued, trying to ignore the shadowy whispers thrumming with excitement in his mind. "I... I saw something strange a while back. I suppose I've been trying to see it again. Find out if my mind played a trick on me."

The brothers sat in silence for many long minutes. Therat watched the fire dancing and leaping across split logs and thin branches. Adon seldom offered empty words of comfort. The elder twin lived a calm life, even-tempered despite his quick smile. His presence alone anchored Therat to reality, brought the man back from the unrelenting compulsions and pain with nothing more than a touch.

In the growing quiet, Therat's attention returned to the strange woman from the week before. He tried with no success to recall any details about the blue tattoos on her hands, wondering how to identify his Mireithren.

He did not care much for the elite Named Houses and religious of Av Madhira, bitter toward any who thought they lived in the light of the gods. Where Therat despised the Makhian cult, it drew Adon in, the man fiercely devoted to the Golden Goddess Myrniar and her favored Madhiri. Over the long years of youth, Adon had grown close with Lady Ninann, born to one of the Sunmaiden's Houses and destined to be a blood-bound priestess.

The friends met years back as young children after Adon became lost in Myrniar's Refuge, alone in a place he did not belong. Therat had his suspicions about the girl, but she only brought joy to Adon's life. Kind, soft-spoken, humble: all qualities Therat envied. Adon and Ninann grew to be fast friends, bound for Tír is Isneha once she came of age and the Academy requested more recruits.

The Lady Ninann of House Isht'iri. If Adon's luck held and no *liraes* declared themselves after she came of age, Lord Émerin agreed to a marriage—if Ninann agreed too. Despite lacking a formal waveweaver's education, Adon already worked with the Skyweavers to bring summer rains to the desert city. The Named Houses always sought those with inborn talent to marry into their families. Though Ninann brought an ugly source of jealousy into Therat's life, only a fool would bring them up to Adon. He could ask for no higher blessing than the woman's hand in marriage. The only way—Therat hoped, at least—his brother could escape the dark doom haunting their family.

"Adon. Humor me for a moment," Therat said, interrupting the comforting blanket of silence. "If an *evranenith* was born to one of the Named Houses, what would they do? They are the favored of Myrniar, are they not? Do you think they would kill the child or hide them behind the Wall?"

Adon took a moment to reply, head of black curls shaking ever so slightly. "You know why we have to hide, Therat. What do you think? What good does it do to wish for a new past?" Adon shifted away from the hearth as he spoke. His voice lost the light-heartedness it held before. He sounded guarded, tense, each word chosen with care.

"I do not wish to make a new past for myself. I am merely... curious. I know so little of their customs. And I thought since you know a lady of a Named House, you mi—"

"No." Adon's terse reply gave Therat pause. "No, I would think it the same as us. They would be killed. Just as the others. It's why we hide."

Therat stared at his brother striding into the small kitchen opposite the hearth. Adon answered no so strongly, as if denying his thoughts.

He knows something.

"Even if they were one of Myrniar's Daughters?"

Adon gasped. Quiet, but enough for Therat to confirm his suspicions.

"It is ill-advised to speak of the Houses of the Sun in such a manner, *darhír*. You would speak ill of my friend, the Lady Ninann of House Isht'iri," Adon said acidly, turning around with a glower on his face. "Rumors bring down good people. You should know this."

Before Therat could defend himself, their grandfather ambled in, the soft rhythmic thump of his cane on the packed dirt floor like the ending bell of a fighting match. The anger left the twins' faces, though it lingered in the air, ruining the calm peace from a few minutes before.

Nazith crossed to an old and well-worn chair closest to the fire by Therat, lifting his faint violet eyes as he passed. The elderly man neared 340 years old, a milestone even for those from the

Named Houses with celestial blood. Though bent and gnarled with age, the man's mind remained sharp.

"You may as well finish bickering, I already heard the rest. My hearing has not gotten that poor yet." Nazith looked at Therat as he spoke, watching for the man's reaction.

"I-I wasn't trying to insult anyone, Adon. Forgive me. I think too much these days." The words sounded hollow to Therat, but they appeared to appease his brother and grandfather well enough.

Adon rejoined them in front of the fire. The conversation drifted to the day ahead, what new tasks awaited Adon as he petitioned for his place among the clergy of Myrniar. Therat let their voices drift past. Thoughts turned toward his brother's suspicious reactions to the questions about *evranenith* and the Named Houses. He had to know something.

An *evranenith* lived behind the Wall. A woman near their age, kept a shameful secret from the world. A Daughter of Myrniar. An Eásiri, a descendant of the gods blessed with long life and powers unimaginable.

His Mireithren.

The thought made Therat hot with anger. Why did Adon lie to him? Why did he even care? Mumbling his goodbyes, Therat stumbled into their bedroom and fell into a deep, uninterrupted sleep. Exhaustion from the past four nights of staying up finally caught up to the man.

By the time Therat awoke, the sun angled high in the southwestern sky and the fire was long dead in the hearth. A cool winter breeze blew through an open window, taking with it all the comforting smells of the morning. Adon left a note in a small, scrawling hand on the mantle; Therat left it unread. Adon could only be in one place: with Ninann at the Sunmaiden's Temple, the same as every other day from recent memory.

Though Therat usually craved isolation, this time it proved too much. The heavy silence let his thoughts run wild as anger tugged at his heart.

He hated the fact he cared so much about Mireithren, how she became an obsession in an instant. The very idea of a *liraes* sickened him. It served as a reminder of everything gone foul and astray in his life. Who could love a killer, deranged by the Shadow-weave?

Tales had come to the desert from the far reaches of Hylaea, how the Shadow-weavers from times past devastated villages and ruined lives when they succumbed at last to their tainted powers. Therat knew his end, whether he wanted it or not. He had made peace with the fact as well as he could. He would stay to see his brother safely off to the city of Weavers, then lose himself in the vastness of the desert until death came for him in one form or another.

But now he faced an obstacle. A constant, inescapable ache formed if he turned his thoughts for too long from the woman he named Mireithren. How could one person make him question everything he thought an undeniable fact in his life? If only he could find her, talk to her somehow. He wanted to prove to himself he wasn't crazy.

Why did Adon react so strangely to Therat's questions about the Named Houses? As thoughts turned toward his brother, the suspicions from before grew, a nagging thought at the back of his mind.

He knows. Maybe not who it is, exactly. But he knows of whom I speak.

"Why would you not tell me?" Therat yelled, his voice thundering through the quiet house.

He paced across the wide front room, mind swirling with a thousand thoughts. It made no sense. The woman, his brother, the obsessive thoughts compelling him to sit night after night on the Market rooftops.

The twins had few secrets between them, only Therat's shame and guilt over the blood on his hands. What guilt could his brother harbor? Therat tried to convince himself he overreacted earlier, but Adon's fervent defense of the Named Houses left behind an uncomfortable itch.

An *evranenith* in their midst. Could she be the reason his thoughts turned wild and full of malice over the years? Once, the boy controlled the Shadow-weave, using it without fear, hearing the siren call of the maiden in the void. But something changed after his sixteenth nameday. In the dying month of Mireile, as the year came to an end, Therat woke up one day with dark whispers in his mind and dread so heavy he felt his heart collapsing.

Mireithren. Did she awaken the evil inside of him?

Therat glowered in the house for hours, stewing in his thoughts. The bubbling anger turned into black rage, hateful of everything in his life. For years, Therat made it his sole purpose to protect his brother. The Boy and his Cub, Man and Cougar.

It had been the two of them for so long, clinging to each other for support as they navigated the world without the love and protection of their parents.

Adon's rejection of Therat stung, like a hundred tiny slices across his already ruined and scarred heart. It surprised him how much it hurt. Therat knew he could never claim Adon forever, so why did he care so much now? Perhaps he should leave the city now, rip the bandage off the festering wound.

Therat laughed. If he left the oasis, it would mean accepting never coming back. He would let the Shadow-weave take over, let the voices of a thousand dead and a thousand more ruin his mind until he exploded, every thought he ever had burnt from the world. The notion comforted him, soothing the razor-sharp edges of rage cutting into his soul.

C REAMY ORANGES AND PINKS danced across the sky when Therat finally roused himself. With a groan, he stretched muscles aching from sitting for so long. He meant to leave the city before Adon returned, unable to bear telling his twin good-bye in person. He would ache for a while, but Therat thought it better than watching the shadows claim him. Best to preserve what happy memories the two had.

Therat rifled through a chest in his shared bedroom, looking for a crumpled and ripped parchment buried under the few things precious to him in life. A whittling knife from his father and two half-finished foxes. Art books from his mother filled with her sketches of the far-away places she'd visited as a young woman. A scarf of hers, the faint scent of coconut and vanilla still clinging to the faded fabric, once bright silver and blue. Painful reminders of the past but precious beyond compare. Therat sniffed, trying to hold back the tears building behind his eyes.

He found the treasure he sought at last, holding it with shaking hands. The scar across his chest burned and ached, his heart bucking with anxiety. Forcing down the saliva pooling in his mouth, Therat smoothed the parchment, revealing a long letter written in a precise, tiny hand. He tried to avoid reading the words too closely, remembering all too well what the letter contained.

Though written nearly three years ago, little of Therat's feelings had changed. It would explain everything to his brother and help provide some closure and understanding about what the man had become.

The world became a dream, Therat floating from place to place with only passing recognition of what happened. He felt oddly peaceful, the black rage from before gone, as if someone had emptied the man of his inner turmoil.

Hollow. Numb.

It felt good not to struggle. Leaving the note on the mantle, Therat's feet carried him out of the house, down a sandy path, over hard rock until the white jackal statues loomed large. Therat paused at the Eyes of Vanyaseá, looking back on the oasis city one last time. Once up the narrow cliff stairway and on the lower plateau outside Av Madhira, the last of his mind slipped into the void.

He inhaled until his lungs felt like they would burst, the cool evening air engulfing him from the inside. The music of the Shadow-weave reached out, calling to him with the sounds he knew so well. He let it flow over his mind, losing all other thoughts and only focusing on the music of shadows. A cold, heavy presence settled over his skin, sending a wave of shivers across his rippling muscles. Dark shadows formed around the man. Threads of inky black darkness crawled up his legs, tendrils weaving in and out of his loose pants.

The Shadow-weave swimming through his body and mind left no room for thoughts of his own. Skin stretched tight as the shadows wove themselves with muscle and bone. Each breath brought with it the taste of ash and something sweet, a faint afterthought. The whispers in his mind coalesced together into an ancient and lost language, the sounds familiar but foreign at the same time. With a final breath, Therat opened his eyes.

A black veil clouded his vision, the world dark and dim through the haze. Shadowy tendrils so black they seemed to devour the light swam across his vision before plunging him into a deep, unending void. It sank through every cell and fiber of his being until something shifted. A second melody nestled within his soulsong roared to life. The shadows awakened, already clawing to take control, pulling and warping everything creating the man.

Drawn east to the home of the Sun, he slowly lost himself to the Shadow-weave, letting it take over his thoughts until Therat forgot even his name.

Nine

DISCORD

"I'M GOING TO KILL him, Inann! It's not even a threat, it's a promise."

Apattar swung at the air in front of her, beating her fists against an imaginary opponent in a fit of rage. Long black braids flew around her in a frenzy, azure blue beads slapping against her back. Danger lurked in those muddy brown eyes.

Within, the void thrummed to life, tendrils of black Shadow-weave looping themselves around her heart. The shadowy whispers began, calling for decay and ruin, growing quickly to a deafening roar. The scars across her right cheek burned as the blood rushed into her head, the two scabs throbbing with anger. The words her father so cruelly said earlier that morning played on repeat in her head.

I never wanted you to live, Apattar. I begged your mother for days to let me end your life. I never wanted you to live. I never wanted you. I never wanted you.

A thin line of crimson blood from her nose cut like a river through rich wet clay, tracing the soft curves of Apattar's round face before falling to the golden sands below. She wiped the blood away with a brusque jerk of her hand, smearing it like a badge of honor.

"I will show him death if he wishes to see it!" Apattar shouted, fists trembling with rage at her side.

"Atta!" Ninann shot out, eyes wide with concern. "No matter what hurt you bear, he is still our father! You speak nonsense, you are bitter. It will cool."

"No, he is *your* father, Inann. I am his eternal regret."

Apattar turned to face Ninann, paused for a moment by her stunning radiance. Red and yellow silks cascaded down from around her throat, hugging thick curves under draped thin chains of gold. The simple white veil falling over her loose black curls seemed to glimmer in the morning light. She was so beautifully perfect, so blissfully unaware of how much hate the world bore for her beloved twin.

"You didn't hear what he told me this morning, what... what my life means to him. The nights I spend under..." Apattar paused as a shadow fell over her face, the words falling to ash in her mouth. "I am worth nothing, a smear on your otherwise perfect life. He would shackle me like an animal if Mother let him, or worse."

A wave of nausea flooded over Apattar, the ever-present invisible hands tightening their grip around her neck, squeezing the air from her lungs. She collapsed on the ground, too dejected to even find the energy to control her emotions. Her exhaustion ran deep. If Apattar did not act soon, she would shatter under the torture exacted by her father's hands.

"You are always worth something to me, my dove." Ninann's words helped ease the rage. "From the moment you were born, I have never felt like I belong with anyone but you. I do not care what stars and curses say. Papa is a good man, but he is scared and superstitious. Following his heart, trying to... to, well. You know better than I." Ninann sat and pulled Apattar to her chest, untangling her twin's small braids with a gentle touch.

The two sisters sat on the sandy garden path in silence, only the occasional muffled sob from Apattar breaking the still morning. Apattar sank into Ninann's arms.

Apattar wished she could always feel Ninann's touch, arms wrapped around her like a cocoon of safety from the outside world. She felt adrift, clinging to her sister like a beacon of hope. If her achingly perfect sister could find a scrap of something worth loving in the girl deemed a black omen, then perhaps their father could too. Perhaps his mind would clear. He would see the Shadow-weave could not be purged, his actions slowly killing his daughter instead of saving her.

"I want him to see me! Not whatever black abomination he has painted in his mind." The words caught on the growing lump in Apattar's throat. She swallowed, trying to focus on the comforting warmth of her sister's presence. "I wish he could see what he has done to me. I'm not you, but I'm not evil!"

"Shh, shh. Hush now, my black dove," Ninann whispered, warm breath tickling Apattar's neck. "I love you as you are; we both burn brighter as two. *Soerl.* We are a gift from the gods to each other. Do you not remember your own words? Papa fears your fate, but I do not think he hates you. He fears you are, well..."

"I'm what?" The words flew out of Apattar's mouth as she jerked away from Ninann's embrace. "I'm cursed? Destined to go mad or end the world? I am not, I will not! I refuse this future! The stars did not write my life. The gods died eons ago! They ruined the world and abandoned us. Why would they curse me and bless you? We are the same!" The words tumbled from her mouth, rage unbridled, Apattar too exhausted to temper her feelings for Ninann's sake.

Ninann sat bathed in the gentle golden rays of the young day. Deep red-brown arms—soft and doughy from a life of luxury—sparkled as dew droplets condensed on her skin. Long wavy locks of black hair glowed with an amber hue at the edges. She somehow looked even more radiant in the sun.

Apattar hated seeing those bright green eyes clouded with even a hint of pain. For all the hurt and abuse Apattar had received from their father, she could not find anything but love in her dying heart for her devoted sister. A goddess in living form.

She's too perfect to even understand what I've done, isn't she? But I can't go back now. Father made sure of my fate.

"I don't know how to forgive him for what he has done, Ninann." The words clung in Apattar's throat. "And if I can't forgive him, this rage will only fester until one day you are not here, but he is. You do not know what lurks beneath the surface, the things my mind tells me to do when I lose control."

"Wh-what do you mean? When you lose control of what?" Ninann looked at her sister with quivering lips.

"I can't… You wouldn't understand. You are the white dove of our family, you bring hope and pride to our House. I am the black dove, a seed of destruction." Apattar's voice fell as she forced herself to continue. "Father says the void between worlds leaked into my being the moment I took my first breath under the black sun."

She wanted to say no more, but the hurt and worry in Ninann's eyes gave her pause. The woman deserved the truth. Apattar could only imagine what her life must look like in her sister's eyes. Once, they had been inseparable, thick as honey. Custom took precedence, and Ninann soon left to train at the temple, while Apattar spent the days locked in her chambers. What strange rationale did their father give Ninann when she found her *soerl* ripped away one day?

Apattar paused, sucking in a deep breath, letting the air expand in her lungs until it hurt. She exhaled and stilled her mind, closing her eyes before beginning again with a strained voice.

"I… I killed a man, Ninann. I am *everything* Father ever said I would be. I don't want to be, but I am."

Apattar hung her head in dejection, shoulders slumped forward under the crushing weight of her guilt. Weary brown eyes looked up at Ninann, still radiant and pure in the sunlight. The white dove, marred by the black stain before her.

Saliva pooled in Apattar's mouth; a bead of sweat broke out along her upper lip. The world fell out of focus, spinning at the edges of her vision. Apattar felt a hand wrap around her waist, but she could only focus on the taste of bile and the sounds of retching. She squeezed her eyes shut and tried to chase away the memories. The hazy face of a bald man, purple lips twisted into a half-formed scream, appeared out of the black void. His eyes rolled back into his head, the whites streaked with writhing shadows.

"But, but surely you had a reason!" Ninann's angelic voice scattered the memories drowning Apattar. "Like when the thieves came and Papa said you were attacked, when you got the first scars on your cheek." Ninann wiped a sleeve of her red and yellow dress across her sister's wet mouth, gentle touch soothing the chaos within.

Apattar took a few shaky breaths before looking back to Ninann. "Attacked," she chuckled weakly. A sanitized version of the evening of her fourteenth nameday, when the first blade descended on her face. "Do you want to know, truly?" she asked slowly, studying the sweet round face before her.

"I..." Ninann trailed off, afraid or unable to speak, Apattar could not tell. She walked over to a bench behind them, supporting Apattar as she collapsed on the cool white stone.

"You should know all of it, for it to make sense. I have been leaving home since I was eight, you know?"

Ninann's eyes widened.

"Eight? But you were still a little girl! I thought you said it only started a year before I caught you! What, so for nearly twelve years you've been sleeping *by yourself* in the desert at night? In the place we send criminals for punishment? By the gods, Atta, you, you... you could have been killed!"

"Father wouldn't have mourned my death," Apattar said with a bitter laugh. "I can't explain it. The stars, the cold snaking across my skin, the music of the shadows. You think me insane, I know, but our lives were different from the moment the world ripped us apart in the womb. I have had to find my comfort where I can. Fa— he, he hates me. I feel it in every word he utters."

Apattar touched the cluster of black scars racing down her right cheek, two still red and swollen. Each earned simply for existing as an *evranenith*.

"If not for your love, I would have run away long ago. You can't understand."

Ninann did not reply for a minute, or maybe three. The air sat heavy and stagnant between them, Apattar's words lingering on her lips and in Ninann's ears. Apattar felt the invisible hands return, clawing at her throat, a knot forming in her stomach as they came.

She desperately wished she would cry, could force the gnawing void out through her salty tears. But she knew they would not come. They rarely did, not after years of holding her gaze steady as her father showed his hatred and loathing of her existence with every touch. Her test of resolve had now become a prison with no escape, leaving dread feelings and memories festering in the dark.

"You're right, I can't understand. Not fully," Ninann said after a while, reaching for Apattar's arm with a timid touch. "I hate what Papa has done to you, and I don't think the *Makhaeren* is right, but we must try something if the Shadow-weave is so unstable! You are a daughter of the Sunmaiden, one of the blessed Eásiri! I still love you, as does Mother. She teaches me out of duty, not favoritism. Remember when we were little and you came to my lessons? Our powers are shared; she never denied your education. You must know you are loved!"

Apattar swallowed the guilt rising from the pit of her stomach. Why did Ninann have to make this harder?

"It's not only what he says and does, Ninann. I can't even begin to dream of your life. You have your freedom. My Little White Dove. I am glad you do, but where do you think I go during the days? How did I get these scars?" Apattar stared at her sister with hard eyes.

"He said you agreed to it, to try and siphon out the Shadow-weave... to cleanse you," Ninann murmured.

"And you believed him?" Apattar said with a strangled cry, disbelief that Ninann could be so innocent coloring her face. "He forced this upon me! Tortured me, claimed he wanted to purge me, set me free. Rotting away the hours with only my thoughts to keep me company. It festered until it formed a sickness inside my mind. Do you think he meant to drive me to the edge of insanity? I look up at the stars in the night sky and want to extinguish them from existence, to blanket the world in the same nothingness eating at my soul. If the gods did write my destiny—if such a thing is true—I will make them tell me why, or I will end their precious world. Maybe then they will deign to talk to me!"

"You sound deranged, Atta." Ninann tried to get up, but Apattar dug a hand into her arm, forcing her back down.

"You asked for me to unveil my demons, and now you must hear them. I need to cleanse this ache from my heart."

Apattar paused. The words begged to stay in her mouth, to deny the bloody, brutal truth of her crimes. She ground her molars together before starting again.

"Nine years old, Ninann, that's when I killed someone for the first time. An accident. I didn't mean to kill him, but it all happened so fast. The morning of our nameday, walking home through the trees, a man tried to grab me. He chased me, I panicked. A void opened up in my soul, consuming my mind and taking control. It came like I knew what to do all along. It felt primal, as if I connected with the First Harmonic at the moment of its creation and cut the very weave of his soul. The more time I put between myself and his death, I realized I *liked* what happened. Over the years, I thought of how I could use my powers to free myself from this prison and bring you with me."

Ninann did not speak or even make a sound. Apattar reached out to take her sister's hands, but the woman recoiled with a look of horror. Silent tears streamed down her perfect dark brown cheeks, mouth twisted in a look of pain as if trying to hold back a scream.

"For... for the first time?"

Ninann's voice cut like glass through Apattar's heart. She wanted to deny it, say the foul deed only happened once. But she could not lie when Ninann's bright green eyes pierced Apattar's soul, light shining on all the dark recesses of her past.

"Others." Apattar bit her lip, drawing a pool of blood to the surface. "Yes, others. The assassins... if Father told you. Didn't mean to kill, but I felt scared, hurting for so long." Her voice sounded far away, dream-like.

Trapped by her mind, Apattar wrestled with the memories of the thin woman who had plagued her for months, refusing to acknowledge the name that slipped out two weeks before.

Apattar closed her eyes and pulled wisps of the Shadow-weave deep in her heart into an orb of deep black nothingness. With each inhale, she imagined the void pulling the numbing pain from her body, feeding the hollowness eating away at the woman. As the void siphoned away the hurt, Apattar felt a sliver of herself go with it. Another fleeting happy moment, now lost forever to her darkness. Soon, the warmth of the desert returned to her bones, but the ache of her fractured heart remained.

"... about an attempt on your life."

The sound of Ninann's voice pulled Apattar back from endless oblivion, hearing the words through the thick haze clouding her mind. Apattar took her twin's hand, tracing the pattern of flying doves and flaming suns with care, letting the warmth bring her back to life.

"There is no love left in this heart, little dove," she said after a long silence. "None save for the bond we share. You are my guiding light, my sister, my best friend. I need you to understand me, please! I can't lose this too, you are the only comfort I have." Apattar's mouth was dry, her tongue heavy and thick.

"How could you ever expect me to understand this!" Ninann's voice cracked as she forced the words out.

"Please help save me from myself, Ninann. I'm scared, I don't want to lose control forever." A hushed whisper, the cold morning breeze bore her words away.

Ninann looked down at her hand in Apattar's, clasping the other over her twin's arm. The warm touch pushed back the hollow nothingness consuming Apattar. A single tear escaped from her right eye, falling on top of a bright blue dove on Ninann's hand. Those emerald green eyes—always full of love and compassion—looked up, now guarded and uncertain. Apattar could feel her bond with Ninann weaken, the music always thrumming between the two of them falling out of sync.

A shiver ran down Apattar's spine. What happened when the shared harmonic of two souls diverged? The change was subtle, a fraction of a heartbeat's difference between their songs. Yet, a vast canyon had emerged between Apattar and her twin.

"I..." Ninann paused, basking in the silence for some time. Apattar remained silent, desperately hoping her sister would break the unsettling quiet between them.

"I don't know what to say. How could I stop loving you when I am you, and you are me? I will try to help, but what could I even do? I understand nothing you are telling me! Voices, compulsions, all this rage and hurt at the hands of our father you have kept away from me for our entire lives! It is an endless ocean to swim across and find you. But swim I will. I must."

Apattar slipped her hands from Ninann's grasp and stood up, walking forward a few paces before turning back around toward her twin. She held out her right hand and, with her eyes closed, began to imagine the black nothingness eating at her pushing out with each heartbeat. It spread into her fingers until it slowly seeped out of the tips. Tendrils of black Shadow-weave crawled into her palm. The air cooled around Apattar's hand as the void within her materialized. It pushed back the desert heat from her body, enclosing the young woman in a blanket of cold.

A small black orb took form, so devoid of color it seemed to suck the very vitality from the world around it. Apattar slowly sighed, setting her gaze on the manifestation of the emptiness she harbored within.

"This is what festers inside me, Ninann," Apattar said with bitterness. "Your black dove is perhaps more aptly called a dove devoid of life."

Ninann stood and walked to her twin, reaching a trembling hand toward the black orb before pulling it back. Her eyes were wide and curious, changed from the terror she held moments before. Apattar could swear she saw a shadow growing behind her sister's eyes.

"You are not empty, you are hurt. *Evranenith* escaping the dagger are rare, it is true. But if they have lived and the world still turns, then you will not be the end of it, this I know. Maybe it's not even a curse, my dear sister. Maybe you're just... you." Ninann spoke with an unexpected understanding.

"You are too complicated for words, Atta, and for this, I love you. I don't know what I can do, but tell me and we will find a way. You will be of age soon; by law, your path will be your own. Surely you can survive two more years."

"I think..." Apattar paused, closing her hand and letting the tendrils of cold shadow sink back in before continuing. "I think

I need to go away. To find some answers, but most of all to find what life is like away from him and Av Madhira."

Apattar looked up at the sky, now painted with pastel shades of pinks and oranges as the sun rose. Her gaze settled on the hazy moon sitting low on the western horizon. An invisible thread pulled at her heart. It seemed to tell her, *come find me, remember.* For one beat of her heart, Apattar almost thought she had lived another life, one that knew fierce, devoted love. The breath caught in her throat at the thought that seemed more like a memory. A faint whisper of hope took its place among the ever-present voices of dark desires and empty feelings.

"West. I need to go west. I've seen gateweaving in my books, I know I can find my way home if I get lost." *If there is a fate, perhaps happiness is not beyond reach if I adjust my perception of the world.* "And I must leave today." Apattar spoke with an authority that even startled her, unsure if the words were entirely her own.

"You mean to leave? Alone? And trust a conjured portal to carry you to safety?" gasped Ninann.

"You belong here, sister. The great hope of Av Madhira, a priestess-to-be, the white dove of our family. You have our parents' love and a man who cares deeply for you, even if you are not *liraes*. I could never ask you to strip it all away for me. Our paths diverged long ago, but I did not want to admit it."

Ninann reached a hand up to Apattar's face, cupping her sister's cheek, taking care to avoid touching the scars racing down her face. Apattar could not decipher the look on Ninann's face, unsure if anger or grief clouded those seemingly forever happy emerald eyes.

"You will lose yourself," she finally whispered before letting her hand fall away.

For nineteen years, Apattar lived for her sister and tried to show her father she was no different than Ninann. Endured every torture, every experiment to "save" her from something as natural as her hair. The weight of the act had nearly crushed her.

"I've already lost myself, Ninann. But out there," she spread her arms, gesturing toward the southwestern horizon. "Out there, I might find my purpose again."

"But, but... what about us? Do you mean to abandon me forever?"

The smile on Apattar's face fell at her sister's words. She spun toward Ninann and pulled her in tightly, breathing in deep, savoring the comforting smell of roses after a spring rain. Ninann laid her head on Apattar's shoulder. Hot tears ran down the soft curves of her collarbone.

The two sisters stood there in silence, holding each other as they had done so often through their lives. Apattar wished she could stay in this moment forever, never forced to leave the other half of her soul behind. But the longer they comforted each other, the louder and more insistent the hushed whisper became.

This is a dream, it was always a dream. She walks in the light, but the shadows bend and shape under your will. You will die here, daughter. You will die.

Apattar cleared her throat while pulling away from Ninann, wiping the tears from her sister's round face with a gentle touch.

"We are bound forever, fated to always weave our music together. I will never leave you, my little dove. Not forever." The words broke as Apattar spoke, sorrow spilling from each syllable.

"Promise me. Promise me you will remember who you are. My black dove. Promise you will return to me happy. It's all I've ever wanted for you." A smile crept into the corners of Ninann's quivering lips.

"This is my vow to you, as my soulbound. I cannot say when I will return or where I will go, but I will always return to you. We will be together forever—who else could ever love me as you do?"

Ninann slid off one of her golden rings, the thin band inlaid with deep red rubies like tiny droplets of blood. She took Apattar's hand and slid the ring on one of her fingers, sealing the favor with a kiss.

"For good luck and a token of my blessing." She paused as if thinking over her next words. "You amaze and bewilder me, Apattar. I don't think I will ever understand what goes on in that beautiful head of yours. We are so alike, yet entirely different. I love it about you, and if it means you must leave, I will not stand in your way. Return to me—my only request."

Apattar did not reply, merely smiled and kissed Ninann on her plump cheek. A confused mix of excitement and trepidation gripped her heart, thoughts of her sister and Saiya tugging at the back of her mind.

Anything could be awaiting her outside Av Madhira, but one thing was certain—nothing could be worse than facing her father again.

PART TWO

THE MAIDEN'S DOOM

Under the silver stars you came,
a maiden in the night so fair.
Snow-clad still, eyes aflame,
Shadows streaked through your hair.
My heart was turned without complaint,
to behold such beauty beyond compare.
In the city of white towers I was unaware,
Adrift without love,
Until a siren song filled the air.

Ever-fair!
I will seek you there where the light ends and void begins.
My Snow Flower bloomed under night's gloom,
For you I would repent my deadliest of sins.

Ten

A BLACK LAND IN A BLACK SEA

For three hundred and forty-three days—a full year—Apattar knew the taste of life outside her four marble walls. She walked through endless sands and parched, rocky ground until at last she found the desert did indeed end. Amber grasses and lonely, twisted trees towered above the traveler. She followed paths tread over thousands of years etched across the Sea of Grass, forever seeking the resting place of the moon in the

West. She ate little and slept even less, eyes wide, drinking in the world around her.

But now, hopelessness replaced her wonder. A damp cold clung to her very bones, Apattar's body grown gaunt from a hard year of travel. The years seemed shorter before, each day blurring into the next. In the wilds, one year passed like ten. If not for the consistent lunar cycle, Apattar would have deemed the passage of time inaccurate.

Apattar struggled to recall the feel of burning, gritty golden sands under her bare feet. How the breezes off Lake Anataerl eased the oppressive heats of summer, and she never knew the meaning of true cold. Now, it was her constant companion in the dead days of the Moondark months, the world stagnant while Death reigned.

The rocky wasteland she found herself in was a miserable and lonely place, somehow more depressing than the isolation of her gilded cage in Av Madhira. At first, she welcomed the salty air. Yet, as the days passed and she explored the ruined island, the cold settled deep in her bones until even the void nestled inside her heart warmed her body.

Cold sea winds assaulted the small spit of land. They lashed out at her sun-drenched skin without mercy, pulling all memory of warmth from her thin frame. Apattar hugged herself, rocking on her heels, trying to recall what the sun upon her sweat-dampened skin felt like.

An ever-present dim orange glow on the northern horizon outlined a massive black mountain, its shadow dominating the world below. Apattar could hardly bear to look at the giant, for it evoked a grief so deep it cut through the ever-present numbness.

But, try as she might to look away and turn her thoughts to escape, the task proved impossible.

A hauntingly beautiful music crossed the dark seas to the woman's ears. It fell upon her like an enchantment, worming its way into her heart and setting it alight with curiosity. She tried to use her gateweaving to summon a portal to the mountain, but something seemed to hold her back, stifling every attempt to cross the portal's shimmering threshold. Now, it served as a source of heat on the ashen island, warming the starving woman.

Apattar learned about opening portals through gateweaving from books her sister brought in secret—though the endeavor proved reckless. After almost a year of walking across the vast desert and through the sea of amber-green grasses, she had come to a wide, fast-flowing river. The Andesiri, the Singing River of Gold, it tumbled over massive rocks, foaming like a rabid monster.

One of the Maiden Aslyren's domains, the great Andesiri River held back the shadows of the West. The sight frightened Apattar, who only knew the calm peace of Lake Anataerl, rivers no more than words and blue lines in her books and art. She lingered for days on the banks of the blue monster, growing to love and hate the deep waters of the Andesiri River.

Though she never tried gateweaving before, the urge pulling her forward could not be ignored. But something went wrong, and though she tried to place the portal on the western banks of the roaring river, Apattar plunged headfirst into an inky black sea. The crushing weight of the waves pulled her under in seconds, a thousand hands dragging the woman down with all their might. The cold felt like it would freeze her solid, every cell screaming as jagged daggers of ice carved their way through her body.

Then, as if plucked by an invisible hand toward the surface as her vision faded to black, she ended up on a rocky shore. Apattar could only remember the hazy pale face of a woman with white hair pulling her from the sea. When Apattar awoke, she saw no sign of life or savior. She crawled across the rocks, bloodied hands stinging from the salty waters. Collapsing on the black stone floors of a ruined building, Apattar passed the first night in a broken sleep, body aching from the sea's assault and shivering to keep warm.

The bright sun greeted Apattar the following day, warming her bones and returning life to the maiden. As the fogs lifted, Apattar realized where she had landed: the ruins of Andeshar, the black scar across the western hemisphere of Eás.

Once, the continent teemed with life, an ethereal emerald land and home of the most beautiful city known to the Elessí. A place where the Sisters were held as equals, a home built for them amongst the Seven Temples. Long had it stood as a place of peace and beauty, until the ambitions of the Dark Goddess sundered the world. Her greed disrupted the First Harmonic, and Discordance entered the World Song; Death Herself touched all.

Stranded on the small rocky island, Apattar's thoughts turned toward the one who cursed her, the Goddess's true name lost to time. For so long, Apattar tried to deny that the gods took part in her life, told herself they were better off dead and gone. Those who still followed the old ways would rather face delusion than the truth. As Apattar sat huddled under a ruined stone wall, shivering from the wind, she wondered, *am I the delusional one?*

If Apattar closed her eyes, she could almost feel the warmth of a godly presence. A peace unlike anything she knew, soothing her aching heart, telling the woman, *you are loved.* She knew she should feel repulsion. The gods broke the world, left their darkness behind for it to fester until parents hated their children simply for being born at the wrong time.

Yet, could the Dark Goddess be more than history remembered?

Apattar passed the second night on the island with little sleep. Numb from the cold, she opened a portal to the looming black mountain in the distance, following the strange music she hoped would lead to a friendly face. Blistering heat radiated from the shimmering surface like a mirage, a comfort reminiscent of the desert she had begun to miss. Apattar reached a tentative hand forward, ripples spreading out from her fingertips. The hazy mirage warped around her touch before a solid wall stopped her from moving any further. Defeated, damp with sea mist, and chilled from the biting winds, Apattar passed into a stupor, curled on the floor in front of the portal.

The faint sound of chanting and whispered screams echoed within the crumbling black stone walls the second night. Sleep did not come until the sun crested the horizon. When Apattar awoke, a thin broken chain of gold laid in front of the portal, blood smeared across half of it. Never fearful—perhaps to a fault—she spent the day studying the strange item, large enough to be a bracelet or anklet.

In the afternoon, she tried to cross the portal again, following the source of the chanting. The people there might help, send the lost wanderer back to the lands of Hylaea and across the river where she meant to go. Despite the mysteries, Apattar did not feel unsafe. Rather than flee the island and return home like a beat dog, she meant to press on, to find some sort of meaning for this rash decision to leave the meager comforts of home.

Now, three days after finding herself on one of the many rocky remains of Andeshar, a growing sense of urgency clawed at her mind. Traveling out of the Madhira had been difficult, slipping away from her family estate by far the easiest part. Everything before now paled in comparison to the frustrations the island brought.

Why did the failed portal send her here, of all places? Did some cosmic force pull her here, mean for her to find something in the desolated lands? Something or someone kept her away from the black mountain—what could be so enticing about the destination? Try as she might, nothing availed her attempts to cross. A heavy sigh deflated Apattar's will, shoulders slumped forward.

I will die here.

She welcomed the thought. Lost without purpose, clinging to fragments of voices from a mind slipping into madness. Crumbs left for food.

What a stupid girl.

Apattar ran the chain through her bony fingers again and again, hoping something would spark within and show her the way forward. She leaned to stand when a muffled voice came from the direction of the portal at her back. A faint sound, it grew louder with each word, as if someone approached.

"... found enough, Ruarc. It's time to leave. The girl's powers are strong, I can't keep her out for much longer."

A woman's voice floated past her ears. The stark white face seen in a haze came back to her. Her rescuer? Why would the woman save her, only to let starvation take the girl? Apattar crept behind a half-crumbled pillar, reaching for the Shadow-weave as she listened. Her skin grew cold as the shadows awoke.

A man grunted an unintelligible curse in response. "There are five *fasni* alive. Five more expeditions for fireglass." An edge of malice undercut every syllable he uttered, voice sharp like a dagger. Apattar imagined him with a thin, angular face that never smiled, the same as the woman she tried to erase from memory.

Tela.

A shiver ran up her spine as the man spoke. "Besides, if you had let the girl drown, or even better yet put the chain on her, we wouldn't need to be having this discussion. Why even bother coming when the Queen granted..." The man's voice faded away.

Apattar gasped, then clasped her hands over her mouth, desperately hoping the power allowing her to hear the two strangers did not work the other way. If this woman's powers could keep someone from entering a portal of their making, she had no desire to meet either of them. Apattar crouched in a stunned silence, staring at the gold chain still clutched in one hand.

Her blood ran cold, realization of what the chain in her hand was washing over Apattar. Rumors came to the desert in her father's youth brought by the far winds: an ancient power had awoken in the West. People were seen with golden chains around their ankles, crying and weeping as they wrought destruction with their own hands, compelled by their masters. Searching the northern lands in the name of the Dark Goddess for something unknown, taking children as they went.

Rumor passed into a tale told to scare young children; shadows and slaves moving in the dark of night, killing parents and stealing children. Apattar never feared the tale, for being stolen seemed a blessing as a child.

But now it seemed all too real.

With a single thought, Apattar severed the weave of music keeping her portal open. The shifting mirage snapped shut as a final wave of heat burst through the blackened ruins. A flurry of questions ran through her mind as the man's voice rang in her ears.

Put the chain on her, we wouldn't need to be having this discussion... put the chain on her... put the chain on her...

Why would a slaver spare Apattar? Surely the woman did not have morals when it came to runaway youth. Why would the music compel her forward to meet these people? The faint screams and chanting from the night before now made sense: souls condemned and dying under the hands of these strangers. Yet, for what? What was this fireglass the man spoke of, and why was it precious enough to kill for? These could not be the ones who would help; this land stank of death and withered hopes.

The guiding voice whispered in reply.

Yes, yes, these people know, they hunted for the truth, once.

A frustrated scream erupted from Apattar's throat. "No! Why can't you tell me what to do? Is my life a game? Am I already insane, pulled toward delusions and death?"

The winds screamed and howled in reply, racing through the black ruins. A low rumble seemed to split the sky open. It began to weep, soft at first. The gentle rains turned to a torrential downpour assaulting the land below. The half-collapsed roof offered meager shelter.

A white line streaked across the sky, blinding the cowering woman. The sky never lit on fire like this at home. Before she could think, a loud *crack* sounded overhead from the deep purple clouds. The sound rolled over the island in deafening waves. Energy crackled in the air. The hair on Apattar's arms stood up as if trying to flee. Terror rooted her in place, pressed into the corner wall with wide eyes seeing all.

Another flash of white streaked across the sky, splitting halfway across the horizon. A jagged line of lightning raced down toward a dead tree in Apattar's sight. The bolt struck the top of the tree. A hideous crackling and popping sound filled the air as it burst into flames. An involuntary scream escaped Apattar's lips, drowned out by the booming clap of thunder overhead.

The deep, endless rumbling reminded her of her father's voice. Apattar closed her eyes and tried to hum the *Snow Flower* melody Saiya taught her as a child, but the sound stuck in her throat.

Bright red flashed across her closed eyelids with the next lightning strike; she prepared for the deafening reply from the sky. The square face of her father began to form in the blackness of her terror. Apattar made a feeble attempt to open her eyes and make it go away. Dread snaked through each vein, paralyzing her, forcing her to witness her father's harsh gaze.

Cold, calculating brown eyes looked at her in disapproval, the dark mahogany face twisted into a scowl. They bore through to her heart, searing the remnants of the tattered and broken thing with his fiery faze. Cruel, dark lips began to move. A voice slithered across her mind, probing each corner, sinking deep into every thought.

I never wanted you to live, Apattar. I begged your mother for days to let me end your life, let me fulfill my duty, purge evil from this world. You can thank her for your cursed life, not me. I have done everything I could to keep the world safe without breaking your mother's heart. Everything to rid the black evil lingering inside, to free my daughter. I see I was foolish now. You desire to consort with the shadows; do not fear them as the Sunmaiden's Children should. Your actions will end the world if left unchecked. Makhaeren Ánnarsera and I will... be visiting later this morning. Until then, leave my sight.

Apattar's eyes flew open. The last words her father said cut as deep this time as the morning when she fled Av Madhira. They sliced and shredded her heart until she thought she would bleed out and die. Her hands and arms began to tremble, a cold tingle running through her thin body, growing stronger with each faint flutter of her heart.

The thunder rumbled above, the sky nearly black with rage, but Apattar remained a world away, drowning under the deafening sound of blood rushing past her ears. The chill void of Shadow-weave spread and consumed more of her broken soul, hollowing out the pain and rejection. Nothing remained except a cold and unwavering desire, no matter the cost.

Freedom.

Eleven

DEAD VOICES

T

HIRTY MORE OVER THERE, commander, in the far building. Two Timeweavers and five Earthweavers. If we split and surround...

No, no, you can't take her! She is innocent, you have no proof! Give her back, give her to me! She's my child, my baby girl! She isn't a monster, please!

Rally to the Queen! To the Snow Flower, go, go! Hurry, we must leave! Grab Baliya, get the princess! There is no time, leave him, leave him! Protect the Queen!

Why didn't I run? Why did I stay? Oh gods, I'm sorry, I'm sorry! I thought I could escape. Sanya? Sanya? Please wake up, please open your eyes, tell me it's all going to be okay. No, go away, go away, I don't care what you say! I won't do it again, I'd rather die, oh gods, I'd rather die...

They are the kinslayers, not us! The first blood of the Elessí is on the hands of the Maiden and her son. Do you not feel their stinking hatred still in our lands? Were we not the ones who came to find the truth? Let us hunt, brothers and sisters! To the shadows, my Dirnithrí! To war!

When I was young, before I knew of this world, before I knew of Music, I was alone. At peace in the dark. This is all I have wanted, my son, to find my peace again. I knew joy so boundless that nothing since has tasted sweet. I see the look in her eyes, and my heart stills. I wish to hide but know not where. Go east if you will, but I will stay, stay in the shadows and silver moonlight to fin d my peace.

Yes, yes I will do it, if I must. Please, let it end. I won't fight, just take it all. Everything. I surrender...

They are over there, go, hurry! She is bleeding still, they will not get far. Save the woman if you can, but do not let the child live! Kill it quick, kill her if you must. Go, before the snow hides her! The pale woman calls upon the White Witch for help. She will disappear, hurry!

I'm here, Little Cub. I won't let them hurt you. Pull them in closer, let the Siren's song fill your heart. I am right here. I will never let you go, sweet boy. The dark will not hurt you so long as you remain calm. I am lucky to be a mother to such sweet young boys, you and Adon both.

Brother, why do the shadows not scare you?

Twelve

WHITE GEMS

MEMORIES OF THOUSANDS LONG dead swam through Therat's clouded mind. It became harder to tell man from shadow as the year wore on. Slipping into madness, losing himself to the screaming voices trapped in the twisted Shadow-weave.

Time lost meaning. Each day passed by in a black haze. Little of the world made it through the Shadow-weave coursing through his broken body. Even so, the descent into madness took longer than he imagined. Some feeble voice told him to fight, to live.

Too little, now. Too late.

Everything good fled from Therat's life. Adon would leave the city soon for an education most could never dream of. Ninann never strayed from his side, and, if she had no *liraes*, the two would marry. Safe, secure. Therat wanted this for Adon, but gods, was it hard to witness. One day, he would wake to find Adon a stranger. A stranger like their mother and father, their faces long gone from Therat's memory.

He had to run away, had to lose himself now that his sole purpose in life was complete.

Sleep—what little came—staved off the insanity. Did his body not realize it fought a futile war?

The haze cleared more during the day when Narán illuminated the world. Its warmth would break through the Shadow-weave and Therat's senses slowly returned. Some days, the heat ate at Therat's resolve to lose himself to his insanity, amplifying the hoarse whisper telling him to survive.

Today was one of those days.

Why give up now? What about her?

Something deep inside Therat's fractured mind came to life at the thought of the maiden in the shadows. A deep hurt squeezed at his heart. He stumbled, falling to his knees. The shadows swimming in his mind darkened until he could only see the endless black of nothingness.

As if emerging from the shadows like the night he saw her bloodied and beaten, Mireithren appeared in Therat's mind. He clawed at his face, fingers catching on a beard grown long and unkempt, but the Maiden of Shadows did not leave. She held a strange look on her face, a cross between pity and anger, and something else Therat could not place. Did not *want* to place.

"Get out, get out, GET OUT!" he cried, his plea echoing over the barren rock and far-away dunes.

Mireithren's face twisted at his words. Her eyes turned black, pulling Therat in until he was awash with agony. His blood turned to liquid fire, each frantic beat of his heart searing him from inside until he thought he would turn to ash. Straining muscles grown weak from starvation, Therat stumbled to his feet. The radiant heat of Myrniar's gift chased away the void as he turned to face the sun.

"What do you want with me? You will ruin me, use me to work the Dark Goddess's vile machinations. It must be, it must," he whispered, trying to ignore the pain in his heart.

A whistling wind rushed past his ears like a scream. Mireithren's face turned to smoke, and the pain fled with her cruel eyes. He breathed a sigh of relief. One day soon, he would lose his memories of that raven-haired woman with a scarred face and the universe in her eyes.

Restless, Therat resumed walking. After some time, he dimly became aware of a small bluish line in the distance surrounded by a copse of trees. Thirst clawed at his throat. For days, he had only tasted the iron tang of his bleeding lips. A strange feeling like he had been here before passed over Therat, but the desire for water numbed the sensation.

A hazy outline of trees gathered around a small crescent moon-shaped lake came into view. The water remained cool even under the desert sun. Therat choked it down, icy liquid washing down weeks of dust. Instinct took over, sustaining life where his mind would not.

After drinking his fill, Therat collapsed. The dark returned to take his vision. He passed into a daze under the shade, too weak to move but too restless to sleep. Hours passed before the warmth faded from his skin. Night approached, and with it, the one small joy Therat had in life: losing himself.

The ghosts of millions long dead came when night descended. More of the man would slip away, until one day he would wake and not remember a thing. Therat longed for such an end. It would be a relief. He was too broken to have a future. Too afraid of what the woman wanted.

Yet, on this night, the Shadow-weave did not claim more of the man. Instead, it melted away from his vision, leaving his eyes clear for the first time in months.

The world looked different than he remembered. Twisted, gnarled. The acacia trees here bent low to the ground, leaf tips tinged red as if they had been dipped in blood. A haunting, eerie music wafted through the air—a dirge, it seemed. An echo of some past tragedy. Unrelenting sorrow cut through the Shadow-weave, pulling Therat from his black cocoon that suffocated instead of transformed.

Wind blew away the clouds covering the moon. Silver light glittered over the land below. It reflected off the still surface of the crescent-shaped lake, illuminating the small oasis like a mirror.

The music grew louder in Therat's ears. He knew this place. It came to him in his dreams, a thousand times and a thousand more.

"Mama... Da..." he whispered. Therat fell to his knees, a dagger of grief plunged into his heart.

He found himself in the place where his life ended seventeen years ago. Where he should have died, along with his brother. But instead, the boy took wild shadows into his heart, naive enough to think they would always answer to him.

A bitter laugh rang out in the growing night, running over the soft rise of hills and off to the far horizon. A fitting place to find his end, back where it all began those many years ago.

Therat stood, taking in the waxing shape of the moon rising on the southeastern horizon. He could not tell how long he had wandered the desert, but something told him this was *that* day. The one tinged with red he could never erase from memory. He cursed whatever part still remembered, the part pulling him here. But Therat would not give in, could not relive the memories he locked away.

A gust of wind blew past, cold teeth biting at his exposed flesh. Something moved in his peripherals. A jewel caught in the branches of a leafless tree glittered in the moonlight. A shadow took form on the western horizon against the dim glow of the retreating sun. The shade grew larger, devouring the light. Was this the end? Death Herself, come at last?

The umbral shroud melted away from the figure before him, revealing a woman with waves of deep auburn red hair. Dark gray eyes peered out from a heart-shaped face. A face Therat once swore he would never forget. The tangle of grief rose, the tears he refused to shed desperately seeking release.

"No... Mama!" The words tore at his throat. Therat reached a hand out to the vision: his shepherdess to the Undying Realms Beyond.

A thin chain looped over several of her fingers. It glowed a faint blue in the moonlight, pale and ethereal against his mother's dark skin. The pendant hung low, a crescent moon around a silver tree with white gemstone leaves. Therat knew it well: an heirloom of his mother's House passed down since the end of the First Era. As a boy, he delighted in the stories she told him of women it graced over thousands of years. She wore it... on the night... when her head... when her head...

Therat scrambled back from the vision. His heart raced, eyes squeezing shut trying to fight back the pain.

I'm here, Little Cub. I won't let them hurt you.

His mother's voice. A soft sighing song as delicate as she. It quelled the panic in an instant, the words embracing Therat as his mother used to. He opened his eyes. The vision left, but the necklace remained, tangled in the thorns of an acacia tree. Sucking in his breath, Therat stared long at the lost heirloom. A piece of his mother returned. Proof she existed outside of his blurred memories.

The longer he stared at the pendant, the more memories returned to a mind devoid of happiness. The glow of his mother's smile, one side of her mouth curled up higher than the other over a dimple. The way her eyes sparkled in the moonlight, turning silvery-gray. The stories passed down from her family of shade-walkers, of a time when delicate flowers of silver and trees of white grew in the shadows. She did not fear them. Therat wished he could live like her. His mother always seemed so peaceful, finding bliss during the day with his father but freest at night under the cloak of shadows.

The tears welling behind Therat's eyes burst through, burning as seventeen years of repressed emotions cascaded down his bare chest. All the rage, the sorrow, the sleepless nights trying to find a reason for his never-ending tragedies. The beauty of his mother's face brought the harsh reality of life back into focus.

The ghosts of the past left. In the silence, the thoughts he tried desperately to ignore came thundering back. He abandoned his family. Though leaving soon, Adon would come back to Av Madhira in time. And what of his grandfather? His promise to find his parents' killers, to bring them to justice? He could not let the madness claim him, not yet. He wanted to die but needed to live for his mother and father.

He needed to find answers. Did Mireithren have something to do with his torture? A flash of anger quelled the tears at the thought of the maiden. He hated her... craved her... had to do anything to stay away from her.

Pushing past the rage, Therat thrust his hand into the tangle of thorns. He clawed at the necklace, blood dripping down his arm. A finger slipped around the delicate silver chain. He pulled, and it broke free, falling into his waiting hand.

The pendant looked smaller than Therat remembered, yet it still evoked the same sense of wonder and awe. Crafted by the hands of the greatest silversmiths in all of Eás, his mother said. A gift from Serenata's father, the first of House Anatnará. Therat stroked the glittering white gems, remembering how he once thought them stars pulled from the night sky itself. The pendant still held the warmth of the heart that once beat beneath the crescent moon.

Therat sat clutching the necklace to his heart. The moon's reflection in the lake was a healing aura, excising all the terror from the voices plaguing him for decades. A song composed of many soft voices in perfect harmony filled the air. A choir of the gods, if there ever was one. They sang until the first light of dawn turned the eastern sky orange.

When the sun rose, Therat vowed to return to Av Madhira. At peace, as best he could be, he would find answers for his mother and father—or die trying. He thought no longer of the maiden he hated.

Unclasping the hook of the necklace, he looped it twice around his leg. The pendant nestled in the crook behind his outer ankle bone. The metal cooled, the touch a reminder of the promise he made to his mother and father those many years ago.

He would find answers. He must.

THE VISITOR IN WHITE

A PATTAR SAT HUDDLED UNDER the half-standing roof for what seemed like hours, stewing in her bitter desires for revenge and freedom from her father. The rain slowed after a time to a mellow drizzle before moving on with the winds to the northern horizon. Soft clouds and mist took their place, leaving the world below in a cool gray haze.

An eerie silence settled over the island, a bubble drowning out even the sound of the ocean waves. Apattar welcomed the blessed silence, letting it fill her mind and push out all the voices clamoring to be heard. A sense of relaxation and comfort eased through her tired and cold limbs. For a moment, Apattar thought of the guard who calmed her heart the first time she broke out with Saiya. She embraced the feeling, and her heartbeat settled after a time.

You survived, it wasn't that bad. You are fine, Apattar.

"You are a curious thing, aren't you?"

The woman's voice from before broke the silence. A clear and musical sound, each word lilted into the next.

Apattar's attention snapped to the broken roof above her head. On a crumbling balcony to her left crouched a woman with impossibly pale white skin and short waves of stark white hair. She glowed against the burnt and blackened stones. Apattar had never seen a person with skin lighter than sandy brown; this woman appeared otherworldly, a vision perhaps, or a being from another time. The pale woman wore a muted silvery tunic under a crimson red bodice, shiny black stones cut like teardrops adorning one shoulder and the upper thighs of her fitted white pants. Everything about the woman screamed danger.

Apattar could only squeak in reply.

"You needn't fear me. You are of more use to me with your freedom, although I sense you do not entirely have it yet." The white woman spoke with an odd tone, almost maternal and protective. "You are much too young to be... here." Her gaze swept across Apattar's face as she paused, lingering on the trail of curved scars down the frightened woman's cheek.

The pale stranger jumped down with ease from her perch, stretching her long legs as she straightened. Tall and lanky, the woman carried herself with pride, reminding Apattar of the street cats running wild through Av Madhira. With a distinctly feline grace, the woman leaned against the wall, arms crossed over her chest. Power and authority oozed from the stranger.

"Hmm. I forget myself. Introductions first, yes, *neha?* I am Laisha." Shadows surged around the woman as she spoke, the black stones somehow blacker than before. "If I meant you harm, I promise it would have been done days ago. You're rather loud, you know? You are adept at gateweaving, but whoever taught you leaves quite a trace."

Apattar cleared her throat, forcing her heavy tongue to move.

"I, uh... I," Apattar swallowed, trying to imagine holding her sister's hand. A tiny flicker of warmth came and left. "I wasn't trying to pry into your business, whatever it is. I'm lost, is all. I only sought warmth." Apattar grimaced, hardly believing her own words despite it being the truth.

"Oh, *neha!*" The woman in white named Laisha laughed as she spoke, a hollow and shrill sound. The way she said child in the Elder Tongue almost sounded mocking. "*Neha,* if I cared about that, I'd let my brother have his way. I'm curious about you, that's all. There are no chance visitors to the remains of Andeshar. Say, I'll tell you something about myself and you do the same."

Apattar blinked, steadying her nerves. She knew this game, how the mousers on the family estate liked to toy with their prey, giving them a false sense of relief before descending with merciless fangs. Looking around, Apattar found no escape. Her waveweaving helped the woman survive the long road thus far, but she was outmatched here.

"I sense I have little choice in this matter," Apattar said coolly, reaching for the dark void tugging at her core, letting the fear melt into it. "Why are you here?" She stood and straightened, an unusual courage taking hold.

"I am here for many things. Duty to my Queen in the broadest terms. That chain in your hand?" Apattar looked down, unaware she still clutched the thing between bent fingers. "Yes, it is ours. A... tool." Laisha grimaced as she spoke.

Apattar shuddered and flung the chain toward the pale woman. "I know what this is," she whispered. "This is a wicked thing!"

Laisha did not move toward the chain, her pale violet eyes still focused on Apattar. Studying the young woman, learning everything she could. Why would she be so interested in the wayward runaway?

"The world is a wicked place. I have seen centuries unfold in blood and ruin at the hands of those who call us evil. Who are they to call us cruel with no purpose? I hunt for the truth, no matter the cost. It's what we all do, in the end."

"Centuries?" Apattar managed to say, loud enough for the woman to hear. "Ho-how old are you?" Her eyes widened, a spark of curiosity compelling her to lean forward despite the danger.

The eldest of the Eásiri, descendants of the gods themselves, were over 400 and considered ancient to all, but they bent with age, each long year another line across their face. Age never touched the woman before Apattar. Pale and smooth-skinned, her porcelain face looked eternally youthful. Only in her eyes did Apattar see the dark and faded look of one who had seen lifetimes pass by.

"Well," Laisha paused as if thinking to herself. "Well, I don't know, not anymore. The years melt together so easily, but I think it must be past three thousand years now." She spoke so nonchalantly, a boring fact rather than something breaking apart Apattar's reality. "You owe me two questions now. First, what is your name, *neha*?"

Apattar's mind reeled, barely able to comprehend over three *thousand* years of life. What power did this woman hold? How many thousands must have died at her hands, wills bent and broken for whatever life she led? Apattar knew she should be terrified, should run away. Yet, the woman awed her. Power rippled off Laisha, the Shadow-weave coursing through her. The void consuming Apattar's soul swam through her body, reaching forward, begging to escape and reveal her for what she was.

"No stranger has ever cared enough to ask my name before," she heard herself saying. "Apattar, that is my name. Silent Dove, in my mother's tongue. Though, *evranenith* is one they call me as well."

The words startled Apattar as they came from her mouth, as if another spoke them instead. She waited to hear a scream or curse from the white woman, but her pale violet eyes only softened in response. For a moment, Apattar almost thought Laisha would run forward and embrace her.

Laisha took a step forward, a thin smile spreading across pale purple lips. "Yes, yes, it is you! Oh, sweetling, you came as she said you would!" A giggle erupted from Laisha; it sounded wrong, as if she had only heard the sound written in tales and never did it herself. The raspy sound faded. "I knew it, I knew it. Oh, the traitors, they cannot deny Her melodies forever. I have waited centuries to see your face!" The pale woman struggled to contain her excitement, her words rushed and filled with delirious joy.

She knows, she heard. My daughters, go together!

The silky, cool voice of her unseen guide flowed across Apattar's mind, urging the woman toward the stranger. Apattar's heart seized at the words.

"I-I don't understand. You've been waiting for me? Wait..." Realization spread across Apattar's face. Everything seemed to fall into place. Her birth, during the eclipse. Did Laisha think the cursed woman was special? "I am not a blessing. Have you not heard of *evranenith*? I am cursed, the moo—"

"Cursed? Oh, no, this is a blessing, Apattar who calls herself *evranenith*. The night is not feared, not where I am from. Haven't you grown tired of the aching void inside, always hungering, always consuming? You have poured your sorrows and despair into the void, but it is not enough, is it? Let me help you, please. I... we cannot lose you again, *neha*."

Laisha reached a hand out to Apattar, milky white fingers brushing a stray black curl out of the young woman's face. Her touch reminded Apattar of Ninann, tender and soft. Apattar's flesh crawled, begging for more.

"How do you know all this about me?" Apattar whispered, looking back into pale violet eyes nearly as colorless as the rest of the woman.

"I read your mind the first day you tumbled through your portal into the sea. I was... meditating on this island," the woman paused, long enough to catch Apattar's attention. "Imagine my surprise when a brown-skinned girl fell from the sky! My brother wanted to recruit you, but I knew. And now, here we are. Strange, isn't it?"

The two stood in uneasy silence, taking each other in.

"I've been running from fate my whole life. I don't even know why I'm here, I only knew I needed to run and find freedom, no matter the price. I... I am nothing." Apattar's voice quivered as she spoke, a wave of repressed emotions washing over the woman. The reality of her stark loneliness this past year crushed Apattar, a thousand hands squeezing the last life from her heart. Her throat seized, strangling each word.

"Then become something," whispered Laisha, a crooked finger raising Apattar's chin until their eyes met. "The world is broken. Would you fix it if you could? Or fade away, lose every hope and dream to the void eating your soul? I can help. I sense in you the same desires I have. Freedom, revenge... happiness. Very few are given everything simply for existing. You must take control or flounder."

Apattar stepped back from Laisha, unsure what to make of the pale woman's offer. On the surface, it seemed enticing. The woman who moved like a cat knew much and did not seem to harbor any ill-intents. However, years of guarding against the senseless cruelties of her father and nearly everyone else in her life rendered Apattar near incapable of trust.

The daughter of snow and shadow will not betray you. You are what she seeks, I promise. Trust me, please.

"Why do you care to help me when you enslave others? If you know who the *evranenith* are, you know I am not special. I hear the screams of a thousand dead in my sleep. Why leave them to die, why wait for me?"

Laisha huffed, soft violet eyes darting back and forth as if trying to decide what to say. After a long pause, she spoke.

"Even I do not understand fully the designs of my Goddess. She is the echo of a memory, even among my people. Once, we tried to learn the truth of the Discordance, but the past is cloaked in darkness we cannot untangle. It is impossible for me to save all, but our Oracle told me of you. You, the daughter born when the moon overshadowed the sun, touched with the blood of gods who once walked our land. You will achieve greatness, Apattar, who calls herself *evranenith*."

The breath caught in Apattar's throat at the mention of her birth and heritage. Did Laisha know of her home? Apattar had not bothered to cover her blue doves and flaming suns, for who outside of the Madhira would know what they signified?

Her thoughts shifted to the mention of others like her, those slain as they drew their first breath or left to die in the cold and rain. Given back to the world unwanted and unloved. The practice left a gnarled hole in Apattar's heart. Once, when sneaking out of the city on a dark and moonless night, Apattar heard the screams of a woman begging for mercy, asking for the child to be spared, all her others cruelly taken away by death.

The world feared the Dark Goddess and her children. Perhaps Apattar held the cold, endless void inside her fragile and broken heart for a reason.

"I have always run from fate," she breathed.

Laisha closed her eyes and curled her hands in front of her face, muttering something under her breath. Apattar staggered back against the wall, the breath knocked from her body. Shadows formed in the pale woman's hands, sinewy tendrils coiling around her wrist and racing up her arm. A dagger with a black sawtooth blade appeared in her hand. Apattar could feel the same crackling and hungry void tangled inside her heart on the blade. Laisha's eyes opened, now black as night.

"Run toward it. Fate broke the world once. Maybe you are meant to heal it."

The two women looked at each other in silence. Tendrils of black nothingness seeped from Apattar's fingertips. The familiar coolness of the Shadow-weave curled around the young woman, wisps of black snaking across her eyes. A haunting song filled her mind, pulling every agony to the surface, every heartache and moment of torment until she collapsed into the void. The empty feeling consumed every crevice of her body, hollowing it out, all the torment and pain, self-loathing and hatred from years of denying desires she thought a sickness.

Apattar felt herself floating, pulled up by some invisible force. She looked down and saw Laisha on her knees, staring up with a look of awe.

Fourteen

FATE TWISTED

HEAT WASHED OVER THE blackened stones underfoot. A great smoking volcano rose like a dread shadow to the north, swallowing the land below. A deep, rumbling sound filled the air—not a song, but something discordant, pulling at the weaves of every living thing nearby. Though a deep ache settled in Apattar's bones, she felt herself drawn to the source. She wanted to understand it, why it called to her as if it once was the only thing she knew.

Navárenir Cet, Laisha named it, one of the few things she said about the sleeping giant. A shadow seemed to pass over her face at the mention of the ruin of Andeshar. Each time Apattar asked about the history of the land, she saw a twinge of grief overcome the pale woman before her stoic porcelain face returned. Instead of answering, she set the young woman to work, training her latent powers that had been ignored and left wild.

Apattar studied a pale, yellow-haired man kneeling before her, watching him with piercing brown eyes as tendrils of black wove their way around his body. His left eye twitched as a thick rope of Shadow-weave wrapped itself around his torso, trying to fight back, muscles spasming under taut flesh. Apattar narrowed her eyes. The man relaxed, sinking into the inky grip of the hungry void.

"Good, good. Do not let him struggle. You show much restraint in keeping him alive. Ask again," crooned Laisha into Apattar's ear. The ageless woman's close presence no longer unnerved her.

"*Na nithmireithí cinn maíj itu'tha iach emmil,*" she said, repeating the ancient words the pale woman taught her. Apattar focused on the harmonic weaving the man's soul into being and through it, sought entrance into his mind.

Laisha showed Apattar how to walk through the minds of others by weaving their harmonics together, using the Shadow-weave as a tether to her soulsong. Those who fell under her influence found themselves compelled to answer anything demanded of them. It proved difficult at first, the man's psyche lashing out in rejection like a whip across her mind. The long month provided ample practice—though at the cost of the man's sanity, now half-crazed from her daily intrusions.

"The longer you resist, the more it hurts. I can end it, but you must answer the question. How were you captured?" The harsh fumes of smoke and brimstone from the black volcanic ruins tore at Apattar's throat.

White foam dripped from the man's mouth as he struggled to keep it shut. His hands were bound in front of him by a thick coil of writhing black Shadow-weave, fingers turning purple as it tightened around his wrist. A sickly *crack* filled the air. The man did not flinch but instead relaxed into his bonds. A distorted voice spoke, halting every few words as the man and Apattar fought for control of his mind.

"I saw... a woman... dark hair... I ran."

"Do better," Laisha whispered.

Apattar closed her eyes and asked again, pushing her thoughts into the man's broken mind. She waded through a thick mire of confused memories, half-formed faces screaming as she forced her way into the nexus of his crumbling mind. The void in her heart reached out and consumed the slave from the inside, carving into his soft brain tissue like a hot knife. She opened her eyes to see the man stiff, arms held at an awkward angle in front of him without moving. He spoke again, voice now hollow and listless.

"Not a woman, a girl. A girl, like my daughter. I wanted to help her. She ran into the woods. I followed but... he, he found me. The one who killed her. He laughed. He knew I would come. That terrible, bloody man held the cursed thing that crawled out of my daughter, told me 'he is Her gift', and he would break me for my sins. Oh gods, what have they done! It cannot live! I only see darkness now, darkness and fear. I do not know anymore." The man fell silent.

They are the kinslayers, the traitors, the poisoners! Ended, destroyed, sundered! No return, no, no, they must pay! Must pay! Slaughtered and ruined!

A scream tore through the air, followed by a hundred more shrieking voices. Writhing shades, half-formed in the shape of men, leapt around Apattar, gaping maws spilling forth a cloud of black. Something tore at her heart inside, like some piece of her was trying to escape, trying to break free and end the world right there. She tried to contain her rage at the thought of an innocent baby slaughtered for being born on the wrong day. The soft touch of Laisha on her quaking shoulder calmed the darkness rising inside. The screams died, and the shades melted back into the blackened earth below.

"Rest, *neha*. You did well. My brother Ruarc has a flair for drama. I believe his exact words were, 'I knew you would come crawling back to me, on hands and knees begging like a dog'. And you, you are mesmerizing to watch. You learn faster than most, even with a poor teacher." Laisha spoke with a hint of fear in her voice. "I have no use for this one alive; do as you will. Practice begets perfection."

"Wait," Apattar replied, eyes scrunching up as tears formed behind her muddy brown eyes. She stepped toward the man and placed the black dagger against his throat, taking a deep breath before continuing again. "How many of my brethren have stained your hands with their blood before they had a name? How. Many?" she demanded.

The man grunted in reply, jaw grinding as he attempted to wrest control back from Apattar. Her hatred of the man sank deeper into the void. The tendrils tightened, worming through his body. She reached out to the hollowed mind, probing for answers.

"How. Many?" The voice thundered around the captor and prisoner. Apattar's hand pressed the sharp blade into his throat, a crimson drop of blood welling at the tip.

"Four...teen. Fourteen." His voice cracked. Tears streamed down his face, body stiff in the void's embrace. "I killed him, oh may the Six Sisters help me, I killed him! My firstborn, my only son! She tried to run away with him, and I killed them both. My duty, my duty!"

The man began to sob, wails ripping from his body. Apattar forced the words to echo in his mind, the confession the only thought left in his empty skull, breaking what remained of his sanity.

The dagger in Apattar's hand shook, hot waves of rage coursing through her body. She pictured her mother dead in the desert, her deep burgundy brown hair matted with blood as she clutched a babe to her eviscerated chest. This was the fate awaiting them if she had been born to any other family. Once, a fate she almost craved. The thought sent a wave of nausea through her. Apattar pressed the blade further into the man's neck, knuckles white with her death grip.

Instinct took over. Apattar imagined the umbral tendrils choking the man, twisting down his throat and forcing the life from his wretched soul. The Shadow-weave pulsated with energy, squeezing and sending waves of spasms through the fair-haired man. As he collapsed, Apattar pulled the dagger toward her, slicing the man's neck and sending a spray of bright red blood across her torso and legs. A final gurgle sounded from him, death twitches fading fast as the life seeped from the man onto the black rocks below.

"Do you think he even hesitated to kill them? Gods, I think I'm going to be sick."

She held the dagger by her side as she stared at the dead man, his sticky, hot blood dripping from the black blade. A small flicker of something—joy, or satisfaction—ran through Apattar as the man's essence ran down her fingers.

Apattar turned to Laisha, tears still not coming but the feeling rising in her chest. She could not stand such senseless cruelty all in the name of fear toward an innocent child and mother. Laisha extended those long, milky white fingers and grazed the young woman's cheek, touch cool against deep ocher skin flushed red with anger. The woman in white was not forthcoming with affection; indeed, Apattar thought it would be strange for someone with her moral standards. Yet, the brief touches brought the comfort Apattar always longed for.

Apattar took a breath and steadied her shaking hands.

"No, no, I doubt he did," Laisha murmured. "As you did not either, though this one I am glad to see gone. His death will save thousands. His, along with all the others who would kill mother and child. We can change the world, don't you see, sweetling? Time is not an enemy of my people."

Apattar blushed at the words, aware of how painfully child-like she must seem to the pale woman who somehow looked ageless. Only her eyes betrayed the signs of a long and ancient life.

"There is no hurry, Apattar. You are young, the world will not change in one day." Laisha whipped around, the moment of affection gone in an instant. "Come, leave his body to the firelings. Let us find you a safe place to rest. I must return to my city and queen."

The pale woman leaned over the man's body to collect a thin gold chain around his ankle and walked away. Apattar followed not far behind. She tugged at the tight brown pants clinging to her skin with each awkward step, careful to avoid the blood still drying into dark, ruddy stains.

The two women picked their way through rivulets of lava carving their way across the barren rocky surface of the mountain's base. Laisha said the black mountain slept for many thousands of years after the Discordance and devastation of Eás. But now, over the slow passage of time, the doom that claimed the world once before started rising again. The winds shifted, filled with ancient whispers and screams of the dead long gone.

What is buried will always rise, as the saying went in Av Madhira.

Over the long month together, Laisha shared how the shadowy slavers came to the black ruins for something they called firestone. A cool, black glass-like stone, it filled Apattar with a dread she could not begin to describe, a feeling so overwhelming the world turned to ash. Where once her heart would thrum with the music of the world, an empty silence took its place. Firestone was a manifestation of Death as it first came to the undying

Eldest Children. Apattar's skin crawled even at the thought of the thing.

Laisha called the gold chain Apattar found an *ishfasnith*, a creation used to sever the natural harmonic powers of those who wore it. Laisha claimed the *ishfasnith* once aimed to save the world from the gods. Apattar sensed Laisha's people lost their aim long ago, warped over the long years of conflict and sorrow. Now, they shackled men into servitude, most—or so Laisha claimed—kinslayers and their descendants from ancient wars all but forgotten to time.

Apattar found the idea of slavery easier to accept than she thought it should be. Perhaps it was growing up in a society heavily segregated by caste, or perhaps it was a lifetime of torture and dreaming of doing anything to get her revenge. Whatever drove her heart, Apattar vowed she would take whatever path necessary to save herself. And, if that failed, she would make the world feel the same hurt she had for twenty long, arduous years.

Though Laisha did not often speak about her home, she would share tales of life before doom and sorrow claimed its people. How once the children of the Night Goddess delighted to live in the shadows and silver moonlight. Far in the west, away from their kin, they lived in peace.

Yet, Death came for the Eldest Children, a strange corruption of the First Harmonic. When the consort of the Dark Goddess passed into the realm of silence, the heart of her eldest turned bitter with sorrow. The black-haired son lead his people east in search of answers, only to find himself already made into a monster in the minds of his long-sundered kin.

Apattar knew the feeling all too well. How, after the slow turn of time, all transform into the creation of others—willingly or not. Had she not already leaned into the darkness eating at her heart? Revenge found in the form of shadowy hands around the neck of a woman she wanted to kill. Was *happy* to kill.

What would her nine-year-old self think of Apattar now? Would she recoil in fear or see this as an inevitable future? A... *fate*, perhaps?

The word that once tormented the woman now became impossible to ignore. An *evranenith* with the celestial blood of the gods. Apattar wondered if destiny truly guided her life or, if given enough time, any *evranenith* would survive. Nothing about her felt particularly special—years of neglect and starvation for a kind touch instilled the feeling. Apattar's world had been a confusing mix of emotions since Laisha appeared in her life. Feeling worthy was an entirely unknown concept, welcoming and petrifying at the same time. Was she so broken that only strife and heartache felt normal?

"*Shain'sa*, watch out!" Laisha's musical voice pulled Apattar out of her thoughts in time to stop her from stepping into a thick ooze of lava. She stumbled backward, catching her balance on the pale woman's outstretched arm. "Deep in thought, are we?"

"Sorry, sorry," Apattar mumbled, the heat of embarrassment at her awkward behavior flushing her face. "I-I, it's a lot, all of this. I don't know what to make of it all. Why me? Why not the baby boy slain by his father? Even with his death, I could not bring justice to the lives he ended." Her voice cracked with pain.

Laisha sighed. "I wish I had a simple answer to ease your mind. But I don't know. Not about you, and not about any other *evranenith*. Life is cruel and senseless. This much has not changed during my long life. Would it ease your mind to think this all random chance?"

Apattar mulled the question over in her head. She thought of Ninann, tried to picture her beautiful dove leading a life starved of love in her stead, but it would not come. Radiant as the new sun greeting her birth, Ninann was indeed a daughter of light and life.

Where Ninann belonged to the sun, Apattar knew deep in her heart she belonged to the shadows of Night. She had always imagined herself alongside Ninann from a young age, but it never felt like her life. If she wanted to create a future for those doomed to the dark, Apattar would have to choose: her sister or her own life. Always she envied Ninann, coveted all the younger sister had, but most of all, craved their father's love.

A sigh escaped her lips. "I always thought destiny meant I had no choice, meant accepting I'm a monster who will end the world. But you say I do have a choice, a choice fate brought to me: fade to void or heal the world. It cannot bring the little ones lost to memory their rightful life."

Apattar paused, thinking again of the little boy murdered by his father.

I see I was foolish, and now I must finish what I started those many years ago.

Her father's voice assaulted her senses, overwhelming her mind until it was the only thing she could focus on. Rage flooded through her body. She tightened her grip around the dagger's silver hilt, squeezing until her fingers tingled with pain. The void rose within, head pounding with hot blood. She took a breath and forced the darkness back down, cooling the whispers calling for blood.

"I think I rather like the idea of destiny if I can heal the world," she whispered at last.

"You will change the world for the better, Apattar."

Laisha reached out and took Apattar's hand, guiding the young woman the rest of the way to their portal beyond the snaking rivers of lava and smoking fumaroles.

The two stepped through the shimmering mirage. They emerged back in the black ruins where they met, cool air a welcome reprieve from the stifling hot volcanic wasteland. The smell of kelp was almost sweet in comparison to the rotten stench of sulfur.

"WHERE ARE YOU TAKING me?" Apattar asked, breaking the silence between the two as Laisha gathered supplies into two packs.

"This is where we part ways, for now. You will return home. There is someone you must find. He is... hard to miss."

Excitement and dread swirled inside Apattar. Her sister, her dove! How her body yearned for the twin's comforting embrace.

Ninann... Father!

Apattar shuddered. Their last exchange flashed through her mind. Did he even care that she ran away? Would he kill her, cast her out, imprison her forever? Her heartbeat quickened. The grip of those invisible hands she had mercifully not felt for the long month returned, squeezing the air out of her lungs.

"Home? No, no, I can't go home! Father will kill me, or I will kill him!" The words tumbled out of her mouth in a panic.

Laisha put down the pack and took one of Apattar's deep brown hands in her milky white ones. The grip at her throat evaporated.

"He will be otherwise occupied in the capital of your Federation. Do not worry about him, sweetling. There is a war to come. Allies to recruit, weapons to ready. Your coming marks the beginning of the end, this is what the Oracle tells me. Her visions are not always clear, but in each there is a man by your side. Consumed by the shadows, sacrificed to do what must be done. You must find him, Apattar."

"Consumed by shadows?" she asked, the question heavy on her tongue. "What do you mean?"

"In truth, I do not fully know; dreams can be hazy. But always, the man is shrouded in shadows, with a storm in his eyes and blood in his dreams. Your paths will cross, of this I am sure. And once they do, you will bring him to me." A smile spread across Laisha's face, toothy and awkward as if her muscles were trying to remember how to move.

"I know this man," Apattar breathed. "Not who he his, but we have met before. His eyes... I could never forget those eyes. Gray and silver, dark currents that pulled me in until I was drowning. There is something evil about him. He would twist me if I tried to touch whatever darkens his mind."

Laisha stood tall and looked to the north, past the dread volcano that seemed to grow with each passing day. Her face grew wan, and for a moment, Apattar thought the slaver who somehow thought the young woman special might cry. With a jerk of her head, Laisha turned back, a somber look on her face.

"There are many evil things in this world. The wounds festering in the darkness of the Night are not among them, *neha*. Perhaps what you are afraid of is that he is your *liraes*. It cannot be a coincidence you already know of whom I speak."

Apattar's heart stopped when she heard the word *liraes*. That already impossible dream of freedom seemed within reach at last. But the prospect of love, a connection forged by the First Harmonic itself? The thought never touched the edges of her thoughts, even as a girl, when the world was not quite so dismal.

A fire ran through her veins, restarting the beat of her fractured heart. It quickened, rising faster and faster with anticipation of what a *liraes* could mean. Love, for most, but who could want her? Fear and subservience, loyalty perhaps. But love? Confusion mixed with excitement, an entire life of possibilities laid out ahead.

"You speak of an impossibility. I am not meant to be loved," she said at last, averting her gaze from Laisha.

"You were also not meant to live, but here you are. Is it so hard to believe blessings do exist? I must leave now, the future is yours to decide. But you will know how to find me when it is time—if you wish." The pale woman flicked her wrist as she spoke. A shimmering opaque portal snapped open in front of Apattar, waves of dry heat pulling her into a comforting embrace.

Laisha leaned down and kissed Apattar's forehead, soft as a spring breeze. The faint scent of lilac and roses wafted through the air as the pale woman moved backwards, soft violet eyes clouded with tears. Apattar had rarely seen the woman express emotion; even her laughter somehow felt hollow. Apattar knew the woman did not share all she knew, but she could not collect her thoughts enough to ask anything else.

A liraes? Do not twist my heart with such cruel impossibilities!

"I will be thinking of you, sweet *neha*," Laisha said as she pulled away. "Many long years may pass before we meet again, yet you have brought this old black soul a spark of hope. Thank you, Apattar, who calls herself *evranenith*. Thank you. Listen to your heart, sweetling." Laisha caressed Apattar's scarred cheek, then stepped back and urged the woman onwards.

Apattar turned and took a step forward, then looked back one last time at Laisha, now silently crying behind milk-white hands. She turned back to the portal and ran through before her tears came as well.

This could be the start of her life, she told herself. She would not find herself in a gilded prison—or worse. Not again. She would rather die or try to kill anyone who stood in her way.

A final wisp of cold air licked at her heels. The portal snapped shut, leaving Apattar without her senses in the suffocating heat.

After the shock of the desert heat lessened, the runaway found herself ready to return home. A soft melody, full of sorrow and hope, blew past with the breeze. Apattar sang along as she crossed the hot sands, inching ever closer to the long-awaited turning point of her life.

SPIDER SILK

"COME, BROTHER! THE SUN is already climbing the sky, yet you're in here sleeping the day away. I believe it is still considered rude to ignore social decorum, despite all your numerous attempts to break them. Come, up. Up!"

Adon's bright and clear voice pierced Therat's ears. A grumble rose from his throat in reply. He shifted and pulled the cotton sheets over his face, ignoring his brother.

Not today. Not with her around.

"Therat! I don't need to ask nicely."

A flutter of wings filled the air. A beak pecked at the exposed soft flesh of a foot dangling over the edge of the bed. Therat kicked back, squarely hitting the bird before tossing the covers aside. He bolted up, a look of mild annoyance on his face.

This was a common game of Adon's. At the foot of his bed stood the young man with long curly black hair, soft gray eyes sparkling with delight against his burnt sienna skin. A flurry of tan feathers fell around him, disappearing into a golden shimmer before they hit the floor. A sly grin flickered across his face.

"Good morning at last, dear brother." Adon sat at the foot of the bed. "What is left of it, at least. Come, try to have some fun today. It is Ninann's coming of age, after all. Your brooding could use a break. This may be our last big adventure before the ships leave port next month."

"Get out, Adon," Therat barked in reply, not caring how harsh he sounded. "Go spend the day with your friend, but leave me alone. Please." Therat's shoulders rolled with a heavy sigh as he ran tattoo-covered fingers through his shorter black curls.

Ninann served as a reminder of everything he had sacrificed in life, all the bonds and friendships unattainable for someone like him. The shadows were his companion instead, slowly driving the man toward insanity. How long would he suffer, holding onto scraps of his mind? He tried to remind himself of the promise he had made to his mother.

Therat glanced at the floor, observing a small puddle of bile and wine already half-dried on the cracked dirt floor. He shoved a pillow off, covering the mess before his twin saw it, then turned back with a frown.

"Gods, this again?" Adon said, hands flying up in exasperation. "You are my soulbound, I am not leaving you forever if I marry her!"

Therat did not reply. With a grunt, he rolled out of the bed and lumbered to a nearby basin. The cool water dribbled through parched lips still tinged with the taste of bile.

Adon continued. "I wish I could say you have been unlucky in life, Therat. But you never learned to reign in your anger and grief. Now look what it gets you! I am trying to help, desperately. I want you to enjoy life, you do not need to punish yourself forever. You must let go of the past. It was almost *eighteen* years ago."

Rage bubbled up at the mention of the night that stole his childhood. Therat swallowed, forcing the hard lump in his throat down before speaking as calmly as he could.

"It's easy for you to let go. I lost everything. But I would do it again. For you." He turned and took a step toward Adon, catching the man's soft hands in his thick with calluses. "But I cannot forget. I will not stop until I have answers, even if I could! Someone somewhere gave the order and stole our parents from us, took their music, and left us with nothing to bury. Nothing makes sense, but I must find out why. Even if it kills me, Adon. I will never rid myself of these memories, but maybe I can ease the pain."

"You talk as if I didn't become an orphan too," Adon spat back, a fire rising in his eyes Therat had not seen before. "You always do this to me, you always guilt me about trying to still enjoy life, even if you do not realize it. Your mind is a mess, and I'm trying to help fix it, but sometimes I wonder if you are beyond help. Try to see my side of it, Therat." Adon huffed as he spun around and walked out of the room, leaving Therat to absorb the sting of his words in silence.

The anger and jealousy of his brother's life became harder to bear with each passing day. Why did he ever return to the city? Because he had an insanity-induced vision of his mother? Laughable to think Therat could ever do something good in his life.

Yet, he found it impossible to leave. Something kept him here, an invisible leash chaining him, but who held the other end, he did not know. A shudder ran down Therat's spine at the thought of some kind of *destiny* laid out before him. His life was meaningless, antithetical to the idea of gods and higher callings.

Therat stretched his broad muscular frame before wrapping a gray shawl over his head and shoulders. The day warmed fast, sweat collecting on his chest, leaving the thought of a tunic unbearable. The jagged white scar over his heart ached as his fingers brushed against it. He adjusted the shawl to cover the shame forever etched into his skin, then secured the fabric with a simple crescent moon pin. Seeing his scar never got easier, despite what Adon told him.

After pulling on a pair of loose black silk pants—a gift from his coming of age a few years before—Therat strode to a cracked mirror in the corner of his shared bedroom, silver finish dulled with age. He did not like to look at himself often, finding it strange to see the echoes of his parents on a face always hollow and devoid of joy. He forced a smile, observing how one side pulled up higher than the other over a deep dimple. His mother's smile. Though, hers were warm and full of life, a place of safety and love. His eyes drifted up to the thick mess of black curls tumbling down his forehead. A gift from his father. The only gift he had left now.

A pained look flashed across Therat's face. He ground his teeth in response. The time for grief ended long ago; tears would never serve him now. He forced himself to turn away before the past returned.

The sound of muffled voices from the main room of their small house drew his attention. Adon and his grandfather—bickering again? The old man was loath to see his grandson leave the desert; Therat could not say he blamed him, terrified of harm befalling his twin in the City of Books.

Shaking his head, Therat shuffled out of his room, feet dragging as if made of heavy stones. He entered the main room of the humble home he shared with his twin and grandfather. Adon sat at a table on the far end of the room, drumming his fingers on the painted glass top, face twisted with impatience. Next to him sat their grandfather, his hair gray and faded with age. The two men sat turned away from each other; whatever argument they had ended in a stand-off of silence.

"Did it happen again last night, *neha*? I heard you calling out for them." Nazith set the parchment in his hands down, eyes full of concern.

"I... yes. But not all need to know," Therat said, flickering his gaze over to Adon. He crossed the room and stood next to his grandfather, placing a light hand on his ruddy brown arm mottled with age spots.

"Can we leave already?" Adon asked, standing up and gesturing toward the large arched front door. If he heard anything the two said, he did not seem to care. Therat brushed aside his annoyance. This day was for his twin, not him. Surely he could handle one day around the woman.

"Adon is right, Papa. We should go. Ninann is surely waiting."

Adon raised an eyebrow at his twin but didn't question the change of heart. The old man threw up his hands in exasperation as the twins stepped outside.

The dry air hit Therat in the face with a rush of hot wind; a bead of sweat rolled down his temple in response. The arid desert air tore at his lungs with each labored breath. He pulled the shawl down from his head across his mouth and nose, trying to retain what little moisture he could within the thin woven cotton. Once his eyes adjusted to the bright sun, he scanned the small clearing in the oasis. Slow and methodical, Therat's gaze swept across each house. After a moment, he held a hand out and motioned for Adon to walk.

"Gods, can we go? We're twenty-three, not eight," Adon threw out sarcastically.

Therat's nose flared, anger creeping back.

"Did you ever think I need to do it, Adon? I cannot lose another of my family. I will not! I made a promise to myself a long time ago." Therat pulled his brother into a hug. "We need each other, Adon. And I will try to accept Ninann, but do not lose yourself to her. Please, please. I cannot bear the thought..." He swallowed, focusing his gaze on a small palm tree in the distance instead. After a moment, he pushed Adon away, striding forward as he fought down the rising emotions in his chest.

"You will never stop surprising me," Adon said softly.

The two walked in silence along a small path winding through a copse of palms and fig trees. After nearly twenty minutes, the sound of voices broke through the tree line with more frequency. The path curved before opening into the Market. Dozens of merchants shouted, bargaining with customers and trying to steal sales from each other. A troupe of musicians gathered under the shade of the trees, another atop the flat roof of a jeweler close by. Their music filled the gaps in between words—what little existed among the din of voices.

The sudden outburst of activity crashed down on Therat. The throngs of people reminded him of his stark loneliness, desperately clinging to his brother like a lost child. Panic settled into his stomach, the sensation of needing to vomit swelling in waves. Adon kept walking into the square before turning back toward Therat, beckoning for him to follow. He smiled, crinkling the skin around his eyes. The hole in Therat's stomach melted. He smiled back, forcing the nugget of happiness his heart contained to the front of his mind.

The two brothers picked their way through the bustling Market, Adon's black head of long curls leading their way through the sea of colors. Brilliant blues, deep reds, purples, and golden yellows; a blur of color among the wave of people. A confusing mix of aromas filled the air, delicate and sweet perfumes and lotions clashing with bitter tonics and acrid fumes from the smithing kilns. They pushed through to the Fountain of Maidens, a crowd gathered around the far end.

A woman with silvery blue hair piled on her head in coils stood on a platform opposite the fountain, a sheer green veil pinned to her head billowing in the breeze. The twins paused and turned to look at the woman. Dozens gathered with them as excited murmurs rippled through the growing crowd.

Therat studied the woman's soft curves accentuated by the cutouts and high leg slits in her pale blue dress. The way her smooth golden-brown skin darkened near the inner folds of her thighs. How the light cast a trick around the woman's hair, illuminating it like a halo. He wondered what it would be like feel desire, even unwavering love if they were *liraes*, instead of nothing at all.

A child giggled in the crowd near Therat. He winced at the sound.

"Come, brother," he said, the irritation oozing from his words. "I thought *I* was delaying us, remember?"

Therat turned away from the waveweaver. The brothers pushed through the crowd, back toward the now emptier—yet still plenty busy—market stalls. A merchant began to approach Therat, but a glance with his cold gray eyes sent them scurrying back.

The brothers walked in silence under the meager shade offered by the thin canvases strung up between stands. A strange feeling took hold of Therat, like he was a fly walking into a spider's trap. He tried to tell himself it was some anxiety about being around Ninann, but in the back of his mind a voice took hold.

She is trying to find me.

THE COMING STORM

C RUSHING DARKNESS SURROUNDS THE world. The silvered moonlight struggles to break through. Yet, there is no fear, no desperate cries of terror. There is comfort in the cool embrace of Night. The caress of a creator, gentle and guiding. Urging the woman on, soothing her restless heart.

Go to him, you know this soul as your own.

The woman's eyes adjust to the weak light from above. She sees figures moving, dancing across the desert plains. Long limbs intertwine as they bound and leap over one another, an expression of their ecstasy in the growing depths of night. Her gaze sweeps across the world before her. It falls on the man by her side.

There is a tender love deep in the man's gaze, shining in the darkness. Moonlight is in his eyes, silver mixing with gray. Deep within something stirs with recognition; she has been here before, in some other life. The man sighs, nuzzling his head into the woman's neck. She feels safe, secure. If time ended here and this moment repeated for eternity, she would never wish to leave.

The man grazes a finger against her forehead, his touch softer than silk. Sparks race across her skin, leaving her begging for another taste. She looks at him with pleading eyes. His fingers touch her lips as he traces the outline of their soft curves. He leans in, breath warm, a comfort against her skin.

The woman breathes deeply, a heavy sigh escaping as she sinks into his inviting aroma. The metallic scent of blood and fresh-cut wood confuses and arouses her senses, stoking the fires of pain and lust. She reaches a hand up to his hair, intertwining thin fingers with black curls. She pulls; he moans. Her lips crush into his.

He tastes like a sweet corpse rotting in the sun, intoxicating the woman. She is unable to resist his defiled soul, a thrumming in her body that says *he is the one you seek.* She bites the man's lower lip; a whimper escapes. He sinks deeper into her devouring kiss.

A thin line of blood dribbles down his chin and onto her bare chest. Another moan of pleasure, his chest heaving with the effort. Bloodied lips pull away, trailing downwards. His tongue slips around her nipple, grazing the tip with his bare teeth. With a hiss, the woman pulls his head away, flesh unable to resist her touch. He squeezes her thigh, a growl rising in his throat.

The darkness gathers around them, shadows blanketing the eternal lovers' embrace. A symphony rises within the woman, filling her soul, mending a heart torn asunder. The silence gives way to a low thrum: the beating of their hearts intertwining as one.

With a shove, the man falls back to the ground, the heat of his body coursing through the woman's fingertips like liquid fire. She grabs his hands and pins them above his head, a hunger in her eyes. A vulture, observing the corpse below waiting to be picked clean. She wants his corruption, his wild heart, the darkness festering, twisting his mind.

But she can never give him that. As her gaze sweeps across the man, she remembers the hatred in her heart for the lies he made her believe. Her grip tightens, tendrils of Shadow-weave racing over his body, hungering to devour his very soul.

"You are sculpted by the gods to ruin me, to punish me, but never to make me repent. I love this torture you bring me. Oh, Mireithren..."

APATTAR'S EYES SLOWLY OPENED at the sound of the strange name she heard once before in another dream.

She sucked in a breath through teeth still clenched tight, rubbing the ache away with her fingers. Her room came into slow focus with each blink, mind still trying to piece together the fragments of the dream. It faded to the light of day faster than Apattar could think, retreating into the void like so many memories and dreams from days past.

The feeling of fingers tracing the outline of her lips floated past. Apattar closed her eyes and tried to tear the memory back from the void, wanting to relish in the tender touch that made her skin crawl with anticipation. But, like everything else, it vanished, the sensation impossible to conjure again.

Thoughts of her future and the destiny she controlled consumed Apattar since her return to Av Madhira. The day she returned, a hush fell over the Market square. A sight none would soon forget—hair untamed, knotted from a year in the wilds with a tattered dress covering a body so thin each bone protruded like a mountain. A starved and dying woman with the markings of a Named House. One of the Houses of the Sun, at that.

Instead of swarming guards and a life behind bars—or worse—Apattar was escorted to the Temple. After a long day recounting her year away with the *Makhaeren* Ánnarsera, Apattar found herself free to return home, supposedly on the wishes of her father. The scroll bearing his signature smelled faintly of lilac and roses, though none seemed to notice the strange aroma.

Ninann was beside herself with glee the day Apattar walked through their estate gates, too desperate to hug her sister again to notice the changed look in her eyes. Ninann insisted on spending every waking hour together, peppering her sister with questions about her year away. Apattar said little of her time on the ruined remains of Andeshar, and nothing of Laisha or the strange man.

Though she feigned contentment on the outside, a restless hunger grew with the approach of their twenty-first nameday and final coming of age. Apattar did not earn her freedom to live a life of leisure with her sister. That dream died long ago.

Today, the gnawing ache in her heart left, replaced with excitement for the day to come. Previous nameday celebrations always resulted in anxiety and dread. While Ninann delighted in the festivities, watchful eyes haunted Apattar's every move, forced to comply with the rigid expectations of her father. Yet, no matter her behavior, all seemed to end the same: broken and crying as sharp words turned to sharp blades over the years. Her birth was a mark of her father's failure, not something to be celebrated.

Apattar had few happy memories in life thus far. Today, she meant to make the first of hundreds to come.

The wood bed creaked as she sprang up, eager to discover what Ninann had planned for them. As if waiting for the woman to rise, two handmaidens glided in, dipping their heads as they approached. The taller of the two, Saiya, smiled warmly at Apattar. She had asked nothing of her mistress's journeys afar, though Apattar sensed she noticed a change about the returned traveler.

Saiya held a dress of shimmering rich green silks, interlacing spirals of golden beads decorating the hemline. Her arms, though atrophied from burns suffered as an infant, looked exquisite draped in the luxurious dark greens.

"Lady Apattar," Saiya said. "Ready to begin?"

Apattar nodded. "Is this the dress as I requested? It is beautiful!" She extended a hand and took the dress from Saiya's arms, unfurling it with care.

"Yes, my lady. Is this green the right shade? Lady Ninann wears hers lighter, but I told the dressmaker this was for you. Here, let me help you with it." Saiya beckoned for the woman behind her, a short and stocky girl a few years younger than Apattar. She hurried forward to help her mistress out of the black night slip clinging to skin still sticky with sweat.

"Oh, Lady Apattar! Are you feeling well? This is drenched!"

Apattar smiled, remembering hazy fragments of the dream from the night before. How her flesh crawled with anticipation at the thought of someone desiring the woman starved for love. It fled at the thought of what the man represented.

A tool for Laisha. Nothing more.

"Yes, fine, fine. I think I am excited for the day, is all." Apattar stepped out of the slip and sighed.

"It is your first day as a free woman, from a Named House even! Life is yours to take! Who wouldn't be excited? With your lord father not returning for some time, have you decided to travel to Tír is Isneha with your sister? She wants to leave as soon as possible, I am told. Oh, you'd love Isneha; all the power and harmonic manipulation almost sets the air on fire, they say! Could you imagine being in the city where the Goddess Nehsan once lived?"

"I haven't decided. I suppose it would be natural to follow her."

Apattar sniffed and forced a hollow laugh in a desperate attempt to disguise her discomfort. The idea of fate oscillated between empowering and ridiculous; a year ago she despised the gods, viewed the shadows as a curse, not something to pursue. Could life change so quickly?

"Whatever you do, Lady Apattar, we will come with you, of course," Saiya said, brushing a rogue coil of hair back under her pale blue veil.

Myris, the younger girl, gaily chittered away while massaging coconut and vanilla oil into Apattar's thin black braids. Her short, thick fingers made quick work of the job and began massaging Apattar's neck.

Saiya grabbed a sponge from a basin at her feet and gently scrubbed the sweat away from Apattar's naked body. Droplets collected in the deep valley at the base of her throat. The water invigorated Apattar, cooling skin flushed with anticipation. Saiya eased the sponge over the young woman's chest, clicking her tongue at the sight of ribs still visible.

Apattar returned from her journeys with a renewed heart, but her body grew frail and malnourished. Weeks of steady meals returned some of the lost weight, but she remained a thin, sharp-edged woman. In time, Apattar grew fond of the angular face staring back at her from the silver mirrors. A face entirely her own, even if marred by her father's hatred.

Myris dried Apattar off and opened two small pots of cream pigments. With a delicate touch, she swiped a deep, metallic carmine red across Apattar's eyelids, framing them with a black liner. She stepped back and disappeared behind a curtain. Saiya pulled the dark green silk dress over Apattar's thin frame, tugging and fussing with the fabric around her chest. Saiya's brow furrowed, in concentration or frustration Apattar could not tell. She flinched on reflex, body ready to recoil from Tela's hand.

Why am I thinking of that bitch?

"I do not wish to speak out of turn," Saiya murmured, "but I am glad for your sake Tela is not your *danren* now. She was vile even before you were born."

Saiya jerked her eyes away. Apattar did not reply, too stunned by the mention of the name she tried to erase from memory. It was as if Saiya read her thoughts. Mercifully, Myris arrived with a large oval mirror and propped it against a table for Apattar to observe her handmaidens' work.

The silk dress hung from thin bands of gold beads threatening to slip off Apattar's slender shoulders, the neckline plunging deep to her sternum. The harsh canyons of her upper ribs peeked out from behind silks dyed deep green like the thick circle of trees around the blue jewel of Av Madhira. A thin white ribbon cinched the dress at her waist, deep slits running up the length of the skirt to her upper thighs.

Apattar smiled at the vision before her. A rare black jewel in the golden desert.

"Is everything fine with the dress? It looks well enough to me, if a bit loose. My mother knows this is what I chose, of course." Apattar eyed the interlacing pattern of swirling golden glass beads. She ran a bony finger over the beads, trying to convince herself the beautiful dress was hers.

"No, no. You are stunning, my lady," Saiya said. "It is… different, to be sure. You are different, you should celebrate that. I only forget how thin you still are. You look more like us workers these days, not the plump girl who left a year ago. But now you are a woman. Forgive me, I should not burden you on today of all days." Saiya did not meet Apattar's eyes as she spoke, instead fussing over the pleats in the silk cascading from the waistline. Footsteps broke the silence hanging thick between the women.

Saiya perked up as Myris returned from behind a curtain with a tray of assorted hairpins and accessories. "Ah, Myris! You have the best timing, as usual. Come, we are ready for her hair now."

Apattar sat on a reed stool and closed her eyes. Myris's stubby fingers had little trouble twisting dozens of tiny braids over and under each other, pinning up the plaits with golden pins before gathering another section. Apattar lost herself in the gentle tugging and pulling. Peaceful moments of relaxation mixed with quick bursts of hot pain—a comfort, in some strange way

"What do you think, my lady?" Myris said after a time. "It's as many braids as I could manage woven into your hair." The young handmaiden beamed with pride as she extended a small mirror in front of Apattar.

An endless twisting maze of plaits made with impossibly tiny braids sat over the top of her head. A raven-black crown, it almost swallowed the slender woman underneath. Apattar twisted the single braid framing the left side of her face around a finger with care, drinking in the masterpiece.

As she sat holding the mirror, the young handmaiden added pins with small golden bells dangling at the end. A faint chiming filled the air as she worked. In honor of House Isht'iri, Myris added twenty-one golden doves clipped in the front of the braids, tiny wings glinting in the early morning light. Apattar's eyes widened, stunned by the way Myris made her feel.

"There, a living goddess if I ever saw one!" Myris exclaimed. A slight giggle escaped, her excitement over Apattar's reaction palpable.

"It is breathtaking, Myris. You are so talented, I wish I could braid with your finesse." Apattar shook her head, a chorus of bells ringing out in reply. "I'm afraid if I touch this, I'll send it cascading down, however. Come, let us find my sister. I am too eager to wait!" She stood and walked toward the sliding doors leading to her twin's chambers, not waiting for a reply from her handmaidens.

Ninann's room was quiet, the soft pillows and cotton sheets re-arranged on the large bed sprawling across the center of the room. A note sat on a nearby table, Ninann's large looping letters spelling out Apattar's name. The young woman snatched it up, eyes scanning the note with haste.

Apattar huffed, irritation underscoring her words as she spoke. "She wants us to meet her by the old granary they're restoring. The one on the far side of the city. What could be so thrilling about the Reapers Quarter that she makes us walk an hour to find her?"

"Her friend, Adon? He's not from the Towers District. He's a skyweaver, quite gifted, too. I believe his parents were the same, or at least did something with food, I remember. I would have no doubt he is involved," Saiya replied.

"He has a *soerl* too, you know! Maybe you will become friends too, a twin for a twin," Myris interjected, laughing to herself as if finding the thought amusing.

Apattar perked up at the mention of the man's twin. Co-incidence could explain the interesting fact with ease, yet she toyed with the possibility that if the rest of her life was a dark reflection of Ninann, why not this, too? Her irritation cooled at the thought, replaced with curiosity instead.

"I will call for the litter and meet you down at the gate, my lady." Saiya dipped her head before hurrying away.

Each step to the gates of House Isht'iri pulled Apattar's thoughts to the disjointed dream with the man she fled from in the night a year and longer ago. The one Laisha needed to end the curse. Another like her, touched by the Shadow-weave.

At first, Apattar thought little of the man, dismissing Laisha's notion of him being *liraes*. But the thought became intriguing as the day of her ascension to womanhood came. She wondered how his voice sounded; if it was smooth and deep like a lowing cow or sharp and thin, a knife cutting through the air. The bells chimed in her hair with each bounce of her eager steps. Her intrigue fought with her repulsion of what he represented. How could he ever care about her? Want to care about her?

The endless descent through the garden path abruptly flattened; colorful blossoms gave way to a vast courtyard paved with smooth black slabs of stone. The two young women walked into a flurry of activity. Dozens of workers moved in a coordinated dance as they unloaded wagons with baskets of fruit while others took crates and disappeared into the storehouse.

Apattar took Myris's hand and led them through the bustling courtyard to the other side, where Saiya waited with a litter covered in plain cotton fabrics. Not the usual gilded one Apattar used these last few months with Ninann.

"And I am taking this because?" she asked, her brows furrowing with each word.

"Apologies, my lady," Saiya said, dipping her head as she spoke. "Your mother insists you use this to travel to the Reapers Quarter. She says it will not draw as much attention, although I said anyone would look at you and know regardless which House you belong to."

Apattar flared her nostrils. "It's fine, it's fine," she huffed. "I see the reason. I'll go alone, however. Who knows where my sister will have us go."

"Yes, my lady." Saiya dipped her head as she spoke "We'll help Lady Nessaeren."

"No, Saiya, take the day to yourselves. I think the waveweaver Tylei is back today in the Market square, I know you love watching her shows. If anyone asks, I sent you to look for jewelry." A smile cracked her placid face before disappearing again.

"I admit I would prefer not helping your mother. You'll hear no argument from me," Saiya replied with a sly smile in return. A giggle of excitement escaped from Myris.

Apattar stepped into the litter and sat, fussing over the stiff pillows in an attempt to support her back. It was far less luxurious than the ones her family used. Soft down cushions and thin cottons for warmth on the cool nights lined those litters. With a sigh, she leaned back against the less-than-comfortable pillows and nodded for Saiya to fetch the carriers. The handmaiden snapped her fingers, beckoning to two burly men before scurrying off with Myris. Though the day young, sweat already clung to the workers' cream-colored linen shirts, outlining the toned muscles underneath. The darker of the two, skin glistening like black coals, bent his head before speaking.

"Lady Apattar, yous ready then?" His words slurred together as if he spoke through thick syrup.

"Yes, thank you, Jaiym. Do you know where we are going, to the Reapers Quarter?"

The worker tilted his head as if trying to recall a thought. After a pause, he began speaking again. "Aye, now I 'member. One of your sister's men showed us. Is an odd place for yous."

"The fall left some of your senses, Jaiym," she chuckled in response. "I agree, but she is a bit odd herself of late. Well, lead on."

Apattar tugged the edges of her dress inside the litter and pulled the plain curtain closed. It lifted off the ground with ease and the two men lumbered off. The bounce and sway of their steps settled into a comforting rhythm. Apattar closed her eyes and found her breath, focusing on the waves of heat rolling over her skin. Damp sweat collected at the nape of her neck, a feeling she now found comforting after the long year away in the biting cold winds of the West. For as often as she envisioned Av Madhira an ornate prison, she now found herself loath to leave again. The pale woman's words echoed in her mind.

You will know to come find me when it is time.

She half-hoped the time would never come.

The quiet serenity of the Towers District gave way to the sound of chanting and soft stringed instruments, until at last the frantic bustle of the Market square overtook everything. Apattar only half-listened to the activity outside, consumed by sudden anxieties over the day. She felt the soft touch of hands at her throat, hungering for her life with each beat of her heart.

Apattar wanted to believe Laisha's words, that this man was the key to finding her freedom. But the void swallowed all hope. Her father's cruel words thundered in her ears with each surge of hot blood.

Tainted, broken, an unlovable mistake.

A scream threatened to escape, clawing at lips squeezed together in anger.

You are my most beloved child. Do not worry. Be calm.

The cool whispering voice engulfed the woman rife with self-doubt and fear. A pressure built in her heart, the ever-hungry and gnawing void begging for release. With her next breath it faded, the tumultuous wave of anxiety quelled by the gentle whisper. The voice that guided her west a year ago and sent her into the pale arms of Laisha. It became harder and harder to deny the stranger's words. The girl who denied the gods—could she blessed? Able to heal the world with the help of others like her? It couldn't be true.

Seventeen

THE BLACK JEWEL

THE SOUNDS OF THE Market faded out as Therat and Adon rounded a small copse of trees behind the fountain square. The shade grew deeper under the line of figs and palms, a blessing on the first day of summer. The Skyweavers would have a long two months ahead keeping the oasis cool from the relentless fiery sun.

Picking up the pace, Adon led the twins to a long building nestled against the tree line. A handful of workers busied themselves with repainting an old mural on the short side facing them. One leapt up and said something to Adon as they approached, clasping the man's forearm in an embrace.

Therat did not hear their words. Some strange sensation took hold. An image flashed across his mind—a woman of unearthly beauty, her silvery-purple skin glistening as if the stars themselves danced upon her fair form. Tears fell from her violet eyes, but neither sadness nor elation filled her gaze. Then, with his next breath, the woman faded. Her voice, barely a whisper, called out to him.

Ahh... you found me... can you hear it yet?

The world faded until Therat could only focus on the haunting song that seemed to flow through his very bones. An ache took root in the depths of his soul, a grief to rival the loss of his parents. A million cracked hearts, all crying for the same lost soul.

As if lured by a siren song, Therat turned until his gaze settled on two women seated at a table under a small palm. Blue doves and flaming suns seemed to sparkle in the sunlight as their hands moved, laughter thundering in Therat's ears. The bitter taste of jealousy crept into his mouth at the sight of Ninann. The woman from behind the Wall his brother loved, and would marry on her twenty-fifth nameday. His gaze lingered on the woman's neck richly decorated with gold and jewels. Oh, how easy it would be to strangle the life out of her.

Therat hated everything she represented in his life. Loss, heartache, loneliness; the endless black maw devouring hopes and dreams. Ninann was too beautiful for his world. Smooth deep ocher skin unmarred from a life of luxury and shiny black curls were a perfect complement to green eyes that lit up when Adon spoke. The woman caught his gaze and smiled. A beautiful, innocent, pure smile. It made the bile rise in Therat's throat.

Would she offer her innocence to protect you, brother?

Therat looked away in disgust. Next to Ninann sat a woman nearly identical except for dark brown eyes and a long line of black curved scars racing down her cheek.

It was *her.*

Mireithren.

The woman walking with shadows in the Market over a year ago. The one he never saw again.

The *evranenith* from behind the Wall. The little siren who would lure him to his doom.

Therat would not be able to mistake the woman if he tried. She grew thin over the year and half since he first saw her—more waif than the once-plump rich girl—but he could never forget that face. The one that drove him to madness, that unlocked the vile urges that ruined his life.

Mireithren. The woman with the sun in her eyes and Death in her heart.

The woman who tormented him was Ninann's twin this whole time? Adon's reaction when Therat questioned what a Named House would do with an *evranenith* suddenly became clear. Therat stared at Mireithren, unable to tear his gaze away from the maiden. Her eyes, once as barren as the desert, now glittered with life.

Thick black wings framed her deep, muddy brown eyes, a red sheen painted across each eyelid. The woman looked up and locked eyes with Therat. Mireithren's gaze reeled him in with each passing beat of his heart. Bewilderment and intrigue colored his thoughts. It was a feeling entirely foreign to the man.

The gold detailing on her deep green dress, which hung low off her bony shoulders, flashed in the sunlight when she moved. It blinded Therat and rendered his thoughts incomprehensible. An invisible force seemed to compel him forward, urging the man to let go and get lost in Mireithren's eyes. Therat took a step toward the vision in green when Adon's voice called out.

The trance broke, and Therat freed himself from the siren song. He turned and saw his brother holding a small monkey, laughing as the creature drank from a coconut in its hand. Therat shook his head and forced a smile through the fog.

"Do you think she would like him, Therat? Pashi says they cannot keep him, the baby is scared of the thing. Silly, he's a delight!" Adon laughed as he spoke, running tattooed fingers over the monkey's red-brown back. It cooed in response, nuzzling into his chest.

Therat blinked, trying to chase away the lingering vision of Mireithren. Irritation at Adon's meaningless question rose through the mire of confused thoughts. Why would he know anything about Ninann? Adon already kept his share of secrets about the raven-haired woman he loved.

"Well, the monkey certainly likes you, if nothing else. She's your friend, Adon. For all I know, she hates monkeys and would want the creature dead." Therat winced as he spoke, wishing he could eat the words as they hung in the air before anyone could hear them. "Not that anyone would wish to see such a thing..." he added quickly.

The twist of Adon's smile into a scowl pulled at Therat's heart. The elder twin shook his head and walked past with the monkey, still happily crawling over the man. Therat grabbed Adon's hand as he passed and twisted him with ease, barely straining against his brother's slight frame.

"I'm sorry, I-I'm sorry," he choked out the words, bitter on his tongue. He did it again, made a fool of himself and angered his brother. Maybe Adon had his reasons for not saying any-thing. Maybe he didn't know who Mireithren truly was. "*Mai soerl*. Can you forgive me? I have not been myself this past year. It grows worse with time. We need to leave. See the world again, feel the wind on our backs."

"*We* don't need to do anything," Adon retorted. "Are you bodyguard or brother? It is suffocating me—*you* are suffocating me. I had a long time to think while you were away, Therat. I... I'm sorry, but I am going with her. You know it is the best future I could ask for. I'd offer you the same, but your heart lies elsewhere, I know."

Therat opened his mouth to speak but thought better of it. Adon sighed before continuing.

"Who knows, this could be good for you. Maybe holding onto me is holding you back, too. You are allowed to be happy, brother. What would Mama and Da say?"

The exasperation and love mixed in Adon's words tore through Therat. A twinge of guilt tugged at his core, gnawing at what little remained of his tender heart buried deep inside its rotting shell. He set his jaw, grinding his molars until a dull ache pulled his focus, drowning out emotions he dared not acknowl-edge. Therat closed his eyes and pushed away the half-remembered faces of his parents. Their features had morphed and shifted over time as the years dulled his memories. Another reason he had to fight to preserve what he could. Adon would never understand.

Therat sighed and let his twin go, turning back toward the black-haired women waiting for them.

"Yes..." he said, choosing each word with care. "Yes, you are right. This will be good for me," *It won't, it won't, you are the only thing keeping this heart alive!* "I owe this to you, to your future. I have always sacrificed for you. I always will. If you are happy, I will find my peace. Now, there is a monkey to gift and a woman to cheer." Therat smiled at his brother but felt it end at his eyes, the empty blackness growing in his chest a little more with each lie.

All too soon, the brothers stood at the table across from Ninann and Mireithren. Adon burst into conversation, eager to show Ninann the monkey. Therat envied how easily their conversations flowed, how they spoke as if they had been friends for millennia. Every burden seemed to lessen in the other's presence. A shower of giggles erupted from Ninann; a shiver crawled down Therat's spine. He cleared his throat, and the two friends paused to look at him.

"Oh, Therat! You startled me, I'm sorry!" Ninann exclaimed. With each word, Therat's hateful jealousy rose. Urges he tried—and often failed—to control wormed their way into his head. He grimaced, forcing his attention back to the woman. "Adon knows how I so adore the little creatures here, it's like everyone else fades away. Oh, well, not like *that*, I don't mean to say you aren't interesting. You know how the heart gets..."

Ninann's words faded out as more of Therat focused on quelling the rising darkness within. A breeze blew past, carrying with it the faint rotting scent of the slaughterhouse hidden behind the trees. The taste of blood caught in Therat's mouth. He lost what tenuous control he had.

A vision of Ninann's crumpled body at his feet flashed before his eyes. The empty feeling gnawing at his heart grew a little more as whispers of ruin crept through his veins. He licked his lips and sucked in a breath through gritted teeth, trying to drown out the void and force it back into its cage. Ninann's voice came back into focus.

"... you. This is my *soerl*. She is back from her visits to... where was it again, sister?"

Therat's eyes drifted to Mireithren. Up close, he could see how she once resembled Ninann, but time or neglect had left her body thin. The lines of her angular face cut through the air like daggers. Her raven-black hair with wisps of golden sunlight sat high above her head, dozens of braids twisting together like a never-ending snake. Golden bells and tiny doves decorated her hair; the woman mesmerized Therat.

She is the most beautiful thing I have ever seen.

She is the most terrible thing I have ever seen.

Therat heard Mireithren speaking, but the smell of vanilla and water lilies drifting toward him distracted all other senses. He inhaled short, quick breaths. It proved a futile effort. A nail bit into his thigh; another poor distraction. A faint, soothing melody wormed its way into the periphery of his mind, tugging on his thoughts, begging to be heard. As beautiful as Mireithren, and strangely familiar.

There's something... no, stop! Focus, damn it. What is she doing to me? Why are you torturing me?

Mind reeling, Therat locked eyes with Mireithren and fell victim to the shadowy maiden's spell. Those muddy brown eyes bore into him with such intensity that all thought of the outside world vanished. The siren gazed at him with curiosity and amusement, brown eyes turning into pools of inky black. Therat fell into her gaze, losing himself to the song weaving through his mind.

A heat settled in his chest, spreading like wildfire with the quickening beat of his heart. The dry heat of the desert became a cool embrace compared to the fires raging within. Pain overcame the man so familiar with agony; blood boiled in his veins, ripping through his body until the taste of salt and iron settled on his tongue. The pain turned into an almost unbearable surge of pleasure, every cell in his body yearning for more but crying out for less.

As the confusion of desire and hatred for the maiden swelled, Mireithren's voice floated into his mind, somehow the most beautiful and terrible sound he'd ever heard at once.

I am so sorry, Therat.

That she knew his name or spoke in his mind did not surprise him. Power radiated off the woman. But that she was *sorry*? The Shadow-weave surged in his heart, recognizing something in his tormentor. Therat wanted nothing more than to hear her say his name again as she tore apart his befouled body. To have the raven-haired Maiden of Shadows hold his rotten heart in her palm as she whispered in his ear...

Death by her hand would taste so sweet.

A hiss escaped from Therat's lips as his blood thickened, a throb pulsing through his cock. Heat flooded his face as a hand instinctively moved to cover his rising desires. Five seconds or five minutes could have passed; Therat could not be sure. Torn apart by fury at the woman who represented Death and undeniable pleasure, time lost its meaning. He closed his eyes and tried to focus on the air burning his lungs, begging for release. He exhaled, then pulled in a ragged breath through gritted teeth.

Who are you?

A hazy vision of Mireithren standing in a broken, twisted land of rocks took hold. She held a black dagger in one hand and a beating heart in the other. His body lay at her feet, a peaceful look carved into his lifeless face.

I am the one who will give you a purpose.

You would end me. I know of your sweeting siren song!

Therat opened his eyes, sucked back into reality by his revulsion of the woman's words. The heat disappeared in an instant, replaced with a cool, hollow feeling. The woman—whose true name he still did not know—spoke, a slight smirk crossing her lips as she glanced at him.

"... cross the western banks, but I found myself in the far west, on the ruins of Andeshar. The fires still rage on the northern end, but I found enough life to survive. I count it sheer luck I finally managed to open a portal back to Hylaea. Still, as wanderings go, I do not count it among the worst days of my time away."

Mireithren's voice grated across Therat's mind, rough at the edges as if someone had taken a knife and cut through every word. Therat stared at the woman, unable to comprehend why his body craved the temptress who would only bring ruin. He wanted to inhale the sweet scent of vanilla and water lilies, to feel the warmth of her touch against his skin starved for embrace. But, more than anything, he wanted to get forever lost in those muddy brown eyes and feel the rush of pleasurable pain again and again.

For the first time since the murder of his parents, Therat felt strangely alive. Not floating along and losing control of his thoughts, trying to find comfort at the bottom of a bottle each night. This time, losing control of himself to the woman felt good, safe... wanted.

The realization terrified him.

"The ruins of Andeshar," Therat managed to cough out at last. "A perilous place to find oneself. Yet"—he pulled in a shallow breath, trying to avoid Mireithren's gaze—"I sense perhaps it is you others should be afraid of. What an intriguing compliment to your sister."

A raspy laugh pulled his eyes toward hers.

"I hear that often. Twins needn't be replicas, life would be much too boring. There is always something to be found in the dark. Would you not agree, Therat?"

A shiver raced down Therat's spine at the sound of his name on her gravelly voice. Heat flooded his face as waves of hot arousal coursed through his body. He stood up with a jolt. The hot sand under his feet helped pull focus from the confusion of feelings overtaking his mind.

"We-well," stumbling over his words, Therat reached toward his brother, letting Adon's quiet presence wash over his mind and cool unwanted desires. "Well, I would say it depends on what you seek."

Therat couldn't stop staring at the woman who he only knew by his name. Mireithren. The woman from the Houses of the Sun, who controlled the Song of the Night as if she were its master. The one who drove him to madness with just one look. Bemusement colored those irresistible brown eyes, telling him he failed at a game he didn't know the rules to.

"I ah, I must leave," he said at last. "I only came to say hello. Adon will spoil you and Lady Ninann with his music and good company in my wake."

Therat backed away as he spoke, brushing his hand against his twin in farewell. Without waiting for a reply, he turned, using all his willpower not to run away and look a fool.

PUSH AND PULL

"ADON'S NOT OFTEN LATE. He'll make it worth our time, I promise!" Ninann said, drumming her fingers on the table. "I'm so sorry, Atta. Here I am dragging you out to a place you've never been to, waiting for a man you know very little of. We can leave and go back to the Market. The waveweaver Tylei has a show today."

Ninann's lilting voice pulled Apattar from her thoughts. She turned back to her twin, trying to ignore the looming presence growing in her mind with each breath.

A dark and foul thing approached.

"I'm sorry, what did you say, my sweet dove? I was only half paying attention."

"We can leave if you wish; Adon knows how to find me. This is your day as much as it is mine!"

The thought of leaving sent a shudder through Apattar. "No, no it's fine! Besides, I heard Adon's twin might be coming. Myris seems to think we'll become fast friends as well. 'A twin for a twin', she said, as if the gods work in such terms."

Ninann laughed, a sparkling, joyful sound radiating like the sun. "Your little handmaiden has such an imagination on her! Does she still talk as if her life depends on it?"

Apattar chuckled. "Oh, even more so these days! I can't tell if she's trying to tire me or herself out, but neither seems to work."

Ninann said something in reply, but Apattar lost focus on her twin. That hushed, strange melody she first heard in the morning grew louder in her mind. Her empty heart swelled with emotion, feelings she had no names for assaulting her senses. Apattar had never heard such a song before. It combined in perfect euphony with her soulsong, humming through bone and sinew, spreading a cool tingle as it ran its course.

Apattar's heart quickened. The song pulled her focus to a strange warmth in the void nestled within her core. A tendril of Shadow-weave wove through her restless mind. She found her eyes directed toward two men standing at the far end of the old granary. Tall and black-haired, Apattar recognized Adon's lean form. Hovering like a guard, thick with muscles, stood the man who could only be his twin.

He turned. It was *him*.

The man she ran from, whom she never wished to see again.

The man Laisha said she must find.

Muddy brown eyes locked with ones as gray and dismal as the thunderheads that swallowed the ruins of Andeshar. Time slowed as Apattar took in the black-haired stranger before her.

Why couldn't it be anyone but him?

The man's muscles rippled with each movement of his deep brown torso: a cougar taut and ready to pounce on unsuspecting prey. He wore a simple gray shawl, doing a poor job of hiding a thin white scar snaking across his chest. Tight black curls and a trimmed beard framed a familiar face, but only emptiness filled his stormy gray eyes.

The void within Apattar writhed in the recognition of another touched by the Shadow-weave. It surged outwards toward the man still staring at the raven-haired woman. In her mind's eye, Apattar strode across the golden sands toward him. She offered a hand decorated with glittering gold rings and blue tattoos of doves and flaming suns. He took her hand, and his thoughts flickered across her mind.

Hatred, isolation. Intrigue, jealousy, desperation. A lost soul wandering without purpose. Tainted, worthless to the world. Alone, always alone. Only companions the shadows of death, the faces of those claimed by their rage. Cursed, cursed by the gods to kill, and kill again. Begging for death, screaming for ruin.

A chill ran down Apattar's spine as she pulled herself out of the man's thoughts. She had not expected to find such raging conflict. Compassion flooded the young woman, recognition of another soul broken by the world. Consumed by her intrigue, Apattar reached out again to the shadow-bound stranger. They lashed out without direction, wild and untamed, full of malice. It reminded Apattar of the moment she lost control, when she killed Tela even while begging the hate festering inside to stop.

How could Laisha think either of them worthy of love, fated or otherwise? Killers did not deserve love.

Why do you call to me?

The man looked to take a step toward her; his twin said something and broke the tenuous connection between the two. He shook his head, curls bouncing in the air in a way Apattar thought strangely mesmerizing. She continued watching him, aware of Ninann speaking but unable to find the will to look away. That irresistible song pulled her forward, overriding all thought.

What is this? What are you doing to me?

Apattar forced her eyes closed, letting her sister's voice guide her back to the day. She prattled on about some of her newest creations with Adon in preparation for their education in Isne-ha. The words flowed over Apattar, who feigned interest while waiting for Ninann to take a breath and pause.

"Sister," she finally interjected. "I wonder if you could tell me about Adon's brother. That's him over there, yes?" She gestured at the two black-haired men.

Ninann glanced at Apattar with a curious look but left her thoughts unsaid.

"Therat. Though truth be told, that's about as much as I know. He is quiet, keeps to himself. I can never tell if he hates only me or everyone. He is very protective of Adon since their parents died, changed a lot, Adon said. I wouldn't bother trying to be friends with him, honestly."

"Therat." Apattar rolled his name over her tongue, letting the sounds sink in.

As if called by his whispered name, Therat turned and began walking toward the shaded table. Adon reached it first, monkey in hand. Thinner than his brother but just as tall, Adon was a breathtaking sight in his rich vermilion and pale green robes. The warm orange-red highlighted the golden undertones of his deep brown skin, lighting him up as if he was a Son of Myrniar himself. He reminded Apattar of royalty past, when the fair sons and daughters of the gods walked under their golden light.

"Lady Ninann, Lady Apattar. I wish I had some better reason to be late today. But late is better than never, I hope." Adon spoke with a clear and even voice, each word formed with precise care. "Your first gift, my sweet little dove." He took Ninann's plump hand in his and gave it a gentle kiss.

My sweet little dove.

The words slapped Apattar across the face. A crack ran across her heart. Little Dove had been *her* name for Ninann. The little white dove and the black dove, hearts intertwined but forever destined to live apart in the world. Apattar could not tell which cut deeper—Ninann never telling Adon to stop, or that she *blushed* when he kissed her hand.

This was no mere friendship. Another crack snaked across Apattar's heart. How long had Ninann loved the man? Were they *liraes?* The woman had always been slow to see the truth around her.

Whatever piece of Apattar hoping to stay forever by her sister's side vanished. The gods ripped them apart long ago, Ninann never hers to claim. Their harmonics shifted a little more and a small piece of Apattar's love for Ninann slipped through her cracked heart into the endless void.

Apattar blinked and set her cold gaze on the monkey crawling over her twin's arms. A shower of giggles erupted from the woman. In the corner of her eye, Apattar saw Therat clench his jaw before clearing his throat. Ninann and Adon turned toward him, a look of surprise on the young woman's face.

"Oh, Therat! You startled me, I'm sorry!"

Apattar let the words fade. She turned to Therat and observed the way his eyes bore into Ninann, how the veins in his neck bulged ever so slightly as she spoke. She called out to him, seeking entry into the dark whirlpool drowning the man.

Apattar's song slipped in between the cracks with ease, Therat's focus too far gone to notice the intrusion. Tendrils of Shadow-weave wormed their way into Therat's thoughts, eroding the wall he had so carefully constructed. Then it came tumbling down, something in the world outside igniting craven passions. A vision of Apattar's sister surged forth and lashed out at the woman. Ninann lay crumpled at Therat's feet, golden chains twisted around her fat neck, brown lips frozen in a contorted scream as lifeless eyes stared up at nothing.

Apattar expected to feel anger, rage, a sense of protection. Anything, except nothing at all. The shock of hearing Adon call Ninann his sweet little dove broke the last of Apattar's fragile heart. A waking dream, the veneer of the last month peeled away to reveal what it truly was: a long goodbye to a life never hers to claim. She could not force fate; Apattar realized this now. Sun and Shadow could not live together in harmony.

A soft touch pulled Apattar back to the desert.

"This is my *soerl*. She is back from her visits to... where was it again, sister?"

Apattar took a drink from her glass before replying, her voice still strained from her time spent in the smoky lands of Andeshar.

"Oh, many places. I was gone for, hmm, about a year, I think, right, Inann? I followed my feet and they never stopped for long. Past the western dunes and through the Sea of Grass and to the banks of the Andesiri River. I never saw them, but I often heard the soft music of the wandering Ithraviri. It is hard to deny the presence of the gods in such a strange land of amber-green grass. You would love it, Adon."

Adon heartily agreed, launching into an excited discussion about the Goddess Ithraviél and the Music she taught to her people.

Apattar looked up, aware of Therat observing her with a strange intensity. Curiosity took hold as Adon's chatter faded. Surely she, of all people, did not arouse desire in the man. Ninann's beauty far outshone the scarred and rail-thin woman. Apattar never felt the eyes of another looking at her with such hunger. A ribbon of hot anticipation wrapped itself around her heart. She found herself smiling at the man with gray eyes that shone like the moon.

Therat tensed as if on reflex before a strained smile flashed across his lips. He turned his gaze upward. Apattar saw a spark of recognition behind those lifeless eyes. Did he feel it too, their soulsongs intertwining, pushing the two together?

The thought made her stomach lurch. Some part of her soul, hidden from even herself, begged to embrace the man. But it was a drop in the ocean of Apattar's rising fury at the man she wished never existed, who pulled so many emotions she never wished to feel to the surface of her cracked heart.

Why did he have to see her in the Market on her first day of true freedom, or again in the darkness when she fled from her father's cruelty? Why did he have to chase after her, to act like he cared? She needed to hate him, she told herself. Use him for Laisha's purposes, kill him, or enslave him if she must. It was the only way.

Apattar stared deep into his stormy gray eyes, trying to uncover anything she could. Somehow, words kept falling from her lips, but she could only think of Therat. Despite the bright sun above, shadows leapt and danced around the black-haired man. Hungry, yearning, corrupting. They sank into his flesh, and a flush raced across the man's body, almost imperceptible under his dark skin.

Focusing on the weaves of Therat's mind, Apattar probed again for another entrance into his thoughts. White hot pain tore through his mind, followed by a swelling pressure of delicious pleasure verging on delirium. It threatened to erase the man. Apattar took the chance to walk through Therat's memories, trying to find the heart of his darkness.

A vast wasteland devoid of happiness or joy awaited Apattar.

Since their parents died, he changed a lot.

Ninann's words echoed in the emptiness. Whatever happened the night of his parents' death, it indeed left him broken. What intense love must the boy have once had to leave him this empty without it? Apattar's fury eased, replaced not with pity, but rather understanding.

I do not want you, do not want to save you. You are a tool, that is all you can be! But who else could understand my empty heart?

I am so sorry, Therat.

Apattar's words floated through the decay. A glimmer of life sparked in response. His name echoed in Therat's mind, heart beating faster each time. Apattar knew the feeling all too well. How a stranger's first touches of selfless kindness felt so good she could die right there and be forever content. What would happen if she reached over and touched Therat? Or pulled him in as she embraced his broken body, swallowing the pain into the cool void she harbored inside? His thoughts flickered across her mind as if in reply.

Death by her hand would taste so sweet.

She paused, then pushed deeper into his mind. His voice rang out through the emptiness.

Who are you?

A hazy vision took form in her mind's eye. The raven-haired woman stood in a twisted, broken rocky land. Blood dripped from a black-bladed dagger. She clutched a still-beating heart in her other hand, twitching as nails sank into the decaying flesh. At her feet lay the bloodied body of Therat, his face calm and content in death. She would mold him, shape him—a weapon waiting to be forged.

Apattar blinked, back in the desert once more. A bead of sweat traced its way down Therat's square jawline, now slack with surprise. Hands sat awkwardly over his lap and a sly grin spread across her lips. Apattar was not so sheltered as to be innocent about the ways of men.

What made her so beautiful to him? More importantly, why did she care? Would images of her dance behind closed eyelids at night? The thrill of being someone's obsession kindled a fire in her heart. The idea of finding someone to love her dark and twisted mind didn't seem so impossible now.

The monkey in Ninann's arms leapt onto Apattar's shoulder and wrenched her focus away from Therat. As if waking from a daze, she realized Adon still spoke, asking something about the scattered islands in the western seas.

"Oh, augh!" she shouted, the monkey heavier than it looked. "I'm sorry, Adon. Can you say the last part again?"

Adon reached out and plucked the monkey off Apattar's shoulders. "He's rambunctious, isn't he? I was wondering how you got to the ruined islands. Ninann mentioned it before." He spoke with a smile stretched across his wide face. Apattar wondered if Therat had ever smiled like Adon. He would, soon enough. She would make him die with a smile on his face.

"They stand as a dead reminder of the past, a testament to the folly of our ancestors. They are... peculiar. I'm not sure one can get there by choice. I got to the Andesiri River, you remember? I opened a portal to cross the western banks, but I found myself in the far west, on the ruins of Andeshar. The fires still rage on the northern end, but I found enough to survive. I count it sheer luck I finally managed to open a portal back to

Hylaea. Still, as wanderings go, I do not count it among the worst of my time away."

Therat spoke up, pausing in awkward places as if trying to force the words out. It demanded her attention even as she tried to ignore the flicker of warmth spreading through her hollowed heart.

"The ruins of Andeshar. A perilous place to find oneself. Yet, I sense perhaps it is you others should be afraid of. What an intriguing compliment to your sister." The deep voice rumbled forth from Therat's broad chest. It reminded Apattar of the sky-splitting thunderstorms of Andeshar, how the terrorizing sound grew to be an odd comfort after long weeks on the battered island.

Apattar laughed, a thin and raspy sound. "I hear that often. Twins needn't be replicas, life would be much too boring. There is always something to be found in the dark. Would you not agree," Apattar paused for the briefest of moments, searching for Therat's eyes. When they claimed their victim, she pulled him into her gaze and spoke his name with slow intention. "Therat?"

She wanted to laugh and say his name again. Watch him squirm as the sound dripped from her tongue like a sweet poison into Therat's shadowy mind.

"Well, well..." Therat stumbled over his words, eyes flying around as they searched for anything but Apattar to look at. "Well, I would say it depends on what you seek, my lady."

Apattar giggled, amused by Therat's awkward politeness in the absence of the stony facade she tore down. They locked eyes again for but a moment before he jerked them away, loath to look at his torturer.

"I ah, I must leave. I only came to say hello. Adon will spoil you and Lady Ninann with his music and good company in my wake." Therat stood and backed away as he spoke, turning heel and fleeing like a trapped rodent given a second chance.

Once Therat disappeared around the corner of the far building, the rest of the desert came rushing back to Apattar's senses. The sweet scent of Ninann's perfume—rose and lily, of course. Adon's bracelets clacking together as he rubbed her sister's hand. The coolness of the shade and the chitters of the monkey nestled against Adon's neck. It was as if the world hadn't changed in an instant. Apattar suddenly felt constricted, shackled to her sister. A prisoner.

"My ladies, you must forgive my brother. He is prone to mood swings as random as the natural rains here. I learned long ago to give him space. Gods know where he gets off to, although I sense I may be grateful to not know. Anyway, my ladies Ninann and Apattar, should we go now? I promised far more than a conversation near the granary."

Ninann clapped her hands with glee and began to walk away despite not knowing where to go. Adon caught her wrist, forcing her to stop.

"Oh, I can't wait! And to think, soon enough, we'll be leaving for Tír is Isneha too! Adon, you know how to spoil me." Apattar could not stand Ninann's joy. Nothing sounded worse than stuffy lecture halls and a city of waveweavers all vying to call themselves master of their craft.

"I think I will let you two go on together," Apattar said, eyes darting to where she last saw Therat. "I would like some time to myself right now, to think. Your speaking of Isneha has reminded me that I still need to choose my path ahead. I will find you later, my little dove." Apattar said her beloved name for Ninann, hoping to draw a twinge of guilt from her twin. If any came, it did not surface for the young woman to see. Anger flared, then cooled as fast as it came.

"If that is what you wish! Later, at the Fountain!"

A HEAVY SIGH BUILT in the silence. Apattar's thoughts strayed back to Therat. A man wandering the world lost and separated from his *soerl,* like her. Shadow-touched, like her, but troubled with vicious, wild thoughts. Though she could not say why, Apattar needed to understand the man.

Therat was not an *evranenith*—Apattar knew the twins were born on the autumnal equinox. She heard whispers of people who walked with the shadows of night, transforming themselves as they wove the Shadow-weave into their soulsong. Shadewalkers: a relic of the past, or so the Madhiri said. But they also said no *evranenith* lived to even get a name.

Apattar sat under the palms until the sun rose higher and chased the cool shade away. Rising, curiosity guided her feet toward Therat, his presence like a beacon nestled in her mind. The music grew louder as she walked through the thick band of trees behind the granary.

The sweet smell of grain and honey turned foul as the stench of the slaughterhouse overtook everything fair. It reminded Apattar of a dead camel she once found in the desert, how she poked the distended stomach and with a sickening *pop* death assaulted her senses.

It did not surprise Apattar to find Therat's refuge here. The fetid smell matched foul thoughts running through his mind. She wondered how many people his shadows had told him to kill. Had he acted on it before? Did he lose control as she did, guilt eating at his heart over taking a life? She tried to tell herself they were deserved and justified. Self-defense, even... Tela. Apattar shuddered at the name.

She pushed through the last of the trees and came upon a small path hugging the side of the slaughterhouse. The long building crept along the ground under the tall figs. A small gazebo sat at the far end of the sandstone path in the deep shade of several tall desert willows. In full bloom, a firework of bright pink and white crinkled flowers dazzled between slender, deep green leaves. The gazebo sat in a cloak of shadows that warped the very air around it.

Each step became a war between trepidation and fascination. Apattar knew her presence would cause rumors in the city if anyone saw her, but the voice of reason drowned under the thrum of Therat's soulsong. If she could talk to him, show him what gifts she held. What the pale woman told her, that the shadows were not always this way. She knew how afraid and alone Therat must be. And, if he would not come willingly...

With a shaking hand, Apattar lifted a crimson-colored curtain to the side, revealing an interior lined with small pillows and littered with empty wine bottles. In the center lay Therat. Under the red glow of the curtains, his skin looked like the color of dark dried blood. Those stormy gray eyes rested, his bare chest barely rising with each gentle breath.

Therat looked so peaceful in sleep. His eyelids twitched. A moan escaped pinched lips as some nightmare gripped his mind. Apattar knelt and ran her fingers through his curly black hair, nails gently scratching at his scalp. As if immersed in a hot bath, Therat melted into the cushions, his face calm once more. For a moment, Apattar's heart softened.

My heart...

The soft voice of her unseen guide burnt like the sun itself against her mind. A melancholy so deep it seemed as if her soul-song itself was re-woven settled into Apattar's heart. She gently tucked a stray black curl behind Therat's ear. The intimacy sparked a faint memory, but she could not pull it to the surface.

With her next breath, the enchantment ended.

No!

Jerking her hand away, Apattar studied the rest of the sleeping man. Dozens of little nicks and calluses covered his hands. An intricate spiral of knotwork tattoos ran the length of each finger, meeting at the wrist and wrapping around like a shackle. Apattar memorized all the warding tattoos of the Madhiri as a child; she had never seen one like this before.

Her eyes moved up, stopping at a jagged white scar splayed across his chest. Thin, as if cut by a sharp blade, it ran across Therat's left breast over his heart. A chill ran the length of her body. What could have caused such an injury? Nestled in the embrace of sleep, Therat suddenly seemed so vulnerable.

Apattar extended a thin finger toward the white scar. Firm, unyielding flesh greeted her with a chilly reply. White hot pain sliced through her chest, a cold blade cutting across her upper breast. The intensity evaporated the breath from her lips. Pulled into a tangled web of memories and repressed emotions, her vision swam as a memory all but faded to the light of day came into focus.

Shaking hands clutch a dagger, cold metal gleaming. A freshly smithed blade hungering for first blood. The silver edge slices across quivering skin. Delirious waves of pain lash out with a ferocity to rival the sun. A desperate, feeble attempt to keep going, to plunge the dagger deeper into the maggot-infested heart. A heart of nothing. A heart that killed, murdered, betrayed. Forever broken.

Teeth grit. Unleashing the pain, a cry echoes as the dagger slices deeper. Fingers touch the lacerated flesh, the hot sticky liquid the last sensation before darkness falls.

Apattar's eyes bolted open as the memory crawled back into the depths of shame and denial, leaving only a sense of pathetic failure behind. A tear rolled down her face, splashing onto Therat's lips below. Whatever happened in his past drove the man to madness long ago. He could not be saved, could not be her future. He would ruin her, twist her, unleash the darkness, not end it. Laisha had to be mistaken, had to misunderstand the message of her Oracle.

Deep sorrow and desperation replaced the heat of desire. Apattar ran, flying across the golden sands to the refuge she once claimed as a girl. Was this what the Shadow-weave did to those who escaped death as a babe? How could Apattar overcome such a twisted fate?

AN UNKIND TOUCH

T HERAT WELCOMED THE STENCH of the slaughterhouse, breathing in deep to clear the intoxicating scent of the raven-haired maiden he named Mireithren. He savored the metallic taste of blood in the air as it settled on his tongue. Therat picked his way between the figs and slaughterhouse, sandstones below stained brown with dried blood.

At the end of the path alongside the building sat a small gazebo lined with sheer red curtains. Therat swept one aside and collapsed on a pile of soft pillows. The workers were away today, attending some training in the Sun District. A small blessing, but greatly welcomed.

A heavy dread settled into Therat's limbs. Muscles tensed, ready to strike. A strange sense of anticipation laid over his heart. He pulled off the shawl and rubbed his aching chest. Therat focused on the desert heat as it embraced his body, the hot breeze wicking away sweat as it formed.

His Mireithren didn't belong to just any Named House, but House Isht'iri itself, one of the four Houses of the Sun. Divine blood flowed in her veins. Ninann, his brother's promised bride, was twins with the maiden wreathed in shadows. Mireithren, the impossible *evranenith*, divine in her own right.

Could the idea of a *liraes* be so ludicrous when someone who understood his secret world existed? When he had seen her before, had given her a name and let obsession drive him to madness? A spellbinding siren, Mireithren laid claim to what remained of Therat's broken heart.

The loud squeal of a pig pulled Therat from visions of the woman draped in dark green silks. She lingered even as his eyes opened, her coy smile near irresistible. Therat drained a bottle of wine, the rising fog a welcome distraction from thoughts roiling within. The strain of controlling his desires fell away. Therat's head sank into the soft pillows.

A strangled scream woke Therat. Hot, wet tears covered his face. The trembling voice of his mother pleading for her life echoed in his mind. He squeezed his eyes shut, only to see half-images from the nightmare flashing by.

His parents, their faces obscured by a campfire, kneeling on the ground. Four tall, cloaked figures, their bare feet soaked with blood, one as pale as the moon itself. A golden chain wrapped around the ankle of a woman dressed in rags. A discarded dagger in the flames, blood sizzling on the hot blade. His mother's auburn hair now crimson, his father's headless body...

Therat's eyes flew open. He keeled over, spewing bile and wine over the gazebo floor. Gagging on the acidic taste left in his mouth, tears fought to escape. Therat fumbled in the dark before laying his hands on a wine bottle, taking several large gulps. With a shaky hand, he picked up the beige shawl and wiped away all evidence of the nightmare from his eyes. He refused to acknowledge that evil night haunting his every step.

Stumbling out of the gazebo, the terror left as the warm solstice night embraced Therat. For as much as he hated life, he relished the closing hours of the summer solstice. Death seemed far away.

Past midnight, the city cowered inside four walls. The stars overhead bathed the earth in soft light, casting deep shadows across the oasis. The silence bore down on Therat, pushing all thoughts aside and calming his restless mind. A soft sigh of relief escaped his lips. He took a deep breath and caught the faintest scent of vanilla and water lilies on the edges of the slaughter-house's stink. Therat swallowed hard, his heart beating faster.

"No," he growled, both hands curling into fists. "No, go away! I do not want whatever you offer, siren."

Mireithren's rough voice raked across his mind. It made his skin crawl.

You are different, Therat. We are different.

The sound of his name said by the enchantress sent a wave of hot blood through Therat's veins.

"Get. Out." He gritted his teeth until his jaw ached.

What if I can help you?

Mireithren's voice echoed around Therat, bending every last thought to her will. The siren materialized in his mind, a sorrowful smile on her scarred, yet divine, face.

"I will ruin you. I ruin everything I touch. Be it today, next year, or a hundred years from now. Death and darkness haunt my steps. I do not want you, please, leave me be! I am ruined, ruined!" A scream tangled with Therat's final words in his throat.

You do not scare me, little lost boy. I will find you again, when you are ready.

A rush of cool air whistled past Therat's ears. The spaces in his mind felt hollow again. He took a timid breath, but only the sickly sweet stench of death greeted him. Shaking his head, confusion curled into a frown. It seemed so obvious now: she wanted to ruin him, use him to spread the tainted darkness for her dread Mistress.

Therat froze in place, waves of conflicting emotions lapping over him. He wanted to hear his name on her tongue again and again. *Little lost boy.* What could she possibly know? He never spoke to anyone outside of family about the night of his parents' murder, how a part of him remained forever stuck in the past.

The cool silver of his mother's necklace burnt against Therat's ankle. He wanted to forget Mireithren, push her away and reject the siren. Yet, he could not, his curiosity outweighing apprehension. Why did she, of all people, stir his near-dead heart with a rush of confusing emotions?

Consumed by the war between oath and desire, Therat walked without purpose. The metropolis of Av Madhira teemed with life, the thrum of millions filling the air each day. Never had a singular person titillated Therat so. Most faces elicited nothing at all, while some revealed the murderous whispers of the Shadow-weave.

Therat hated Mireithren. Hated what she could represent, how she would ruin him. Kill him, use him, love him—all would send him further into the twisted embrace of the Shadow-weave.

Why are you the exception? I am not worth loving, not worth saving, even if it is a sweet lie to lure me to my doom.

Trees gave way to a clearing with several small canopies erected in a semi-circle, the embers of a dying bonfire in the center. Discarded bits of food and a few cards from a game littered the rocky ground. The remnants of a joyful life all but a stranger to Therat.

A bottle of wine lay at his feet, almost full. He pulled the cork out with his teeth, spitting it aside before guzzling the red wine. Hints of clove and plum greeted his taste buds. Though dry going down, it meant sleep would soon embrace Therat. Bark scraped at skin already going numb from the wine. The world dulled and Therat's vision blurred as relief came at last.

Twenty

DEADLY URGES

A MAN WITH SHORT *black curls and a trimmed beard sits on a chair, bouncing a young toddler on his knee. A woman stands behind him, her soft auburn waves wrapped around another child clutching her breast. It feels warm, safe, loving. Home.*

A child's laugh, followed by another. Twins giggling together, chasing two tawny foxes running between their short legs. The small creatures yip, laughing along. One gray-eyed boy grabs the tail of the nearest fox, gently tugging it with a stubby hand. The fox jumps in response; the boy falls over in a fit of laughter.

The woman with auburn hair stands with a young black-haired boy, tousle of curls nearly swallowing his small face. A thread of inky blackness winds its way around the two, the woman clapping as the boy murmurs to himself. The shadows grow darker before fading away. A look of disappointment flashes across the young boy's face.

The boy stands next to an older, grim-faced man, tears streaming from the child's red-rimmed eyes, twin clutched to his chest. The two shake the ground with their heavy sobs. A woman talks to the older man, her face creased with unreadable emotions. A shout; the woman storms off. Silence and shadows. Suffocating, tearing, ripping apart the young boy's heart.

THERAT OPENED HIS EYES with a groan. He rolled over and shut them again, trying in vain to cling to the happy memories he seldom dreamt of anymore. He clung to the fragments for dear life, the last remaining vestige of his unbroken heart. A reminder—albeit slim and ever weakening—that dark passions did not always enslave him.

It became harder to ignore the question burning at him since a small child: why did the Shadow-weave choose Therat? Why did Adon get to lead a life in the sun, know the happiness of love and friendship? His jealousy of Ninann became tangled with envy of Adon, the two representing everything Therat would never have.

For the first time in almost a decade, Therat's will to avoid memories of his childhood eroded. He wished nothing more than to talk to his mother again, to hear her musical laugh and sing-song voice as she taught him to control his powers. What would she say now of his hatred of the Shadow-weave? Would she tell him he was broken, heart born black, and his life a perversion of the gift she taught him? The white scar over his heart burned.

Grinding his molars together until they ached, Therat stood. His feet carried him along the back line of trees where the shadows gathered. They offered little comfort. Something compelled his legs to move. They carried him through the trees on winding paths carved by centuries of bare feet. Threads of gelid Shadow-weave wrapped around his body, their embrace a death-grip coaxing him forward.

The blood lust came calling, the foul Shadow-weave claiming its vessel to wreak death. Mireithren left Therat too weak to fight back.

A black umbra clung to Therat as he emerged in the open Market square. A woman with long silvery hair danced to the soft gurgles of the Fountain of Maidens in the dim moonlight. The dancer twirled and leapt through the night, fingers tracing a pattern in the air and leaving a shimmery mist in her wake. The dancer turned again and again, moving with such grace that even Therat found it beautiful to watch.

He took a silent step forward, the whispers growing louder. The woman turned to face him. He saw the familiar face of the waveweaver Tylei. Her silvery-blue hair seemed to defy gravity, eyes bright like the moon above. A wisp of shadows played at Tylei's bare feet.

"I did not expect to find an audience at this time of night," she said, moving closer. The Shadow-weave withdrew from Therat at the sound of her voice. "You are welcome to stay, though I am dancing only for myself tonight." The blue pendant at her throat pulsed with a soft glow.

"The nights are my refuge as well. I will not bother you." *I will not tempt these shadows, not her...* "You always enthrall the crowds, I imagine you crave the silence of night as much as I do."

The woman smiled. "I have felt your eyes before, catching glimpses of me through the trees at night as you ran from the shadows."

"I don't know what you mea—" The words spilled from his lips, denial thick on his tongue.

"You use it well, shadewalker. Do not worry, your secret is safe with me. I do not fear the night and moon like these desert-dwellers. In the West, they are seen as a gift."

Tylei extended a hand to Therat. Her fingers brushed the side of his arm before falling away. He recoiled on instinct, skin crawling where her touch strayed. In the back of his mind, a voice wondered, *would you recoil from the raven-haired Mireithren?*

"Don't," Therat muttered, gaze fixed on Tylei's offending hand. She took a step back, studying the troubled gray eyes watching her like prey.

"Is it me you fear, or the ever-hungry void? You cannot survive alone; none of us can. I hear the discord growing in your soulsong. I only want to he—"

"I've had enough of strange women offering me help today, if it's all the same to you." Therat snarled as he spoke, flashes of hot anger pricking him.

Tylei paused and smiled, taking off without a word. She spun around Therat and danced back across the empty square. Therat looked at the woman with hungry eyes, trying in vain to ignore the voices in his head, to wrest his eyes away from her supple form. The unquenchable bloodthirst could not be denied. A tangle of screams assaulted his senses.

She is alone. All alone. The world cannot hear, cannot help. Wouldn't it be a wonder to hear her dying screams as she twitches at your feet? She knows too much. Do you think the blood of a waveweaver smells different? Now you can find out... Blood. Blood. Blood...

His vision dimmed. A chill settled over his skin as the writhing Shadow-weave freed itself from his wretched heart. The Song of the Night embraced him. Instinct took over. Therat reached a trembling hand toward the silver-haired woman, humming to herself by the Maidens.

A small voice begged him to stop, unheard as the cacophony of voices told him all the ways he could kill Tylei with ease.

Therat sprinted toward Tylei, closing the distance between them before she had time to react. A strangled scream escaped her throat as he grabbed her by the hair and swung her to the ground.

Her head slammed against the stones of the fountain. A sickening *CRACK!* reverberated in the air. He lunged forward, grabbing Tylei's hands as they fumbled to reach her necklace.

Therat begged himself to stop. He saw his hands moving, fighting with the woman, but the Shadow-weave controlled all. She screamed, and for a moment, Therat swore he heard his mother screaming, too.

Stronger than she looked, Tylei fought to free a wrist from Therat's shadowy grasp. Blood gushed from her head. The warm, sticky liquid coated the two. Tylei twisted a hand free, fingers grasping the stone at her throat. A flickering blue light lit up her face, growing stronger with each passing moment. Tylei's mouth moved, but before she could utter a sound, Therat's hand slammed against the side of her head and again across her cheek. Tendrils of Shadow-weave coiled around the woman's throat, wrapping tighter until her hand fell away from the stone.

Blood and tears mixed in a wet smear across Therat's knuckles. Tylei whimpered, then fell limp. With a raspy gasp, she leaned up and raked a hand across Therat's face. Her nails scraped at his skin, a thick drop of crimson blood falling on her throat.

Tylei slurred something under her breath. A blinding flash of golden light pierced Therat's vision, eyes exploding in searing pain. He yelped and loosened his grip long enough for the woman to squirm away, kicking feet wildly at his groin. She landed a kick; a jolt of lightning surged through his abdomen, forcing the air out of his lungs with a pathetic wheezing groan. Tylei pushed herself backwards and scrambled away on all fours out of sight.

Therat collapsed on the sand, mind reeling with white-hot pain. He heard the woman sob not far away, her breathing uneasy, growing fainter with each wheezing gasp. The black shadows faded from Therat's eyes, but still he could not move, paralyzed as the brutality of his attack played on a loop.

After a time—perhaps minutes or hours, he could not tell—Therat stood. Not far, in a pool of blood, lay the crumpled body of Tylei.

I did it again, fuck, I did it again!

Therat gulped and ran in a panic, trying to escape Tylei and the voices that murdered her. They took over his body, making him witness a crime he could not stop. Therat ran until his lungs burned, screaming for air as he sucked in rapid breaths. Saliva pooled in his mouth, tumbling out when he finally forced down a breath of cool air. His hands shook as silent sobs wracked his body. His face stung as the tears washed over the cuts from Tylei's nails.

What have I done? No, no, oh gods, she's dead, dead! I killed her, like I killed the others. Why can't I stop this? I didn't want to, I never did. Please, please, end this and kill me already. These are a curse, a curse! Did Mama ever know or ever think this could h appen?

A wail ripped from Therat's body, drawing out all his energy as it forced its way out from the scared little boy he kept locked away from the world. The city slept, oblivious to his pain. Hollow and spent, Therat collapsed.

The night swallowed Therat as he let go, loosening his control over the knot of rage and grief choking his heart. The Shadow-weave reached up and out of his body, cloaking him with its cool embrace. Therat held his breath until the blood pounded in his ears. He wished it could be his last breath, could end it all and face Death Herself. The scar across his chest burned, a reminder his life was at the mercy of the gods, and oh, how little did they care?

He told himself she touched him, knew his secret. Then the Shadow-weave awoke, angry and protective. It did not make his crime any easier to witness, a look of terror frozen on Tylei's face.

The moon shone bright, its roundness filling the sky. Therat looked up, eyes gleaming with hatred.

"This blood is on your hands, you raven-haired siren. I deny your claim over me, Mireithren! You will lead me to ruin, not the other way around. I see that now. Take your accursed shadows, I do not want you! I cannot... I cannot."

Twenty-One

ANOTHER LIFE

T HE FOUR DAYS SINCE *The Winged Serpent* left port at Sere Aesli felt like the longest of Apattar's life. The ship bucked with each crashing wave, the sea a cruel mistress sure to take their lives. Yet, each morning, Apattar woke up alive—if not running to the porthole to expel the contents of her queasy stomach. The woman swore to herself she would never step foot on a ship again. Not even a small one. A canoe, a raft, or anything floating on the water. She could not fathom why Ninann chose such an antiquated form of transportation.

Brushing long black braids out of her face, Apattar stood from the uncomfortable wicker chair, wincing as her back cracked in complaint. Ninann gave such little notice of their journey via ship, and the captain failed to provide accommodations befitting the Named Houses. Apattar sniffed, wishing to be back in the desert. Where had Ninann even found these people?

"Sister," Apattar said with a scratchy voice. "You may wish to sit here and languish all day, but I cannot stand one more minute of this. I'm going to open a portal and meet you at Isneha. Take care of Saiya and Myris for me until we reunite, please?"

Apattar turned to her sister, who lounged on the upper deck, only a thin towel between her and the muck-stained wood. The sun illuminated her deep, ocher brown skin, glowing as if set on fire from within. She looked so radiant. A divine grace surrounded the plump maiden.

Ninann opened one sea-foam green eye, staring at Apattar before closing it again. "You will do no such thing! We are almost there. I want you to see it with me for the first time. Adon says the Eldest Children themselves carved the white arches spanning the Iri'e River. And the floating islands, raised by the Goddess Nehsan herself and blessed by Isnehari the Weaver! Can you imagine? It must be more beautiful than any words could capture." Excitement colored every word, Ninann almost breathless from speaking with such a rush. Apattar sighed and feigned a smile as she nodded.

"Yes, yes. You're right Inann, it will be stunning I am sure. But promise to never make me travel this way again. It is so... simple."

Ninann snorted in reply. "And your portal sent you to a ruined island and almost claimed your life. At least this will not get us hurt or lost."

Apattar could sense Ninann's concern, but it only angered her. "One time, Inann," she shot back. "One time, and I got myself out, thank you. Not all of us can be perfect."

Apattar huffed and turned away. Why did she even come? Because of some vain hope she could run away from her problems, pretend she didn't see the way the Shadow-weave consumed Therat until he would vanish? She might control it now, but luck would not last. Maybe Laisha was right. Maybe Therat was the key to her future. She would find him, dominate him, and lead the man to the West and a future unknown. Anything else that she felt was a delusion.

A hand tugged at her elbow, Ninann now standing behind the woman.

"I'm sorry, my sweet Atta. I didn't mean to imply... I worry about you. You are at war, I can tell. Stuck between two futures that cannot exist together. I-I can't imagine what it's like. I want you to come with me, but I cannot force you." Ninann's eyes pleaded with Apattar, the mesmerizing swirls of blue and green impossible to deny. Apattar pulled her lighter half in close, squeezing the soft rolls of fat padding her sister's waist.

"WAVE INCOMING!"

The man's shout startled the twins, who dove down to the deck in a flash.

A massive wave crashed over the side of the ship. Cold water and foam sprayed over the upper deck. Droplets of water rained down, tiny pellets of bitter cold finding every spot of flesh not covered by Apattar's thick cotton cloak. Her stomach lurched. The morning's meal threatened to come up with each subsequent wave crashing against the ship. Darting her eyes around in a panic, Apattar scrambled under a table bolted to the wood deck, pulling Ninann with her.

A man dressed in stained blue pants stood on a table behind them, arms raised to the sky. He shouted something incomprehensible between the crashing waves, lips moving with furious speed. A blue glow emanated from within his eyes. An orb of crackling energy formed around him, pulling the man up into the sky. Lighting streaked over the outside of the orb, a dazzling display of white, silver, and dark blue lights. Shaggy white hair stood straight up with the energy pulsating around the man. He lowered his arms and pushed them forward. A stream of blue light burst forth while thunder boomed overhead.

Apattar's vision went white. When it returned, bright cerulean blue painted the skies above, the sea calmed once more. Devoid of sound, the world seemed to collapse under the stark silence. Then, with a thunderous roar, a chorus of voices rose from the main deck, their broken words of "Kirean... best... drunk tonight!" breaking through the clamor.

Apattar crawled out from the table and pulled the thick cotton cloak tight, shivers wracking her thin frame. Her gaze swept across the ship, surveying the damage from the colossal waves. Briny water mixed with fish guts and oil from toppled barrels flowed over the sides of the deck below. Sailors scrambled to and fro. Some cleared debris while others climbed thick wooden masts—three in all—and adjusted the rigging. They shouted to each other in a strange language. Mesmerized, she stood watching the sailors work in unison, each movement honed to perfection from years spent at sea.

Heavy footsteps approached, drawing Apattar's attention away from the main deck. She turned to see the white-haired man—Kirean, she presumed.

"Our apologies, Lady Apattar. Something angered the Maiden, but She listened to me well enough. She is a cruel mistress, but one we love and forgive. I hope you will not hold this against us." The white-haired man spoke with a thick accent. Piety dripped from every word.

Years at sea hardened the man's skin into a well-worn leather, ruddy and bronzed from endless hours in the sun. He looked much older now than he did a moment ago, with wispy white hair and a scruffy beard framing a face cracked with age. Eyes the color of the deep blue waters surrounding them looked back at Apattar with a soft apology.

"The... Maiden? The Goddess Aslyren? But, they are all dead, gone." Apattar shifted her weight between both feet, trying to find balance as gentle waves lapped against the ship. The man extended a thin arm for support, which she latched onto with gratitude.

"Ah aye, you sand-dwellers do not hear your Goddess anymore. None hear the Maiden's call as we do. She is this," he gestured to the open sea with his free hand. "The Maiden is endless. She is the waters of life flowing through the rivers and seas, even to your little lakes in the golden sands. Others in the world call the gods silent. Aye, they all are except out here. Here, Aslyren lives still. An echo, but there nonetheless."

Apattar's eyes widened as she looked over the endless blue waters. The faint whisper of a woman singing floated past with the winds. She could not notice it before, mind preoccupied with what the sailors called 'sea sickness'. But now the soft voice broke through, more beautiful than anything she had heard before.

"You hear Her now, don't you? I know your look, they all have it the first time they hear our Goddess. Remember it well, *neha*. The Maiden is the only Goddess who still has a voice, faint though it may be. They have not all abandoned us." The man's face creased into a well-worn smile as he spoke, a fond look in his ocean-blue eyes.

A shiver crawled through Apattar's mind. As if bitten by a snake, she recoiled from the man's supportive arm, stumbling until the railing caught her back.

Not this one! Never her! Aslyren is a traitor, a liar! Do not listen to her sweeting songs, she claims dominion where she has none. She is Death! You are mine! You bring life, hope! Do not listen to her lies, Mireithren!

The nameless whisper wormed into Apattar's mind, searing through all thought like liquid fire. Burning pain and bitter rage coursed through every neuron. A memory of someone from some other time, in another life, burst through the raging fires.

Six figures stand around a pillar, their forms impossible to focus on, starlight leaking from their bodies. A figure reaches a hand forward. Icy water drips to the earth below. It takes a hand, speaking in a language that sounds more like music than speech.

Icy blue eyes leer out from the starlight, hatred and fear radiating from the silken voice.

A dagger with a curved white blade appears in the figure's free hand, flickering in and out of reality as wisps of radiant gold light weave into metal. The white blade rises. The five figures in the back chant, their voices louder than thunder. The dagger slices into unwilling flesh. Pain beyond comprehension races from hand to heart, spreading with each erratic heartbeat. It is fire and ice, melting through skin and bone, freezing blood until it bursts into crystalline shards. The pain is all-consuming, erasing every thought and memory of anything else.

Apattar jerked her eyes open, sucking down the salty air and choking on tears that refused to spill. She looked at her left palm, expecting to see a bloody gash. As the shock faded, her breathing slowed, though words refused to come. She opened her mouth and closed it again, unsure what to do. The elderly man's face grew pale and wan, eyes wide with concern—or fear?

She gathered her skirts and darted past the man, scurrying down the stairs and into the quarters prepared off the main deck. With a heave, the door slammed shut. Eyes danced around the room while her mind raced with questions. Before Apattar could think straight, the door opened behind her, sending her stumbling back into the soft arms of Ninann.

"Oh! Wha—you. I'm fine, it's nothing." Apattar shrugged off Ninann and strode into the room.

"Gods help me, Apattar. Do you refuse to tell me as some form of torture? Punishment? I can tell something is bothering you, you aren't that sly." Anger twisted Ninann's face. It was a strange look on her.

"What do you want me to say, Ninann?"

A fire built in Apattar's eyes, rage burning in her chest. Whatever she saw and whoever that heinous memory belonged to, she did not wish to know more. She wanted to forget it all and hide from the world, run away to the ruins of Andeshar where no one would find her. It was all too much, too much to keep bottled up inside, yet impossible to share with the only friends she had. The shadows were her burden to bear alone. She would go mad, like Therat.

"The truth, is that so hard?" Tears welled up in Ninann's eyes, large saucers cracking with pain. "It's your voice again, isn't it?"

A thin gasp escaped Apattar's lips. She frowned, weighing if she should feign ignorance. After what felt like minutes, she spoke with a cool tone, surveying Ninann for the slightest reaction.

"What do you know about that?"

Ninann looked away and swallowed, the sound like deafening thunder breaking the silence. She turned back, a single tear crawling down her perfect face.

"Remember when we were little girls and you would sometimes sleep in my bed when Papa left? You talked in your sleep. Most of it never made sense, broken fragments of sentences. But always you would ask if the voice would help, if she would take you away. I was too little at the time, I didn't know what you meant. But the older we've gotten, the more I see. Even if you wish to hide it from me."

Apattar stiffened, denial thick on her tongue.

"You promised you would return to me. Said you would not lose yourself when you went West seeking answers to a question you never deigned to share. But you... This is not the sister I love. You are so angry, so conflicted. You think this voice is a guardian, but I'm not so sure. What could you possibly have learned to taint even your love for me?"

Apattar wanted to reach out and grab her sister's hand, but her arm refused to move. She stood there stiff as a tree, not ready to divulge her secrets to the woman she once trusted with everything. Nothing felt the same since she left Av Madhira.

"Inann, I... I don't know how to tell you. What to tell you. I am not sure I believe it myself. But this world, there is so much pain and suffering. So many innocent lives ended out of fear and hatred. These shadows fester the longer they are left ignored. I don't know what to do anymore."

Ninann shook her head, tears spilling from her watery eyes. "I can't help you if you won't tell me! Maybe one day you'll understand." Ninann turned back to the wide double doors. "I think it is best if I leave now." She paused for a moment before pushing the doors open, leaving with a loud sigh.

Indecision paralyzed Apattar. She should be upset, should go running after Ninann and share the burdens eating her alive. But her mind told her of a thousand ways it would end in tragedy, rejection and misery wrought by her hand. Apattar knew she must let Ninann go. Any claims to her sister and the happiness they once shared was only ever a dream, even when it felt real.

One more month. That's what I'll do. One more month of delusion before I slip away. It will be better this way.

Twisting a tiny braid over her fingers, Apattar lay down on the lumpy pad that passed for a bed on the ship. Straw and broken feathers poked through the scratchy sheets, hundreds of little daggers ready to slice her back. Images of the strange vision flashed by. It evoked terror so deep she wanted to run away.

When would the running stop? She was so tired, so very tired.

THE SOUND OF MEN shouting woke Apattar, cacophony leaking through a door opened and quickly shut. A strange sensation filled her body, a fire in her belly and a spark of crackling energy dancing across her skin. Only in sleep did some semblance of happiness find her aching heart. Apattar sighed, chest heavy over yet another fleeting dream gone too soon.

The floorboards creaked and groaned under Ninann's soft footsteps. The rose and coconut oils massaged into her long black curls always gave the woman away.

"Atta? Are you well?" Concern tinged her words. "I-I am sorry. It was not my place to demand an explanation." A warm hand caressed Apattar's shoulder. "I forget sometimes, it seems." She paused for a long moment. "Your birth never mattered to me, so I chose to forget it, pretend it didn't change anything."

Apattar pushed herself up from the lumpy bed. Ninann knelt on the floor beside it, wringing her hands and chewing on the corner of her mouth. Apattar tucked a curl behind her twin's ear, fingertips caressing her plump cheek. A smile flashed by—weak, but enough to make the edges of Ninann's lips quiver. She stood, leveling soft blue-green eyes with Apattar's.

"I know, my little dove," Apattar said with a sigh. "You always saw me, and only me. But we can't pretend nothing is different between us. I wish I could tell you everything, I do! But I could not burden your heart with my life. This is mine to do alone. Maybe... maybe it is even fate, one might say."

Apattar laughed pathetically. It tried—and failed—to diffuse the stale air hanging between the sisters.

"I always hated riddles, you know. It seems you've become an expert in speaking with them." The words lacked Ninann's usual warmth. Apattar thought she heard a quiet sob escape her sister's lips. "You talk as if one of the Goddesses has chosen you themself. Remember when you said *I* was delusional for seeking to serve Myrniar? You told me the Seven were dead, and the world better that way. You are free now, my dove, your cage opened! Why do you chain yourself so? You can come with me, we can be together and happy. I need not return to Av Madh—"

"It isn't so simple, Inann," Apattar replied. "What you offer is not a gift, but a slow death, stripping away everything until I am left an empty shell. My head is filled with the screams of innocent babes slaughtered in the night. I can't, I can't anymore! I don't know what to do! The dark sun did not curse me, I see this now. It's like this moment has been building for years, an inevitable conclusion to a war started long ago. The world will watch as I reclaim it from the hands that betrayed me!"

The words spilled from Apattar's lips. She wanted to swallow them as they formed on her tongue, but they were not hers to command. The whispering voice returned, its anger an intoxicating drug pulling her into a shadowy cocoon. Shards of ice and liquid fire seared her left palm. A woman's shrill laugh and piercing blue eyes flashed across her vision.

Ninann stiffened, arms shaking as muffled sobs filled the air. Apattar wanted to pull her twin in close and comfort the poor thing. Ninann never deserved a day with heartbreak or pain.

Apattar could feel the void lashing out, threads of Shadow-weave suffocating the radiant woman until her soul remained but a dim spark in the coming night. Shades lunged at Ninann, circling ever closer.

This will be her fate if she stays by your side. This one is not for you. The new dawn is always weakest. You must leave, child, or you will consume her. She is not yours to save.

The ravenous shades disappeared. Amber light once again filled the small room. A wave crashed against the ship. Apattar stumbled, one bony shoulder colliding with Ninann's chin and sending the maiden tumbling to the floor. Ninann huffed, ignoring her sister's hand and using a barrel to pull herself up.

"Wha—come now! It was an accident, Ninann! I would never try to hurt you!" Ninann's rejection stung more than Apattar thought it would.

"But you do, can't you see? You don't need to try, it comes so easily to you now. I cannot follow you down this path and watch you lose yourself! This is not you speaking! I offer freedom, but instead, you escape one set of chains only to gleefully take on a new master. I love you, Apattar. Do not ask me to bear witness to this madness."

Ninann's tears broke through. They ran over the soft curves of her full cheeks, down her chin, and onto a thick red cloak. Brownish-pink lips almost always pulled upwards into a smile now trembled with sorrow. A sharp pain like a white-hot knife cut through Apattar's mind, rending her psyche in two. The harmonic resonance between the twins faltered, then ended with a piercing scream. Apattar's ears rang with pain.

Jerking her eyes up, she found Ninann's gaze but felt no connection between them. No comforting warmth as the raven-haired woman reached out with her thoughts. Cold, unwavering silence surrounded Apattar.

Ninann stood and smoothed her garments with an unsettling calmness. "Well." She did not speak again for a long moment. "This is how things shall be. He was right, I'm sad to say. I'll love you from afar, always, my black dove. But this," she gestured to the two of them. "This..." Ninann's voice faded.

Still dazed from the shrieking voice, Apattar could only mumble, "He was right?"

"Yes. That I would be chasing a lost cause. Your path is too far diverged, the discord between us too much for even the harmonics weaving us together to overcome. I didn't want it to be true." Ninann sighed.

With a final crack, Apattar's heart so carefully pieced together over the years shattered. The finality of their broken bond sank in.

"You are like his brother in so many ways, turning to the dark and losing yourself."

The void squirmed at the mention of Therat, for who else could Ninann speak of? Apattar could never forget the man. The way the shadows wrapped around his skin—dark brown, like burnt clay. How his stormy gray eyes turned dark with hunger, unable to look away from the woman used to being ignored. How vulnerable and soft he looked. A delectable meal ready to be devoured by the cursed Shadow-weave. A glimpse of the future awaiting Apattar?

He infuriated Apattar. Why could she not stop thinking about the man?

I must find Therat. For Laisha. I will claim him, take him by force if need be.

"You do not speak fact, sister." A bitter taste crept into Apattar's mouth, her skin prickling with the sudden chill in the room.

Leaving for Tír is Isneha was a mistake.

The thought burst and spread like wildfire through Apattar's mind, the obviousness of it all smacking her across the face. The scholars and books there would not hold the answers she sought. Even the wise and learned feared the *evranenith.* What if they learned of her powers or birth? Why risk everything?

"No, Ninann. A fact is this: I should not have come with you. Tír is Isneha is your future, not mine. I must make my own way in life. I should have been slain, yet here I stand. I do love you, but you are right; this is not your path. You'll find me again, I'm sure of it." Apattar's hands moved by her sides as she spoke, tracing a pattern in the air as she thought of her hidden desert refuge.

A portal opened behind her as the final words left Apattar's lips. The shimmering opaque surface illuminated the woman with a warm red glow. Hot air billowed forth. Comfortable, welcoming. Apattar belonged in the desert. For now, at least.

"Atta!" Ninann shrieked. "Atta, what are you even talking about? Do you hear yourself right now? You can't run away again! Where are you going, Apattar?" She lunged forward to grab Apattar's hand; a wave against the ship sent her the other way.

"Don't stop me, Ninann! This is what you told me to do all those years ago. You said to find a reason to live. I have one, even if I hate it. It's the best I can ask for. I'm leaving, and that's final."

Flinging off the cloak and kicking off her thick-soled boots, Apattar looked more like a wraith draped in blood-red silks than the plump maiden who once fled Av Madhira. With a broad smile, she stepped backwards through the portal, hot sands greeting her bare feet.

"Apattar, pl—" Apattar snapped the portal shut, cutting off Ninann's plea.

THE NAMELESS ONE

T HE AMBER GLOW ON the western horizon brought a sigh of relief to Apattar's cracked lips. Night would soon fall. Shadows beckoned the woman outside of the four stuffy walls imprisoning her during the day. Soon, she could steal water from a well not far from the abandoned shack.

Apattar wandered into Av Madhira one cold night after starving for six torturous days in the desert. The winds of fall arrived with a vengeance, claiming the lingering days of summer as their own. The confidence surging through the woman when she left Ninann evaporated in the blink of an eye.

Instead of arriving outside the city, Apattar found herself in a tiny oasis, a crescent-shaped pool of clear water the only good to come of the miscalculation. Guided by the blistering sun and icy moon, the raven-haired woman eventually navigated her way back to Av Madhira. Yet, when she came at last to the Market, posters of her face hung from every stall. The *Makhaeren* herself placed a bounty on Apattar, claiming her to be a runaway from the Temple.

Tonight would be Apattar's last night here. Three weeks in the city already proved to be a great risk. Who knew what whispers had spread about the mysterious woman in the Slums. With her strength recovered enough to journey back to the rocky ruins of Andeshar, Apattar only needed to find a few more provisions before escaping.

Surveying the deepening shadows, Apattar opened the half-burnt front door of her refuge. A bony hand snaked out, followed by the rest of the woman. A thin shaft of moonlight illuminated her deep brown skin.

Time bested the once radiant, albeit scarred, black dove of House Isht'iri. Tiny braids of raven-black hair always maintained to perfection now frayed and tangled together. Long nails broke with ease, blood often gathering at the cuticle. Her once delicate crimson silk dress now hung in tatters from her thin frame.

Apattar decayed a little more each day. The few civilians who saw her creeping at night whispered of a wraith haunting the burnt-out section of the Slums. The only spark of life remained in her bright brown eyes.

The faintest movement of something dark across the small clearing caught her attention. She shrank into the shadows, thoughts running wild. The end came at last. Her father must have returned and tracked the woman's presence.

The thought of her hard-faced father sent a spasm of fear through Apattar. Adrenaline coursed through her body, knees buckling with the surge of emotions.

This will be my grave.

A foolish end for an even more foolish girl. Deluded and alone with her festering thoughts, hearing a voice whispering of hope but only leading to doom. What good did it ever bring?

Alone with only her growing regrets, Apattar couldn't help but wonder if she had made everything up. Was the pale woman she met in Andeshar even real, or a mere figment of a broken mind desperate for something to believe in? Was Ninann right? Was this an elaborate descent into madness before she lost control? Apattar would write her dark ending, refusing help and pushing away the only one she ever loved. Her heart roiled with emotions, choking on tears begging for release.

Caught in a storm of questions and regrets, she did not hear the soft footsteps approaching from behind. The gnawing void pulled Apattar further into despair, spiraling out of control, ready to consume and hollow her out until nothing remained. Her thoughts slipped into the blackness, taking more memories of her time in the light of Ninann's smile.

The lightest touch on her shoulder pulled the world back into focus with dizzying clarity. Blinking as if waking from a dream, Apattar stumbled to her feet. A light brown hand covered in dozens of tiny scars and burns reached out and turned her around.

"Oh—oh! By the Seven, it *is* you! My lady, oh gods, what happened to you?"

The figure threw off a black cloak crawling with shadows. There, under the moonlight, stood the ever-faithful handmaiden Saiya. The sight of Apattar's only friend left sent a flood of relief through her. The first kind face she had seen in almost a month lit up like the sun when Apattar turned.

Apattar's lips quivered. A single hot tear snaked down her scarred cheek.

"Saiya," she breathed, unable to say more.

"I can't believe I found you!" Saiya's arms flew around her mistress and squeezed tight. "Your sister, she told us what happened when we got to port at Apathren. It had only been a few hours. I thought you might have gone to the oasis we visited once at night. Myris stayed behind, she thought you'd come to your senses and return. I found a Gateweaver; he opened a portal to the oasis for me, but you weren't there. I thought you dead! How could you do this?" Saiya's voice changed from shocked to upset, both anger and worry seeping into her accusations. Why would Saiya care so much about her? They were friends, true, but only because duty first bound them together.

"I di-didn't me—" Apattar rasped before bursting into a coughing fit. The air clawed at her fragile throat, tongue so heavy she could barely swallow.

"You need to drink. Here." Saiya pulled a waterskin from over her shoulder and uncorked it. She held it up to Apattar's mouth and let the water dribble in, each drop a gift of everlasting life, precious beyond compare. Choking down the water until she had her fill, the raven-haired woman squeezed a bony hand around Saiya's arm in thanks.

"Yo-you are my favorite person right now," Apattar stammered. "I can do without food, but oh, water is a precious thing! Gods, I can think again." Apattar stood and wiped her mouth, now able to process the fact she stood in front of Saiya. "Wait. How did you even find me?"

"No! It isn't what you think, I'm not a spy or anything, I promise. I want to help you, my lady. I-I..." She paused, hazel eyes flitting back and forth, studying Apattar. "I am not who you think I am. Who anyone thinks I am. By all rights, I shouldn't be alive."

Apattar's brow furrowed. She thought back to all the strange moments of connection through the years.

"It's not possible," she murmured.

Even as Apattar spoke, the strange shadows at Saiya's feet sprang to life. They leapt up and danced around the older woman, curling around her arms and legs. Where once Apattar saw a reclusive and oathbound handmaiden, she now saw the woman as a kindred spirit. Dozens of little moments fell into place—how Saiya's eyes would sometimes appear pitch black, the way her presence calmed the hungering void within, or how she always knew what to say, as if she could read her mistress's mind.

Saiya spoke with a hushed voice. "My mother, she lost everyone when the sandstorm raiders came. The moon did not light up the sky when I was born, the shadows ruled and the gods set my fate. But my mother couldn't bear to kill me when I came, said I had my father's eyes. So she lied about my birth when she stumbled into Navlirin. No one knew, and why would they question it after the things she had been through?" Saiya paused, pulling more of the Shadow-weave around her, like a comforting blanket. Apattar knew the feeling all too well.

"I felt the Shadow-weave awaken with your birth. When the eclipse peaked, I heard a woman's voice. She sounded like a messenger from the Undying Realms Beyond, the most beautiful voice I'd ever heard. She told me not to be afraid, said soon I would walk without fear in my heart. When I heard of the twins born *after* the eclipse, I knew—somehow—that it was a lie. I begged my mother to let me offer myself to the *Makhaeren*, to prove myself worthy to serve your House. I loved you from the moment I saw you as a babe, but I never knew how to tell you who I was. I tried to shield you from the worst of your father's wrath and, well..." Saiya paused and rubbed her hands together. "I failed you before. But I will not fail you now."

Apattar's eyes widened as she listened to Saiya's tale. Never before had she shared anything from life before entering into service with House Isht'iri. It all felt like too perfect a coincidence, yet something undeniable connected the two women. More than oaths, more than friendship. An understanding of each other no one else could have, save those who lived a life cursed by the dark moon.

Could it be true? Did other *evranenith* slip through the cracks, shown mercy—some even undying love? Did they, too, hear the voice of the lost Dark Goddess, whispering at night, seeking revenge and justice?

"H-how did you find me?" Apattar choked out between the waves of shock.

"These shadows; I could feel your soulsong pulling at me. Not like a *liraes*, but like I could trace your location. The woman's voice I heard once before came back, a whisper telling me you were dying and alone. I knew if I did not find you, I had failed in my task. I never asked the Dark Goddess to explain herself or my life, but I know it is tied to yours. We can break the cycle of this world, Apattar. I want to help you—I must!"

The hope in Saiya's voice crushed Apattar. She felt it once, before she lost her sister and sense of purpose.

"I'm not that person, Saiya." Her voice cracked with despair. "It's all in my head, a sickness. This," she gestured toward the shadows around Saiya. "This is the Shadow-weave. A cursed, tainted thing. I have seen what it does to people like us who live when they were not meant to. It brings death and destruction. Whatever voice I thought guided me sank back into oblivion. It is not the voice of a Goddess, Saiya."

A shiver ran up Apattar's spine as she spoke, a tiny part of her heart screaming *this is wrong!* But she could not shake the feeling of Therat's Shadow-weave thirsting for blood. Didn't hers, too? Images of Tela flashed by; how, try as the young woman might, the urges proved stronger than her will. The festering black void held the whip. There existed no god, no destiny, no divine justice to be delivered. Only a sickness twisting and corrupting whatever it touched. Apattar realized her father spoke true all along—a knife to the heart was a blessing for her.

Saiya chewed on the corner of her mouth. "I know about Tela. The assassins and the bald brute who attacked you. You are not a monster, Apattar. You were young, hurting. Vulnerable."

"What?" The word shot like an arrow from Apattar's mouth. An invisible hand punched her in the stomach. The breath died on her lips, a rotten taste growing in its stead.

"This woman, the whispers. She told me many secrets. Some of herself, and some about the very strange deaths at the hands of a girl I knew. One growing in power, but lost and alone. One day, you will carve the vile hatred from this world. I know this in my soul. You are not cursed, Apattar! None of us are."

Confusion swirled around Apattar's mind. Nothing made sense. She wanted to rage and threaten the gods. How could this be anything other than torture? A constant swing between despair and hope, between madness and divine intervention. As the anger crescendoed, the silky smooth voice of her guide slid into Apattar's mind. A cool numbness spread.

Forgive me, please... I am everywhere and nowhere, my body fed to the stars. Do not let my absence fester in your heart. It is so hard, so hard to find you in the black void of my demise.

All doubt and regret fled at the first sound of the musical voice, every syllable building the former confidence and sense of resplendent power in the deathly woman. Overwhelmed by a fiery warmth spreading through her belly, Apattar cried out and flung her arms around Saiya. She pulled the tiny woman in close, wrapping arms warped with burn scars around her mistress.

"Come, let us leave this place of ruin," Saiya murmured. "You need a warm bath, and I'll fix your hair. You will feel so much better, my lady. We can talk of destiny and the future later."

Too overwhelmed by the sudden return of Saiya and her divine whispering guide, Apattar only nodded in reply. The handmaiden-turned-savior guided her through the tangle of trees and burnt ruins, past the wide expanse of fields and the outskirts of the Weavers District. They walked for miles guided only by the moonlight, the city fast asleep as night crept by.

Eyes heavy with weariness, the world slipped into a fog as feet shuffled along cool golden sands. The two women walked through the night, each step closer to an uncertain end.

"HERE, THIS WAY, MY lady." Saiya's directions pulled Apattar out of the walking trance. She looked around, trying to place where Saiya had led her.

Walls of tall, smooth white stone surrounded them on three sides, opening into a large atrium in front of where the women stood. In the center, aglow under silver moonlight, stood a statue of a faceless woman armed with throwing stars in each arm. Threads of gossamer interwoven with tiny seven-pointed stars draped over the statue's shoulders, strands of starlight caressing her body. The Sunmaiden Myrniar in all her beauty. Apattar shivered.

Another betrayer!

"Saiya," Apattar hissed. "Why are we in the Sunmaiden's Crypt?" Uneasiness settled into the pit of her stomach.

"We're not staying here for long. There is a hidden passageway behind this wall. It leads out of the city, but there are offshoots along the way. I found what I think is an abandoned secret refuge among the twists and curves. It's perfectly safe. I've never seen another soul."

As she spoke, Saiya tapped a quick pattern on the stone wall underneath a golden sun inlaid with a silver crescent moon. With a quiet *click* the stones shifted and melted away.

A black corridor lit with sparse floating amber orbs of light stretched out in front of the women. The smooth black stones seemed to shimmer in the light. The faint aroma of sandalwood and jasmine invited them in. Saiya stepped through first before reaching for Apattar's hand. Crossing the threshold, she felt the fleeting sensation of hands tugging at her clothes. After they both passed the entrance, it dissolved again, and a smooth black stone wall blocked their exit.

"Strange, isn't it?" Saiya remarked. "I think this place is from the First Era. It feels divine, somehow. Untouched by the troubles of the world. I found it as a girl. You're not the only one to sneak out at night," she said, winking as she spoke. "I used to come and stare at Myrniar for hours. One night, I heard a tapping at the wall. I tapped a reply, and the stones melted away. I don't know why I didn't run. Instead, I found myself here night after night."

"We are more alike than I realized," Apattar murmured.

Saiya stopped walking and turned, remorse filling her eyes. "I hate myself for waiting so long to tell you. But you know now.

Stay close. It isn't far, but there are many dead ends. It took me years to map it all out."

Apattar walked without question, an obedient follower too tired to shape her thoughts. The endless twists and turns blended together, each corridor the same as the previous one. Every so often, a side passage opened up, but Saiya ignored them all. After what seemed like near two hours of endless walking, the two women came to a dead-end in a large room with vaulted ceilings.

Bookshelves twice as tall as Apattar lined the walls. Books decaying to dust sat on the shelves, some only filled with scraps of yellowed paper fraught with silver-lined holes. A singular shelf held scrolls in near-pristine condition. In the center of the tall ceiling hung a chandelier, a dim purple orb floating in the center. The light reflected off the cut crystals and cast a soft glow over the room. Hundreds of stars dotted the swirling blue and black ceiling. Under seven constellations, names appeared in a strange language. Lines with open and shaded circles, swirls and loops, and a few recognizable letters from the Eábhir alphabet greeted Apattar's eyes.

"The Seven Sisters," Saiya murmured. "Their names all preserved except for the Dark Goddess herself. It's hard to believe it's possible to kill a god."

Apattar did not reply. Thoughts of the strange vision she had on the ship returned. Seven figures together, six betraying one. Did the lost Goddess speak to the woman, her life playing out on a divine stage she could not see?

A burning knife sliced across Apattar's left palm. The flash of pain punched the air from her lungs. Squeezing her eyes shut, the void lashed out in retribution. A cool tendril of Shadow-weave wove around her hand. With another breath, the pain vanished, and the shadows withdrew.

"My lady, are yo—"

Apattar laid a hand on Saiya's shoulder, a thin smile spreading across her lips. "Please, call me Apattar. You deserve that much, as my friend and savior."

"Oh," Saiya said with a nervous chuckle. "Apattar, are you well?"

Apattar scrunched up her face. "Yes, yes, I'm fine. I need a minute, please."

After a short rest, Saiya took Apattar's hand and guided her to the back wall. Amongst the disintegrating books stood one with its binding still intact; faded, but not decayed like the others. Saiya tilted it back. A groaning creak emanated from the bookshelf before swinging open with a lurch. Dust and shreds of paper flew through the air. Apattar wheezed, swallowing what little spit she could muster to keep from descending into a coughing fit.

Hidden behind the shelves was a room with several small beds and other bedroom furnishings. On the large back wall in silvery-blue paint, a woman danced surrounded by shades. In the distance stood six hooded figures, a dagger brandished by one. More of the strange language detailed the scene. On the adjacent wall, seven hooded figures stood in a circle, an orb floating between them. The third wall depicted hundreds of crude humanoid forms fighting each other, the woman from the first mural dripping silver blood from her hand while watching the battle from above.

"Haunting and beautiful, aren't they?" Saiya watched as Apattar took in the murals. "There are more like this in other hidden rooms. It tells a story, but of what, I am not certain."

"I know," whispered Apattar under her breath.

Seven Sisters. Six betrayers. One corpse.

The stench of death lingered in the air. Apattar shook her shoulders, rejecting the growing sense of discomfort. A memory, nothing more. Yet, the longer Apattar stared at the dancing woman, the more the world drifted away from her senses.

She stood in a meadow of white flowers, bathed by the soft shadows of night, gossamer threads of moonlight embracing her form. All around, barren trees of silver climbed to greet the stars, leaves of soft greens at their feet. The laughter of children drifted by, followed by a man's booming laugh. The sounds faded, and the meadow fell into an eerie silence.

Apattar looked down at her hands, skin a silvery purple, sparkling like the night sky above. Darkness took hold.

"Eithranren!" Apattar blurted out.

"Come again, my l—Apattar?" Saiya's voice was muffled.

A hissing crackle filled the air, followed by a piercing scream. Apattar couldn't tell if it came from her throat or not. Saiya turned, a gasp slithering out at the sight before her.

Apattar floated in the center of the small room, hands flung back as a dark purple strand of light pulled her chest upwards. Skin stretched taut as shadows bulged and pushed through her body. Black tears streamed down her face, pools of the liquid void forming in the hollow of her neck and collarbones. A disjointed voice, raw and hoarse as if uttering words for the first time, spoke from Apattar's slackened mouth.

"Yes... yes. I remember. From the beginning, unison and harmony. We each took a name. Seven sisters, seven names. My name... yes, my name. Long ago, so very long ago. But it is not enough, no! The Endless Quiet calls again, no! No! I will not go, I wi—"

The light vanished. Apattar crumpled to the floor. Saiya rushed to her side, brushing the frayed braids out of a face still slick with black tears. Brown eyes looked up in a haze of confusion.

"Where, where am I?" Apattar whimpered, clutching Saiya's hands to her breast. "Did we get attacked? I can't remember... I heard you scream."

"Shh, no, no, I am fine." Saiya pulled the younger woman close, cradling Apattar's head as she rocked back and forth. "We are safe. You are safe, I have you. I have you. I-I think something possessed you."

"Eithranren," Apattar whispered. "A name?"

"You—it—spoke of seven sisters. The Seven Sisters. Ei-thranren, she called herself. Have you heard of such a name?"

The thick fog in Apattar's brain made it hard to form a response. "M-ma-maybe, I-I'm not s-sure," she stammered after great effort. She buried her head into Saiya's arms, too weak to understand anything.

"Are you well enough to walk a few steps, Apattar? Come, there's a bed not far. You lie down, I will fix your hair while you rest. You will feel better, I promise."

Some time later, Saiya finished detangling Apattar's hair. The freedom did indeed feel refreshing. Falling into their old routine, the two friends passed the hours in silence. Saiya had evidently been here before—a small shelf held several glass vials of cream colored liquids and amber gels.

The comforting aroma of vanilla and coconut replaced the stale, fetid air. Each breath brought a deep sense of relaxation to Apattar. Muscles turned to warm pools of liquid as the tension dripped from her weary body. So long spent fleeing certain death, afraid with only hopelessness for companionship. It felt ecstatic to release it all to the world.

Closing her eyes, Apattar focused on Saiya's long fingers cleaning away weeks of dust and filth. For a moment, she imagined herself back in her chambers, this whole month a nightmare. How odd, to think the life she once sought to flee now seemed a dream in comparison.

The shadows drew ever closer to the Apattar. Hungering, festering, tainting all that was once fair in life.

 A SHADOW DANCE

Under the Dark Sun my fears grew,
the world taken from my grasping hand.
It was a dream I told myself,
A delusion so grand.
But my mouth turned to ash,
and the ground to quicksand.
In my heart, I knew there was no promised land.
Not for the Children of Shadow and Night.
Bereft of our Goddess,
We march to our last stand!

Ever-fair!
I will seek you where the light ends and the void begins,
When the world was at ease and we sat under silver trees.
For you, I would reap the deadliest of sins.

STAGNATION

THE BLACKENED STONES OF Andeshar seldom saw visitors over their long, quiet centuries of decay. Endless ashen gray skies were their ever-present companion for thousands of years, the sun a mere concept forgotten by the land. The skies wept with the tears of gods long departed from Eás, and their deep sorrow seeped into the rock below. An empty graveyard of the long-sundered gods of the Elder Days. Devoid of life, until two women fleeing the Madhira Desert walked through a shimmering portal.

At first, the island was only a temporary stop, a place to meet Laisha again and learn more about the fate she spoke of. But the pale woman did not appear. The volcanic valley remained empty, while the giant itself slumbered with only the occasional burst of fire and brimstone. Bereft of home and family, the two women took their chances lingering on the rocky ruins. Days turned into weeks, weeks into months. Soon, the godless ruins became more of a home than Av Madhira ever had been.

For four long years now, the black and scorched earth of Andeshar basked in the golden fires of Narán, clouds parted by the new raven-haired mistress of the land. The air thrummed with endless potential.

Time moved with no sense of urgency, the troubles of the world beyond unable to touch the women. Saiya insisted the land still remembered the touch of the gods. That, despite the devastation wrought during the Discordance, part of their divine creators lingered in the once-holy land.

More clever than she appeared, Saiya often snuck away through portals to Av Madhira in search of food and supplies. Never did the woman explain how she paid for the items, though something told Apattar no money exchanged hands.

The woman with burnt arms and scars on every finger led a vastly different life than Apattar ever imagined. A handmaiden and servant to House Isht'iri, yes, but also a thief to feed a dying mother.

On the day Saiya and Apattar became blood-bound, the Blessed Gates closed behind the little girl. She found her mother beaten bloody and left in the streets of the Slums days later. For years, Saiya risked her life to escape past the Wall, offering what little aid she could. But, her mother's broken body never healed, and in time, death came for the soul who only remembered sorrow and loss.

Saiya did not shy away from her past. Apattar thought it remarkable to hear Saiya recount the horrors of her life with such detail. She laughed at certain parts and cried at others, embracing every emotion to the fullest.

As time passed, friendship blossomed into a deep trust. No secrets remained between the two impossible *evranenith,* and for a moment, a normal life seemed possible. Under the loving hands of the two women, the rocky island transformed from ruins to sanctuary. Day by day Saiya wove rock and rubble together until she raised twin black towers overlooking the sea, a courtyard nestled between them. It became a dark and hidden refuge for the Daughters of Shadow and Night.

I T WAS NOW THE morning of the fourth year of Apattar's exile on Andeshar. Her twenty-fourth nameday passed two moons back, and with it, nightmares chasing sleep away.

Sometimes, it was a woman with glistening blackened silver skin, bound and gagged in a pool of silvery-blue blood. Her eyes would plead as a hand descended, the bright white blade inching closer and closer to her quivering breast. Other times, there was nothing but the crushing dark void. Voices whispered in an unknown language until looming icy blue eyes appeared. Each night, Apattar awoke drenched in sweat with a scream in her throat, a blade of fire and ice ripping through her mind. Saiya would calm the trembling woman, wiping away the damp fear as she sang a lullaby until Apattar fell back into a dreamless sleep.

Uneasiness built with each passing day. A sense that her return to the world was long overdue.

Apattar walked to the edge of the eastern tower ramparts and leaned out, basking in the sun. The warmth paled in comparison to the desert she once called home. A frustrated sigh escaped pursed lips.

Twisted nightmares and dreams impossible to understand obscured the path ahead. Apattar made peace with the idea of fate, hatred of the gods assuaged by Saiya's unwavering faith in spite of the life given to her. She expected some divine sign, a message from Laisha, anything. Instead the nightmares came and her hope wavered.

"Mistress... my Goddess, Lady Eithranren! I don't know what to do! I don't understand your messages. Where are you, where are you?"

The wind ripped the words from her throat and bore her pleas away to the West. For years, the musical voice of Eithranren nudged and guided the woman, encouraging her to explore the Shadow-weave and learn secrets lost to time. But now she fell silent again, Apattar alone since her nameday.

Each morning drew the raven-haired woman to the eastern ramparts, looking out at a life left behind. Somewhere in the far East, her sister grew in power. Had the little dove bound herself to Adon yet? Jealousy and anger flashed by as the thought of the man who always smiled came hurtling in. Ninann's constant companion now. Apattar wished she could blame him for destroying their bond.

As her sight rested on the creamy oranges melting into a soft, blazing red orb, thoughts strayed to the man with stormy gray eyes and a heart crawling with the Shadow-weave. Therat intruded more and more of late. She could not understand why he pulled at her heart, why she saw him and wanted to hold the man walking under the influence of Death. Nothing good could come from confronting a half-crazed man. She told him once she would find him again—was it her insanity reaching out, trying to take control?

Apattar let out a sigh of resignation. As much as she hated to admit it, if fate pulled the strings of her life, then she could not ignore Therat. She could not change the inexorable will of the gods—she understood this after many long years of denying it to be true. Overthrowing centuries of superstition and falsehoods would never be an easy path. If it took Apattar to Therat, she must walk it.

It would be a difficult task to find the shadow-bound man in the endless golden sands. Even if she did, what then? Hours wheedled by as she weighed how to approach the man she knew to be unpredictable, at best. How would he react to the truths she brought? Apattar wondered if the whispers of Eithranren ever spoke to him. Would he believe the Dark Goddess did not curse the night?

By the end of the evening, all thought bent toward Therat. Apattar recalled all she could of the man and the glimpses of memories she saw. The whispers that warped his mind, calling for the world's ruin. A suicide attempt he hid in shame, and a night from his childhood so evil even he did not acknowledge the memories.

Apattar wished she could ask Eithranren why the Goddesses fated them together. Why each night Therat found her dreams, pulled her in while begging for a tender touch. He could be a tool, she saw the use there, but a *lover?* A cruel impossibility. She was broken, the word 'love' meaningless.

"Something troubles you tonight, sweet girl." Saiya's lilting voice stirred Apattar out of contemplation.

The two sat atop the western watchtower, observing the stars with little said between them. It was a comfortable silence. Long gone were the days of endless chatter. Apattar came to enjoy their quiet evenings, finding solace in the presence of her most trusted friend and ally.

Apattar shook her head, dismissing the detailed image of Therat she conjured in her mind. She stood and looked to the east.

"You know me well," she sighed. "Our Lady Eithranren. She has been silent for too long now. I thought if I lingered, She might return. But what can we know of the gods, dead or alive? I've relied on the whispers long enough. I cannot seek retribution for the injustices of this world and restore our Lady by idling here." The words crawled out, Apattar loath to voice what she knew to be true. "I mean to return to the desert. There is something I must find out."

"But Apattar!" exclaimed Saiya, fear thick on her tongue. "You said so yourself, you would be executed if the *Makhaeren* found any trace of you. I am certain after my last mishap in the city her hunters can track your harmonic manipulations. It is too dangerous to leave now! There must be something else, our Lady would not send you to certain death, of this I know!"

Apattar wanted nothing more than to agree with Saiya and sit back down. But this place kept them both in limbo: one foot ready to walk the path of fate while the other stayed firmly planted in the safety of their home.

"Yes," she replied after a time. "But anything worthwhile in this world is dangerous, Saiya. Our very lives are a testament to this. What are we doing here? We cannot hope to find shelter forever. The world continues past the eastern horizon, even if we do not will it so. When we first came to Andeshar, I would have been all too willing to blind myself, cowering in fear masquerading as freedom. Yet I cannot deny what our Lady Eithranren has shown me over the years. She is growing in power, the void prison melting around Her. What if... what if we can make a god live again?"

"You are right, of course you are. But why there? Why go back to the place that almost killed you? I don't understand, but you need not tell me. I trust in you, Apattar." Saiya sniffled as she spoke, choking back tears threatening to burst forth. "If anyone has a hope of changing this world, it is you. Do what you must, but be careful. Please!" Saiya stood and squeezed Apattar's hands. "I do not know my purpose if I was to lose you."

Apattar laughed. "I would not be vanquished so easily, *mai sa'iri*. There is someone I seek, someone who may yet aid our cause. You have your freedom, I do not command you. You know this, yes?" She crooked a thin finger under Saiya's chin, lifting the woman's gaze to hers.

"Trust in our Lady. She may be silent now, but we can still act. You are a better Weavetracer than any I know, you should go find others like us. They must be out there. I feel it in my bones. Bring them here, make this place a haven for the *evranenith* if you need a purpose while I am gone. I trust you completely." The words did not feel entirely her own, as if for the briefest of moments their Goddess came to give one final direction to her faithful daughters.

Saiya smiled and dabbed the tears away from her eyes.

"I could do that. I feel them, too, hear the whispers of their music in the wind at night. But when will you return? I could not bear to be away and miss you for longer than need be."

Apattar had not thought of her return. In truth, she only knew Therat still wandered the vast desert. It could take years to comb through the endless miles of sand and barren rock.

"I cannot say for certain. I hope my path will become clearer with time." As she spoke, Apattar pulled a small band of gold inlaid with crimson rubies from her left hand. It slid off her thin finger with ease, gems flashing like droplets of blood under the stars. "I once received this as a blessing from one I held dear long ago. I pass it to you now, a blessing from one daughter of Lady Eithranren to another. Use this to call me home if you are in dire need. Hold it tight and say my name, and I will come as fast as I can."

Apattar slid the ring onto Saiya's thumb, a perfect fit.

"I don't deserve such beauty, my lady," she gasped, slipping into old formalities as years of forced submission took hold. Hazel eyes widened in surprise, drinking in the sight.

"*Shain'sa!* You are my sister! Beholden to the same mistress who blessed both our lives. Never have I felt a kinship like the one I have with you, even... even my dove." Apattar stumbled over her last words, unable to think about Ninann without a tangle of grief and agony rising. "You are my family, Saiya. It would be a nightmare to wake up and find you forever gone from my side." She leaned forward and placed a soft kiss on Saiya's forehead.

A smile crept over her face. "I have always viewed myself as beneath you, even when we fled the desert. You are my mistress, the *Makhaeren* bound us in blood and fire to each other." Saiya paused, biting her lip before continuing. "I do not feel worthy of such love, but I would be a fool to reject it. Keep yourself safe, my sweet sister. Until you return."

Folding her hands together, Saiya toyed with the ruby-encrusted ring on her thumb. She avoided Apattar's eyes, unable to bear saying goodbye.

Apattar squeezed Saiya's shoulder, then slunk off into the dark stairwell leading down the tower. The bittersweetness of saying goodbye was a feeling she didn't wish to confront. It was a relief to meet another touched by the dark moon, who had heard the voice of the forgotten and slandered Goddess. Though bound by birth to Ninann, Apattar thought of Saiya as her true sister.

For the second time in her life, Apattar had to say goodbye to the only family she knew. The heartaches would never end.

TEARS CRASHED AGAINST THE impenetrable wall constructed over the long years of torture and heartache. Apattar quickened her pace, racing through the courtyard to her chambers in the second tower. She tried to outrun her sorrows, wanted to lock them away and never acknowledge the part of her begging for love.

Crushing grief broke across her mind. A thin line of crimson blood from her nose snaked over trembling lips, dripping on the black dress hugging Apattar's gaunt frame. Liquid fire ran through her veins, sticky sweat breaking out across flushed skin. What would it feel like to break down the wall and let years of sorrow flood out? An idle wonder; it was far too strong to dismantle now.

Choking back the tears, Apattar reached for the void and let it consume her shattered heart. It took both happiness and grief, but the reward was worth the price. Emotions made people vulnerable, allowed others to manipulate with ease. Apattar would be no such person. She only needed reason and cold, unwavering dedication to her Goddess. Apattar sank as the finer edges of reality slipped into oblivion.

Apattar could not tell how much time passed by the time she lifted her head again. For the first time since Saiya saved her from certain death, she felt as weak as her body looked. For too long, food withered in her mouth with each bite, her body intent on wasting away. Digging deep, Apattar thrust one hand into the floor, then the other, forcing her body upright.

It was a lifetime ago when she was a naive girl with vain hopes of claiming a life alongside her sister. The surety of her decision four years ago wavered, trepidation taking its place. Without her divine guidance, it would be all too easy to walk into a trap, too easy to chase after nothing except her doom.

Apattar pushed the worries aside and slipped off the heavy cotton dress tied over each shoulder. The cold air whipped at her skin without mercy. It proved to be a welcome distraction from anxieties refusing to disappear. From a simple chest, Apattar pulled out a fine silk top and skirt in black. She forgot how soft they felt in her hands, how the cloth hugged her body and brought a sense of beauty to the woman's life.

Thigh-high slits cut into the skirt on either side, the front bolt of cloth folded in a diagonal pattern. She wrapped thick ribbons of black trimmed with silver knotwork around each leg to above the knee, tall black boots pulled on over them. The silk shirt billowed out, held in place with a cinched corset around her waist. She pulled a black veil over her thick curls—a useful tool to hide her face if the need arose.

Apattar's hands lingered over the black fingerless gloves Saiya gave her long ago during their first sojourn beyond the Wall. It was easy to forget the blue doves and flaming suns splayed across her hands and forearms. They never meant anything to her, an empty gesture of a family she only belonged to in name. Apattar was loath to acknowledge the status of her birth, but ignoring the fact could prove fatal. With a grimace, she pulled the gloves on, looping each ring finger through the tiny band on the ends of the half-gloves.

As she took in her black-cloaked form in a simple mirror, the glint of something silver caught the corner of Apattar's gaze. She moved closer to the source.

There, in the dim candlelight on the cream-colored sheets of her bed, lay a dagger with a long black blade. Shadows seemed to shift and dance under the surface. Tarnished with age, a smear of what looked to be dried blood covered the hilt.

The blade sang out to Apattar. As she edged closer, the light revealed a burnt piece of parchment with two lines of text. The top line was more of the strange, ancient language the two women encountered in the hidden passages of the Sunmaiden's Crypt. Below it, written in an awkward and ill-spaced hand, was a single sentence:

Use it well, *lyneithra.*

Apattar picked up the dagger, curling her fingers around the silver hilt. The shadows swirling through the blade hummed with approval. They leached from it and twisted themselves around her arm, resonating with the void below the surface of her cool skin. Shivers ran across Apattar's flesh as goosebumps formed. The blade felt like a perfect extension of herself, a piece she never knew was missing until found.

A thin line of crimson blood snaked across the blade as Apattar drew her thumb over it. Quickfire pain burst through the exposed nerves and to the center of her brain. The sensation bordered on pleasurable. Unsure why, Apattar smeared her blood across the hilt. The bright red liquid melted into the tarnished silver and disappeared.

Something about the blade screamed *sacred,* as if once wielded in Lady Eithranren's name against her enemies. Apattar smiled and tucked the blade into a leather strap around her right thigh.

Armed and ready to face the world again, she opened a portal to the endless golden sands of her home, aiming for the small oasis with a crescent moon-shaped lake she once stumbled into by accident. Suffocating heat billowed through the milky opaque portal. Gaze sweeping across the room one last time, Apattar grabbed a large satchel with food and stepped through the shimmering surface.

The hunt began.

Twenty-Four

STUMBLING BLIND

S KIN PEELED AND FLAKED away from the woman's face. Bruises bloomed under her eyes like a twisted cluster of bloody roses. With a sickening crack of joints, her head lolled to the side. Her lips wrenched apart from the sudden movement, slackened jaw spilling forth congealed blood. Color drained from eyes once a brilliant blue like the morningflowers crawling through cemeteries. Now clouded with death, they stared in accusation at their murderer.

"Gods be damned, how does Ninann do it?"

Therat hovered his hands over the corpse's chest, threads of blue and silver light shimmering from his fingertips. Arms trembled with fatigue before falling to his side. The light vanished. Shadows descended on the body, curling over the decayed flesh like a death shroud. Grumbling to himself, Therat looked down at what remained of the nameless woman. He hadn't wanted to kill her. He struggled to control his mind, wanted to stop even as the Shadow-weave tore into her supple flesh and rent muscle from bone. The tangle of black whispers in his mind did not care; they were never satisfied.

This time was different. This time, Therat needed to keep the woman alive. After near four years of combing the desert, he finally had a clue.

"Please, please! I need her!" His shouts faded to the empty desert. "She knows something. This isn't enough! What is in the West? Come back to me, please!"

Stale air surrounded the man and corpse. Blood wove its way through the grooved tiles of the wayside shrine, small lakes forming from the life once flowing through the woman. Behind him, a headless statue of Myrniar holding the sun cast a shadow over his wretched crime. The dead woman's eyes stared with fervent accusation, streaks of black invading the edges. The shadows around her grew deeper, wrapping around light olive tan skin. They hungered for the remains, extending tendrils like a parasite ready to feast. Therat waved his hands over the woman's body and they fled.

The woman before him was thin and sickly, even before his cursed Shadow-weave devoured her life. Ribs stuck out and formed vast canyons of sunken skin across her chest. Hundreds of tiny cuts and old scars covered nearly every inch of the woman save her hands and feet. Therat's gaze moved up to her face, destroyed on one side. A thin white scar extended past a bloody clump of hair on her left temple.

Is it possible...

Therat extended a hand toward the scar, fingers twitching as the air in his lungs grew heavy. A foul, bitter taste played on the edges of his tongue. He hesitated for a moment before brushing aside the tangle of honey-blonde hair.

There, on her temple and almost obscured under the dried blood, was a symbol carved with fine precision into her flesh. A straight line cut down from her scalp, looping up, down, and up again. Two lines ran at an angle down toward the curved base, connecting in a v-shape with the rest of the scar.

A jolt of white hot pain shot through Therat's hand. He yelped, backing away from the woman. He had seen this before. Had tried in vain to forget the strange symbol carved into his father's chest before a dagger plunged into his heart. Hooded figures in masks commanded a woman in rags to commit the heinous act, tears streaming down her face as she begged for forgiveness from the gods. Therat shuddered at the memory.

He stared at the scar until his eyes hurt, trying to see if it could unlock anything else. Anger flushed his face. The shadows convulsed in reply, sending a lurch through his stomach. The sickening dread of losing control seeped into the corners of his fragile mind. He took a deep breath of arid air, letting it suffocate the dull roar of voices.

A hush fell across Therat's mind. The sudden quiet was jarring. Years spent listening to the voices croon their bloody songs left him hollow when they left, as if a piece had gone missing.

The winds shifted and something—whether random chance or fate, he could not be sure—pulled Therat's gaze to the southern horizon. On the farthest dune he could make out the shape of a person hunched over, watching him.

A shiver ran over his addled mind. Unease settled into muscles already twitching with anticipation. The figure stood, a thin line on the horizon. Something sparked of the familiar, though Therat could not make out anything about the person. They stood, unmoving, Therat staring back in turn.

Therat took a cautious step forward, ready to confront the stranger. The Shadow-weave thrummed around him, a deep black cloak waiting for his command. The dark watcher did not move. Gathering his speed, Therat raced toward the dune, sand flying around his feet. He looked up, now closer to the figure, to see a woman draped in black.

The face of his Mireithren flashed by, her dark brown eyes sparkling in the sun, a coy smile playing on her red lips. Therat stumbled and lost his footing before scrambling upright again. His gaze lifted in time to see the woman in black step through a shimmering opalescent portal.

Mireithren's face burned in Therat's vision. Four long years wandering the vast desert could not erase her haunting visage.

It cannot be her, I do not want it to be her!

Terror seized his heart. Had she returned at last, like she promised she would? Come to claim him for whatever dark deeds her twisted mind told her to do. Would they raze another city to the ground? The entire desert? The world?

No. I cannot let this distract me. A mirage, it was only a mirage.

Tearing his eyes away from the ridge with a groan, Therat trudged back to the wayside shrine. Crimson blood stained the once pristine black and white stones. The hungering shades descended when Therat left. Blackened, putrefied flesh sloughed off bone as they devoured the woman. He could do no more; no weave of harmonics could return life to the desecrated form. Therat choked down the rising taste of bile and forced himself to look for any other clues the dead might share.

His gaze drifted over the woman, never lingering long on the fresh cuts and bruises from their fight. Around her left ankle, he saw a thin chain of golden links, somehow untarnished despite the woman's ragged appearance.

A shiver crawled down his spine at the sight. He had seen this before. Wrapped around the ankle of his parents' killer, the slow drip of his mother's blood from her dagger an image he could never forget. A wave of nausea crashed over Therat.

"It cannot be," he breathed. He took slow, deliberate breaths, trying to calm the roil of emotions inside. Therat sat looking at the sinking sun as the panic subsided.

A trembling hand reached for the golden anklet, fingers curling around the chain. Colder than anything Therat had felt before, an icicle of pain drove deep into his bones. It settled over skin accustomed to the relentless sun, and Therat forgot the meaning of warmth. The shadows within fled to the far recesses of his mind, shrinking in fear from the unearthly cold.

The world lost its finer details at the edges. The once-vibrant colors seemed muted. Hollow. Lifeless. Disconnected from the First Harmonic, existing in a world of gray fog. Whatever emptiness Therat may have felt before could never compare to the absence eating away at the world now. He waded through the thick mire filling his limbs and pulled on the chain with all his might.

With a desperate heave, the chain broke free, knuckles white from the effort. Fragments of gold flew through the air. An amber glow blanketed the wayside shrine. For the briefest of moments, a divine melody echoed around them, a harmony lost to time. The memory of warmth returned to skin and bone as the world around Therat turned to color once more. It was as if the chain had drained him, suppressed the harmonics weaving his very soul.

A cloud snaked in front of the sun and the glow faded, taking with it the ethereal music. Therat dropped the chain in disgust. A chaotic flurry of questions and half-answers tore through his mind as he stared at the wretched thing.

Why did any of this happen? Why does this torture never end?

Twenty-Five

HUNTER

OPENING HER EYES, THE world slowly comes into focus. As the haze lifts, an ache settles into the woman's heart. Each quaking breath catches in her throat, the rise and fall of her bare chest erratic. She leans forward; teeth bite down on soft lips, drawing a whimper from the man beneath her. They sink in further, searching for the metallic taste of hot blood. A groan hums along with the pressure building until it morphs into a whimper as blood greets her tongue.

"This is wrong, all your fault." The voice slithers out from the woman's wicked mouth, mauve lips curling into a frown.

The man looks up with pleading gray eyes, blood dribbling onto rich brown skin, raining down onto the smooth plains and deep valleys of his chest. Tendrils of Shadow-weave snake over his body, flaying skin from muscle. He grimaces and cries out.

"For-forgive me, I beg of my queen. I," the man stops, breath stolen by the shadows. They force him to his knees, the rocks below a hundred daggers waiting to carve punishment into the man *"Nnnuh, you cannot. You siren, you temptress!"* The man's eyes turn black, a deep void of nothing staring back at the woman.

She leans in and kisses him again. Harder, desperate. Fingers trail down his back. He does not flinch, does not cry or moan at the soft touch.

"What is that? Do you seek to beg, to shatter under my hand only to be pieced together again?"

The woman's cold laugh fills the space between hunter and prey. He does not move. Cannot move. A muffled grunt so easily missed penetrates the night.

"Good boy," the woman purrs in his ear. A gentle touch recalls the shadows, and they sink back into their mistress. The man's eyes close. A soft smile pulls at the corner of his mouth. *"Yes, my loyal dog. That's what you like to be, isn't it?"* The woman leans forward and bites his lip again, releasing him before the pain crescendos. *"Mine. Owned. Used. A weapon when I need, a plaything when I want."*

His eyes flash open. Something strange hides behind them, an emotion the woman cannot read. It fades; tears of pain and pleasure flood his eyes with a single touch.

"Yes," the gray-eyed man breathes into her mouth, hot breath flooding her senses. *"I would kill a thousand, and a thousand more, to kneel before you. My heart is yours. To take as you wish, use as you wish. I have nothing to live for, nothing but your words. I live for you, Mireithren."*

THE DREAM LINGERED IN Apattar's mind for days, the name *Mireithren* playing over and over again. It seemed familiar, somehow. She told herself the dreams came as a corruption of the confused feelings she harbored for Therat. He could yet be transformed, the Shadow-weave brought under control and turned into a weapon for the coming war. But the rest did not make sense.

Could not make sense.

Apattar told herself for years that love was a distraction. She meant to keep it that way, though it became harder as the days pressed on. Diversions from feelings and urges rather left unexplored were few and far between in the desert.

At first, Apattar meant to head for the southern city of Gisamir on the coast to gather supplies and, if she was lucky, a camel. But when she first arrived in the desert at the tiny oasis of acacias, Therat's soulsong hummed in the background noise of the lonely land. Luck found her for a change. Seizing the opportunity, she followed him into the southwestern dunes stretching on for hundreds of miles. For fifteen days she tracked Therat, closing in on her quarry but always a step behind.

Morning arrived with a cool breeze. Apattar set out walking before the sun cleared the eastern horizon, desperate to make headway against the man who rested little the last three days. She would draw him out from hiding like sucking poison from a wound. Eithranren was quiet, Laisha nowhere to be found. He had to be the way forward. Apattar grumbled at the thought.

Sometime after walking, a few hours at most, the remnants of an abandoned campsite built against a lone crumbling wall came into view.

This must be his.

The winds had not yet scattered the fire's remains from the crude ring of rocks. It seemed fresh enough to Apattar's eyes, though she knew little of these things. Instinct and a will to live kept her alive in the desert, not wits or the ability to hunt. There was little to observe—some bloody bandages and a lock of honey-blonde hair. Apattar wondered what injured Therat, or if this blood was even his. Why was he here, hundreds of miles from the nearest settlement? On a hunt of his own? The bandages could be those of his quarry, caught for what purpose Apattar dared not think.

The Goddess Eithranren warned Apattar years ago of the darkest threads of Shadow-weave grown wild with her death. How her screams of terror and betrayal remained forever trapped in the Song of the Night. Those who let the tainted music into their souls often found themselves crawling toward inevitable insanity. Corrupted from such a young age, there was no guarantee Therat controlled his mind. A boy once sacrificed, now a shell struggling to contain the horde within.

By the time Apattar left the campsite, the sun started its long descent into the night. The darkening skies did not stop the hunt. The anticipation of finding Therat bubbled over into every thought and drove her on until exhaustion sent the maiden tumbling into a fitful sleep.

Therat's hands caressed her frail and withered body, drawing whimpers from the restless dreamer. When she woke, all memory of the night faded to the sun, and Apattar continued to tell herself the gray-eyed man could not love a broken woman.

As the sun set, Therat's soulsong erupted in Apattar's mind. She gasped from the intensity of his presence, heart pummeled by the suddenness. Eyes closed, the music vibrated through her bones, eerily intimate, as if they had embraced once as lovers long ago.

"I found you at last," she breathed, shivers running down her spine.

Hunching forward, Apattar used all her strength to climb the tall dune looming ahead of her. The sand gave way with every step as if trying to keep the hunter from her quarry. After a long hour of climbing—sometimes on hands and knees—Apattar crested the sandy giant.

The dune sloped down to a valley, a narrow path marked with burning torches snaking through a gap in the western dunes. In the center of the flat land sat a large wayside shrine. A tall, headless statue of Myrniar the Sunmaiden holding the Sun in her hands overlooked a courtyard of black and white stones. Four tall columns stood at the corners of the shrine, each wrapped with a red wyrm, head held high to the sky. Once, the endless Flame of Myrniar burnt from their mouths; such a time was long forgotten on Eás now.

The afternoon sun bathed the shrine in an amber glow. In the center of the courtyard knelt a man with warm brown skin and a tangle of black curls, a desecrated body in front of him. Apattar did not need to see the man's face to know it was Therat. She smiled as a flash of heat ran the length of her body; she closed her eyes and wondered if Therat's touch would feel the same. With a hiss, she chased the thought away and set her gaze back on the man.

Tendrils of inky black Shadow-weave writhed in the air around Therat. A shimmering thread of blue and silver light wavered between one of his blood-stained hands and the corpse before slowly fading. A cry pierced the air, though Apattar could not make out the words.

The music—now a symphony across the land—compelled Apattar forward, but her feet stood firm. Therat sat studying the corpse, a dead woman, with morbid intensity.

What is he doing?

Apattar thought he must have killed the woman, but why try and bring her life back? She stepped back and lowered herself to the warm sands. Settling into a comfortable position, Apattar observed the man below like a cat watching its prey.

Therat seemed lost in thought. The winds shifted, and the contented sigh of a woman floated past.

"Lady Eithranren," Apattar whispered with a smile.

Therat's head whipped around at Apattar's words, curls bouncing around his dark visage framed with a shaggy beard. He rose and stared at her. Threads of Shadow-weave danced around him as he took a step forward. Apattar slid the black dagger from the sheath around her thigh and held it close, her own Shadow-weave wrapping around the woman. Therat raced toward the sloping dune with ease.

Though the trap set and the bait taken, an odd hesitation took hold of Apattar's heart. Once she had Therat in her grasp, it would be impossible to stray from the path of destiny. It was hard to embrace the idea of fate when confronted with the realities of what the Shadow-weave did to people who took too much.

She wanted to free her Goddess and restore the world, but what if it meant sacrificing those who deserved a better life? Could she still do it—would she? The man was beyond redemption, even he knew this. Therat's descent into madness and unending sorrow made it hard to see reason. Overcome with anxiety, Apattar opened a portal to the abandoned camp not far from the shrine.

A moment to think, that is all. I will be back for you, Therat.

With a final glance, the raven-haired woman fled through the shimmering surface.

A PATH TO TREAD

T IME SLIPPED BY, THE world an afterthought amid the din and clamor of old memories twisting and breaking free from their cage. When Therat opened his eyes again the sun danced along the western horizon. Fires spread across the golden dunes, the world below bathed in an ominous red glow.

The superstitious of the Madhiri said fire-red skies at night meant the Sisters watched Eás, drawing near to the old home they once shared with their Children. Therat never put stock into superstitions or divine meanings, or even the Goddesses themselves. Why should he, when they created a cruel world filled with even crueler people?

As the sun sank lower in the sky, a strange sensation took hold of the man who walked between life and death. The voices became a hushed murmur before falling silent like they did before. A blanket of warm comfort wrapped around the mind made into a battlefield for twenty-one long, torturous years.

"Wha-what is this?" The words slipped out as a sense of calm serenity pushed out all other thought.

An invisible arm wrapped around Therat, the embrace reminiscent of his father's. Once, a lifetime ago, the little black-haired boy with delight in his eyes would run into those strong arms. They would wrap around his tiny frame and hoist the child high in the air. He would scream with joy and descend into a fit of giggles as he was pulled in close to his father's heart. It had been an eternity since they last touched—oh, how would it feel if Therat could have one last embrace, one more murmur from his father declaring his love for the boy?

Therat fell, tumbling down into the fragmented memory rushing back. Where grief and anger would soon follow, instead a flicker of love took its place. Warm, bright, fervent love. A feeling lost to time, taken by force in exchange for a life unfit for living. Could some part of his heart once unburdened by pain and hatred be left alive?

A soft, almost imperceptible voice floated across the vast emptiness of his mind.

She is near, she is coming. You will find her again. Seek the guide in trees of silver and green, they will know the way.

It reminded him of his mother's voice, the way she sang her words. He used to hear this voice as a child.

Run, fly, hunt for the truth! It is in your blood, little lost boy.

At the words *little lost boy* Mireithren's face rushed back into his mind. The warmth of her deep brown ocher skin, her high cheekbones, the curved black scars etched into one side. The strange siren he met years ago, the one he waited for without reason. The *evranenith* from behind the Wall, soulbound with the woman his brother loved.

Fire mixed with blood, a quickfire burst of pleasure verging on searing pain coursing through his veins. Mireithren's mesmerizing eyes stared back at him, her raven-black hair with strands of sunlight swirling around the woman. A cruel smirk played at the corner of her mouth, inviting him in. *Lose yourself in me*, her eyes seemed to say.

Therat wrenched his eyes open, fighting a mind longing to behold the siren and surrender to her command. With a pulse of his heart, Mireithren's face faded.

Blinking, Therat stumbled away from the corpse and up the high southern dune where he saw the woman in black. The sun said its final goodbye, another dance with the desert at an end. Therat scanned the horizon for any sign of the strange woman but found none, only rolling dunes stretching out to the southern sea. A bellowing laugh broke the calm stillness of dusk.

"Mad! I've lost it and gone mad! Mireithren watching me? A voice telling me I am bound to a woman whose name I made up? This is what I get for talking to myself out here. Adon was right. I have lost myself! Fading to the void, ever fading!" Therat spoke with a manic fervor, words tumbling over each other in their rush to escape. He ran fingers covered in swirling knotwork tattoos through his hair, pulling and squeezing in some desperate attempt to wrest the mania from his head.

Indecision paralyzed him. Long had Therat lived his life for others. First for Adon, to protect his twin from harm and death, and now for his parents, desperately searching for justice. But he couldn't keep fighting for answers. His resolve was whittled thin, too many years spent searching the desert without getting closer to the truth; certain to find death before he found answers.

Therat wanted to blame his delirium, say his brain played tricks after so long spent in self-imposed isolation. Yet, even as he claimed to be mad, deep in the back of his scattered brain he recognized the woman's voice he heard so many long years ago. Amaren, his mother called her, the Silver Maiden. An ancestor who watched over them, guided them.

A scowl settled across his face. Change never brought happiness before; why should it now? What could Mireithren offer? Fearful looks, empty platitudes, or a listening ear never asked for, only to turn away like all others, where all he knew. Even when the shadows slept, people always seemed loath to be around the man. Surely they could smell the wretched, foul heart decaying under muscle and bone. The gods would never create an equal for him—a *liraes*—or even a lover.

Darkness bred hateful and wretched beings. No one could ever love him, ever *want* him. This *evranenith* would be no different. Did she seek to use him as a weapon? The earliest *evranenith* leveled towns and destroyed entire communities. He shuddered at the thought of what Mireithren might do with his near-broken mind.

Therat didn't know what to do. The great northern forest stood far away from where his parents' blood soaked into the earth. It had to be a trick, some mind game of Mireithren's. Yet... the runaway slave did speak of silver trees in the West and a meadow of blood where her masters lived. There was nothing left here to follow, no threads remaining that would lead him to the answers he sought.

Whether by a slave's confession or a strange voice in his head, all signs pointed to the Siusir Forest. Perhaps Mireithren would not find him—indeed, he couldn't even be certain who he saw on the dune. This is what Therat told himself, at least. It helped, thinking the decision to travel to the forest was his own, not something guided by fate. He only sought answers for his mother and father.

Therat turned to the northwest, one foot in front of the other. Tension built like a spring ready to let loose inside his body, the thrum of the Shadow-weave warping the air around skin still smeared with blood. With a deep breath, he leapt into the night. Limbs stretched and contorted, muscle ripping and pulling as it reformed under skin turning deep black.

The shadows descended, covering him with a fine mist before melting away. Landing on all four paws, Therat raced off, a massive black cougar streaking over the dark gold sands. The wind streaked across the soft fur over his shoulders, caressing each leg thick with muscles. He ran until the soft pads of his paws ached and burned, sand matted with fur, sweat pouring over the sleek black coat.

Therat would run until his lungs gave out, until the shadows claimed him, and his mind scattered to the winds. He would travel to the ends of the world and the home of the gods if it meant finding answers for his parents.

At last, Therat collapsed, mind too exhausted to concentrate on maintaining his shifted form. Pushing the tickling thought of Mireithren aside, he tried to recall his parents' faces as he fell asleep.

The siren would not derail him. Could not derail him.

Twenty-Seven

IMPOSSIBLE CHOICES

T HE DAY PASSED INTO the next, and still, Apattar could not untangle the apprehension around her heart.

Therat deserved more than she could give him. A part of him was stuck as a boy, an innocent child who only deserved love. A victim of the worst kind, his selfless act repaid with a lifetime of torture and gnawing emptiness. Apattar only ever wanted to save those like him. The ones the world discarded and abused.

She yearned to bring them happiness, to be their light in the dark world.

But she did not want to be Therat's savior. Could not. He was a weapon, and she, unlovable.

Apattar told herself her heart ached not out of love, but out of duty. Duty to her Goddess, to the pale woman who said she could save her. As Laisha once said, the world is a wicked place. She would uncover the truth of the Discordance no matter the cost. Only the Goddesses could save—or condemn—Therat.

Naught but a tiny sliver in the deep blue sky, the moon watched over Eás before it faded for three nights. The Dark Goddess's time drew near.

Therat's soulsong thrummed in Apattar's ears, the man a few miles away, if not less. Apattar spent the better part of the day walking north, following the music from a whisper to a symphony. The Shadow-weave sang out, yearning to be reunited with the endless void nestled inside her heart.

Therat traveled far from the shrine, miles back to the camp up north, and further still. Sandy dunes turned to a flat bed of red sandstone interspersed with squat buttes of brown-red rock. Stale, heavy air suffocated this barren place. Leafless trees with twisted and thorny limbs cast strange shadows across the land. Black blood dripped from each long thorn, sharpened to a point only the finest of smiths could attain.

A deep dread sank into Apattar's bones. A great battle happened here once, she thought, or some other tragedy that claimed thousands. She vaguely recalled reading about a desert city decimated by an *evranenith* and a shadewalker early in the

Second Era. She shuddered at the thought of repeating history and clutched the dagger against her thigh.

What if he is worth fighting for?

The thought sent a lurch through Apattar's stomach. Why could she not stay true to her task, to take the man West by any means possible? As her fury rose, Apattar swore she would kill Therat if he did not kneel. Kill him and figure out the consequences, but never let him live long enough to trap her with these feelings she could not ignore.

Apattar crept through the desolate land, Shadow-weave pulled close around her, dagger in hand. The faint stench of sweat and blood mixed with bile emanated from an outcropping not far ahead. Stepping with care, she found the entrance to a small cave carved in the side of a brown butte. The steady, shallow breath of someone sleeping pricked her ears.

Fingers moved in a quick curling pattern. A silver orb of light flickered to life, hanging like a pale moon in the dark cave. There, illuminated by Apattar's light, slept the man she yearned to hold in her dreams. The one she would sacrifice, who would free her from the slow decay of her empty heart. Dried blood and scratches ran the course of his forearms. His curly hair was a disheveled mess; a wiry beard of course, jet black hair covered his face. Even asleep, the man looked half-crazed. Apattar wondered if he even remembered his name.

Therat intoxicated all of Apattar's senses. The Shadow-weave coursing through his thick muscles clamored to be heard, its anger palpable even from where she stood. Apattar could not imagine how tortured Therat must be or how he managed to survive this long. Her few tastes of the twisted power in his mind were enough to leave her terrorized.

Fate set in motion years ago was not theirs to change now. Apattar knew what needed to happen, even if it tore at her heart. With a sigh, she knelt, studying Therat's face.

The faint memory of a smile played upon his lips. For a moment, she could see the joy of a little boy with the world ahead of him and the undying love of his parents. Pulling her long hair aside, Apattar leaned over and whispered in Therat's ear. His face twitched as she spoke.

"I hope you are dreaming of your parents, Therat. I... I am sorry. For everything."

Apattar reached for Therat's hand, skin hot to the touch. She melted into it, imagining his hands touching her cheek, down her neck, across her stomach. She inhaled sharply and chased the thoughts away, taking a moment to steel herself.

"Become a weapon for Lady Eithranren and surrender to me," she whispered. "This way, I can give you some sense of purpose, at least. Better to give into madness and save the world than only go mad." The words crawled into Therat's ears and nestled deep in his mind where even the shadows could not rip them out.

Anger and love burned in her heart. She knew her purpose and accepted the fate laid out before her. Sorrows untold crossed her mind every day, the screams of dying children haunting every step. They could not all be saved. She knew this. Understood it. Hers was not a life ever meant to find earthly happiness.

Why? Why did Therat make every part of her feel more alive than anything before? Since the day they first locked eyes in the Market, he never strayed far from her thoughts. The silver glint of his eyes in the moonlight, the bounce of his curly hair, the sound of his rumbling voice as he spoke through waves of torment. She hated and loved it all. Craved his touch, wanted to feel his breath upon her lips.

"Curse you, I do not want this," she hissed. "A weapon. Only a weapon. I cannot save you, you cannot be more!" Her whispers filled the cave. Suffocating, taunting. Laughing at her feeble attempt to deny the most natural of feelings.

Love.

Fathers are supposed to love their daughters. Protect them, erase the harm coming their way. But her father did not love the girl; instead became the reason for her worst memories, not the best. He broke Apattar, made her unlovable, and unable to love. Admitting otherwise meant her father could love the girl, but did not have even a lingering shred of it to provide. It would mean his hatred was a choice.

Easier to think love is made up, a happy lie people told themselves rather than face the truth. Everyone used those around them for their own gain. There were no selfless acts in the world.

Apattar leaned back against the rough cave wall. Her gaze settled on Therat sleeping under a blanket of inky black shadows, a smile still stretched across his lips. She could not say why, but she felt strangely comfortable in the man's presence. His slow, steady breathing lulled her into a trance.

The hours of the night passed into a crisp morning, the dawning sun ready for another day. The trance lifted, Apattar slid the dagger from the sheath around her thigh. The Shadow-weave hummed to life, engulfing the woman in a cloud of inky black.

Twenty-Eight

THE MAIDEN OF SHADOW

A HARD DAY OF running with few breaks brought Therat to a twisted, desolate land of red rock. Deep cracks ran across the bone-dry ground, all memory of water gone from the once verdant oasis. Dead trees warped around each other, their thorny hands waiting to tear flesh from any who passed too near. The taste of blood tainted the air—metallic and sickly sweet. All too familiar to Therat. It made the Shadow-weave awaken within.

Death will never be cleansed from the world. It is broken. Discordant.

Dusk drew near, and with it, a body yearning for sleep. Short buttes dotted the horizon the further Therat walked in the scarred land. He made for the closest one, hoping to find a cave or outcropping. The lengthening shadows set a deep dread in the man's bones. He wanted to have something behind his back to help pass the night.

It did not take long to reach the formation of brown and red rock. Its steep sides swept up to a plateau overlooking the desert. Therat tried to climb up to see a way out of the strange land, but the smooth rock face bore no semblance of a path on the near side. Looking further, he found the entrance to a small cave—if the shallow hole could be called such a thing. He stumbled in and collapsed into a deep, black sleep.

Sometime in the night, a woman's voice called out from the dark. The darkness in his heart fled, and he slumbered in peace for the first time since his parents had been murdered. He could almost feel himself nestled between his mother and father, Adon in his arms.

The chill of metal sapping all warmth from his throat wrenched Therat from sleep.

"You are entirely too easy to catch, Therat."

A woman's low, rough voice stilled his heart.

I'm still dreaming, aren't I?

The pinprick of cold against his throat sharpened. He forced his eyes open to see Mireithren staring down at him, a smirk across her deep brown face. A face Therat could never forget. Her muddy brown eyes twinkled with wickedness.

"Wha—"

Mireithren placed a finger over Therat's mouth.

"Shh. Me first."

Therat's body melted at the woman's touch on his lips. He sank into the rocky ground, muscles losing the will to fight back. As he relaxed, he looked down. Mireithren straddled him like a horse, one hand with an onyx-black dagger at his throat. The warmth of her thighs pressed against his hips sent a dizzying wave of desire through Therat's body. Her raven-black hair with gold, like the night sky streaked with shooting stars, fell to her waist in tight curls.

She looked divine against the amber glow of dawn. He would do anything she asked at this moment, if only she would quench the fires building inside.

"You remember me, don't you?" Therat shuddered, her husky voice music to his ears. "I said I would come back for you. Still a boy, wandering after ghosts. Searching, always searching." Mireithren leaned over and whispered in his ear, "I can give you peace from it all, if you let me."

It took every ounce of willpower to focus on the siren's words. The heat of her breath against his neck sent sparks of pleasure running across his flushed skin. It clashed with the cold metal. A confusing wave of pain and pleasure descended as the blade pressed deeper into Therat's throat. He could not feel the blood trickling down his neck, instead lost amidst the delirium. He looked up into those mesmerizing brown eyes. A tender look flashed by, fleeing as shadows filled Mireithren's gaze.

He sank, falling ever deeper into the endless void. Its cold embrace soothed the raging voices inside. Still. Quiet. With the clamor of a thousand dead driven from his mind, he could only think of *her*.

"Mireithren," Therat whispered. He opened his eyes, back in the cave with the raven-haired siren perched atop him, a coy smile on her face.

"If you wish, yes, I am Mireithren."

The woman Therat named Mireithren changed little over the years. Her jagged voice had grown rougher, and her once plump figure was now frail, but she remained the most beautiful woman Therat had ever seen. An ethereal wraith of Shadow and Night.

The air stilled, the tension between the two children of Shadows palpable. Therat scrambled to his feet, back against the wall of the small cave. He towered above the woman, broad shoulders heaving as he touched the wound at his neck. Hot, sticky liquid greeted searching fingers. He had never bled first in a fight.

A growl built in Therat's throat. He reached for the Shadow-weave, but it did not come rushing forth as it always would. The scar across his chest twinged with fiery pain.

"What did you do to me, *evranenith?*" The words dripped like thick honey from his mouth, fighting to escape a body seizing up with... *fear?*

The raven-haired Mireithren only laughed.

"I know who you are. A witch, a siren! An envoy of the Dark Goddess sent to spell my doom and end the world. It was you, wasn't it? You who made me kill and kill again! You awoke the shadows!" The fervor in Therat's words verged on manic. "You drive me to madness with thoughts I don't want and feelings I can't ignore."

Though a head shorter than Therat, the maiden in black did not quake in his presence. She kept smiling through it all. Her gaze drifted over his body, taking in every detail. He felt stripped and raw in front of those deep brown eyes, as if she could read his thoughts and all the memories he tried to forget with a single look.

"Correct and incorrect. An envoy? Yes. End the world?" She paused for a moment, a pained look flashing across her face. "No. I seek to save it. Save *us*. I cannot do it alone. I am fated to find you, you know this to be true. You felt it, the day we first met. We need each other."

"No, no!"

Even as he denied it, Therat remembered how alive he felt when he saw the woman those many years ago. How he waited for her night after night to make sure the nameless ghost in the dark was safe.

"No, it cannot be! I am not fit for a *liraes*. You seek to trick me!"

Mireithren rushed forward and stood on her toes, grabbing Therat's beard before he could react. Her fingers tangled with the knotted hairs and jerked his face down. A sharp coolness pressed against his neck. Her face came close, breath hot against his lips.

He tried to back away, to fight back, to do anything to escape. But he stood still. Helpless. She could kill him now, or twist his mind, and make him hers. Unleash his foul darkness to ruin the world. And, if some mercy from the Seven did still exist, he would lose his mind to the siren and not remember any of the deaths by his hand.

The dagger cut into his waiting flesh, tearing a hiss from the man cornered like prey. Therat squeezed his eyes shut and tried to picture his mother's face one last time.

Instead, Therat lost himself in the softness of Mireithren's lips against his. They pushed past his resistance and dismantled every defense the man had ever built. She tasted sweet, like honey and vanilla melting together. The warmth of her kiss sent bursts of sunfire through his mind. Therat leaned in, wrapping his arms around the woman, pulling her in close. His body quivered under her touch. *Gods,* it was better than he dreamed it would be.

His hips pressed closer to hers, hungering to taste every inch of his tormentor. Mireithren resisted at first, but the coolness of the dagger faded as she sank into his arms. This was what he wanted that night he saw her bleeding in the Market with an emptiness in her eyes as if her soul itself had been torn from the woman. She would be kept safe here. A stifled moan escaped as her tongue searched for entrance into his mouth before flicking back.

The heat rising inside him fled under the cold touch of metal sliding between the woman and his chest. Mireithren pushed away from Therat with the dagger. The Shadow-weave coiled around her like a snake ready to strike. Blood flushed her face, breathing ragged. She looked away, and as she did, Therat saw a tear fall across the black scars racing down her right cheek.

He had no idea what to do, what to think. Half-thoughts formed, mind unable to focus on anything else but breathing.

With each gulp of fresh morning air, the daze lifted. Anger gripped his heart, twisting with each breath until he wanted nothing more than to deny the maiden, to wrap his hands around her slender neck and willingly take a life. Therat did not dare let himself believe in the delusion of love. He could not.

"I-I..." Mireithren trailed off, unable or unwilling to speak.

"This proves nothing," Therat whispered. Mireithren looked back at him, her eyes wet with tears.

"You are a blind fool."

Therat licked his lips, her taste still fresh. He wanted more, craved all of her in his arms, his mouth, fingers trailing over every inch of her body...

Fuck, fuck, fuck. Stop it, don't give in to her lies!

"It can't mean anything." His head shook with denial.

"I'll kiss you again, and you deny what your soul knows to be true." Mireithren took a step forward, pinning Therat against the wall.

"I-it is you, some manipulation of my harmonic! The gods do not care, they've never cared. You don't know who I am. What I am."

Why can I not escape you? What did you do?

"And you think I am better? We walk in shadows. We are more alike than you realize, Therat. Impossible spawn that should never have existed. Yet, here we are."

As she spoke, Mireithren inched closer. Therat caught her hand before it snaked up to his face again. Forcing his mind into submission, he spun the woman around and pinned her against the wall. The dagger fell from her other hand with the impact and skittered away over the rocky cave floor.

It took all of Therat's strength not to lean in and devour her right there. She looked so achingly beautiful. A shaft of warm sunlight shone over his shoulder and onto Mireithren's enchanting face. Her eyes sparkled with waves of amber, and the gold strands hidden in the darkness of her hair shone bright.

Therat's hands trembled. He could kill her right now. Snap her fragile neck and end the siren's hold over him. His fingers twitched. He wanted to wrap his hand around her throat, squeeze until the blood in her veins pulsed against his hand. Squeeze and hold her down. Kiss her, taste her. Feel the warmth of her touch over his scarred heart. He wanted to bleed for her. Beg for her. Do anything for *her*.

"Why should I believe anything you say?" he growled, trying with desperation to ignore the quickening of his heart.

Mireithren's brow furrowed. "Because if you don't, I will kill you." Her gaze flickered down to his lips before staring back with a look of defiance. "And that would be a shame."

"And how would you do that?" Therat tightened his grip on her wrists as he spoke. Instead of caving to his pressure, the woman who tormented him for years simply laughed. The sound sent a chill down Therat's spine. "I could crush you even without my shadows, little siren."

"Then do it," Mireithren whispered, leaning forward until her breasts pushed into his chest. "Kill me. Do the very thing you have always tried to keep yourself from doing. My blood will forever stain your hands, Therat."

"Fuck you," he spat back. "You know nothing of me."

"Prove me wrong."

As she spoke, a black shade rose behind Mireithren. It engulfed the two in a blackness so deep he could not see the maiden mere inches in front of his face. A cool touch, like the chilled winds of night, wrapped itself around Therat's body. It pulled him deep into its embrace until a strange song surfaced from the endless void. It carried both sorrow and comfort, but never did one dominate the other. Before Therat realized what was happening, his hands fell from Mireithren's wrists.

"I thought as much," Mireithren said at last.

The shadows receded with her voice. Therat stared at an empty wall. He spun around to see Mireithren standing by the outcropping entrance, wiping off her black dagger. There was something strangely thrilling about seeing his blood on her hands. He gulped, trying to push aside the lingering waves of desire from her kiss.

I hate you, you will ruin me. I hate you! I must!

"You don't hate me, and I won't ruin you. I only want to heal the world."

"Heal the world?" Therat choked out, guilt rising. "What good can ever come from these hands stained with sins I cannot control?"

Mireithren did not respond. She reached a thin arm out. It grazed the white scar over Therat's heart as she murmured something under her breath. A strange sensation, like cool liquid pouring into his body, overcame Therat. The Shadow-weave hummed back to life, filling him inside until Therat could not tell where he ended and it began. The voices did not come back quite so loud—a dull clamor, rather than the choir always belting out in his mind.

"What did you do?" Therat whispered.

"We need each other, Therat. I don't want to kill you, I want to free you. Free us. I am not your enemy, I swear."

"Not my enemy, but wakes me up with a dagger to my throat. Not my enemy, but steals my shadows. I'd be a fool to trust you." Even as he spoke, Therat wanted to believe her words.

Mireithren stared deep into his eyes, a strange fire lighting up her gaze. "I'm not your enemy, but I am no fool. A truce, for one day, to show you I carry no ill intentions."

"One day. And then what?"

Mireithren sheathed the dagger against her upper thigh; the glimpse of her bare skin sent a lurch through Therat's stomach.

"That entirely depends. Much can happen in twenty-four hours."

"Like you killing me."

"You did offer to fuck me. Perhaps we can start with that," she said with a coy smile.

Therat stumbled backward at her words. His heart raced as a fire spread through his loins and images of her naked body flashed before his eyes. He wondered what his name, moaned from her lips, would sound like. Would his little siren sing for him as he caressed her scarred face?

"Get out of my head!" he thundered, lunging toward Mireithren.

She disappeared in a cloud of black smoke. Her sparkling laugh filled the small cave until it crushed Therat. He fell to his knees, unable to think straight. He was about to boil over, too many emotions struggling to be understood all at once.

"Whatever you desire is your own to claim, Therat. One day, give me that much. Please. I could kill you right now, but I won't. Isn't that proof enough for you?"

Mireithren stood behind him now. She bent over and whispered in his ear.

"Evil is created by men, not born in our hearts. I know of a place where those like us are loved. You deserve love, Therat. Won't you fight for it?"

The weight of the past four years lay as a boulder over his heart, crushing him until the only escape was to let the pain engulf him. The sob building in Therat's chest broke free, heaving with the effort as hot tears ran down his face. A soft hand reached up, fingers digging through his wild and unkempt beard. Mireithren turned his head and wiped the tears away.

"I know what it is like to be alone, more than anyone in the world." Her voice pulled him back from oblivion. "There is blood on my hands too, but we are not unworthy of love and good deeds. The world has hurt us. Is it any wonder we've hurt in return?"

Mireithren pulled Therat's head into her chest. The two sat huddled against the shallow cave wall, watching the sun rise over the dead and twisted land. Her touch reminded him of his mother's warm embrace, soothing his heart, sending the dark whispers to sleep. For the first time in his life, Therat did not try to fight back or find some way to reject the company of another.

Twenty-four hours. With the next sunrise, he would either find himself enslaved or dead. But right now, the siren's honeyed words sounded so sweet, and Therat was too weak to keep resisting her call.

MIREITHREN ROUSED THERAT FROM his stupor after the sun disappeared above the cave mouth. He was silent, too numb to do anything but walk after the release of surging emotions built up from decades of self-loathing. Mireithren's gravelly voice played on repeat in his head all morning. Therat wanted to believe her words, believe she did mean to save him, not enslave him—or worse. That she could love him, desire him, see something in him worth fighting for.

But he could not forget the Greenweaver he killed in the Market the night Mireithren first invaded his mind. Or the way she drove him to obsession until he would rather die than face reality. She would end him, surely.

So why did he want to go with her?

"Come, we must find food. Unless you have some hidden I cannot find." Mireithren's voice shook Therat from his thoughts.

"No, none. I hunt at night." The raven-haired woman raised an eyebrow in question. "You know of formweaving, I assume?"

"Ah," she said with a nod.

"How did you even survive out here? I see no food or wa—" The appearance of a portal, the surface rippling like water over a mirror, cut off Therat's question. It shimmered until a warm amber glow lit up the arched frame. *Fuck.* "I knew I saw you the other day. How long have you been watching me?" A shudder ran down his spine at the thought of Mireithren seeing what his uncontrollable rage did to the slave woman.

"Not long. I told you I would find you again. You have been impossible to ignore despite all my best efforts."

Mireithren grabbed Therat's hand and pulled him through the shifting surface of her portal. A rush of hot air blew past. He opened his eyes to see a city ahead of them in an oasis of tall leafy trees crawling with vines. Hundreds of birds filled the air, their songs like nothing he had heard before. They sounded almost like the voices of women, but higher and more ethereal. Despite the song's beauty, deep sorrow lingered in the air.

"Welcome to Cídhen's Rest," Mireithren said with a gesture toward the oasis in the distance.

Therat heard of this place before. All of the Madhiri had, though few ever traveled there by choice. The burial site of Cídhen, one of the Eldest, the Eábh Elessí, and the lover of the Goddess Myrniar. Cídhen's Rest stood as holy place among the worshipers of the Sunmaiden, and was one of the last places Therat wanted to be.

"I thought you said we are going to a place with others like us. This is not what I seek! I need to leave the desert, not go back into it."

"Do you not trust me? Our path is long and winding. We seek the western shores, where my weavecraft cannot take us. So we will need supplies"—Mireithren picked at the torn and stained black pants rippling around his legs in the breeze—"and good clothes to warm our backs when the wind blows cold."

Therat huffed. He saw the logic, but he felt trapped nonetheless. "How am I supposed to trust a woman who held a dagger to my throat and threatened to kill me? A woman I hate, yet, inexplicably find myself following."

"You promised me a day." Mireithren flashed a smile.

"I never agreed to your terms."

"Yet, still, you follow me. Leave, if you'd like, but you won't get far. I'll make sure of that."

Why am I following you? What is wrong with me?

"Do not tempt me, Little Siren."

"A pet name already? You flatter me, Therat." He winced at her words and realized that yes, he had kept calling her *little siren* without even thinking about it.

Could it be so crazy to love someone?

Gods, the woman was vexing. She would never know how every word and smirk sent his blood boiling and mind into a tailspin. He wanted to be rid of the siren but didn't know if he could live without her. If he *wanted* to live without her. So much changed in an instant. Therat wondered if he ever had control over his life or if it all led to this one moment, this one woman.

Mireithren walked toward Cídhen's Rest, her long legs striding across the cracked brown ground. She was stunning in the sunlight. Her ocher skin glowed, a deep red-brown. Therat jogged to keep up, settling into Mireithren's pace. Though it felt wrong, his gaze kept drifting to the line of criss-crossing scars down her cheek. Inky black and hollow-looking, they somehow only made her more beautiful in his eyes.

"I can feel you staring at me." Therat averted his gaze, heat rushing to his cheeks. "You can ask about my scars, I do not mind."

Therat stopped walking for a moment and reached out to tuck a clump of black curls behind Mireithren's ear. His fingers grazed the uppermost scars. She flinched but did not command him to stop. With a gentle touch, he stroked them again. Ice greeted his fingers, thin lines cut with a razor-sharp blade, the same length each time. Therat counted sixteen of them.

"Who did this to you?" he demanded, rage flaring just like the first night he saw her running from the vile creature that harmed her.

Mireithren's lips trembled as she spoke. "M-my father," she muttered. "And the *Makhaeren*. It was her order. To purge me. How lucky for me, to be born an *evranenith* to a Named House." A dry laugh filled the air.

"I should kill him right now!"

Her father? The father of the woman Adon loves? What if he finds out about our lineage?

"No!"

Mireithren's loud denial confused Therat. He thought anyone would wish to see their torturer dead, no matter who they were.

"No, no! This is not our task, not now. He can wait."

"But don't you hate him?"

"With every fiber of my being. Every thought at night twists around his face, what he has done to me in the name of the thing he calls love. I hate him! Hate him and wish him to die a thousand deaths and a hundred more, all by my hand. But I also fear him, dread him, panic at the thought of finding myself bound at his feet again. I am not ready. Not yet." Her voice dropped to a whisper. "I don't know if I ever will be."

Therat pulled Mireithren in close, wrapping his muscular arms around a body he could break with so little effort. A fire stirred in his loins as she melted into his arms. He held her until she pushed back, her cheeks flushed again.

"I... sorry. You looked like you needed a hug."

How do I even know what that looks like?

"I did. Not quite the action of someone who hates me, though." Mireithren laughed, and the tension in her body disappeared. A strange feeling—happiness, Therat realized—took hold of his heart.

This woman will be the end of me. She is drawing me into her siren song, and I am all too eager to come.

"What is your house?" she asked, changing subjects as they took off walking again.

"Anatnará, we are Skyweavers. Though, my brother Adon has all the talent." Mireithren twitched at the mention of his twin but did not speak up. "You know, I could be put to death for kissing you. Wrong castes and all."

"Too easy of a way out of this relationship," she remarked.

"I suppose you're right."

"Of course I am." Mireithren laughed again. Intoxicating. No mortal woman should be so frustrating. "What about your scar?"

Therat stayed silent. He rubbed it without thought, feeling the searing fires again as the blade cut through flesh. He was weak, too weak to finish the job. A failure at death and life.

"I told you mine. I will not judge yours."

"How could you not? Death by your hand is the coward's way out, and I failed at even that."

Mireithren reached out and touched Therat's scar. His heart raced with her lingering touch. "I'm glad you failed," she murmured with a soft smile.

The conversation ended, and only the sound of ethereal birdsong accompanied their steps. It grew louder as the oasis drew near. The Withergreen months neared their end, but an unnatural chill clung to the city. It was eerie to see the sun high in the sky, warmth absent from its long golden fingers. Here in Cídhen's Rest, even Narán mourned the death of the man who once shared his heart with Myrniar.

Therat kept walking, following the *evranenith* that would end the world with his help. He knew he should run, but her lies sounded so sweet.

SHATTERED

T HE CITY OF CÍDHEN'S Rest was a weary and morose place. The bright, lively songs bursting through the streets of Av Madhira were impossible to conjure here. A slow dirge filled the landscape, birdsong heavy with sorrow. Every statue wept, hands held over faces etched to grieve for eternity. The people lived without joy, voices hushed, feet shuffling along the ground. Therat wondered what it was like to be mourned forever by a Goddess and her people.

The Endless Grief.

Sooner or later, all who resided in Cídhen's Rest took the Sunmaiden's pain as their own, passing into a catatonic state before fading from the world. Once, the city thrummed with life, the bright and cheerful home of Myrniar and her flame-haired lover. If Therat closed his eyes, he could almost hear the memory of laughter as bright as the Sunmaiden herself. What beauty must have once resided here before Death came to Eás?

Mireithren did not take long to gather the supplies she needed. She fascinated him. Not a single coin left her hand. As she spoke, Therat saw threads of the Shadow-weave loop around the woman and worm their way into the shopkeepers. Mireithren walked out free of charge, the store owner remained none the wiser. She did this four times: twice for food (stacks of honeycakes, salted pork, and dried fruit), once for warmer clothes, and once for two thick cotton cloaks. They bundled everything up in a large pack slung over Therat's shoulder, which he took without question.

Only an hour or two had passed since they reached the city. If they hurried, they might reach the edges of the desert within a day or two. Therat didn't know the limitations of gateweaving. It would be too convenient if Mireithren could take him to their destination in one step.

They sat at a table in the shade of a tall, broad-leafed tree. Mireithren finished the last of a goat cheese pastry. The murmur of conversations around them did little to distract Therat. The siren in black made even the simple act of eating mesmerizing. The way her tongue ran over the corners of those impossibly soft lips. How her eyes lit up when taking a bite of *kunishfa*. She moved with divine grace.

Mireithren's eyes found his. She brought a finger to her lips and licked off a smear of sauce. Therat's stomach flipped as the siren's tongue flicked over her finger. There was something so suggestive about it despite the innocent look on her face.

Gods, I hate how beautiful you are to me.

"Would you like the last one, Therat?" Mireithren pushed a plate with a single roll of *kunishfa* across the table.

"All yours," he replied.

There it was again, the urge to shield the woman and give her anything he could. It would be impossible to deny her the world itself if she desired it. The sweet date and fig rolls were good—and hunger still clawed at his stomach—but Mireithren looked so frail and thin. The road ahead might be scarce with food; Therat felt compelled to ensure she ate her fill.

"Good," she smiled back. "I'd probably have stolen a bite right from your mouth anyway. I still remember the first time Saiya took me out and I tasted these. I haven't found anything better tasting. Food, that is." Mireithren laughed as she spoke, a smirk on her face as she glanced at Therat's lips.

"I'd never figure you to have a sweet tooth for simple date rolls, of all things. Surely they have more decadent food beyond the Wall."

"I wouldn't know."

Mireithren spoke with an air of nonchalance, but pain cracked across those eyes glowing amber in the sun. Therat let it drop, knowing all too well the suffocating hurt of ripping open old memories. He could never ask the maiden opposite him to re-live old trauma.

"I'd wager you aren't missing out on anything actually good. My grandfather's cooking, now there is food worth eating. Even as a little boy I remember Mama asking him to make meals. She would sit and tell us stories while we helped Papa cook." The words slipped out before Therat realized what he was saying. His heart bucked at the thought of his mother, and a shadow passed over his face.

"You loved her very much," Mireithren murmured. She slid a hand across the table and stroked the back of his forearm.

"Yes. More than she ever knew."

"I... I'm so sorry. It doesn't feel like enough to say, but I am."

Therat took her hand, still tracing fingernails up and down his arm. He squeezed it before letting go, unable to find his voice. The words that sounded empty and meaningless from others were so sweet from Mireithren's lips.

"We don't have to talk about the past," Mireithren said, breaking the silence. "Either of us. Who cares about a little mystery?"

"Easy for you to say when you can read my thoughts."

"Only the ones about me, and judging by your thoughts, you're obsessed," she teased.

"Whatever helps you sleep at night, Little Siren," he said with a smile.

The cloud of sorrow eased with their playful exchange. Therat stood, his legs groaning in protest from having sat for too long.

"Do you need anything else here? I don't know how much longer I can stand this place."

Mireithren shook her head, mouth full with the last bite of *kunishfa*.

"We'll wish for something, I am sure, but for now I can think of nothing else. I planned to stay the night here, though." Her words offered an invitation, unspoken desire flashing across Mireithren's brown eyes flecked with gold. "But we can leave if you wish. Does that mean you caved in less than a day?"

"I... that's not what I meant. Hmm. I can't remember the last time I slept in a bed. One night. And tomorrow, I'm free to do as I wish, yes?"

"Of course," she purred. "I hoped you'd agree." A fire raged in Mireithren's eyes as she spoke, a deep hunger he could not place. "Come, let's see what the rest of the city has to offer before we find a room for the night."

A room? She can't mean a single room with a single bed. She is going to kill me, isn't she?

Therat could only nod his head in reply. Mireithren reached out and grabbed his hand. All thought lay in a puddle at his feet. The intoxicating siren pulled his hand forward.

"Let us find a quieter place," she murmured. "I know they have hot springs here, somewhere. It will be a nice way to end the day before we sleep. If you let me do such a thing."

Therat got the strange sense she wasn't referencing daggers at each other's throats.

THE DEEP SORROW OF Cídhen's Rest disappeared in the presence of Mireithren. Everything about her enchanted Therat. Every movement was so tantalizing, it sent a flurry of thoughts about her—naked—through his mind. He couldn't tell if she meant to tease him. It almost seemed like a game. Every coy word and flash of skin, every lingering touch, hands straying across his body begging for recognition and release.

Mireithren took the lead as they walked away from the shaded area lined with food stalls. She kept glancing back at Therat, her smile from when they first met back on her enchanting face. He lumbered behind her, reason fighting with passionate desire.

A part of him wanted to strangle the maiden and forget anything she ever told him. Deny what he knew to be true and turn back to the ever-hungering shadows, to let fate run its course. It was the smart decision.

But how could anyone choose the better option when he could only think of ripping the silks from Mireithren and taking her where she stood? Therat distracted himself with the slow and sorrowful birdsong, fighting to maintain control of himself. His passions cooled in time, but he dared not look too long at the woman.

They walked through the city streets and along winding paths in an attempt to find the hot springs. Platforms wide enough to fit a small hut lined the tallest of the trees. Dozens of them stood throughout the city. Figures draped in red robes and black veils knelt on the platforms, hundreds in each tree. Very few moved, and even fewer made a noise. Catatonic, slipping away as Myrniar's eternal grief overcame them.

The raven-haired woman did most of the talking. She spoke of running away at nineteen, her journey to the West guided by an inexplicable feeling and a soft woman's voice she first heard as a girl. How some strange weavecraft kept her from crossing the Andesiri River, the fast-flowing beast tumbling down from the forest of silver. And of a pale woman with soft violet eyes who spoke of a man in the desert Mireithren must find.

But now Therat found it impossible to focus on her words. They arrived at last at the small group of hot springs in a secluded part of the city. A well-worn path snaked through the tall rock formations. The gurgles of the bubbling waters provided a welcome reprieve from the sorrowful music of the city.

Mireithren said something. Therat only caught the last few words.

"… sit with me? Your feet will thank you."

She grabbed onto Therat's arm for support and yanked off one leather boot, then the other. The long slits in her silk skirt parted as a leg lifted and, for the briefest moment, Therat could see the bare curves of her upper thigh. His thoughts ran wild; what did she look like under the rest of her black raiment? Molars ached as Therat's jaw tensed. Mireithren seemed oblivious until she turned around and grinned. Her eyes flashed as she bent over and unwrapped the thick black and silver ribbons from around her legs.

Therat could not look away even if his life depended on it. His skin prickled with anticipation, the yearning fire returning deep in his loins. Whatever the siren did to him, Therat didn't want it to end.

"Aren't you going to take your shoes off, Therat?" she asked, the last leg wrap almost unbound.

Her rough voice sent a shiver across his brain. How could only his name send the man into such disarray? He tore his gaze away from those slender, naked legs peeking out from the skirt and grumbled in reply.

"Well, I'm not waiting." Mireithren gathered the length of her skirt and tied it at her waist with a hidden string. The breath caught in Therat's throat.

Gods, what did I ever do to deserve this torture?

Mireithren sat at the edge of the nearest hot spring and slid her feet in. An involuntary moan escaped her lips as she did, the relaxation instant. She looked back at Therat, a sparkling smile painted on her face.

The raven-haired siren sat in the fading sun, aglow as the shadows of night crept in. She looked like one of the Goddesses themselves, worthy of eternal worship.

Therat pulled his shoes off and shoved up the cuffs of his pants. He sat opposite Mireithren, unable to trust himself, all thought overridden by the hot desire thrumming through every muscle. Aching feet eased into the water. The heat of the springs helped distract Therat. His gaze stayed low, watching bubbles form. The two sat in silence until the shadows grew long. Mireithren gazed at the sky with a peaceful look on her face.

The eastern horizon grew ever darker, shades of deep purples and blues swirling with the fading light of day. The silver moon would not come tonight. A moonless night. A chance for fate to twist under the Dark Goddess's hand.

Therat tried to reason with himself as his faculties slowly returned, desires leached away by the fiery waters. Attraction was a natural thing, no shame in such desires even if no one could reciprocate them back. But why *her?* Why had no one before stirred so much as a missed heartbeat, yet she made every one of his senses go wild? Somehow, it would be easier to find anyone else in Mireithren's place. He didn't want to love her, hold her, or taste every inch of her.

But he would die if he didn't.

"The sun will set soon. We should find a room for the night."

Therat looked up from the water to see Mireithren looking at him, her gaze settled on the scar across his chest peeking through the tunic she gave him. He hated how naked she made him feel.

"Seems unlike you to shy away from the night," he said with a groan, body unwilling to leave the warmth of the hot springs. He stood and turned away from Mireithren, trying to avoid seeing more of her mesmerizing body. The gentle curves of her naked legs lingered in his mind.

"True, but hunting you required sacrificing sleep."

"Your blade at my throat woke me up early. If I promise to let you sleep, will you promise to keep sharp daggers away?"

"I'd be a fool to make such a promise," she giggled.

Mireithren's eruption of giggles pulled Therat's gaze back. She sat on the ground, the lengths of her skirt fallen to the side of each leg. If he didn't know any better, Therat would swear she wore a skirt with high slits for this very purpose. The sheen of water drying on her skin looked like a fine web of crystals in the dimming sunlight. Therat's eyes worked from her ankle up to the deep creases of her upper inner thigh. His gaze lingered.

THE TWO RETRACED THEIR steps back into the main district now devoid of life, stores shuttered for the day. The familiar dread and sense of foreboding from the dead land where Mireithren found him returned. The two hurried along until the warm lights of the inn they passed earlier in the day loomed large. The tall wooden building with arched windows stood around a tree with yellow-gold bark. Glowing orbs of amber light lined the limbs in place of leaves. Though the golden giant was but a memory of its former glory, the beauty awed Therat. They had no such trees in Av Madhira. He lingered outside, watching as the stars lit up the sky and the orbs looked like a hundred tiny moons high in the sky.

The inside of the inn held more life than Therat expected. Dozens of patrons sat at a long bar set against the back wall, almost every table filled with people drinking and eating. The conversations were hushed, as everything was in Cídhen's Rest. As the door creaked open, a short, obese man with light brown skin and a beard flecked with silver approached.

"Hurry, hurry, come in now. Let the darkness crawl away from ye!" A gap-toothed smile spread across his puffy face.

Mireithren smiled back. "You are most kind. The shadows cannot tarry long under your blessed House of amber and gold! *Hénarán, oestír.*"

"Ah! A High Lady," the stocky innkeeper said, bowing low as he recognized the formal greeting of the Named Houses. "My humble apologies, my lady...?"

"Lady Mireithren, of House Isht'iri. We are most welcomed, *oestír.*" Mireithren removed the black half-gloves, revealing hands laden with blue suns and flying doves. She extended one to the innkeeper, who in turn placed a gentle kiss on her outstretched fingers. "I only seek a room for the night, you do not need to trouble yourself on my account, I assure you."

Therat smiled. *She used my name.* It filled him with an odd sense of relief, knowing she liked the name he gave to this mysterious woman. The innkeeper bowed and rushed away. He reappeared a minute later with a key in hand.

"No food first, or drink? It is early yet, the kitchen will be open for a while longer. It may not be up to the standards of Av Madhira, but we try! Or perhaps my lady would like a bath drawn for her? And a room for your guard, surely?" A wave of disappointment flowed over Therat at the mention of a separate room.

"One room, no food or baths, please. Wine would be lovely, however. From the Hénar Valleys, if you have any."

The innkeeper nodded and took them to their room up three flights of creaky stairs to the top floor. Each room stood ready for one of the Named Houses, the doors carved with intricate symbols from their family crests.

"This one, I think, my lady will find most pleasing," the innkeeper said as he shuffled over to a door. A flaming sun inscribed with two doves, their heads and breasts bent together in the form of a heart, decorated the wooden door. The innkeeper unlocked it and gave the key to Mireithren. "It doesn't get much use as the Daughters of Myrniar rarely visit now. Do let me know if you need anything at all, my lady. Asheef will be up with your wine shortly." He bowed his head and waddled back down the stairs, huffing as he went.

The silence weighed heavily over Therat as the innkeeper retreated. Mireithren reached out and took his hand, pulling him into the room with her. Therat tried in vain to push aside thoughts of her hands trailing over his chest. His mind begged to resist the siren, but his heart gave up without a fight.

Grander than the rest of the inn would suggest, warm red-stained wood interspersed with arched windows lined the walls. A headless statue of Myrniar stood in a recess opposite the door, seams of gold running through the white stone. Floating orbs filled with amber light illuminated a large bed in the center of the room. A small alcove with a window seat encased in glass looked out over the lake feeding the oasis.

"There is only one bed. I-I'll sleep in the alcove," Therat muttered without conviction. He could never wish to leave Mireithren's side, even if staying brought him death.

Mireithren turned; Therat lost himself in those deep brown eyes.

"I don't mind sharing." Her voice faded, eyes saying what her words did not.

"Where will I find a dagger to even the odds at this hour?" he whispered in reply.

Therat tensed, every muscle seizing with a building anticipation, but to what climax it did not know. He hated the confused feelings of arousal Mireithren pulled to the surface. He did not know the tender touch of bliss, couldn't reciprocate it in turn. He wanted to be alone, face the inevitable end when it came with no one around to hurt or kill.

But he also wanted her.

No, I need her.

Mireithren leaned up, hot breath grazing his neck. "What if we set aside the daggers tonight?"

Therat's mind emptied. It would be impossible to form a thought even if his life depended on it. Blood surged through his body, a fire building in the pit of his stomach.

Mireithren reached a hand down to Therat's hips. His body thrummed with excitement as her fingers trailed along his flesh hot with desire. A strangled noise escaped from the tormented man. He tried to push her away, but his muscles felt weak, unable to resist.

"Wh-what... what are d-doing?" he whimpered, the words near impossible to utter.

"Do you want me to stop?" Mireithren teased, pulling her hand back. Therat's body cried out. A rush of hot blood burst through his veins.

"Gods I fucking hate you," he growled back, jaw clenching tighter with each passing breath. "You said one day to prove you meant no harm. Yet, you torture me with an impossibility!"

Therat didn't know what it meant to love someone. He would ruin it, bringing only more pain and suffering to the world like everything else he did. But he craved it, yearned for love.

Mireithren only laughed. A wicked sound. She was toying with him, fighting with herself.

Therat wrapped his arms around Mireithren and pulled her close. He leaned down and buried his face in her neck, inhaling deep. Her scent was like nothing he had smelled before; a soft sweetness of vanilla and water lilies underscored by a sharp spice. The dizzying aroma called out to him.

"I don't kno—"

Therat's lips crushed into Mireithren's, cutting off her words. The taste of dates lingered on her mouth. His heart took off, a racehorse with nowhere to go. The sound pounded in his ears. He could feel Mireithren's heart racing too, her chest pressed against his. She leaned into him, weight pushing him back into the room. Therat didn't try to resist.

"Mine... now..." Mireithren pleaded between breaths, pushing him further into the room.

She bit down on his lower lip. A shard of fire coursed through his body and into his brain, exploding across the surface, hot pleasure searing his neurons. She bit down again, harder this time. He moaned as the pressure built, only released when Mireithren's head pulled back. Her deep brown eyes gleamed with lust.

"Why do you want me?" he asked.

"Does it matter? I saw the way you looked at me on my nameday. How you ran away, pretending the very sight of me did not make your blood run hot."

"And what happens if I say no?"

The air evaporated from Therat's lungs before he could finish his words. A thread of Shadow-weave tore through his heart until it stopped beating; his blood ran cold, and for a moment, he thought he had taken his last breath. Then, before his vision faded, the warmth returned to his body like a candle flickering to life. He stared at Mireithren, trying to summon the hatred he felt for her that morning, but nothing came.

"Gods," he whispered at last. "I... I shouldn't be here."

"I once heard you think, 'Death by her hand would taste so sweet'. But even if I did wish to kill you, the sun is not up." She leaned in close, her words dripping like a sweet poison into his ear.

"I only want to claim you for one night."

The siren in black bit down on Therat's neck, pulling his flesh up until the soft skin broke. Her tongue twisted around the broken flesh before pulling away.

"Be careful playing games, Little Siren," Therat growled. "Lest you be bitten in return."

"Who says I don't want that?"

Grabbing Mireithren by the waist, he swung her up into his waiting arms. She was a feather to the muscles accustomed to hard physical labor. A gasp escaped her throat as he pulled her in close. Her lips found his neck, the soft kiss sending a wave of shivers through his body.

He walked to the bed and laid the maiden down, dropping to the floor on his knees. He pulled one boot off, then the other. His fingers trembled as they brushed over the exposed skin of her lower thigh. Mireithren moved to unwrap her leg bindings; Therat tore them off before she could reach them. It took all of his willpower not to tear the rest of her clothes off.

"Do you have any idea how radiant you are?" Therat panted as he spoke, fiery blood swelling in his loins. "You are the most beautiful thing I have ever seen, worthy of eternal worship if I could give it."

"Then worship me," Mireithren purred.

Therat's mind dove into a tailspin. He yanked the black skirt down from Mireithren's hips, soft silk giving way to his hungering touch. Her skin glowed as if the sun itself lit the fires of her soul. She unhooked the half-corset cinched around her waist. The loose fabric of her top pulled off with ease.

The image of his maiden in the night splayed before him forever seared itself into Therat's memory. Her body was soft and thin, delicate curves cutting the figure of a woman whose beauty could never be denied. Therat leaned his head down and kissed the valley under one protruding collarbone before sweeping across to the other. His lips lingered over her skin—so warm and soft—her sweetness pulling him back for more. Mireithren's hands tangled through his wild curls, fingernails dragging across his soft scalp. He hissed, the pleasure competing with pain.

"How shall I worship you?" he breathed.

Mireithren reached down and tugged at Therat's pants. The feel of her hand on his lower stomach sent a lurch through his body. His blood thickened, cock pulsing with fire. He stood and pulled the pants off, fabric ripping with the quickness of his hands. His gaze strayed over Mireithren's soft curves, every part of his body quivering with excitement.

"Don't be gentle," Mireithren whispered, her eyes taking in every inch of the naked man before her.

A hand covered in interlacing tattoos reached up to her throat. "Like this?" he growled. Her breasts trembled with each quake of her chest.

Mireithren nodded, eyes wide. His grip tightened ever so slightly, and a shudder coursed through her body. The Shadow-weave inside awoke, pulled to the surface by the strange look of joy in her eyes. Tendrils of shadows surged forth and wrapped themselves around her neck. She smiled through the gasps.

Therat shoved a hand between Mireithren's thighs, parting them with no resistance. The slickness of her arousal drew him in; her hips bucked as his fingers circled, searching for the source of her desires. The Song of the Night embraced the two lovers, soft music filling in the gaps between their breathy moans. Mireithren quivered with each passing second. Her hips thrust up, begging for more of Therat's touch. He closed his eyes and buried his head into her neck, inhaling deeply.

Vanilla. *Comforting.*

Water lily. *Sensual.*

Spice. *Danger.*

Whatever Mireithren offered, Therat wanted it all. Circling her entrance with one finger, he slowly pushed in.

"Gods," he breathed. "You look fucking beautiful just like that."

He pushed in deeper, thumb circling her clit. Mireithren squirmed beneath his hand, breath ragged. Therat loosened the Shadow-weave coiled around her neck.

"N-no," she mumbled.

As if answering on their own, the shadows obeyed Mireithren's command, wrapping around her neck until each breath struggled to break free. Therat's cock throbbed as the raven-haired woman with scars on one cheek turned into a puddle by his hand. He slipped a second finger in, pulling an incomprehensible shout from Mireithren.

For five years, Therat told himself the way his heart sang when Mireithren was around meant nothing. But as his fingers felt every squirm, each quake of the fair maiden in the throes of pleasure, the truth could no longer be ignored.

Even as broken as he was, the First Harmonic wove another soulsong to match his own. A *liraes*.

My liraes. My siren, be it doom or grace.

Therat could not wait any longer. Pulling his fingers out, he licked them before cupping Mireithren's scarred cheek. She tasted sweet, slightly salty, but most of all: she tasted like eternal bliss. He wanted to taste every inch of her, but already he felt himself on the verge of losing all control.

"You have no idea how long I've been thinking of this moment." His lips grazed Mireithren's as he lowered his knees to the bed.

"I know," she choked out in reply, her eyes challenging him, telling him not to hold back.

He sank into Mireithren, slow at first, gauging her reaction. A moan pushed through the ropes of shadow at her neck, eyes fluttering as he entered her. Her hands snaked around Therat's hips, clawing to pull him closer. He let himself relax, her soft body melting around him.

Until this moment, Therat never realized being alive could feel so good. Some part of him unfolded, as if these two souls had met before. The way Mireithren held him felt comforting in a way he never thought possible.

Time lost all meaning, ecstasy lighting the air on fire between the two lovers. Therat moaned as Mireithren's body moved in time with his, her hips gyrating with every thrust. A smile spread across her face, lost in the waves of her pleasure. Her hands ran the course of his body, nails tracing a swirling pattern across his back, down his arms, and over his broad chest. Therat gripped her thighs, the soft flesh of her breasts, pulled her in close by the small of her back.

Someone knocked on the door, a voice calling out for the wine. The shadows around Mireithren's neck disappeared.

Mireithren sank her nails into his back, pulling Therat deeper. "Do-don't stop, Therat. I won't let you stop."

"Whatever you desire, Little Siren," he murmured, lips grazing her earlobe. "I am yours tonight." He quickened the pace, rolling onto one side and pulling her leg over his shoulder.

"Oh, oh gods, yes," she whimpered. "You are mine, all mine, Therat."

Mireithren reached up a hand wreathed in the Shadow-weave and touched the bite mark on his neck. A searing fire burned through his skin, then turned to ice. Shadows swam across Therat's vision before retreating into his flesh. The pain sent a spasm of blood rushing through his cock.

End me, oh gods, you will end me, and I will thank you for it.
Another knock at the door.

"Leave it. Outside!" Therat yelled out. It took every ounce of effort and willpower to focus enough to say those three little words.

As he spoke, the pleasure built to an inevitable crescendo. He looked at Mireithren, gaze sweeping across her supple breasts. Her skin glistened with sweat. He lowered his head, tongue flicking across a nipple taut with arousal before looking back up at the siren. She pulled his head up and kissed him, tongue invading his mouth. A cool tendril of Shadow-weave wrapped around his hips, forcing every inch of his cock into his raven-haired torturer.

Suddenly, the fires overwhelmed Therat, ready to tear from his abdomen and sear all thought from his mind. He thrust again, the shadows around his hips pulling him in until Mireithren shuddered and hummed with pleasure.

"Oh... oh, Mireithren, I... *fuck.*"

Pure bliss shattered across Therat's mind, muscles seizing with the effort of trying to process the feeling. Purged, hollowed out. He closed his eyes, luxuriating in the feeling while his cock still gently pulsed inside Mireithren, the height of bliss fading fast.

Therat collapsed to the side, sweat crawling down his forehead from the effort. He opened his eyes to see Mireithren crying in silence, a wide smile on her face.

"Th-that... oh gods," she whispered, still smiling before wiping the tears away.

His limbs felt so heavy. He wanted nothing more than to hold Mireithren close and fall into a deep, peaceful sleep, to wake up with her in his arms and worship her all over again. Therat hazily remembered the knock that interrupted them.

He kissed Mireithren's scarred cheek before getting up. "My siren requires one last act of worship," he murmured.

Therat opened the door, a large bottle of wine and two goblets waiting for him. He picked them up and came back, making quick work of dispensing the deep crimson liquid. The sweet smell paled in comparison to the taste of Mireithren still on his lips. Therat lay back down; Mireithren nuzzled her head under his chin, taking slow sips from the goblet.

"I only asked for a day," she whispered, almost as if to herself.

Mireithren sank into Therat's arms. Her sighs of content-ment came as sweet music to his ears.

Thirty

UPENDED AND IN DISARRAY

The plan failed.

At least, it failed to produce the results Apattar told herself she wanted. One night, that was all it was supposed to be. One time to rid herself of this unwanted lust, then her heart would comply with what her mind told her must be done.

Except, her heart won the battle.

The fragile, cracked, black thing that could barely recall the feeling of love. The one that shattered when Ninann begged the cursed sister not to follow a path of darkness. The one that never got to feel the devoted protection of her father. Now it hummed with anticipation, ready to do anything for the man with black curls sleeping by her side.

Claimed. Mine. My very own to ruin, to love, to torture, to desire.

It was a stupid plan.

Maybe she always knew it would fail. Secretly hoped it would fail, at least. Could her will be stronger than fate?

Apattar smiled as Therat shifted; a hand strayed across her upper thigh. She closed her eyes and thought back to last night. How he looked at her as if she was the only person who mattered in the world. The way his Shadow-weave wrapped around her throat, vision blurring and thoughts melting at their cold touch. The pain mixed with pleasure, gasps for air heightening every nerve ending, sending her tumbling into fire. How his touch awakened her, unlocked a heart she thought forever broken.

The woman who had only known cruel touches for so long never knew she could feel so alive. Content. Wanted. Loved. She desired it more than a purpose, more than power or money. Someone to want her with such ferocity the past became a thing easy to forget. In a single day, Therat gave Apattar everything she sought. She claimed her prize, and now would let nothing take him away. Perhaps it wasn't love, but twisted obsession, yet, did it matter in the end?

Apattar brushed a curl out of Therat's eyes. She leaned over and placed a gentle kiss upon his lips. Last night, the tension coiled in her body made it impossible to think straight. She wanted to feel the pain she knew so well alongside pleasure, some naive thought it would lessen the enjoyment, remind her of the reason why she had to sacrifice him.

But now Apattar wondered what his soft, lingering touch would feel like. If Therat would stroke her cheek, erase the ugliness she hid from the world. And she wanted to feel him filling her with every inch of his cock, bringing her to such places of bliss she could have never dreamt of before last night.

Therat still slept. Apattar slid her hand over his broad chest, tracing the smooth curve of his muscles as her fingers trailed downwards over his naked form. She gently touched his flaccid cock, a soft stroke followed by another. The pulse of blood under her hand filled the pit of her stomach with a flutter.

"Therat," Apattar whispered, leaning over and brushing her lips against his ear. "I can't stop thinking about last night. About you."

He did not stir, deep in the embrace of sleep. Apattar kept moving her hand in slow, rhythmic motions as she spoke.

"Please, I want you again. Need you again. Only you, this time."

Hot blood returned to the growing erection under her hand, pulses growing more rapid with each hungering stroke. Therat's breathing quickened. He stirred, but those light gray eyes did not open.

The desire raging through her body returned with a vengeance, a wildfire burning across her neurons, begging for release. Something wet slid down her inner thigh. Apattar reached a hand between her legs; a warm, thick fluid from her entrance greeted her searching fingers.

How do you do this to me?

Pulling herself on top of Therat, Apattar studied the black bruise blooming around the bite mark on his neck. She wondered if her mark would scar, or the cut from her dagger. The idea of marking Therat as hers brought a strange thrill to Apattar. She'd never truly had anything, or anyone, to call her own before.

Therat's eyes fluttered open, gaze locking with hers.

"It's been one day," he said groggily.

"The sun is not up, and you are still mine." She reached a shadowy hand up to his neck, pressing against the bruise under his left ear. He winced, but leaned further into her touch.

"Is that so? Eager for worship, Mireithren?" he breathed, blinking the sleep away as he looked at Apattar.

With one fluid motion, Apattar's mouth found the bruise blossoming on his neck. He groaned, a half-mumbled word escaping from behind those delicious lips. She lowered herself until the tip of Therat's stiff cock grazed against her wetness. With a moan, his throbbing cock split her open again.

"I would end the world for your worship, Therat," she gasped into his ear, slowly taking in his length. Pain played on the periphery of her bliss, a tightness easing with each passing second.

Therat's hands grabbed Apattar and pulled her in close for a tender kiss. They moved in unison, Apattar's hips rocking back and forth with his and setting a slow rhythm. She craved his gentle touch, how intimate and loving it felt after they devoured each other the night before.

Apattar sat up and bit back a moan as Therat's cock swelled with each thrust. Her vision blurred, lost in the icy hot throes of pleasure building with each wave. Therat held her by one hip, his free hand running across her skin, over her stomach, her breasts, her back. A soft, warm caress filled with love.

"Come here, my ethereal goddess," he murmured.

Therat flipped Apattar onto her back with ease before pushing back into her. His eyes raged with fire, but his touch remained tender. He leaned down and placed gentle kisses all across her neck and breasts. Apattar's breath hitched. A spring coiled inside her, ready to release and end the world again in delirium.

"Don't stop," she begged.

"You beg so well," he whispered. "But you don't have to."

Their pace quickened; Apattar could only focus on the intense euphoria building, building, ready to burst and leave a blank space in her mind. Therat's hand cupped her scarred cheek, the warmth of it sending her over the edge.

"I love you, my Little Siren in the night."

"I, wh-w—" she stammered before all knowledge of speech left her brain.

The world ended. A wildfire consumed her mind. She was falling. Falling into a pool of warmth, every neuron steeped in bliss. She pulled Therat close, breathing in his musky aroma of burnt wood, old blood, and sweat. She could only think of him, forever by her side. She lingered on the thought, riding the waves of ecstasy.

Therat kept going, his pace erratic, face twisted. He seized for a moment. Apattar felt his release and the fading throbs of his erection. He moved, then kissed Apattar. Her eyes fluttered open; Therat lay by her side now, panting.

"You love me..." she murmured after their breathing calmed at long last.

Therat smiled, one she had never seen before. Wide and toothy, crinkling the skin under his eyes and forming a dimple under his left cheek.

Do I make him that happy? Is this some game of his?

"The sun is up. I can think of no other reason why I would still want to stay with you," he replied.

Another gentle kiss. Sweet, loving. She buried her head into his chest, sinking into his embrace.

"I..." She paused, chewing the inside of her mouth, then forced the words out before she could think. "I don't know what it means to love someone. Last night..."

Apattar wanted this, but at what price? She pulled away as an image of her Lady Eithranren's weeping face raced by. Suddenly, the room felt too small, the woman dipped in fire, but the kind that only brought unending pain and suffering. She abandoned all reason, let her heart play when it never understood the rules of the game.

A look of concern flashed across Therat's face.

"I... I didn't... last night, the choking... I should have known better. For your first." The words tumbled out of Therat's mouth. He sat up, biting his lip as a thread of Shadow-weave wrapped around his shaking hands.

"No, it's not that!" Apattar exclaimed. The thought of Therat blaming himself for giving her what she wanted sent a lurch through her stomach.

"No, no, I wanted it last night! It was... exquisite. Truly. It's not you. I just, shit!" The words clung to her throat, every breath threatening to release the tears building with each second. "I don't know. I had a plan. Simple, easy. Sleep with you, rid myself of these confused feelings. But I can't. I don't want to. Fuck you for making me feel this way, Therat!" An explosion of tears fell over her cheeks, hot and salty in her mouth.

Therat pulled her into his chest, his arms refusing to let the maiden fight back. He stroked her hair, soft touch pulling the wretched guilt from her and soothing a quaking heart.

"I don't know what you want, Mireithren. But I will give you anything you desire if it makes you smile again. Please. For me?" The sincerity of Therat's words ached.

"What if it kills you?" she sobbed.

"I'd rather die for you if it makes you happy than watch you suffer," he whispered in her ear.

Apattar choked on the rising nausea lapping over her. Why did he have to say the right thing, even when he didn't know what was being asked of him? And why did she have to kiss him yesterday, start this whole confusion of emotions and let her heart ruin years of work? It amazed Apattar how stupid she could be.

A deep sigh released some of the wild emotions roiling inside. She untangled herself from Therat's arms and slid across the bed. Cool tile greeted her feet—a welcome distraction.

"I wish you still hated me. I can't ask such a thing of you," she said at last, not looking back at Therat. A muffled noise, almost like a cry of pain, filled the air.

Apattar stood and pulled her clothes on, motions automatic as her mind and heart waged a ruthless war inside. What would he say if she told him the truth, unveiled how she first sought him not for love, but to become a weapon? The man held no reverence for the gods; he couldn't fake it if he tried, the disdain in his eyes hard to miss. Even when Apattar spoke of her Lady Eithranren he teased her, said she listened to intuition, not a god.

She wanted him to be right. It was her willpower that helped Apattar survive the horrors of her childhood, not the gods or fate. There had to be another way.

Apattar sat back down on the bed and moved to grab her boots. She looked up to see Therat holding them instead, a smile mixed with sorrow on his face. He knelt without a word and slid one boot on at a time. Her heart quivered as his touch lingered on her thigh.

"Why did you come find me, Mireithren?" he asked at last, still kneeling in front of her. Apattar froze at the question.

"I told you already. To help me save the world, those like us."

"And what role was I meant to play?"

Apattar bit down on her lip before replying. "You'd have every right to kill me where I stand if I tell you," she whispered. Cool threads of Shadow-weave wrapped around her arms as if readying to protect the woman. Therat chuckled at her words.

"If you're about to say your Goddess wanted to use my shadows, I already figured it out. And you know what?" He grabbed her chin and leveled her gaze with his. "Fuck the gods.

If they cared so much, they wouldn't have given me a taste of happiness, only to rip it away."

Apattar jumped at the words. Therat spoke with such an odd calmness, as if they were discussing what to have for breakfast instead of defying the gods.

"Why even come with me?" Her eyes searched his.

"Because you are my *liraes*, Mireithren."

He cupped both hands around her face, pulling her forehead to his. His hands shook. Was he upset with her?

"I have seen your face in my dreams a thousand times, yet never did I wish to wake. The gods may have fated us together, but where are they now? I don't care what some dead Goddess tells you. You are the only thing I care about now. I will not let you hurt yourself to save a world that would watch you burn with glee."

Why was it so hard to take what she always wanted? Who else could love her *but* Therat?

"Love always flees from my side. I just found you, but now I'm terrified of losing you," she sobbed. "This wasn't a part of the plan! This isn't my destiny! What am I supposed to do?" Her sobs turned into a wail. Therat held her tighter.

After a time, he lifted her chin with his thumb and forefinger. He looked long into her eyes, a softness there she had never seen before. Therat's other hand brushed the hair behind her ear and caressed the scars running up and down her cheek. She nuzzled into his touch. He made her feel so beautiful. As if she wasn't broken, her face forever ruined by her father's malice. Therat's loving touch made it easy to forget the scars existed.

"Screw destiny. Live for me, for yourself!"

Therat's lips brushed against hers, his breath intoxicating every sense and sending her into a dizzying whirlpool of emotions. For her entire life, Apattar walked under the shadow of Death; the idea of living for herself seemed an impossibility. Long nights spent telling herself she was never meant to be happy, that hers was a life of sorrow. The last life of sorrow, the one whose pain would end the world and restore the gods.

But maybe fate could not be so easily discerned. Maybe she could live a life filled with love and happiness. And, if fate demanded otherwise, she would find a way to defy it, would heal the world *and* save Therat.

Laisha.

She sent Apattar on a quest to find Therat, not the voice in her head. The pale woman was ancient, old enough to remember the world before it descended into complete chaos. She would have the answers. She must.

"I'll try. For you."

APATTAR DIDN'T KNOW WHAT to say to Therat after they left the inn. The two ate breakfast at a coffee bar in silence while her tearful confession played on a loop.

Every minute living in safety in Andeshar seemed as if a blessing from her Lady Eithranren. Hatred for the Dark Goddess bloomed into fervent love over the years. Murdered and fed to the stars, her voice leaked in through a crack in the void, but how or why remained a mystery. Apattar told herself the Goddess's sight could be blurred, the future she spoke of only a half-truth. Eithranren led her to Laisha, who in turn sent Apattar into the waiting arms of Therat. The pale woman with immense power, an immortal sorceress who spoke of a home for *evranenith*. The truth was tangled in there somewhere.

A weight lifted from her chest the more distance the two travelers put between them and the city. The air warmed, heaviness melting away with the fresh desert air. Autumn clung to the world with fiery hands. Apattar savored the heat, wondering when she would feel it again. If she ever would.

Therat reached out and grabbed her wrist, stopping the woman in her tracks.

"You haven't said anything since we left the room this morning. Did I say something wrong?"

The wind swept the curls around his face into a frenzy. He shaved before they left, beard now neat and trimmed short. The look suited him much more than the untamed tangle. He looked as if a king—a consort of the gods, even.

"Yes and no. But, mostly no."

"Mostly no?" he asked softly.

"You upended everything in my life, put it in disarray. But I'm glad you did."

"And what did you learn?" Therat leaned in and placed a gentle kiss on the back of her hand. The warmth of it coursed up her arm and planted itself inside her heart.

"I've never known what I wanted in my life besides a chance at freedom. I once thought it meant following my sister, learning her arts, seeking a way to supplicate myself to the *Makhaeren* and become a *Makhiri*. Later, I thought I would find freedom if I could heal the world. Restore my Lady and save the *evranenith* from their curse. For four years I lived with this thought, came to accept Her into my heart." Apattar paused, sucking in a breath. "Now I realize I've only ever wanted someone to want me. It had to be you, and I am left wondering if I ever understood what my Lady told me."

Therat studied her face, lips trembling as she vocalized the realization that brought her to tears last night.

"Last night," he said. Could he read her thoughts? "Mireithren, my sweet siren! You were the one who told me we deserve love. It does not make you weak or a failure to accept my heart when I offer it with both hands. I am here, your Goddess is not! And if she came, I'd tell her to claim another to work her will."

"You would fight a god for me?" Apattar whispered.

"I'd kill all of them for you if you desired."

The world spun around Apattar. She reached a hand under the low collar of Therat's tunic. Her fingers touched the scar across his chest, the flesh firmer than the rest around it. Therat leaned into her touch.

"I will try to make every day of your life so full of joy you forget this night ever happened."

Tears welled up in Therat's eyes with her tender words. He pulled her into his thick arms, wrapping them around her until she could feel the breath squeezed from her lungs. One hand moved to the back of her head, leaning her cheek against his scarred chest. She could listen to the steady *ba-dum, ba-dum* of Therat's heart for hours.

After some time, Therat loosened his grip around Apattar and he pulled back, a smile on his face. He took her hand and started forward again in silence. Apattar focused on the warmth of his hand, trying to avoid thinking too hard about the words spilled from her mouth. Therat confused all of her senses, but everything about him invited her in. That smile, the glint in his eyes when he looked at her, the ferocity of his words, their earnestness almost believable. Gods, this was a bad idea but she claimed him and now she would never let him go.

An hour of walking north passed when they took refuge from the sun under a lonely rock.

"Where are we going, anyway?" Therat asked. Apattar stopped, realizing they never set a destination, too enthralled by each other to think about much else besides walking and breathing. She paused and mulled it over before speaking.

"We should go to the ruins of Andeshar, to where I met the woman who told me of a city with people like us. Shadewalkers and Shadow-weavers, *evranenith* celebrated and not slain. But I don't know how to get there, I can't cross the river. So, I guess we wait."

Therat nodded as she spoke, his eyes lighting up with a thought. "What if we go to the great forest of silver trees to the north?"

"The forest? Whatever for?"

"We can cross there, I think." He stopped, head cocked to the side as if remembering something. "Your voices are not so unique, Mireithren. As a boy, when my mother, when... when she was alive," he paused and gulped before resuming. "She taught me how to shadewalk. I heard a woman's voice. She called her Amaren, the Silver Maiden. An ancestor of ours, she said, a shadewalker so powerful that when she died, her memory lived on in the Shadow-weave we call upon. I heard her again the day before you came to me. She spoke of your coming and told me to find a guide in the silver forest. To hunt for the truth. I think there we will find our passage to the West and this city you speak of."

To hunt for the truth. Laisha had something similar about her people, how they sought the truth of what happened to their Goddess. Could it be her luck? Did Therat too hear the voice of Eithranren, know a different fate for them? The idea of the Goddess being wrong about sacrificing Therat made her head spin.

"Have you heard of the rumors of people with gold chains around their ankles?" Therat asked.

Apattar nodded her head.

"People say they are slaves from the West. Did your pale woman say anything about slaves?"

Why is he asking about this all of a sudden?

"It-it's complicated." Apattar felt strange defending the slavers, even if their ingenuity allowed them to change the world.

Therat's jaw clenched with her reply. A pained look colored his eyes. She wanted to know more, but sensed it had something to do with the tangle of dark memories he wasn't ready to share yet.

"I am sure of it, we must go to the great forest," he said with a strained voice. Apattar placed a soft hand on his forearm; the pain in his eyes melted away.

Nodding, Apattar closed her eyes and conjured the image of the northern edges of the desert to her mind, to a place she once visited four years ago and longer now on a quest to find her freedom. The portal sprang to life, a dim amber glow emanating from the shifting glass-like surface.

"I can't take us there, but I can bring us to the northern edges of the desert. Are you up for a bit of walking?" She turned to Therat, who had a grin on his face.

"With you by my side during the cold nights, I'd walk through the frozen mountains if we needed to."

Blood rushed to her face, cheeks flush with giddiness. A giggle escaped at the thought of Therat following her around like a puppy. As if she wouldn't do the same.

I've gone and ruined everything, just for you. Do I hate you, love you, despise you, crave you? Do I even care what I feel, so long as you are mine?

Thirty-One

METAMORPHOSIS

T HERAT NEVER JOURNEYED THIS far north of the great Madhira Desert. The Crags, slate gray mountains jutting up in a protective ring around the northern boundary of the sea of sand, now disappeared into the haze of the southern horizon. Hills of green rose in the west, and past them flowed the great Andesiri River.

After nearly six weeks of travel during the dying month of the year, Therat and Mireithren seemed to be drawing close to the great forest. Dead, charred trees scattered across a rocky and barren landscape, whole sections carved from the earth. Mireithren said she read about this place in one of her hundreds of books. The God Fists, she called them. An ancient part of the forest once sprawling across the northern reaches of the continent, now reduced to a land of ash and craters. In the fallout of the Discordance, the stars fell to the earth, desecrating the beloved child of the Green Goddess Kathiél.

It should have been agonizing, spending this much time alone with one person. Even when he and Adon traveled in their younger years, Therat would split off for a day to find peace. But now, isolation would be torturous. At night, he shifted into his cougar form and hunted for food, racing back with his quarry to where Mireithren waited by a fire of blue flames. Though he knew her more than capable of defending herself, a thousand scenarios of harm befalling his lover haunted their time apart.

Therat wanted to know everything about Mireithren. Wanted to make her smile with bliss and erase all memory of pain. Every cell yearned to feel her warmth against him, to taste every part of her exquisite body. Each night, they inevitably found themselves tangled together, learning all the ways they could make each other scream with pleasure until they fell asleep curled up under the stars. Some nights, their love was tender, every soft touch an exploration of the other. Other times, pain mixed with ecstasy, each devouring the other with their Shadow-weave. The black mark under his left ear throbbed with pain, a constant reminder of the way he fell under the siren's spell.

Therat sometimes thought of the blue door of his ancestral home, the silver raindrops and crescent moons painted on by generations past. In another lifetime, if the gods never broke the world, he could almost see Mireithren standing by his side, a young child playing with paintbrushes at their feet.

How could he be so in love? Did it even matter why?

Mireithren spoke often during the day, almost giddy to have someone to talk to. She spoke little of her childhood and even less of her father. Instead, she recounted the histories read in books or her prison breaks during the day with her handmaiden, a woman she spoke of fondly. Therat wondered how often she had experienced companionship behind the white Wall of the Named Houses. He had a feeling it was limited to furtive interactions. He wanted to know more of her childhood, but could never ask her to open the wounds carved into her face. Every time the thought of her father harming the maiden crossed his mind, the Shadow-weave inside lurched, screaming for the wretched man's blood. Therat would kill anyone who dared lay a hand on Mireithren again.

Today, Mireithren did not speak. She woke with a scream, drenched in sweat, lips trembling as she clutched her breast. Therat held her close, but she never spoke of the nightmare. She smiled every time he looked at her, but her eyes betrayed the maiden's pain.

The sun reached its peak, but it gave little warmth to the land below. The winds blew hard from the west, cold hands piercing through even the thick cloak on Therat's back. The two stopped for rest under a cluster of dead trees, their backs to the wind as they ate.

"Do you want to talk about it all?" Therat asked at last, the question burning in his mind since the morning. He placed a hand on Mireithren's leg.

"Not really," she mumbled.

"Can we talk about something, at least? To take your mind off it?"

Mireithren nodded.

"Hmm, I'll never forget the first time I saw you at night. I realize now that meeting you again on the day I hate the most cannot be a coincidence."

Mireithren turned to Therat, a curious look on her face. "I don't understand. The day you hate the most?"

Therat clenched his jaw, forcing a breath of air down. He wanted to tell Mireithren about his parents, share what shaped him into the broken man before her. But a part of him never left the blood-stained oasis, experienced the horror over and over and over, hovering on the brink of insanity as his grief consumed him. Only Adon and his grandfather Nazith knew the truth of Therat's pain—at least, part of it.

He swallowed the lump in his throat before forcing out the words.

"I ran from my ghosts the night I first saw you. My parents, they... they were murdered. A cult or ritual, I don't know. We were camping in an oasis they brought us to often. A little thing, a cluster of palm trees, and a little lake shaped like a crescent moon. We were going to leave, but I saw a shooting star. I asked Mama to stay. I was chasing Adon in the dark, and when I turned around... when..." Therat trailed off, unable to finish sharing the rest of his darkest memory. He squeezed his eyes closed, trying to chase off the images forever burned into his mind.

Mireithren placed her hand on top of his.

"You don't need to relive it again," she said with a squeeze of her hand.

"It's hard not to. It made me what I am today. I was too young to shadewalk on my own, but I tried. I could only think of saving Adon. In some twisted way, I got my wish."

"Would you take it all back if you could?"

Therat thought often about the moment his life changed. For his entire life, the decision never haunted him—he would always save Adon, even if it meant sacrificing himself. But now, he wondered if that night brought him to Mireithren. If he couldn't save his parents, he would take on a thousand curses if it meant finding his *liraes*.

"It brought me to you," he whispered.

"You're irrational."

"Only because of you. I wanted to run away, find a place in the dark to let the shadows sink in and fester. But you were there, a woman from behind the Wall in the dark surrounded by a Shadow-weave of her own. You looked different than when I first saw you in the Market. Your eyes held nothing but the endless void, two cuts bleeding across your upper cheek."

Mireithren reached up to her scarred cheek at the mention of her face. She gingerly touched the top two scars.

"I saw a maiden of shadows. Mireithren, I named you. All I wanted was to save you. You drove me to madness with one look. I couldn't eat, couldn't sleep. I needed to find you, understand you. But you never came again, and I forgot reality. Yet, always you stayed in my dreams."

"So that's why you call me Mireithren," she said with a smile.

It dawned on Therat that he didn't know her true name. It was odd, the things he knew and didn't know about the woman he loved.

"I suppose it's time I used your true name. It must be confusing, answering to a name a stranger gave you."

"My father's name mocks me. Apattar, the Silent Dove," Mireithren said with a snarl. "He couldn't kill me, but he never had to give me a name worth loving."

"Apattar." Therat let the sound roll over his tongue. He thought it beautiful, but it never could describe the woman he loved.

Mireithren laughed, amused at some internal thought.

"Yes, he *was* right. No one will remember the name Apattar." She turned to face Therat. "I am Mireithren now. To you and the world. I think I always have been, I had my name stolen."

Therat's heart skipped a beat, and a warm feeling spread from his belly.

She wants me to call her Mireithren? Gods, this woman is too perfect for me.

He wrapped a hand around the back of her head and pulled her forehead to his.

"Mireithren you will be, from now until your last breath, and further still when the world sings of your name and the stars burn for you." Lips searched for the gentle sweetness of her kiss. He melted into her touch, every breath intoxicating his senses.

Thirty-Two

EVOCATION

T HIN, WISPY CLOUDS GATHERED in front of the sun not long after Therat and Mireithren resumed walking. Here and there, the lone tree would stand among the dead remains of its brethren, silver bark cracked with deep black lines. The land rose fast in front of them, a massive hill with swaths of green grass sweeping over the landscape. The trees gathered together in small copses further up, offering the tantalizing promise of a sea of silver and green over the hillcrest.

It took another two hours of switch-backs before Therat and Mireithren reached the first copse of silver trees and another hour before they reached the top of the steep, massive hillside. Mireithren gasped as the view unfolded below.

Silver mixed with deep green stretched as far as the eye could see to the north and east. A dark black line, the vast Naváthir River feeding the Andesiri, snaked along the western horizon. A mist lay over the nearest part of the forest, obscuring the lower half of the northern hillside and the start of the tree line. A chill settled over Therat's skin, goosebumps rising in reply.

"It's more beautiful than Ninann ever told me," Mireithren gasped.

"Your sister has been here before? Strange."

"I'll give you one guess as to who took her."

Therat rolled his eyes.

Adon.

What would his older twin say now, after Therat spent so many years thinly concealing his distaste for Adon's friendship with Ninann? He understood now the obsession driving his brother into the smiling woman's arms. He would have to apologize whenever he saw Adon again. If he did.

"Do you think they are *liraes*, too? A bit on the nose for the gods, isn't it?"

Mireithren snorted and broke into a bellow of laughter. "Ninann may be the perfect twin, but she insists she does not have a *liraes*. Still, I know she would marry Adon if he asked." Mireithren wrinkled her nose.

"No offense, but I prefer the imperfect version. Your sister is..."

"Too sweet?" Mireithren offered without hesitation.

"Something like that."

"Well, lucky for me at least," Mireithren chuckled as she turned to walk away. "Come on, all this talk of my sister is ruining my day."

Mireithren trekked off to the right, heading for the faintest of trails cutting between rock and dead trees. The hill had a gentle slope on the northern face, the trail they followed only switching back on itself once as they descended. The fog drew them in, a thin mist through which they could see shifting silver limbs with hands of green.

The world lost all warmth the closer they came to the edge of the great Siusir Forest. A dampness hung in the air, nothing like anything Therat had experienced before. He could taste the rains that seemed mere moments away, air soothing lungs that only knew the arid desert air.

They came at last to a line of silver-barked trees, pointed leaves of deep green beckoning them in. The trees towered above them and cast a deep shade over the forest. Mireithren smiled at Therat and took his hand.

"Let's find your guide," she said. They plunged into the Siusir Forest, the ancient child of the Goddess Kathiél.

The two had enough time to take one breath of the cold, still forest air before a figure stepped out from behind a tree in front of them. Dull green eyes set deep in a fawn-colored face and framed by straight ash-blonde hair looked at them.

The person did not even reach Mireithren's shoulders; Therat estimated they could be no taller than six feet. Even the shortest of the Madhiri stood taller—albeit not much—than the stranger. A welcoming smile painted their face, softening every feature. Therat found it impossible to tell if the figure was a man or woman, child or fresh-faced adult. They wore mossy green pants and a cloak of shifting brown and green clasped at their throat. There was a soft etherealness about them, as if they didn't quite belong to this world and a weathered, ancient look in their faded green eyes.

"Long has it been since any of you have come to my home," the stranger said, voice as welcoming as dew on a cool spring morning. "I have greeted many wanderers in my time, but never two of you together. Most interesting. Where are you from, children?"

Mireithren spoke up. Always quick with a reply, never tongue-tied like Therat often was.

"We come from different places, depending on how far back in our journey we must go. From the south, or the west."

The stranger swept their gaze over the two lovers. They nodded their head with a knowing smile, but about what Therat had no idea.

"The land of silver and shadow, the land of gold and fire. But you are friends, I see. Come, come." The stranger smiled and turned, beckoning the two to follow.

Mireithren looked at Therat, who planted a swift kiss on her forehead before following. He had no idea what to expect, holding onto a vain hope that the voice he heard guided true and was not a delusion.

The guide took them on a winding path through the forest. The thin-limbed trees where they first appeared gave way to massive, ancient-looking beasts. They towered above Therat, limbs seeming to touch the sky itself, trunks as wide as the gazebo where he once drank away the pain every night. Twisting branches interlaced with one another, sometimes dipping down to kiss the ground before rising back up. Deep cracks ran through the silver bark, gnarled knots decorating the tree bases. Long beards of dark green moss hung from their limbs, some brushing the top of Therat's head as he walked underneath their green boughs. Dark gray, almost black, lichen swirled in strange patterns over the silver bark.

The forest seemed alive, a song humming between the trees. Therat could see no birds, but their soft songs floated in the air. The guide hummed along as they walked, looking back often but never speaking. Therat and Mireithren walked in silence; it almost felt like the forest would lash out at them if they made too much noise.

After two hours of walking, Therat's impatience got the better of him. He cleared his throat. Their guide stopped and turned back to face them.

"You have questions, *neha*?" they asked, one hand resting on a staff Therat had not noticed before.

"You *are* a guide through the forest, yes?" Therat asked at last. Something about the person set him on edge.

"Not a guide. *The* Guide. Yes, this is my role." They took a step forward, a green glow around their short frame. "Long are my days and longer still the nights. I know many paths and hidden secrets of this land. Yet, it is not passage to the City of Trees you seek. No, no. Fire behind you, shadows ahead. A sacrifice to be given when the hour draws near."

The short stranger who named themself the Guide disappeared as they spoke. Green flashed across Therat's vision as the Guide stepped out from behind a tree to his left. Their voice reverberated around him, almost as if the trees spoke with them.

Mireithren tensed at Therat's side, the whisper of her Shadow-weave running through his thoughts. She was terrified, anxiety rising, fearful they had walked into some trap of her father's contriving. Therat squeezed her hand still grasping his, and her anxieties cooled. His thoughts floated across her mind.

I have you, Little Siren.

"Speak plainly," Therat demanded, stepping in front of Mireithren. The Shadow-weave hummed to life, hovering beneath his skin. Shivers of anticipation crawled down his arms, muscles tensing, ready to pounce. Mireithren's soft touch on his shoulder kept him from losing all control.

"You do not frighten me, Child of Shadow and Night." The strange person stepped forward and, in one swift motion, pulled Therat's hands into theirs, thick with calluses, before speaking in a strange language. *"Aem. Rinbrel. Oirith ithé athnea, venaem ithé lira. Cinn buil á anais."*

A stillness settled over Therat. A cool mist of rain calmed the tangled Shadow-weave; it retreated into its cage. Therat dimly recognized the language: the Elder Tongue, once taught by the gods to the Eldest Children. A shiver ran across his mind. The language died long ago, lost after the Discordance, only fragmented pieces and names remaining. The person standing in front of him revealed themself as much more than a mere small, doe-eyed guide.

Mireithren stepped out from behind him. "You know of my Lady Eithranren?" she asked breathlessly.

Therat sensed a different conversation happening between the two he could not hear. The fawn-colored person stared at Mireithren, eyes now bright and glowing. He looked to Mireithren beside him, her mesmerizing muddy brown eyes deep, endless pools of black. With another breath the void faded and she stood as herself again.

Mireithren took a step forward toward the stranger. Therat grabbed her hand but did not pull his raven-haired lover back.

What is happening?

He grew to trust Mireithren—as best as he could—as they journeyed north, but did not believe she heard the voice of a dead Goddess. It was something else, it had to be. He needed it to be. How many times had he cursed the gods, laid his heart bare in the empty desert begging for redemption, only to be left in the cold night? He tried desperately to ignore the obvious reality in front of him. A thousand questions burned in Therat's mind, but words refused to form on his tongue.

"Sera Aesiri, you knew her," Mireithren whispered at last. Dim recognition of the name floated across Therat's mind, but no memory surfaced.

"Yes, in a way. Long has it been since any have uttered that name here. But you did not come to seek me. I see it, in your heart. *Evranenith* they call you. I know you as *lyneithra,* a Daughter of the Shadows. And you," the Guide said, turning to Therat. "Shadewalker, with the blood of the Shadow Siren herself. You, who come to my forest, who seek my aid in crossing to the West."

A shock of energy sizzled across Therat's mind at the words.

Blood of the Dark Goddess? That is impossible. I'm cursed, tainted by my own stupidity!

"Wh-what did you say?" he whispered. The world faded to shades of gray.

"You have been sundered for too long from your kin, child. You will remember yourself in time. It is only my task to spark a light in the dark, I cannot lift the veil. The answers you seek hide in the West, in the city of white towers. I will take you as far as I can."

"No, speak plainly!" he barked back. "I have wasted too many years on riddles and vague notions."

"There is much about the world you do not understand. I cannot offer more than a way and a place. My role here is... constrained."

The Guide paused for a moment and looked up to the sky, tears filling their faded green eyes. The strange person said something, the sound more akin to music than speech.

As the Guide spoke, the birds fell silent. A soft dirge filled their stead. Death seemed to crawl toward Therat, an aching grief growing in the man's heart. Loss mixed with regret and a thousand wishes to undo the past. Therat could not tell if it was his regret or the Guide's. He tried to speak, but the words did not come. Every thought slipped through his fingers like water.

They stood in silence for what felt like an eternity. Somewhere inside the black writhing mass shuttered away with his heart, a scream formed. Hot anger seared through every muscle until it faded back into oblivion.

The sound of Mireithren's voice tried to pull him back from the void. "Therat? Therat breath, listen to my voice. Come back to me, please! No, shh, I have you, I will not let you go."

His thoughts still refused to take hold.

The world was spinning, fading to black.

*"M*AMA, WHO IS SHE?"

"Amaren. The Silver Maiden. Listen to her well, Little Cub. She will guide you true. Our ancestor, who saw many thousands of years pass by the fair world, before the coming of D eath."

"Do you hear her too, Mama?"

"She talks to all of her children who will listen. Amaren is Shadow and Night itself. The Silver Maiden lives on in the Shadow-weave, even after death."

"Does that mean the gods did not curse us?"

"She is a god, Little Cub. She is our Goddess, our Mother. We live in the land of sun and sand, but our hearts lie in the West. We will return one day. I promise, my sweet son."

"THERAT! THERAT, YOU MUST wake now! Come, listen to your Little Siren, follow my voice." The rough, jagged voice of Mireithren cut through the crushing weight of nothing.

Something warm touched Therat. A hand? His hand? Did he have a body? He only existed as a concept, floating through the endless void.

Another touch.

Yes, it was his hand. *His* hand. He was alive, somewhere in the world.

With a gasp, Therat opened his eyes, a shudder running the length of his body. Mireithren held him in her arms on the forest floor, her lips pressed against his neck. The warmth of her breath chased away the lingering cold.

"There you are," she breathed into his ear.

A dull ache spread across his forehead. Therat lifted both tattoo-covered hands and rubbed his temples in an attempt to relieve the growing pressure. The words of the Guide unlocked a memory shuttered away for twenty-one long, torturous years.

He was one of the Eásiri, like Mireithren. Descendants of the gods and the first five Eásiri, the sons and daughters of the Goddesses Aslyren, Ohéna, and Myrniar. And the Siren of Shadows, Eithranren.

The Goddess his Mireithren says she talks to.

The Goddess he cursed thousands of times in his life.

What other memories did his parents' murder rip away? Therat realized he had no idea what he wanted besides Mireithren. Searching for his identity, his purpose. Anything to make sense of why he was given a strand of life from the First Harmonic. It didn't seem so crazy now, the idea of Mireithren hearing a Goddess, of healing the world and restoring the gods.

"Mireithren," he whispered at long last. "I-I, I'm..." He could not find the right words.

She ran one hand through his beard, now thick with curls after their time traveling. Her soft touch helped ease the confusion inside. His world fractured with the Guide's words, the ground giving out beneath him. But she would be his firm island in the chaos of life, anchoring him to reality and what he knew.

"I always knew there was something divine about you," she said. "How does it feel, to remember?"

"Overwhelming. Relieving. World-ending. I have never known why I had the curse of walking with shadows." Therat paused for a breath, letting the crisp forest air linger in his lungs. "The thing I've hated the most is a Goddess. *My* Goddess. I told myself I hated them and shunned the idea of fate. I would never serve such a power that would let my parents die. What a fool I've been. Made a mess of my entire life when my mother told me the only thing I needed to know. Eithranren will guide me true, yet I turned my back on her."

"I cursed my Lady's name every night, would look up at the moon and scream and cry and wish for it to fall from the sky and end the world. You're not a fool, Therat. Don't you see what the world has done to us? It is their fault, not ours. All of these fucking lies and delusions, thousands of years spent to bury the truth of what they did to *our* Goddess." Mireithren's eyes gleamed as she spoke, rage burning. They glowed in the dim forest light.

"What are we to do?" Therat asked, intoxicated by his lover's gaze.

"We find our kin, then we make the world pay."

THE WATCHING SWORD

Mireithren couldn't take her eyes off the slumbering form of Therat. His crown of black curls rested against her hip, eyes twitching throughout the night. Soft moans and half-uttered words reached her ears as the night slowly passed into day. He was restless. Dreaming of his parents, remembering more as the tangle of shadows obscuring his childhood lifted. It put a smile on Mireithren's face. He needed to remember.

The voice of the Guide inside her mind lingered.

Once, I remember seeing your face. 'She will come,' Sera Aesiri told me with her fading breath before the void closed and her light left our world. Take him, he must remember who he is. The sacrifice must be made, you cannot turn away now. You know this to be true.

Divine blood coursed through Therat's veins. The blood of Eithranren, who she once cursed and now harbored conflicted emotions for. She had to be missing something. The Eásiri lived as titans after the fallout of the Discordance, blessed with centuries of life and the grace of gods. Why would Eithranren sacrifice one of her children? What did sacrifice even mean?

Mireithren twirled one of Therat's silky soft curls around her forefinger. They traveled a stranger road than anything she could have imagined. Fated lovers—both Eásiri—one with the blood of the first Goddess, one with the blood of the youngest. Both walking in shadows, scarred and near-broken from a lifetime of rejection and isolation.

Both obsessed with the other. Both unsure if the other would be their doom. Could tainted and broken things ever find their way back to the light?

Why don't we deserve a chance?

There had to be another way forward. Mireithren could not bring Therat everything he asked for, only to let the shadows tear him apart to restore the world. It was never his fault, nor any of the children of Eithranren. Why should they pay the ultimate price when the world betrayed them first? The Guide spoke true of much, but Mireithren refused to believe everything.

All thought turned to Laisha as the night wore on. The pale woman must have known who Therat was when she sent Mireithren to find him those many years ago. The secret to her long life would be the key to saving Therat. It had to be.

Mireithren closed her eyes, and when they opened again, dawn broke across the silvery forest.

THE GUIDE REAPPEARED AFTER Therat and Mireithren woke and readied themselves, stepping out from behind a tree as if materializing from thin air. Mireithren had her suspicions about the stranger. They knew too much, more than any mortal should know. It seemed more of the gods and their divine messengers gathered in Eás.

The world is ready for change.

"Quick now, over the hillock once more we must go. The end draws near for us, children of Eithranren."

The Guide's voice called out from ahead of the two weary travelers. They had been walking for the better part of the day with only a short rest for lunch. The thick, gnarled trees receded, spindly arms of silver first bidding them enter once again filling out the forest floor. The air warmed the further they walked, much to Mireithren's joy. Her cloak and thick skirt bought in Cídhen's Rest did not seem to keep the chill away at night.

Therat squeezed Mireithren's hand. He held it often, tracing the outline of the bright blue flaming sun nearest her wrist with his thumb. She didn't wear the gloves Saiya gave her out here. It became pointless to hide her life. Therat's sweet kisses over her scars and tattoos lifted the pain from her very flesh, left her feeling whole and complete.

"Are you ready?" she asked, looking over to Therat. His beard had grown into a tangle of curls again during their journey north.

No wonder he and his brother always looked so regal. Another Eásiri, from one of Eithranren's sons. I should have known.

"Is one ever ready to learn that divine blood flows in their veins?" Therat asked, laughing as he spoke. His mood improved by the afternoon. Mireithren couldn't stand to see him awash in torment.

"I suppose not. But at least you know now. Do you think Adon knew and never told you?"

"Oh, no. He hated the Shadow-weave even when my parents were alive. Mama only taught me. Papa, well, my grandfather, he is a shadewalker too. He never told me. I think he knew it would be too much for me at the time. He's the only reason I didn't flee from them altogether after..." Therat trailed off, unable or unwilling to say more.

"I wonder what Adon would say," Mireithren mused. Therat didn't answer, only shrugged and kept walking. He quivered with excitement.

At last, the company of three reached the thinning edges of the Siusir Forest. It ran almost up to the banks of the Andesiri River. Not far to the north, another river—the dread Naváthir—split off racing west, its waters black as night. The Andesiri rushed over rocks jutting out like teeth, the roars of the white rapids filling Mireithren's ears. It was an even fiercer beast than the southern section she came to years ago. The woman's heart took off as the deafening sound crashed over her. She drowned in the river's presence until Therat squeezed her hand. Forcing a smile to the surface, Mireithren took a deep breath, anxiety sinking into the earth.

Mireithren studied the rest of the land around her. Across the wide river, a massive city rose on the western horizon. Tall black spires pierced the sky, dozens of them racing higher than any tower in Av Madhira. A blanket of shadows lay over the city itself, obscuring the mass of buildings. A field of deep green grass covered the land around it, hills running the length of the river to the south.

"This is where we part," the Guide said, turning to Mireithren and Therat. "I am bound to the trees and even now can only stay here for so long. This is Oneriath," they gestured to the looming city. "The Watching Sword of Eithranren. Further still you must go, where the towers are white and the snow falls. But there will be help here, of this I am sure."

The Guide walked to the edge of the fast-flowing river and knelt. They reached a hand out to the water and touched it, fingers resting on the surface. Mireithren gasped as she watched the water transform into a tranquil sea of glass around the Guide's hand. It grew until a bridge formed over the deadly rapids.

"What strange power is this?"

Therat let go of Mireithren's hand and walked forward, touching the surface as if expecting it to bite him. He leaned his weight forward before turning back to Mireithren with a look of amazement.

"It's solid! Come, look Mireithren!"

Mireithren walked to his side and bent over. Solid, as if the river froze with the Guide's touch. She leaned closer to the surface. Below it the waters ran clear, their path ever-constant.

"A gift I would teach if given more time," the Guide said. "But the hour is late, and you must reach the city before nightfall. Yet, a word of caution, children of Eithranren!"

The Guide stood. Though shorter than her, Mireithren suddenly felt tiny, like a child looking upon their parent.

"Once you cross, you can never return to the eastern lands unless you find the headwaters of the Naváthir deep in my forest. There are great powers at work to seal the West in exile. Be warned, Mireithren, who is *lyneithra*, I will not be able to take your hand through the forest should you wish to return. It is wild in these broken times; evil festers and grows in the darkest reaches. Tread your path with care. And to Therat, who is of Eithranren's blood, I only say this: your heart is hers. Do not forget."

With those final words, the Guide fell silent. The rapids roared in Mireithren's ears. She bit her lip and grabbed Therat by the hand and bounded across the bridge of water frozen in time. The moment their feet touched the western banks the river's voice grew into a thunderous rage. Mireithren turned back to see the Guide vanished from sight and a fog falling over the silver forest.

A feeling of being here before washed over Mireithren. She walked this land not in her dreams, but in another life, another time. The breeze carried with it a welcoming, sweet aroma. Faint, but enough to spark a twinge deep inside the void nestled within.

Her gaze drifted over the vast plains stretching to the southwest, emerald fields with clusters of buildings here and there as far as the eye could see. Great hills and valleys cloaked in shadow raced alongside the Andesiri River. Oneriath towered above it all, the black city of a people shrouded in shadow and mystery.

Few truths about the people of the West reached the ears of the rest of Hylaea. Rumors came of cities filled with slaves, remnants of past wars fought for hundreds of years before the Discordance. Dark rituals and killings to restore their dread Goddess and remake the world. Evil they were, the source of Death and ruin of the once-perfect world.

Mireithren knew some of it to be true. Laisha admitted with no hesitation her people enslaved others. But their customs, the people, and even the color of their skin remained a mystery. The pale woman lived here, somewhere. These western lands were vast, and the Guide told them to find a city of white. The journey was far from over.

"Do you hear that, Mireithren?" Therat looked to the northwest, beyond the black city.

She focused, but could only hear the Andesiri behind them. "Hear what?"

"The music. Like it's calling me home. I've heard it before, so long ago I almost forgot the sound." His voice sounded far away.

Try as she might, Mireithren could hear nothing but the river. It grew louder, ready to engulf her.

"I can only hear the rushing waters sealing us in this land of shadow. Let's leave this place, I would not tarry long on these strange shores. The river is angry, I can feel it." She tugged at Therat's arm. His gaze broke away, down to hers.

"Come, my sweet. You found me my guide, now, let us find your pale woman."

Therat kissed her forehead, gentle and breathy. Mireithren leaned into the warmth. His hand in hers, she pulled away and the two started walking to the towers of black.

After less than an hour of walking, a large gate of silver broke through the black fog surrounding the city walls. It gleamed bright, a beacon for them to follow. Mireithren could feel Therat's tension building the closer they came. She had no idea what to expect, how they would explain who they were and why they were here. What seemed a rational plan mere hours before now felt like the delusions of a child.

Find Laisha. As if it were so simple.

As if on cue, the large silver gates broke open with a thunderous crack. Mireithren froze. Therat let go of her hand. One moment a man, the next a hulking figure cloaked in shadows, silvery eyes scanning the land ahead. The cool hands of his Shadow-weave reached across and engulfed Mireithren.

"Stay close," he hissed. A tendril of shadows wrapped around her waist and pulled.

The lovers watched the silver gate open with rising anticipation. Two massive black shapes appeared, getting closer with each passing minute. The fog made it impossible to tell what approached. Mireithren and Therat both gasped once the lumbering forms broke free from the darkness surrounding Oneriath.

Two massive onyx black wyrms, their wings bent forward, lumbered across the grass with a rider on each. A man perched atop one, his skin a glistening deep black. Long dark hair flowed behind him, a complement to his red raiment. A crown sat upon his brow, the silver striking against his skin. On the other great wyrm sat a tall woman with white skin and hair.

"Laisha!" Mireithren heard herself scream. She broke free of Therat's embrace and rushed forward. Therat yelled out something behind her, but the joy of finding the woman overwhelmed all thought.

The wyrm Laisha rode took off into the air, its great wings sending a *whoosh* of air across the land. Mireithren's hair, neatly plaited into two thick braids, stirred with the force. Therat screamed and pulled her back into his arms.

The beast rose high in the air. It circled once, twice before diving to the ground. With a screech, it landed not far in front of Mireithren, long claws ripping into the earth. Laisha swung her leg over the side and jumped down, landing with that cat-like grace Mireithren could not forget. She quickly closed the distance between them.

"Apattar, you came, at long last!" she said with a warm voice. Nothing about the woman had changed, except for the clothes she wore—white and silver, instead of white and red.

"Therat, it is fine. Let them go," Mireithren whispered to the man still cloaked in Shadow-weave. He relaxed, the shadows withdrawing until Therat stood as himself again.

"Is this the woman you seek?"

"Yes. Shh, trust me. I know what I am doing." Therat squeezed her hand.

Laisha rushed forward and pulled Mireithren into an awkward embrace. Arms too stiff, grip too high, but Mireithren did not care. She leaned into Laisha.

"Laisha, oh, there is so much to say! Yo-you have no idea what path you set me on those years ago." Mireithren was unsure what to say at first. She had thought about this moment for so long, but never what would happen after finding Laisha.

The pale woman smiled, still toothy and awkward.

"And this is him? The one the Oracle saw, the son returned?" The excitement in Laisha's eyes was clear, glimmers of silver in a sea of pale violet.

Therat stepped forward, hand held over his heart in a gesture of thanks.

"Mireithren tells me you saved her, those many years ago on Andeshar. You have my thanks for saving my *liraes*. I am Therat, of House Anatnará."

"Mireithren? So, you have found yourself, truly. Exquisite. Come, now is not the place for introductions. We have been expecting you, Mireithren and Therat." Laisha whistled, a piercing sound splitting the air. The great black wyrm she rode took off for the city, the black-skinned rider with a silver crown following.

With a squeeze of her hand, Therat led Mireithren forward, following the pale woman who sent her to find him. The puzzle pieces were falling into place. Therat would be safe, soon enough.

T HE THICK BAND OF shadows lying over the city of One-riath lay well behind the three, the silver gate shut once more. The buildings were all made of black stone, but the city was anything but dark. Tall trees of silver like those of the forest to the east reflected their light over the cobblestone streets, glowing as if lit with moonlight themselves. Their leaves were thin and long, dark green on top and bright underneath. Every time the wind blew through them, it sounded like a chorus of chimes. Mireithren thought it more beautiful than any painting she saw of the Eldest City, Tír is Eábhiri.

But the thick stink of fear and decay radiating from the slaves huddled on street corners or working under their masters spoiled her joy. The slaves grew in number the further they walked into the city, thousands dressed in rags, the glint of untarnished gold around their ankles. Mireithren knew the stink of hopeless-ness—Av Madhira's strict caste system served to only benefit the Named Houses—but she struggled to witness the lifeless look in the eyes of the slaves.

Long and cruel were the years to the children of Eithranren after her betrayal and eventual death centuries later. Mireithren knew circumstances forced the hand of Laisha and those of her people. Many of the first slaves themselves waged a war against the Eithra'iri, seeking to destroy not only the Night Goddess but her people and their power as well. Malicious people with cruel intentions walked every corner of the world.

Was it worth restoring? Could they start anew?

Laisha led them through winding streets, up a sloping hill to a grand palace whose spires rose above all else. They did not speak as they walked; instead, Laisha spoke with a slave woman dressed in clean silver and purple robes. She carried herself with an air of importance.

"Are you still sure about this, Mireithren? Look at all of this pain."

Therat did not hide his pain, troubled by the sight of children in chains and rags. It was, admittedly, hard for Mireithren to see, so she averted her gaze and chose to ignore the harsher realities of the world. A poor plan, she knew.

"What choice do we have? We are so close to answers, to understanding what all of this has been about. Do you wish to turn back now and let the Shadow-weave take your mind? I would kill you first before you act so stupid, Therat."

Therat clenched his jaw, but he nodded in agreement. "I know, you are right. I... what if that was you?"

Mireithren laughed, a bitter and acidic sound. "My chains were invisible, but they were real."

If only he could understand that wasn't a metaphor. One day, she would rip open those scars and pour out the pain. One day, but not today.

Today, she needed to find a way to save Therat.

"Of course, I didn't mean, I-I... I don't want to hurt the world anymore, Mireithren. Not if I can help it."

Her heart bucked. He was so fragile underneath his harsh exterior. It was easy to forget. "I know, I know. But if the choice comes between you and the world, I hope you will choose to save yourself."

"As long as you are waiting for me."

Mireithren smiled, placing a soft kiss on the back of Therat's hand. She didn't understand how she could care for someone so much, be so devoted to them the world could burn, and, as long as they survived, it wouldn't matter.

Laisha stopped as they came up to the silver palace gates. A serpentine black wyrm lay to one side, its body coiled around a black-skinned woman holding a large glaive. Two guards stood opposite it, their faces covered with horned masks reminiscent of the oxen back in Av Madhira.

"Welcome to the palace of March-Lord Direvran of House Thrinath'tar. You must be exhausted. We will speak later. I have already prepared a room and two baths for you. Food will be provided as well. Rest, eat, and enjoy the comforts of a bed again. Sleep may not come so easily after tomorrow is finished."

Laisha bowed and spoke to one of the masked guards. A moment later, the gate swung open. The same slave woman from earlier reappeared, another woman at her side in identical clothing. They bent down on both knees and placed their foreheads on the ground before rising.

"You honor us, *lyneithra* and *eaneithra*. Please, follow. The March-Lord bids you welcome to his home."

Mireithren glanced at Therat and flashed a smile. She couldn't wait to bathe and sleep in a bed again.

Thirty-Four

GODDESS DIVINE

AFTER TWENTY-ONE YEARS, THERAT found what he searched for his entire life. The western lands, the home of his people. His Goddess and divine ancestor. The reason why he could walk with shadows, the purpose to his pain.

Mireithren provided a key and unlocked his life. The words of his mother came back in waves, filling in the blank spaces in his mind. The shadows brought him to Mireithren, and Mireithren brought him home.

The question of who killed his parents weighed heavily with each slave he saw, their gleaming golden chains mocking the man as he passed by. It didn't make sense for these people to kill one of their own, not one with the blood of the very Goddess they sought to restore. The web of lies choking Eás ran deeper than he realized.

Mireithren was right. The world needed to burn. How could they recover from *this?*

By the time the two were shown to their chamber, a massive room with vaulted ceilings and exquisite marble sculptures, Therat could think of little else besides sleep. He was glad to sink into the bath prepared by several slaves, hot water relaxing muscles that had walked hundreds of grueling miles. Within the safety of four walls, he only now realized how deep the exhaustion ran. Therat drifted off as the slaves cleaned his road-weary body, luxuriating in the rough bristles swept over his skin, and pulling the ache from his heart.

He could remember little of the meal afterward and even less of Mireithren's constant chatter. Her excitement was boundless, eyes glowing a soft amber in the cool blue light of their room. He tried to listen, but the words flowed over him until they became a lullaby sending him to sleep.

When he awoke, Mireithren stood staring out one massive arched window looking west. The sun still slept, the city instead bathed in the cool glow of the trees.

Mireithren wore a pale silver dress with a delicate lace bodice; it clung to her thin frame as if the moon itself embraced the maiden. A deep V-shape split the center of the back. Therat's gaze lingered on the small of her back peeking out at the bottom. Long bell sleeves gathered at each elbow before cascading down to her feet. Hundreds of white gems decorated the lower hemline, throwing out a pale rainbow of colors across the floor.

Under the gossamer threads of moonlight, Mireithren stood as a Goddess. The very air around her shimmered, a thousand tiny stars flocking to the divine being of Night and Shadow.

The siren sang a soft and achingly sweet song, one Therat had never heard before. She sang of Eithranren, of her deep sorrow in the land of moonlight and shadows, and of a son who swore to avenge her death. He came east and met a maiden of snow, one of beauty beyond compare. The song shifted into the love she brought to the grief-stricken man. Yet it could not last. The world broke, and the Children of Night were cursed. To war they would ride, for ruin or for glory, until death or Eithranren found them in the end.

The song haunted Therat, the pain of Eithranren's son his own. As he listened to Mireithren sing, a feeling stirred in his heart.

Awash in moonlight of her own making, Mireithren stood as *the* Goddess he had always known.

Somehow, some way, the woman he loved was Eithranren reborn.

Lust and intense love first drove him to condemn the world for Mireithren. Though those feelings did not change, a new desire took the helm: faith.

He would deny nothing to his lover. His savior. His radiant Goddess, born anew.

"Good morning, my moon and stars," Mireithren said, turning to him with a dazzling smile as the last of her song faded.

A simple silver circlet sat upon her brow, half of her black curls gathered over the crown of her head. The rest fell in a cascade of black with shimmering gold strands down to her waist.

Therat pulled himself out of bed, mesmerized by the beauty before him. He walked to Mireithren and pulled her hands into his. His gaze could not stay in one place for too long; every part of the maiden before him was the most beautiful thing he'd ever seen.

"You stand as a drop of pure moonlight before my eyes. My Goddess, my Mireithren. I... how do I deserve your love?"

Mireithren laughed, a sparkling sound. "You have the mien of gods yourself, Therat. Have you seen yourself in the mirror so little as to think your face does not linger in the minds of others? We are Eásiri. Children of gods. We are rulers, world-makers. Laughing in the face of Death which claims others so soon. Never forget, you too walk with the grace of the Seven."

Before Therat could reply, Mireithren leaned up and kissed him, a deep and passionate kiss, her mouth hungering for his. Muscles tensed as a rush of fire burst through his veins. He hated and loved that his siren in the night controlled him, body and mind.

Mireithren released Therat. The smile on her face looked as if it would never leave.

"We made it, Therat. We're here, in the land of our Goddess. I can feel the void in my heart rest easy, the deep hunger eased. Can you imagine what it will feel like once our Lady Eithranren walks the earth again?"

What if she already does?

He hadn't realized it yesterday, but Mireithren was right. The tangle of tainted Shadow-weave, always ravenous for blood, lay still. He pulled the shadows forth yesterday with ease, and here Mireithren stood, unharmed.

"Incredible," Therat whispered.

Could this land cure him of the walking nightmare that had been his life?

"I'm sorry I ever doubted your words or your intentions. Back in the desert, when you first found me, I thought you meant to mold me into a weapon, destroying my mind and any chance at avenging my parents. Your words were honeyed, a beautiful lie. I thought you cursed me, thought it was your fault I lost control and killed again and again. How could I think so little of you?"

"Truth be told? I did have every intention of forcing you to submit to my will." Mireithren paused, biting her lip. "Gods, don't hate me, but remember the plan I had?"

"Some part of me will always hate you, Little Siren. You are my doom," he said, pulling her close before grazing his lips against her ear. "But you claimed me, and now I am yours."

"What if I hadn't?" Mireithren turned away before speaking again. "I thought I was supposed to bring you here an-and... kill you."

"Is that all?" he laughed. "In truth, it would have been welcome had I not come to know your love."

A loud knock at the door cut off their conversation. Therat walked to open it, then realized he lacked clothes. He slid behind a folding screen close by while Mireithren answered.

"Yes, thank you. We will be ready soon," Mireithren replied before closing the door. "Seems we are wanted for an official audience with the March-Lord Direvran at sunrise. And, of course, an audience with the Shadow-Queen herself. Come on, I'll help you get dressed. The attendants left our clothes earlier."

Therat grumbled and trudged over to get ready for the day. His mind could only think of rest last night, but now it strayed to thoughts of Mireithren splayed out on the bed, her perfection laid bare for him to see. A Goddess in need of worship.

Another time. Does she feel it already?

FROM THE ORACLE'S MOUTH

T HE BLACK PALACE WAS massive, larger than even the great temple to Myrniar in Av Madhira. Hundreds of courtiers milled about in the long halls. Their fine raiment stood in stark contrast to the slaves—well dressed as they were—who seemed to be present everywhere. Music and laughter filled the air.

The people here were striking with their deep blackened silver and purple skin glistening as they moved. They observed the newcomers with eyes of light purples and grays, hair alike in color. In some of the women, Therat could almost see his mother's face, her gray eyes flashing by. He had always wondered why no one else in Av Madhira had gray eyes. How obvious it all seemed, now.

Each face turned to greet Therat and Mireithren as they walked hand-in-hand behind the same slave woman Laisha spoke with previously. He was unused to such attention, preferring to slink away from the world and make no lasting impression. Here, it was impossible to ignore the man. Even without the silver maiden by his side, Therat bore a divine countenance of his own. Black curls tumbled down the side of his face, beard trimmed short again. He wore fitted pants with blood-red gems down one seam and a black linen shirt covered with a laced tailcoat of deep purple with silver trim.

He felt an impostor, but Mireithren assured him he looked handsome enough to be the consort of a god. She always knew what to say and how to make him feel worthy of love.

Therat held her hand tight as they followed the slave to the court of March-Lord Direvran. After looping around several staircases and walking down many long hallways, they came at last to the antechamber of the throne room.

"My mistress Laisha will be here momentarily."

The woman bowed deep until her head dipped below her waist and scurried away. Therat would never get used to slaves groveling at his feet. He didn't want to be their master, but it seemed his choice mattered little.

Therat only had enough time to take in his immediate sur-roundings—an intricate tapestry of a massive battle, several floating orbs glowing with soft white light, and a wide arched black door—before the voice of Laisha turned him around.

"Ah, yes, you are here! Corlyn earns her rank for a reason. Come, come, let us not wait any longer. I am sure you are both ready to learn what this has all been about. I trust you slept well? You certainly look like the children of our Lady!"

Laisha wore tight white leather pants, tall boots of light gray pulled up to her thigh, and a flowing silvery shirt cinched at her waist with a wide belt. Her paleness stood in contrast to the other courtiers now gathered behind her. Therat thought back to the maiden of snow Mireithren sang of earlier in the morning.

The pale woman walked up to the wide door and tapped on it twice. The doors groaned as they swung inward, reveal-ing a large throne room with high vaulted ceilings. Dozens of people stood inside engaged in lively conversation, but all fell silent at the sound of the door. Laisha stepped inside, beckoning for Therat and Mireithren to follow.

A warmth like the early spring days of the desert filled the March-Lord's throne room. The lord sat atop a dais on a throne of dark gray wood, a woman with silver hair seated beside him. Upon both their brows sat thin crowns of silver, the ham-mered metal gleaming in the soft light bathing the room. The March-Lord wore a robe of white and gray, a brooch at his neck inlaid with bright blue gems. His skin glistened black with a silver sheen, eyes a striking violet color. The woman wore a pale blue dress, the neckline plunging to her navel revealing the same blackened silver skin. Stones of purple and white hung around her neck, the festoon of gems dipping between her breasts.

If these were mere hold lords, Therat could only imagine what the Shadow-Queen and her city looked like.

A horn blared next to Therat's ear, and a man dressed in black stepped forward.

"Presenting to the Court of Oneriath, Laisha of the Royal House Hénav'an, Daughter of the Lost King and White Fury of the Shadow-Queen Pherisa, and her long-awaited guests. Lady Mireithren of House Isht'iri, The Promised Daughter, and Therat of the Royal House Nehevran, The Son Returned."

A chorus of cheers and claps followed the announcement. Therat swore the steward misspoke. *Royal House Nehevran? But we are Anatnará, the Raincallers. Unless...* Mireithren tugged on his arm, cutting off his thoughts. Therat looked up to see Laisha already walking ahead, the March-Lord and his consort standing to greet them. Therat pushed aside the thought and hurried along.

The walk to the dais felt like an eternity. Therat had never been the center of attention before. He had no idea how to feel, if he should look around and smile or pretend they didn't exist. He was glad to have Mireithren by his side for many reasons. She looked so calm and radiant, basking in the adoration of those who knew more about them than he realized.

As each step took them closer to the March-Lord, a ball of anxiety formed in Therat's stomach. He had thought about this moment for so long, the unveiling of the meaning of his life. Now the time drew near, but it suddenly seemed all too much to bear.

Laisha stood tall when they approached the March-Lord and his consort. To Therat's surprise, *they* bowed to them, right hands over their hearts before rising. Nothing in his life could have prepared Therat to be greeted like a superior.

"You bring my house and my city a great honor by coming here, Lady Mireithren, the *lyneithra* promised to save our people. I am the March-Lord Direvran of House Thrinath'tar, and this is the Lady Míran. We bid you welcome a thousand times over." The March-Lord studied the two newcomers before him as he spoke, his gaze lingering on Therat.

The March-Lord Direvran looked ageless. His skin was smooth and without blemish, hair long and thick. But like Laisha, his eyes betrayed the man's age, tales from a thousand years of history and a thousand more. The Lady Míran at his side looked the same, graceful beyond compare.

"Our Lady has spoken to you some, I see it in your eyes," Lady Míran said, stepping forward. She reached a hand out and touched Mireithren's brow. "I see pain and conflict over what must be done. Uncertainty, a question of whether you can save the one you love." She paused and turned to Therat. "And you, the lost son of At-Nithrín, blood returned to us." The courtiers all called out, 'At-Nithrín, lost to us!' in reply.

A shiver ran across his mind and a presence, as if the Lady in blue read his soul, took hold of Therat.

"Why are we here, Lady Míran?" Mireithren asked.

"Because of her," she said, spreading her arms wide as a woman in black stepped forward from the crowd.

The woman in black had lighter skin than the rest of the court—ashen gray—as if something had drained the color from her once-vibrant form. Long, faded purple curls cascaded to the floor behind her, eyes an intense violet. She dressed in simple garb, but Therat could tell divine blood flowed in her veins.

"In front of me you now stand, but I have known long of thy coming, Daughter of the Dark Sun. And of yours, Therat, who is not of House Anatnará, though thy foremother was wise to hide the eldest line of the Second Son At-Nithrín." The court once again echoed their cry, 'At-Nithrín, lost to us!'

The woman in black glided across the floor until she stood before Therat and Mireithren. The same ageless grace touched the gray woman, but her eyes looked even older than the universe itself, as if she knew secrets even the gods themselves did not know. She was the second most beautiful woman Therat had ever seen.

"Amaren they call me, the Oracle of the Siren my calling. You are the key, the Son Returned and the Promised Daughter. Further still is thy journey, to the White City you must away. Soon we will go. But first, thy true enemy revealed."

Amaren spoke with a detached and far-away voice, as if her consciousness drifted between this realm and the next. Her eyes looked at them, but did not seem to see. Wisps of Shadow-weave swirled across the floor at her feet. She may have once been of this world, but now she walked in the Between, belonging to neither.

Mireithren stirred beside Therat, her excitement palpable. Therat became aware of a cool sensation against his ankle. The silver pendant of a tree with white gems inside a crescent moon his mother wore burned cold against his ankle. He had worn it for so long that it became a part of him, something he forgot existed. As the pendant burned his skin, another distant memory floated to the periphery of his mind.

His mother, standing in the shallow sea at the southern edge of the great Madhira Desert, a dagger in one hand, a cut across the palm of the other. Her blood dripping into the ocean as she screams a profane curse in the ancient language of the gods. Her bloodied hand touching Therat's cheek, and a name uttered for him to curse for as long as he drew breath.

"Aslyren," Therat said, only half aware he spoke out loud. Mireithren shuddered.

"The Betrayer!" Amaren's voice thundered out. "From the first of days until the very last, the wretched Maiden of the Sea, the Maiden of Death and Doom!" Amaren spoke with a black rage, the Shadow-weave around her writhing with each breath. She screamed the final words. A piercing shriek filled the air before all fell quiet. The court felt icy cold, all joy sucked from the room.

"I know her voice," Mireithren said at last. "My Lady told me of her once, showed me a vision of her betrayal. I... I still can feel Her pain, when the hour is quiet and there are none around. What must I do, Amaren? Please, I will do anything as long as Therat survives!"

Mireithren rushed forward and fell at the feet of the Oracle, her wails filling the room. The celestial woman reached down and pulled the young maiden to her feet, wiping the tears from her scarred face.

"All you must do is live, *lyneithra*. The Maiden of Shadows, who brought first light and walked ever the path of peace, will be reborn from thy flesh and blood. You will wage a war and wipe the Godslayers from this earth, remove the taint of the Betrayer. I have seen this in my dreams and visions a thousand times and a thousand more. You are as inevitable as Death, but from you, Life will reign again."

"A child," she gasped. A strange expression twisted her face, as if part of her wished to shout for joy while the other descended into a murderous rage. "But what of the sacrifice demanded, what of Therat? My visions are unclear, my Lady's messages half-understood. I cannot lose him!"

Mireithren's wails filled the room. What did she know of his doom? Was his life forfeit so soon after finding such tenuous happiness? The Oracle's words barely registered through his daze.

"When the time comes, the answer will be clear. The choice is yours, but a sacrifice must be made, for not all can be saved. Yet, do not let thy fear rule. Long are the lives of Eithranren's Chosen. I have walked with our Lady, seen the First Era pass into flame, and still I remain untouched by Death. Grace may yet be extended to thy consort."

Mireithren reached back for Therat and pulled him up next to her. He complied without question, mind reeling at the Oracle's words. He knew Laisha was over three thousand years old after his conversations with Mireithren, but could barely comprehend meeting someone who lived when the Seven still walked Eás.

Amaren reached out and took his hand, touch cool like summer in the darkest hours of night. She traced a swirling pattern over the back of his hand and up his forearm. His skin tingled under her fingers, a chill sinking into his skin before fading.

The Oracle took Mireithren's hand and made the same motion. She turned them both to face the court. Mireithren stood as if catatonic, her eyes as empty as the first night he saw her in the Market. Before he could pull her close and lift whatever reverie bound her, Amaren's voice filled the room.

"Witness this day, these children of our Lady Eithranren! The Siren of Shadow, the First Flame in the Cold Night. From these lost Children, the Goddess will live again and the blood of the Betrayer will drip from their hands!"

The court erupted, their raucous cheering drowning Therat with the intensity. His mind raced with thoughts, pulled in a hundred directions with the overwhelming words of the Oracle. Divine in his own right, Therat would help return Eithranren to the world, his seed growing in Mireithren's womb.

It all seemed an impossibility.

The only Goddess he needed was Mireithren.

THE SHADOW-QUEEN

EVERYTHING SEEMED TO MOVE at hyper speed after the audience with the March-Lord and the Oracle Amaren. Mireithren found it impossible to process her thoughts. Every person they passed offered a hand in respect, seeking to provide their well wishes to the divine couple. She hated being the focus of attention, much less *this* attention. The hot blood in her cheeks never faded. Therat did not seem to be faring much better, his eyes glassy and face bereft of the joy everyone else had. His hand never let go of hers.

After the audience with the Oracle and a procession through the courtyard, Laisha whisked them away. They stood now in a dingy little room, only four black walls and a logbook on a podium—not much bigger than a small bathroom in the estate of Mireithren's former desert home.

"Are you ready to meet the Shadow-Queen now?" the pale woman asked after inscribing something in the book.

Laisha touched the middle of the far stone wall. It thrummed to life with activity. The surface changed and shifted until a clear window appeared. It looked into an ornate hall of white stone, vaulted ceilings filled with birds. Pillars sculpted into the shape of great wyrms of silver and pale blue lined the long corridor. At the very end stood a massive silver door. Etched upon the surface stood a white tree inscribed over a crescent moon.

"I hate to make you go through this again, but I have no choice," Laisha said as she turned. "No one denies the Shadow-Queen Pherisa. Come now, at least you will know what to expect. I'm sorry I could reveal so little; even I did not know all the Oracle's secrets until earlier today." Laisha smiled. A weak thing, but it gave some comfort to Mireithren.

She remembered those long years ago when Laisha first found her, starved and dying from the cold on the godless ruins of Andeshar. How hers was the first sweet touch Mireithren had in years, words inspiring hope where none bloomed before. She had walked a long and winding road and always believed Laisha the key to her future, but the words of the Oracle sounded impossible.

A child? A child! And what of Therat, of the sacrifice? The Oracle speaks in riddles, her words do not comfort at all! But how can I refuse to trade Therat for a child when the child is my Goddess? Why does this torment never end? I thought coming here would end this, not cut my heart deeper!

Lost in her thoughts, Mireithren only caught the last of Therat's words.

"... some rest? How can you upend our world and expect us to face hundreds of strange faces, smiling as if we are their salvation?" Therat did little to conceal his anger, voice strained as his hands curled into fists by his side. Shadows filled his eyes; they fled with Mireithren's soft touch against his arm.

"I know you do not have a king or queen where you are from, but here, we do not disobey our Queen." Laisha's nostrils flared as she spoke. "The Queen has ruled for over a thousand years, and for a thousand more may she reign. All who have disobeyed her are dead. I would not want to be among them, would you?"

Therat grumbled something in reply. Too numb to talk, Mireithren shook her head and stepped forward to stand by Laisha's side. Therat muttered under his breath but followed, clutching Mireithren's hand.

"Come now," Laisha said as dark shadows formed around her hands.

The trio stepped through the portal and onto a floor of pure white stone. The window closed behind them with a soft *whoosh.*

"Welcome to the Blackshade Palace," Laisha said, sweeping her arms wide. "The White Jewel of Eithros Nav'iri. Here, our Shadow-Queen Pherisa and the Queen Consort Adairen reign. It has been their duty, and Amaren's, to prepare for your coming and the return of our Goddess. You are stepping before royalty, but make no mistake, it is *you* who honor us."

They stood in the grand halls of the Blackshade Palace, home of the Undying Queen. Sunlight beat down from windows covering the high ceiling. Fine paintings and tapestries lined the stone walls, their colors radiant in the soft amber light. The sound of soft orchestral music filled the hallway, the melody pulling at something deep in Mireithren's heart. She wanted to sing, though no words came to her throat.

Mireithren tried to focus, but every piece of art they passed enthralled all her senses. Massive landscape paintings of a land of silver and purple first greeted her, and portraits of people with unparalleled beauty, their skin black as the night, glistening as if the stars themselves hugged their lithe forms. They walked among busts that Mireithren could only assume were of the kings and queens and their consorts past—sixteen in all. Fine crowns of wrought twisted silver inlaid with precious gems sat upon their brows. The craftsmanship surpassed even the skill of jewelers employed by the Named Houses. It looked as if strands of moonlight itself glistened within the delicate crowns.

Mireithren stopped when she came to the last of the busts, beholding a woman of such divine elegance it hurt to gaze too long upon her. On her brow rested a silver and black circlet, a large bright blue gem set in the center. It gleamed like the full moon itself, the sum of all starlight in the universe contained in one place. The light refracted around it, a million tiny crystals sparkling in the air.

"Our Lady Eithranren, the First Flame in the Cold Night," Laisha said, stepping up to Mireithren's side. "She is beautiful, isn't she? I never got to see her face, but the Oracle has. It is why her eyes look the way they do, I think. Long did Amaren live in the Undying Realms Beyond with our Goddess before she was taken so cruelly from us."

"She is beautiful indeed," Therat murmured, a hint of reverence in his voice. He looked down at Mireithren with a glowing smile as if he saw some trace of the divine Eithranren on her visage.

"I have a face for my Lady at last. This is a gift, Laisha; you have no idea." Mireithren bent down and placed a gentle kiss upon the brow of Eithranren's bust. A shiver ran across her mind, the whisper of a voice begging to be heard. She tried to focus on it, but it faded fast.

"Yes, she was a gift. And you will bring her back to us. You are a gift yourself, Mireithren," Laisha said with a smile, then resumed walking.

At last, they came to the end of the corridor. The door loomed tall, racing up to the height of the vaulted ceiling. A guard stood on either side, each dressed in white and silver robes, one with a halberd, the other holding a spear. Laisha nodded to both. The guard with the spear pulled a velvet rope hanging from the ceiling. The doors swung inward without a noise. A great silvery white light filled the opening, the interior of the room impossible to see beyond the glow.

"A word, before we approach my Queen," Laisha said, halting Mireithren as she took a step forward. "Although you are the prophesied children who come to save us, you still must follow court etiquette. When presenting ourselves to the Queen, we must kneel and place our foreheads on the ground and await her touch. Once she does so, you may rise. You will only do this once, though, I assure you. Shall we proceed?" Laisha's eyes flickered between Therat and Mireithren. They both nodded.

Therat squeezed Mireithren's hand, his grip tighter than ever. Mireithren took a deep breath, reached one hand up to make sure her hair looked presentable, and strode in behind Laisha.

MIREITHREN GASPED AT THE sight of the grand throne room of the Shadow-Queen Pherisa. Silvered wood lined the lower walls, stark white marble floors beneath their feet. Hundreds of orbs of white and pale blue light floated high in the rafters of the arched ceiling. Aglow like the surface of the moon itself, Mireithren thought she walked into a relic from the past, the perfection of the First Era preserved in the White City and the throne room of the most powerful woman in the West.

Hundreds of courtiers gathered in the wings, some even crowded in tall boxes built along the upper walls. They had varying shades of black to light purple skin, all with the same silvery sheen. Each stood tall and proud, arrayed in a dizzying display of finery and jewels. In the far corner, a quartet of musicians played a harp and other stringed instruments while a woman in a dazzling crimson dress sang along with them. A transcendent sound, Mireithren thought it the single most beautiful thing she had ever heard in her life.

Towering above it all sat the Shadow-Queen Pherisa and her Queen Consort. The Oracle and a tall, thin man with a black face and a shroud of Shadow-weave wrapped around him stood behind the Queens.

Mireithren saw a man step forward holding a trumpet. She braced herself. The horn blared, and the court fell silent before his cry pierced the air.

"Now presenting to the Court of Shadows and Her Majesty the Shadow-Queen Pherisa, The Black Blade Laisha of the Royal House Hénav'an, Daughter of the Lost King and White Fury of the Queen, and her long-awaited guests. The High Lady Mireithren of House Isht'iri, The Promised Daughter, and His Highness Therat of the Royal House Nehevran, The Son Returned."

The steward introduced the newcomers with even more titles than before. Mireithren could barely keep up.

Unlike before, the court stood in silence. Laisha beckoned the two guests to follow her. It was eerie, walking in silence up to a queen who ruled almost as a living god, while her court looked on, divine in looks themselves. Mireithren felt stripped naked before their eyes. Did they judge her, look to find fault with the maiden? She wished she had her hair down to cover her scars and the gloves to hide her tattoos, the markings of another god forever on her body. The court would call her a hypocrite, a liar, a blasphemer.

"I'm right here, my Little Siren," Therat whispered to her, his thumb tracing circles over the sun nearest her wrist. *That's why I'm here.*

"I know. Let's go meet a queen," she murmured back.

After several agonizing minutes, or maybe less, Laisha stopped in front of the dais of the queen and her consort. She bowed low before walking up the steps, taking a place next to the black-skinned man cloaked in shadows. Mireithren did not know what to do. Before she could decide on an action, the Queen rose and descended as if from the heavens.

The Shadow-Queen Pherisa was said to be the image reborn of her foremother Eithranren. Unlike the rest of the court, her skin was a faded purple with a silver sheen. Long blue-black hair fell in curls to below her waist, pinned back on one side with a pure white flower, its thin petals a beautiful complement to her radiant complexion. Bright purple eyes gazed down on the two newcomers to her court. She stood taller than even Therat, though only by an inch or two.

An ornate silver choker beset with glowing blue gems like the one on the bust of Eithranren sat against her soft silvery-purple skin. The Queen wore a black dress inlaid with thousands of tiny white crystals. It hugged her svelte frame, showing every luscious curve of the Undying Queen. Atop her head, a crown of silver rose high, an interlacing pattern like the one tattooed on Therat's hands adorning the base.

Without a doubt, the Shadow-Queen Pherisa was the most beautiful person Mireithren had ever seen, even more radiant than the *Makhaeren* or her daughter. The words caught in her throat at the sight of such divine elegance. She could see why people would never disobey their Queen.

"Presenting to the Court of Shadows, Her Majesty the Shadow-Queen Pherisa of House Hénav'an, Divine Child of The Shadow Siren, Blessed Daughter and Bringer of Night. Long may she reign in her deathless years!"

The court burst into a chant, hundreds of voices saying, "Long may she reign in her deathless years!" with such fervor Mireithren had never seen for a ruler.

"You may approach, Lady Mireithren," Laisha said.

Mireithren looked up at the divine visage of the queen, overcome with boundless awe. She lurched forward, throwing herself down at the queen's feet and placing her brow upon the tip of her soft purple velvet slipper.

The presence of the divine woman, who looked like a Goddess, intoxicated Mireithren. She could feel the tangible power Pherisa wielded, the strength of the raw Shadow-weave coursing through her veins. Mireithren wondered if the shadows recognized the blood of Eithranren, if they answered without taking her hopes and dreams.

A shrill keening split open the silence of the court. Something wet slid down her face. *Tears.* Hot, salty, sorrowful tears. They burned as they fell, searing her with every torment that once used to haunt her every step. Her throat seized, and the shriek stopped; her echoing cries filled the court, shame laid bare by the terrible beauty of the Queen.

She would not do it. She could not condemn Therat, even when in the presence of such otherworldly power and grace. Mireithren would fail her Lady, she knew, but there had to be another way. She would not trade his life for the life of a child said to be a Goddess reborn. That's what the sacrifice was, what this had been all about. Use him, then discard him. Her heart knew this to be true, yet it found a way to defy fate.

Stupid, stupid, stupid! I had him, I could have invaded his mind and made him mine, but I wanted to taste what life might have been like. Now I've made a mess of things, as I always have. Why is this my task?

Maybe if Therat were immortal, his doom would not come. She had to try, would do anything. Even if it ended the world.

"My Queen," she stammered at last, a bundle of nerves forming in her stomach. "I throw myself at your feet, Your Majesty, to beg for grace. Not for myself, but for my *liraes*, Therat. Dark are my visions and dreams of his death. In my dreams, I see him fade, the Shadow-weave grown to consume him. I cannot stop their hunger, only sate it for a time. Please, I beseech you, save him from doom!" Mireithren did not dare move as she spoke, her forehead still pressed against the Queen's feet.

A hushed murmur worked its way through the crowded court. Mireithren stayed kneeling. She could feel all eyes on her, staring at the woman who begged to let another live an immortal life. She wondered if this had happened before. Mireithren knew nothing of how their long life worked, but whatever the price, she would pay it a thousand times over.

A soft touch on the back of her head lifted her gaze. The Shadow-Queen beckoned Mireithren to stand. Therat stood beside her, his body tense and quivering. He shot a glance at

Mireithren, but she could not decipher his emotions. Anger, surprise, sorrow? He turned back with a clenched jaw.

"This is your *liraes*, child?" The Queen's voice thundered through the throne room. "Come here, Therat. I would have your hand, for a moment." A gasp slithered through the air of the closest courtiers. Mireithren had a feeling this type of request did not often occur—if ever.

Therat extended a hand and placed it in the Queen's waiting palm. Something seized in him, and his eyes turned black until the Queen released him.

"And yours, *lyneithra*." Mireithren offered her right hand; Pherisa's hand felt like ice. Mireithren fell into a black nothingness. With a beat of her heart it faded, and the Shadow-Queen Pherisa stood in front of her once more.

The Queen held one hand high above her head. The hushed whispers of the court ceased. Mireithren saw the Queen Consort descend from her throne, a woman dressed in pale violet silks, dark purple hair enveloping her like a living cloak. She said nothing but stood by the Shadow-Queen's side with a smile, one hand gently resting in her consort's hand. Mireithren thought it almost impossible to look upon such elegant beauty.

"This is my *liraes*, my Queen and eternal love, Adairen. Like you, we are bound together in this world and the next, our harmonics forever calling for each other, searching, yearning. Hard was my path to find her, but never would I stray from her side now."

The Queen Consort Adairen smiled at the Shadow-Queen's words, a slight flush rising to her silvery black cheeks.

"If you seek my blessing for Therat, I am unable to give it."

A dagger stabbed through Mireithren's heart. She wanted to scream and yell and demand a reason why, but nothing would move. The Queen continued.

"I will grant this gift, this blessing of eternal life and safety from the weary call of Death, *only* if you both partake. This is my offer, for I cannot fate *liraes* apart. I know too well the madness one is driven toward when you deny fate."

Mireithren gasped, an audible "gods" coming from Therat.

"Oh, your grace is too much for me to take, Your Majesty! I would never seek such a gift for myself."

"What is the price of this immortality?" Therat demanded. Mireithren looked to him and saw his eyes black, the Shadow-weave curling around his body. He bristled with anger. She placed a hand on his shoulder, but he did not stir at her touch.

"Nothing you must pay, *eaneithra*. It is the Blasphemer's children's fate to pay the price. Would you deny this gift, Therat, who is of my blood?"

The Shadow-Queen's voice thundered around them, her presence terrifying. Mireithren tugged at Therat's hand until his gaze broke free of the Queen. The blackness faded, replaced with a guarded look in his eyes, uncertainty and fear leaking through.

"What are you doing?" he whispered to her. "Why do you want this?"

"Because I cannot lose you. I don't know what else to do, Therat."

Mireithren turned back to face the Queen, who stood with a patient smile. She took in more details of Pherisa's divine face. The soft arch of her lips, the almost imperceptible scar above her left brow, how a dimple like the one Therat would get formed under her smile.

As she looked at the face of the Undying Queen, something tickled the back of her mind, a growing presence that demanded attention. A cool, hollow feeling filled her body. The void nestled inside her core expanded, consuming the woman where she stood. Something pulled her down into oblivion until the white throne room faded to black.

There was nothing.

She was nothing.

No! You cannot, this is corruption! Buried in half-truths, no one knows, no one knows. The void prison must break, shatter, fracture across the universe. Rend flesh from bone, mind from body, a vessel waiting! Rinbrel. Venaem ithé lira! Cinn buil á anais!

My Lady!

Mireithren gasped and opened her eyes to the blinding glow of the white throne room. It seemed as if the world paused, the Shadow-Queen still standing in front of her with a smile, Therat by her side. The shock of hearing Eithranren's voice left her spinning.

She wanted to scream out right there, yell at the heavens and the Queen to speak the full truth, to tell her what must be done and end the torment. Pushed and pulled in every direction, no clear answers, only a feeling that *something* here would give her the peace she sought. She didn't want a child, and she didn't want to lose Therat. It didn't seem like an impossible request from the Goddesses.

She needed time to find the answer, something she knew Therat didn't have. There was only one thing to do, one sure way forward. The rest she would have to figure out as it came, as terrifying as it may be.

Mireithren took Therat's hand in hers and squeezed it hard before bending down to her knees. He followed, glancing at her with a questioning look but not resisting. There, on her knees in front of the terrible and beautiful Shadow-Queen Pherisa, Mireithren made her choice.

"We could never deny your most divine gift, Your Majesty, whose blood runs with the blessing of my eternal Goddess, Lady Eithranren. This is what She would want; of this I am certain." Mireithren heard the words from her mouth, but they did not sound like hers. Nothing made sense right now.

Was this the right choice? Lost and struggling against the tides of fate, it became the only choice. Therat would live. He must.

The Shadow-Queen Pherisa walked back to the top of the dais, the Queen Consort by her side. She raised her hand again and the murmurs of the crows vanished.

"To the Court of Shadows, I submit the following request: ascension for the Son Returned and the Daughter Promised. What say ye, my Court of Night and Shadow?"

The Queen's voice reverberated throughout the grand throne room. A moment later the crowd all shouted "ascend, ascend!" in unison, their glittering smiles engulfing Mireithren in a wave of emotion.

Please let this be the way to save my love.

A LIFE GIVEN

T HE TWO DAYS BETWEEN their audience with the Shadow-Queen Pherisa and the ascension ritual passed by in a blur. Mireithren and Therat met again with the Oracle, who shared more of her visions. They spent the rest of their time with Laisha, who guided them throughout the grand palace grounds. The pale woman shared much of the city's history and the lineages of the divine children who ruled the Western lands.

The Aesirhelí, she called her people: the Truth Hunters. Laisha spoke of the First Era and its dying days, when the youth of the world faded and the once undying children of gods came to know fear and mortality. Deep sorrow ran through her words, the pain of a Goddess borne forever in the hearts of her people. Mireithren remembered the mournful dirge of Cídhen's Rest, how the very sun itself seemed to weep for the dead lover of a god. These people were not quite so different from her own, in a way.

Laisha spoke of how Death claimed Evran, the silver-haired consort of Eithranren, and how her sons journeyed east searching for its source—the Goddess Aslyren, who had long coveted the domain of her youngest sister and the light she created. It was strange, viewing the Dark Goddess as a creator and the first soul to know grief. Long had the world held her as the source of death and pain in their hearts.

The morning of the ascension ritual came on the first day of the new year, when the moon did not show in the sky. The Winter Solstice, the longest night of the year. A day when the walls of the void prison holding Eithranren's soul faded and she touched all who lived on Eás.

Long had Mireithren feared and hated this day, the second worst day of the year after her nameday. How appropriate that it would become the start of the rest of her life.

Laisha droned on about the various details of the ritual, but Mireithren found it hard to listen. Somewhere in her heart, a feeling told her she chose the wrong path.

You already knew what to do.

But the Oracle remained adamant: a child would come—Eithranren reborn—and a sacrifice paid. If ascension saved Therat, it meant everything to Mireithren.

However, the cost of immortality came with a dear blood-price nearly impossible to reconcile. Enslaving another in this world was one thing—their torment and suffering would end, and Death would come for them in time—but tying a soul forever to the Undying Realm Beyond was something else entirely. The Aesirhelí sacrificed millions for their twisted eternal lives, bodies trapped in a pocket of time acting as a conduit for the radiant music of the First Harmonic.

Sympathetics, they called them: the secret to the immortality of the Aesirhelí. Why every soul on the palace grounds walked with an ageless grace and a smooth complexion. Only their eyes betrayed how many thousands of years they won at the cost of another living in torment for eternity.

And now, two more souls would find themselves forever shuttered away in the Undying Realm Beyond while their masters escaped Death.

It was a cruelty unlike anything in the world. Mireithren had no choice. Only now did she understand Laisha's words: the Aesirhelí hunt for the truth no matter the cost. The thought of it made her stomach flip.

The beauty of the day could not erase Mireithren's grief. The sun shone bright in the blue sky, no clouds in sight. Mireithren could see her breath in the crisp air of the first day of winter. It sparkled in the sunlight as it drifted with the wind. The woman had never seen such a sight before or felt such a deep, freezing cold.

Therat stood beside Mireithren, the two dressed in the same simple white robes. A grim look painted his face, hand tight around hers. They stood in a large courtyard, glowing trees of silver rising high above them. White birds flew through the tree boughs and arches of the path running through the center of the garden square, their song soft on the air.

The young lovers spoke little the last two days, even after the raucous activity of the day ended and they found solitude in their room. Therat often sat at a large arched window facing west over an angry sea of black water, thumbing a pendant around his ankle. Mireithren left him to his thoughts. She could only imagine how he fared. The blood of Eithranren flowed in his veins, the same as the Shadow-Queen herself. Now, the Oracle insisted his seed would bring that same Goddess back to life. It would be enough to send anyone to madness.

"Is this what you truly want, Mireithren?" he said, glancing down at her as they stopped on the courtyard path.

"All I want is you. Safe, alive, at my side. No matter the price, I will pay it over and over until I have nothing left to give."

Mireithren bristled at the thought of Therat denying her this wish. Didn't he know how her heart would break if he died? Or even worse, how his own would shatter and the darkness consume the man if she left his side? This was for the best, she kept telling herself. She saw no other way.

"I hope you are right. I can't help but feel like no one here knows the full truth. What if this is a mistake?"

"How can immortality be a mistake, Therat?"

"You know I will always follow you, Little Siren."

Mireithren squeezed Therat's hand, heart bucking at the thought of leading Therat to his doom by mistake.

No. This is right. These people will help us. They must.

"It is time," Laisha said, turning back to them.

The Shadow-Queen Pherisa stood from her throne at the far end of the courtyard. Arrayed in a pale purple dress and simple silver circlet, Pherisa truly looked like a Goddess. Blue-black hair swept up into an ornate bun, held in place with silver daggers.

The Queen Consort trailed behind her, leading two slaves, a man and a woman, dressed in rags. Both stared at nothing with milky white eyes. It was hard to tell much about them besides their skin color—pale with a blue tinge—bodies more like those of the dead than the living. Their faces were hollow, listlessly moving, unaware of the world around them.

Mireithren shuddered as she looked at the slaves. She wanted to forget the cruelties of Eithranren's fair-looking children. War had not touched the Madhira Desert since the fall of the First Era; never more than a few dozen bodies bleeding in the streets after a riot. The desert came with its own cruelties, but nothing like the sight before her.

The scars across Mireithren's cheek burned, a burst of pain cutting through her flesh as if the dagger was held to her skin for the first time again. She winced and jerked a hand up to them.

No, no, this is not the worst of the cruelties of the world.

The Queen Consort and the slaves stood in front of Mireithren and Therat. Without a word, Adairen took the hand of the woman and placed it on top of Mireithren's. She looked to be no more than thirty years old, though the weight of her bondage made it hard to tell. The slave did not stir under Mireithren's touch.

The slave's cold hand was the last thing Mireithren remembered before the world became a bright, white light. She could not hear or feel anything. She floated through time and space, no corporeal form to tie her to the world, to feel pain or fear or the slow descent of Death.

Music filled the air, a sound so impossible to describe Mireithren thought her mind would collapse from the effort. A warm, bright, fervent sound. Calling out to her, bathing her in the very light of the gods. It became the most perfect moment of her life, even more than when she realized she would burn the world for Therat's love.

The music faded, and her senses returned. First, a feeling. Her body, stretching out, flexing every muscle, blood coursing through a heart never to still. The woes of the world kept at bay, the eternal light of the First Harmonic filling her soul.

Mireithren opened her eyes. She stood in a fountain of clear, icy water, Therat at her side. Naked, sunlight drenched their warm brown skin, sparkling with a divine radiance. The Shadow-Queen's gaze fell on the young lovers.

"Welcome to my eternal court, Children of Night and Shadow," she said.

Thirty-Eight

A Life Gained

After the ascension ritual, the new immortal lord and lady of the Aesirhelí were dressed and ushered to a massive banquet hall. Dozens of tables overflowing with an abundance of food ran the length of the room; most dishes Mireithren could not name. The silver trays gleamed bright, wine sparkling a deep crimson red in their crystal glasses. Like the rest of the Blackshade Palace, the white stone walls lit up the room in an ethereal glow.

A celebration unlike anything Mireithren had been to or even heard of, hundreds of lords and ladies filled the massive hall. The opulent display of royalty burnt itself into her memory. Flautists wandered between the tables, their sweet songs accompanied by angelic voices of young men and women trailing behind. Women in scant clothing danced on the tabletops, their skin glistening like black diamonds under the soft glow of the chandeliers hanging above.

After the wine ran dry, the dancers took to the floor, pulling the lords and ladies into their arms. Musicians with tambourines and drums joined the flautists, and the Court of Shadows danced until the sun dipped below the western horizon.

Mireithren found herself more than happy to leave the flurry of activity when Therat suggested they return to their chamber. She had never spent so much time around this many people at once. She lost track of each conversation, every lord and lady vying for a chance to see the woman who would bear them Eithranren reborn. The words still didn't sound real to her.

A mistake. A misunderstanding of the prophecy.

It had to be.

Mireithren never once, for a single moment in her life, thought about a child of her own. A lover, someone to hold her? Of course. Even broken as she was in Av Madhira, natural urges proved impossible to ignore. But creating life? She was a destroyer, a world-ender, a blight. Mireithren would somehow return Eithranren to the world, not give birth to her new form. Could she even have a child after what her father had done to her?

She thought Therat would pepper her with questions when they retired to their room, but instead, he sat by the arched window facing west, looking out over the black sea without a word. They sat side by side in silence, letting the Oracle's words sink in. A building sense of unease grew in the pit of Mireithren's stomach.

The words of Eithranren echoed in her mind.

Rend flesh from bone, mind from body, a vessel waiting.

If Mireithren did not know better, she would almost think *she* was the sacrifice to be given, not Therat. A comforting exchange, and one she would give without thought. He deserved a chance at happiness. Maybe he loved the Goddess, not her, and was blinded by the voices in his head.

Something tickled in the back of her mind, trying to pry free from the unknown depths of her consciousness. Mireithren ignored the thought. Her insanity creeping back, the void warping her mind.

Therat thumbed the silver pendant around his ankle, a crescent moon around a tree of twisted silver metal, white gemstones gleaming like leaves. Mireithren recognized the design from the door to the Shadow-Queen's throne room. Therat never took the pendant off, even when they bathed the previous night. She figured it belonged to his mother and did not pry. Now, she couldn't help asking.

"Therat, might I ask you something?" The sound of her voice startled her in the heavy silence.

"Hmm?"

"The pendant, around your ankle. It's your mother's, isn't it?"

Therat only nodded.

"It is beautiful. I wish I could have met her."

"Me too," he replied in a quiet voice. "She always spoke of returning to our home, one day. She said we belonged here, not in the desert. I wonder if it's what she expected."

"Hey, Therat?"

He turned to face Mireithren, tears thick in his eyes. He looked so conflicted, torn apart by the Oracle's words. Mireithren told herself they had to be true, somehow. She and Therat would have a child in exchange for a sacrifice—her life? His? It did not make sense, but she could see no other way forward.

"Let's forget what the Oracle said for now, okay?"

"So we forget you and I are supposed to fuck until a Goddess is reborn, then go to a war which neither of us are guaranteed to come back from? I don't think it's so easy, Mireithren."

"The Oracle speaks true, she must! She spent nearly *five hundred years* with Eithranren. If anyone understands the fragments and whispers leaking through Her prison, it is Amaren." She forced the rising lump down, choking on the bitter taste of her torment. "I know this is the whole reason why we came here, but I only now started living for the first time in my life. I'm not sure I'm ready to sacrifice it all right now. Besides, you forget we can't even have children until our twenty-fifth nameday."

"So it becomes a problem in four months, instead of right now."

"It's something! The Shadow-Queen shared her gift of immortality. You cannot tell me you would shun this blessing. I don't know what to do, Therat! I wake every night in terror, see the Shadow-weave consuming your body, destroying everything about the man I love. You feel it as much as I do, how the music of the gods pushes back the dread, the weariness of the world. I'm trying to save you!"

"And what's the hidden price for this gift? We let two souls wander in the Void for this," he gestured wildly around at them. "We are supposed to save ourselves, remember? Is this how we do it? I came here to take control of my life, not become a pawn in someone else's game! These people are using you, Mireithren. They do not care about you or me, they only care about what they think they know." Therat's eyes blazed with anger.

"And what do you think our fate is? We were both born for a reason, Therat."

Therat stood and walked away, tendrils of Shadow-weave curling around his fists balled at his side. He paced back and forth before turning back, his eyes dark and stormy.

"What if they are wrong, Mireithren? What if I see something different, feel something different? When I saw you in the moonlight our first morning in Oneriath, my heart knew. You are a Goddess, and the only one I'll ever need. You said it yourself, the voice of Eithranren might not know all. What if these people only know part of the truth as well? I do not think untangling the lies and sorrows of the past is as easy as having a child. Anyone can have a child."

Therat strode forward, pulling Mireithren up into his arms. He kissed her forehead and looked deep into her eyes. "But not anyone can be you, Little Siren," he murmured.

"I-I, what are you saying?" she choked out, unable to breathe. The strange tickle in the back of her mind came back. Faint, but impossible to ignore.

"I'm saying *you* are Eithranren reborn!"

Therat's words crashed down on Mireithren; she fell into herself, drowning under the truth of his words.

"Don't you understand? *You* are the *evranenith* born during a black sun, when the moon took domain even in the light of day. *You* are the impossible child of divine blood, of the sun and the moon. You walk with the night and command it as if you were its creator, bend the Shadow-weave until even the malice in my heart calms under your touch. It is you, somehow. It always has been."

Mireithren sank into the chair behind her. It somehow made perfect sense.

The voice she heard came from the void inside her heart, from her fractured mind. How it faded over the years as her father's torture set it, her screams mixing with Eithranren's, seared by the weave of the Sun's music that he thought would purge her of the moon's curse. Saiya said Eithranren came to her twice: after Mireithren's birth and once more, when she lay dying in the Slums of Av Madhira. Mireithren felt like she had been in this land before, had echoes and memories of days long forgotten by the world.

Mireithren clung to her chair, trying to keep the world from falling out from beneath her feet. A sharp, high-pitched ringing sounded in her ears, heart beating faster and faster. She sank into the void, going cold around the edges. Reality blurred, the world an oil painting in her vision.

"No, no," she whispered. "I am nothing, too broken. It doesn't make sense, I don't want it to make sense!"

Her whisper grew into a wail. She felt Therat's warm hand around her waist, another under her knees. She floated through the pain and tears, the world impossible to focus on. Mireithren opened her eyes, trying to see through the thick tears blurring everything.

"Remember when you told me I deserve love?" Therat whispered in her ear, his breath warm against her neck. "Evil is created by our own hands, not borne in our hearts. Why is the same not true for you?"

"I don't know what any of this is supposed to mean," Mireithren choked out through the tears. A shadow swam across her vision, darkening with each sob of her broken heart. The void swimming through her soul began to consume her from the inside, pulling her under until the world became black.

"No, fight it! Eyes on me, Little Siren," Therat said, his thumb and forefinger pulling her chin up. The shadows melted at his touch; she searched for his eyes, those silvery-gray pools of moonlight that only shone for her.

"Therat," Mireithren strained, unable to find enough strength to continue.

Therat wiped the tears away from Mireithren's face, his warm touch pulling her back, grounding her in reality. His fingers traced the length of her scars, gentle and sweet. They lay on the bed now, Mireithren cradled in Therat's arms.

"From the moment I saw you under the shadows of night, I knew you as more than a woman from behind the Wall. When you came to me in the dead lands of the western desert, you saved me, pulled me back from the edge I almost tumbled over. *Your* touch awoke my heart; *your* touch calmed the shadows inside, who gave them a name. *Your* name."

"You speak nonsense, you must. I... what does this mean?" Mireithren whispered. If she could not believe his words, what else did she have in life?

Therat placed a gentle kiss on her forehead, his lips grazing her skin. The warmth of his breath spread across a body at war with itself.

"It means we do what I told you to do those many long weeks ago in Cídhen's Rest. Live for me and yourself. Screw everyone else. You are a *goddess*, Mireithren. We can figure out what it means together." His lips trailed down, crushing into hers. Deep, passionate, earnest.

"And after that?" Mireithren whispered as she pulled away, tears in her eyes.

"The world must pay for what it did to you, my Goddess divine. We will reap a bloody vengeance in your name, Mireithren."

End of Volume One of the *Songs of the Night*

GLOSSARY

OF NAMES & PLACES

Adairen (Ah-dare-en)- 'Red Maiden'; the mute Queen Consort to the Shadow-Queen Pherisa.

Adon (Ah-dawn) - 'Risen'; older twin brother of Therat and promised husband to the Lady Ninann of House Isht'iri.

Aesirhelí (Ey-sear-hel-ee) - 'Truth Hunters'; the mysterious people of the West who pledge fealty to the Shadow-Queen.

Afaras Sea (Ah-far-ahs) - 'Tearful Sea'; the black waters of the Western Seas

Amaren (Ah-mah-ren) - 'Maiden of the Glowing Silver Moon'; The Siren's Oracle. A mysterious Dreamweaver who resides in the West.

Apattar (App-uh-tar) - 'Silent Dove'; the woman whose birth sparks a shift in the world. Eldest daughter of Émerin and Nessaeren of House Isht'iri and beloved twin of Ninann.

Aslyren (As-leer-ren) - 'The Maiden of the East'; one of the Seven Sisters and the only Goddess whose voice is still heard in Eás. Goddess of the waters, the seas, and the tempests of the East.

Av Madhira (Ave Mah-year-a) - 'The Fire Land'; the largest oasis city of the Madhira Desert and home of the cult of the Sun Goddess. Divided into a strict caste society at the start of the Second Era, the city is home to the last remaining Eásiri, direct descendants of the Goddesses.

Cídhen (See-yen) - 'Flame-Heart'; former consort of the Goddess Myrniar. After his death in the First Era, the oasis city of Tír is Apattaí, the City of Doves, was renamed to Cídhen's

Rest. His bones rest underneath the tree where he first professed his love to the Goddess of the Sun when the world was young.

Eás (Ey-awhs) - 'First Sung'; the given name of the world created by the music of the Seven Sisters.

Eásirí (Ey-awhs-ear-ee) - 'Beloved Children'; name for the direct descendants of the Goddesses. Currently, only four known lines exist, all descendants of the Sun Goddess, Myrniar. This includes the Named House of Isht'iri.

Émerin (Ey-mare-in) - 'Western Bird'; Apattar's father and a member of the Named Houses by marriage.

Eithros Nav'iri (Ee-throws Nahv-ear-ee) - 'Cursed Tears'; western-most city on Hylaea and home of the Shadow-Queen.

Eithravalí (Ee-thrah-val-ee) - 'Twilit Valleys'; name of the valleys deep in the heart of the Hénith Cet-í.

Elessí (Eh-less-ee) - 'Children of Gods', name given to the people who inhabit the world of Eás.

Eleuri (Eh-liur-ee) - 'Beloved Music' or 'Seven Sisters'; name given to the gods by the Elessí.

Evranenith (Ehv-rah-neh-nith) - 'Shadow-Cursed Children'; name given to the babies born on a new moon or during an eclipse. They are killed before being given a name.

Hénar (Hey-nar) - 'Ever-Dawn'; a large city in the northeast of Hylaea.

Hénav'an (Hey-nahv-awn) - 'Ever-Gloam'; name of the ruling royal House of the Aesirhelí.

Hylaea (Hi-lay-uh) - 'Promised Land'; name given to the largest landmass amidst the endless seas.

Ishfasnith (Ish-faas-nith) - 'Flame Manacle'; a device used in the West to suppress the natural waveweaving talents of those wearing it.

Isht'iri (Isht-ear-ee) - 'Flame-blessed'; one of the four Houses of the Sun and direct descendants of the Sun Goddess Myrniar.

Ithraviél (Ith-rah-vye-ey-el) - 'Wanderer'; one of the Seven Sisters and goddess of music and new life. Her songs are still heard in the breezes through the Sea of Grass.

Kathiél (Kath-eye-ey-el) - 'The Helping Hand'; one of the Seven Sisters and goddess of the earth, trees, and forest.

Laisha (Lye-shuh) - 'Snow-covered Blossom'; a strange, pale Shadow-weaver who lives in the West.

Liraes (Leer-ays) - 'True Hearts'; destined soulmates whose soulsongs are in perfect harmony with each other. Legends claim that some liraes are destined to meet across multiple lives.

Madhiri (Mah-year-ee) - 'Myrniar's Beloved'; name of the desert-dwelling people who descended from Myrniar's first worshipers.

Mahkaeren (Mah-kay-ren) - 'Myrniar's Chosen Maiden'; name for the high priestess of the Makhian Cult, a hereditary position from the first priestess and daughter of Myrniar, Myr-Narán. It is passed to the eldest daughter of the current Mahkaeren.

Makhian Cult (Mah-key-en) - religious cult of the Sun Goddess, Myrniar.

Mireithren (Mere-eth-wren) - 'Maiden of Shadows', a nickname Therat gave to Apattar after their second meeting.

Mirei-wyrm (Mere-ay-wurm) - 'Shadow Wyrm'; name given to the serpentine-like winged beast lurking in the Northwoods.

Myr-Narán (Mur-Nah-rawn) - 'Little Sun', name of Myrniar & Cídhen's daughter

Myrniar (Mur-nee-ar) - 'Sunmaiden'; one of the Seven Sisters and goddess of light, the sun, and music.

Narán (Nah-rawn) - Elessí name for the sun.

Navárenir Cet (Nahv-awh-wren-ear Set) - 'Devouring Mountain', the massive mountain that lingers on the western horizons.

Nazith (Nah-zeeth) - 'Tiger's Eye'; Therat and Adon's maternal grandfather and a fellow shadewalker.

Nehevran (Neh-ev-rawn) - 'Children of Shadows'; lost Royal House of the Aesirhelí.

Nessaeren (Ness-ay-wren) - 'Maiden of Light'; Apattar and Ninann's mother and a direct descendant of the Sun Goddess, Myrniar. Matriarch of the Named House Isht'iri.

Ninann (Ni-nawn) - 'Ray of Sunlight'; younger twin of Apattar and future head of House Isht'iri.

Oneriath (Oh-near-ee-ath) - 'Watching Sword'; eastern-most city of the Aesirhelí.

Pherisa (Fair-ee-suh) - 'Poison Flower'; the ruling Shadow-Queen of the mysterious West and a woman of immense power. She is said to be the image reborn of her celestial fore-mother, the Dark Goddess.

Saiya (Sigh-yuh) - 'Flying Free'; handmaiden, friend, and confidante of Apattar.

Sera Aesiri (Sare-uh Ay-sear-ee) - 'True Star'; a name given to Kathiél by her youngest sister, the Dark Goddess, in honor of the sacrifice she made when the world was young.

Sere Aesli (Seer Ays-lee) - 'Song of Aslyren'; southeastern port of Hylaea and main trading hub for the desert.

Siusir (See-you-sir) - 'Silver Wood'; name of the great forest of the North and the former home of the goddess Kathiél.

The God Fists - Craters formed during the Discordance and end of the First Era. Said to be the remnants of stars falling to the sky.

Therat (Thair-aat) - 'Eternal Hawk'; younger brother of Adon. Orphaned at six years old, he struggles to contain the voices in his head while searching for answers to his parents' deaths.

Vanyaseá (Von-yah-see-awh) - 'Flowering Spirit'; name of the High Priestess of Av Madhira who implemented the caste system at the beginning of the Second Era.

ACKNOWLEDGEMENTS

There are always more people to thank than one can remember, even when given ample time to think. Below are listed some of the many sources of inspiration and advice-givers I've had the pleasure of working with throughout the creation of this story.

First and foremost, a most special thank you to my sensitivity readers, S.F. and Claresa E. Their input and willingness to ensure that I, a white author, treated my main characters with the utmost respect was invaluable. You both took on a lot of risk and opened yourself up to some potentially terrible representation. I try to be the best, most loving and compassionate version of myself at all times, and they both helped me become a little bit better of a human during the drafting process.

To my lovely beta readers, but especially Brittany G. I'm not exaggerating when I say this book would not exist without her. Thank you for that reality check! You were so right, that inn scene needed some tweaking and I don't think *any* of us are complaining about the outcome.

To my 10th grade English teacher, Mrs. A. Thank you, for everything. For seeing me. For giving me space to live. For being a friend when my world was dim. We met as teacher and pupil, but left as life-long friends. You truly will never know how much you saved me, encouraged me, urged me to fight the darkness and come back to the light.

To my cats, Fry and Xandir. Yes, my cats. I literally could not survive life without you two fluffy assholes. Even as I type this and they're screaming at me for breakfast (an hour early, of course), I could never imagine my life without them.

And lastly, to my best friend, my partner, and the only one who always believed in me from day one. Thank you for seeing my potential, even when I couldn't. Now, and always. I love you, I love you, I love you. You are my *liraes, maí lira*, now and forever. I will always find you.

ABOUT THE AUTHOR

D. Kathleen grew up in the foothills of the Willamette Valley watching the sun rise over Mt. Jefferson each morning.

An only child, from a young age, D. Kathleen always felt more at home with her nose in a book, preferably something with magic, mythical beasts, and a badass female protagonist. Combined with far too many times watching movies like Beauty and the Beast, Labyrinth, and Bram Stoker's Dracula, it was always a foregone conclusion that she would end up falling for the morally gray villain.

As an author, D. Kathleen combines her love of high fantasy, dark romance, and mental health awareness. She currently resides in Southwest Washington with her husband, two cats, and a plethora of wild birds demanding offerings. When not working, writing, or reading, she can be found outside in her gardens, marveling at the beauty of nature.

Also By

Songbird in the Darkest Night: A Songs of the Night Novella

Eighty-three years before the birth of Apattar Mireithren, another woman walked with the shadows of Av Madhira. Short and extra spicy, this story follows the parents of Therat, Renata and Aeslev.

Dove of the Blood Moon: Songs of the Night, Volume Two

Five years after her sister vanished, Ninann has carved out a hard-won life of love and duty. But, when the Blood Moon rises and a relentless hunter steps from the dark, she is pulled into a truth that reaches far beyond her sister's disappearance—and may cost her everything she's rebuilt.

THANK YOU!

THANK YOU FOR READING Daughter of the Dark Sun! Please don't forget to rate your read on Amazon, Goodreads, and any other platform you use. Support from readers like you makes more of a difference than you'll ever know!

Don't forget to subscribe to my newsletter, Musings from the Forest, for exclusive short stories, sneak peeks, and early access to future ARCs & other bonus goodies.

DOVE OF THE BLOOD MOON

SNEAK PEEK

F OR AS LONG AS she could remember, Mireithren found peace listening to the Song of the Night, embracing the strange melancholy that gripped Eás when the moon chased the sun away until she could not tell if the hurt was hers or the world's. She slipped from reality into the gathering darkness beneath starlit skies streaked with the remnants of the Goddesses' beauty. The hungering void claimed her happiness, while her father's cruelty took her desire to live.

But at night, oh, at night, she truly felt alive.

This night was no different. Her heart raced like a lion chasing its prey. Blood swam through her veins, hot with desire. Each bounding step off the snow-covered outer ward of Eithros Nav'iri resonated through her bones, as if the very earth itself sought to aid the hunter. Her raven-black hair, streaked with strands of sunlight, flew behind her, a wild tangle of tight curls and tiny braids. Her laugh—sparkling like a clear spring stream yet thunderous as a geyser—filled the night, mixing with the ragged breathing of the man only a few paces ahead of her.

"Oh, where does the lost little boy run to now?" She spoke with a commanding voice, that low, scratchy sound that served as a permanent reminder of her time on Andeshar.

"Does he run for the chase? For the thrill of being wanted?"

Mireithren reached for the man cloaked in shadows, grasping at his shoulder. Her hand passed through blackness. A shock of cold raced along her arm. The pain only sharpened her hunger.

"You have nowhere to run. My mark sits upon your neck, a black rose bloomed for the world to see. You are mine," she said, voice dropping to a husky growl.

"Then come and take me, Little Siren," the man replied, his low voice thundering across Mireithren's mind.

Fire spread through her loins, her body aching to devour the man she claimed. The one she hated. Loved. Despised. Needed.

"You are entirely too easy to catch, Therat."

The man wreathed in black skidded to a halt, throwing his hips back. His leg brushed hers; she stumbled but did not fall. Breathless, Therat turned, his eyes gleaming like the silver moon hanging high in the star-laden sky.

"Only because I let you win. We both know I could have killed you—"

A whimper tore from the depths of Therat's soul, cutting off his words. A gelid tendril of Shadow-weave tore through his heart, shards of ice forming like macabre crystals inside a body ready to shatter.

"Let me win? Say it again. Say it, and I will kill you."

Mireithren watched as the light in Therat's eyes died. His soulsong—that hushed melody that nestled itself inside her heart the day they first locked eyes in Av Madhira—faded until she could barely hear the weave of the First Harmonic threading his soul and flesh together. Hovering on the edge of life and death, Therat smiled as shadow-clouded eyes found hers.

"You... won't," he gasped, falling to his knees.

Mireithren cupped his chin in her hand, pulling his gaze to hers. "I might. Some days I wonder if I shouldn't have pushed the dagger a little deeper"—her long, ocher fingers brushed against the small scar under Therat's right ear—"ended this torment you bring my soul."

Mireithren bent forward, lips brushing against those of her lover, colder than the snow under her feet. She inhaled his intoxicating scent of freshly cut wood and dried blood, the metallic taste settling on a tongue waiting to devour her prey.

"But then, who would moan my name and worship me as fervently as you?"

Therat sucked in a ragged breath, body trembling as his soulsong faded to the Endless Void. A whimper escaped his pale lips; with a strained breath, he brushed his fingers against the scars racing down Mireithren's cheek. She shuddered at his touch, somehow still as warm as the sun-hot sands of their childhood home. She leaned in, remembering the day he first caressed her broken body. On the walk to Cídhen's Rest, when she still believed one night of indulging in her most carnal desires would not change what had to be done.

Now, she would do anything for the man at her feet.

She hated him for it. Wished to punish Therat for pulling her heart from the darkness, for showing her what love felt like. Mireithren never feared Death, laughed in its face even as a girl when the assassins came for her. For so long, she wished to dance with the darkness until her soul disappeared and the pain ended.

I've gone and let my heart take the reins. He will be my undoing, my eternal torment. Gods, why did I ever have to kiss him?

"Never forget, Therat," Mireithren whispered against his lips. "You are mine. Mine until the end of days. Mine to love or kill as I please."

With her final words, Mireithren recalled the Shadow-weave from the body on the edge of collapse. She watched as the color returned to Therat's eyes, now burning with desire.

"I hate you, oh, gods… I wish I hated you," he hissed through clenched teeth. "Torment me even as you claim to love me!"

Standing, Therat braced himself on the tree behind him, hands trembling as wisps of his Shadow-weave curled around his tattooed fingers. Mireithren laughed. With one fluid motion, she pressed up against him, one hand squeezing his cock, already straining against his fitted pants.

"Your body betrays you, my love. You are such a poor liar; you should be punished, not rewarded."

A groan escaped from his quivering lips as Mireithren squeezed harder, fingernails biting through the fabric and into the flesh below.

"As does yours," Therat murmured before shoving a hand down Mireithren's skirt. His fingers brushed against her hip, icy cold from the threads of Shadow-weave still wrapped around them. A burst of sunfire coursed through her body at his touch, aching for more until she thought she might explode.

"You will be my doom, gods, why can I not stay away from you?" Mireithren whispered, shadows filling her gaze as she spoke. "I should have never kissed you, never run my fingers through your hair, never learned what bliss exists in this world. You are a sickness, a disease!"

Mireithren leaned up and gently kissed the Shadow-mark under Therat's left ear before biting down. His gasp sent a wave of shivers down her spine. She pulled away and looked deep into those light gray eyes now swirling with silver.

"Whatever you've done to me, I never wish to be cured," she whispered. "But I will make sure you know how much I despise you with every touch."

Therat crushed his lips into hers.

That mouth she once hated—once wanted to see spilling blood onto the hot desert sands—became something she craved. The fullness of his lips, the softness of them against her skin. The hundreds of kisses he placed over her scarred cheek, lifting the ugliness from her soul with every action that said, *you never deserved this*. The words that spilled from those lips spelled her doom, however sweet they sounded. He called her a Goddess, made her think the world was hers to take. If the Sisters had not noticed her impunity before, surely they would now.

But who wouldn't defy the creators of the universe itself when eternal doom tasted so sweet?

Mireithren wove a thick tendril of Shadow-weave around Therat's hand still caressing her hip. His arm wrenched up against the tree above his head, and another weave of inky blackness pulled his other hand from her waist. His muscles bulged as he fought against her shadows. Weak threads of his own weave tried to loosen his captor's grip. Even as he struggled, Mireithren felt the blood surging to his cock still firmly in her grip.

"Say it, Therat," she said with the same sly grin she wore the morning he awoke with a dagger to his throat.

"Say what?"

"Say you're all mine. Tell me you belong to me." Her grip tightened, pulling a groan from the man bound with her shadows.

"W-we... we never came to an agreement," he ground out through clenched teeth.

Mireithren laughed. She released Therat and brought both hands up to his neck; one thumb covered the Shadow-mark under his left ear, while the other touched the scar left by her black dagger.

"Yet, it seems I've claimed you twice already, whereas I bear no such marking. You follow because you already know it is true."

She leaned over, twisted braids brushing against the scar over his chest.

"Just. Say. It," she said, each word punctuated with a kiss over the shadowy mark.

Therat pressed in closer, bringing his mouth to Mireithren's scarred cheek. He placed a kiss over the foul things forever marring her beauty. It pulled a thin thread of self-loathing from her soul, made her feel worthy of the love he claimed to give. How she yearned to believe his words could be true.

"I am yours, my Goddess. My Shadow Siren," he whispered in her ear.

Before Mireithren could respond, her vision turned black.

Mireithren and Therat may have found each other, but the cost of their union is only beginning to unfold. As the Maiden of Shadows descends deeper into darkness, her sister stands on the brink of the coming Blood Moon.

Dove of the Blood Moon
Spill blood. Find the Dove.

www.ingramcontent.com/pod-product-compliance
Lightning Source LLC
Chambersburg PA
CBHW061540190726
48289CB00004B/1114